RON

Philip Payne

ISBN; 9798455389184

Cover design by: P Payne
Library of Congress Control Number: 2018675309
Printed in the United States of America

A special thanks to Sarla, aka "monster"
The only other person to know Ron as
intimately as I do

CONTENTS

ONE

Her silk covered thighs clamped tightly around Ron's neck and forced the stubble on his chin to back in on itself. Arching her back, the woman in pink desperately tried to off balance him and bring him to the floor where she could then control him. Although the move was well rehearsed, she had clearly underestimated the size of her quarry this time. Ron stumbled a little but remained standing.

The Hurricanrana was a fancy superhero move, seen in Hollywood movies that combined gymnastics with martial arts. The legs were clamped around the neck in a vice like action in order to topple an opponent in a fight. In reality, although the move looked good, it was risky if it didn't work. On this occasion, all she had achieved was to cause him to drop the whiskey bottle he had just stolen. Now, she dangled helplessly, upside down from his neck, unable to bring him down in order to face justice for his petty crime.

Ron noticed two Japanese Sai daggers strapped to each of her thighs, ready to skewer him should he resist. Why was life so damn unfair he thought as he struggled against the vice like grip of her thighs?

It had taken less than two weeks from being released from prison, for a crime he hadn't committed, for his life to return to rat shit once more. His parole officer had just managed to get him fired from the job he had been forced to take, and losing his job meant he had lost the crummy apartment that came with it too. No job and no fixed address meant, through no fault of his own, he had broken his release conditions. To top it all, now he had a pink Lycra clad super heroine hanging off him, out for blood. He spun her around, trying to prise her clamped legs from his neck.

Wannabe super crime fighters were popping up everywhere these days. The nation had become divided on whether to love them or hate them. When the police department cracked down on them, the crime rate rose, but if they did nothing they ended up sorting out the trail of destruction in their wake. Half the public wanted them left alone, the other half wanted them dealt with severely. It had become a politician's nightmare.

Ron sensed his attacker's ankles begin to loosen their grip as they pirouetted like ice dancers. Once rid of her, he planned to hot foot it up the road. An unexpected dull thud radiated from the inverted woman but the momentum of the spin carried them another half a turn before her legs finally gave up their grip. Ron looked down in horror at the lifeless, pink catsuit clad body, now lying by the edge of the alley with her neck at almost a right angle to her shoulders. In his haste to free himself, he hadn't spotted the lamp post, just within the vigilante's turning circle. Instinctively, he glanced around to check for witnesses but saw none. Technically, he could argue that it had been self defence, or even an accident, but he knew no one would believe him. With one last check, he pulled his collar high, tucked his head down and strode from the scene. With no job, no fixed address and a death by his doing, he knew he was in deep shit now.

His parole officer had well and truly stitched Ron up by getting him fired from his job. It wasn't as if he liked working in the abattoir but at least it had been a source of income. Because his parole officer had also done a dodgy deal with the abattoir owner, the job had been linked to his accommodation. No fewer than six ex-cons worked at the slaughter house, all with rooms over the main processing plant. No doubt, for each monthly rent the owner took, his parole officer would be better off too.

That same parole officer was *supposed* to be the one looking out for him; instead he had just got him canned by shooting off his mouth. The slime had thought it funny to reveal that Ron had gained the prison nickname "The pig sticker." For a parole officer to let that slip to an abattoir boss of all people was unforgivable. It may have been OK to let the nickname slip if Ron drove trucks or cut down trees, but working in a meat processing plant!

Ron felt the nickname was totally undeserved anyway. It was yet another case of him being in the wrong place at the wrong time. Like most prisons, if you kept your head down and behaved yourself, you could usually land yourself a nice cushy job. He had done just that and eventually the screws had rewarded him with the privileged role of prison farm helper. Whilst not the most exotic job, it did at least allow him a bit more freedom to access to the open air rather than being stuck inside the laundry room like most.

One of the other inmates, serving three consecutive life sentences for murder, had chosen to remain working in the laundry, even though he had been offered several more sought after roles. They called him *The Still* because of his uncanny ability to distil almost anything into some sort of eye watering alcoholic spirit. The only reason The Still had chosen to remain in the launderette was because of the distilling rig he had secretly set up, hidden within the boilers. It was the most widespread kept secret within the prison. No one dared enquire what the raw ingredients were, but the end product was always potent. If ever the wardens caught anyone under the influence, prisoners knew that the consequences of squealing on their supplier could prove fatal, even if they had lost their eyesight from the alcohol.

Ron regularly exchanged fresh eggs and animal feed for the odd slug of moonshine. He didn't particularly enjoy the taste but the shady dealings did give him the chance to believe he had a modicum of control over his life.

On one occasion he received a shampoo bottle full of moonshine from The Still that had a lingering taste of Vagisil. He knew the taste as he had once brushed his teeth by mistake with the stuff at an old girlfriend's house. Although Ron retained no recollection of the incident, he had somehow managed to drink the whole contents of that shampoo bottle then collapsed inside the prison farm. Eventually, the prison guards came across him, naked and straddling a prize Vietnamese pot bellied pig. As a result of his antics, not only did he lose all farmyard privileges, he was also labelled *"The pig sticker"* from then on. He never regained any memory of the episode but was damn sure he didn't partake in any romantic activities with the pig, had it even been possible.

The memories of his time in prison only darkened Ron's mood deeper as he walked in no particular direction, constantly looking over his shoulder before deciding it was safe to stop. Sitting down on a broken bench, he knew he needed to get his head together and decide what to do next.

Close by, a handful of kids were playing a game of one-on-one at an overgrown basketball court, shadowed by the high-rise apartments. The faded back board clearly showed the signs of abuse and the missing hoop had been ingeniously replaced by a bottomless shopping basket. Rag tag kids played against each other with their heart and souls as if playing at the NBA try-outs. None of the kids paid him any attention as they bounced the cheap soccer ball about in their ageing fake Nikes bound up with duct tape.

He knew, if he handed himself in to the police and explained the accident, he would never have his freedom again. They would pin murder one on him in a flash. Who would believe that a dainty little woman had instigated an attack on a two hundred and thirty pound ex con? Another option would be for him to drop out of the system altogether. He could get a casual job, but with no social security number, he knew he would get exploited. No doubt, at some stage he would get sucked into a life of crime.

There was always the possibility he could track down his sister, Candy, and stay with her for a while. The more he thought about it, the more he realised that was probably his worst option. After all, they were not exactly what anyone could call close any more. It hadn't always been that way though. When their mother had turned to the adult entertainment business in order to fuel her drug dependency, social services had put them both in care. His sister had looked out for him while they were in the foster home. It was only after she left that he found out from the other kids that his mother had been a hooker and his father could be any name from the phone book.

He learnt a while later that Candy had somehow tracked their mother down and convinced her to take her in. Their mother had shacked up with a guy ten years her junior, who had been dumb enough to support her drug fuelled lifestyle. Ironically, he eventually took more of a liking to Candy and ran off with her.

The sound of whooping and hollering brought him back from his thoughts. The kid with the taped up Nike trainers was jumping about having just won his game. He felt a pang of sorrow for them. It was unlikely these kids would be doing anything different ten years on. Maybe if all the up and coming vigilantes who were prepared to tackle petty crime put their efforts into helping these kids, they might make a difference. Real super heroes were the ones that could give these kids a better future and steer them away from getting into crime in the first pace.

His stomach gave an audible rumble. He knew of a soup kitchen on the other side of town but did he really want to eat with all those bums? Who was he kidding, he *was* one of those bums, he thought.

Standing up, he began the long trudge across town. He knew he could easily hop the turnstiles and ride the subway for free but knowing his luck, there would be another Min-hero waiting to jump on his back.

That's what the press had named them, "Min-heroes". Any vigilantes acting outside the official law enforcement agency were worshipped by the media. Television programmes just dedicated to vigilante activities were becoming big business. Many wannabe crusaders did it for the thrill of being seen on camera, others did it for the adrenaline rush and a few were led by a sense of self righteousness.

His steady walk across the town took a couple of hours but it didn't really matter. It wasn't as if he was going to be late for a date. The soup kitchen lay just between the poorest and richest sides of the city. Sceptics argued this was because the wealthy didn't want the low life on their doorstep but they also didn't want to go too far when they felt charitable. After all, it wouldn't do to travel all the way into the middle of a dangerous territory just to dish out soup.

By the time he reached the old Christian hall it was nearly eight o'clock and the last of the early crowds had drifted away. The hall was mainly used as a parent and toddler venue during the day then converted into a soup kitchen by night to bring salvation to the poor unfortunates. Ron tagged onto the short queue, waiting for a bowl of a grey looking liquid and a bread roll. To describe it as soup must have contravened some law or another but he took the offered bowl anyway. As he sat down at a wooden trestle, amongst all the other down and outs in the hall, he realised this was rock bottom. At least in prison, he had a roof over his head and two warm meals a day. Freedom wasn't all that it was cracked up to be and he started to understand why criminals re-offended.

As he casually stirred the contents of his bowl, he watched the rich little old lady hauling another cauldron of gruel to the counter. The pearl necklace around her neck couldn't be any more inappropriate if she had studied inappropriateness at Harvard. Even a low life back street pawn shop would offer a year's keep to the bum that slipped it from her. Her gnarled and arthritic hands clutched at the pot tightly, but Ron could see it was only going to end up one way. In an uncontrolled act of chivalry, he quickly made his way behind the serving counter to prevent the impending accident. The sound of silence was deafening. All eyes within the room suddenly turned towards Ron, as he hurriedly encroached into the sanctuary of the do-gooders side of the serving counter.

'Let me help you with that,' he said, taking the heavy load from her just before her strength gave way. Pulling his sleeves over his hands he awkwardly took the pot of dubious substance from her. Swiftly, he set the burning cauldron down on the counter then blew on his fingers. His sleeves had been no match for the little old lady's oven gloves but he didn't make a scene about it.

'You are a sweet dear,' she said with her million dollar smile. 'I was struggling a little wasn't I?' she added.

Ron said nothing but returned the smile. He thought it was a smile at least. He had done it before but couldn't quite remember when. Without a word, he turned and headed towards the poor side of the counter once more.

'Don't sit back down yet,' she called, beckoning for him to return to the counter.

Ron knew he should never have intervened. This was how trouble always started. He would try to do the right thing but, without exception, he would end up worse off for it.

Doing the right thing was how he ended up in prison in the first place. He had been in a bar, innocently having a quiet beer after work when a fight broke out. At first he had let the two guys sort it out between themselves but eventually the smaller one ended up unconscious, lying on the floor. It should have been the end of the matter but when the brute kept kicking him, he decided enough was enough.

'Hey buddy, I think it's over,' he had said, pulling him away from the unconscious man.

That was the moment things turned sour. The big guy had immediately rounded on Ron and pushed his arm away just as a police officer had appeared on the scene to break the commotion up. Ron's elbow flew back and connected with the officer, breaking his nose, and prompting all hell to start. Before Ron could apologise, half a dozen cops had jumped on his back in an attempt to bring him down.

The headlines in the papers described the incident as "Drunken brawler attacks two police officers". Truth was, he had only drank half of his first beer when it all started. Even though he had offered no resistance whatsoever, cops just piled onto him to take him down. He ended up being charged with two accounts of grievous bodily harm. The first cop with the broken nose and a second who had cracked his own head open on the foot bar in the process of dragging Ron down.

Now, still reeling from his last act of decency, he knew he had just set himself up for another fall. The little old lady detected Ron's reluctance to return.

'Come on, I don't bite you know,' she said, enthusiastically.

Like a prisoner walking the green mile, Ron

reluctantly obeyed the summons. The lid that had covered the mystery pot now lay on the counter as little "Agnes" rummaged around the base with a large ladle as if she was panning for gold. Ron stood, fixated as he watched her fish out the only chewable chunks and put them into a fresh bowl for him.

'Just what a growing boy needs,' she said, offering him a wink.

Ron gave her another token smile before making off with his "reward" before any more trouble arose.

Returning to his seat, he noticed someone had taken the liberty of relieving him of his original soup and stale roll. The theft felt more like a blessing in disguise and he wondered if his luck was changing for the better. He placed his new bowl down and went in search of a drink half hoping someone would be brave enough to take his second helpings. Freshly ground gourmet coffee wasn't high in his expectations but he figured as long as it was hot it couldn't hurt.

On returning to his seat, he noticed two unexpected things. First, his soup remained where he had set it down, lumps included he assumed. Second, an official looking guy in a black suit sat opposite it. Ignoring the newcomer, Ron picked up his spoon and tentatively took a taste of the brown slurry. Knowing he was being watched, he tried to show no sign of weakness but Ron involuntarily winced a little as the food attacked his taste buds. The corners of the well dressed man's mouth curled up a little at Ron's discomfort.

'Ronald Sebastian Hawley,' the official said, in a slightly squeaky voice.

Ron said nothing. He figured, as he hadn't been asked a question yet, there was no need to reply. There were only two types of people who would address a person with their full name. An angry parent, or a government official. Somehow, he couldn't imagine the guy turning out to be his father.

Ron took another mouthful of soup to demonstrate he wouldn't crack under pressure.

'Enjoying life on the outside yet?' the official asked, full of sarcasm.

Ron ignored the question and carried on chewing the meaty chunk that was putting up a fair amount of resistance.

'We've had a bit of trouble over in the Bronx earlier this evening,' the official said, nonchalantly looking at his manicured fingers.

Ron knew he was being scanned for a reaction.

'I also hear you lost your job this morning,' the man in the expensive looking black suit added, folding his arms in front of him.

Ron noticed a damp stain immediately appear on the man's sleeve, as it soaked up old spilt coffee off the trestle.

'I'll get another job,' Ron said, battling the chunk of gristle in his mouth. He figured if the suit was here to arrest him, he wouldn't have come alone.

'Might prove a little tricky without an address.' The satisfaction of reading Ron's predicament made his squeaky voice rise another octave. Disappointment began to show on the official's face though when Ron showed no response. 'I have all the answers to your problems though,' he continued.

'Like a sort of fairy godmother?' Ron asked, straight faced.

The official looking man searched for signs of

being ridiculed, but lacked the awareness he believed he possessed. Nonetheless, he pressed on.

'You can stay here and enjoy this gourmet meal or I can take you to a restaurant up the road where they serve real food and I can tell you all about my offer,' he said, obviously relishing having the upper hand.

Ron sat chewing the unidentified morsel a little longer, now worried that he may be engaged in an act of cannibalism. He knew he would regret taking up the offer but as options went, they were few and far between. Accepting the inevitable, he spat the indigestible morsel into a napkin and stood. No offence to little old “Agnes”, but he suspected CSI might be more interested in the contents of her cauldron. He had nothing to lose. Yet.

'OK, let's go.'

*

It never ceased to amaze Ron just how cruel and insensitive those with an abundance of money could be to the poor. Some went about their lives in their happy little bubbles, getting on with their daily routines, occasionally stepping over the stray beggar without even noticing them. Others realised they were blessed with a good life and genuinely tried to help those less fortunate, but a few were just damn right spiteful. They were the ones who parked their brand new Cadillac alongside the beat up old wreck when the parking lot is empty. The ones who would light a cigar with a hundred dollar bill while standing next to the homeless guy. The restaurant Ron was just about to enter was predictably owned and frequented by that very type.

The swanky restaurant, although not very deep,

stretched all along the side walk, offering views of the common people going about their pitiful daily lives. Although not in the roughest part of town by any means, it offered views of the transient poor on their way to the soup kitchen. The rich could safely exhibit their opulence to salivating onlookers behind a glass, like tourists in a zoo.

As Ron followed the suit into the restaurant, a maître d' came rushing towards them with a look of sheer panic on his face. Ron's unshaven face and his forty eight hour abattoir clothes signalled he was on the wrong side of the glass.

'No, no, sirs. We cannot accommodate you,' he said in some sort of European accent, whilst frantically waving his arms.

Without uttering a word, and with obvious satisfaction, Ron's guardian angel quickly flipped open a leather bound wallet that contained some sort of badge. Ron guessed, by the fluidity of the manoeuvre, that his new buddy had spent hours on end in front of the bathroom mirror practising the sacred badge flash. Whatever it was that lay inside the wallet, it did the trick.

Reluctantly, the maître d' led them over to one of the furthest tables, away from the coveted window seats, all the time casting Ron with looks as if he was being forced to let him date his sister. Once shown to the table, the maître d' quickly dashed off to block other riff-raff from entering. Ron suspected that had they been his usual clientele, he would have faffed about pulling chairs out and laying napkins in their laps.

'Shall we start afresh? My name is agent Landon. You can call me Frank, however.' Frank held his hand out across the table.

Ron did the decent thing and shook the proffered hand. It was like rescuing a week old fish from behind the fridge. He held his tongue but made a mental note to wash his hands at the first opportunity.

'Ron,' said Ron, in reply.

Agent Landon was clearly pleased at the broken patch of ice in front of them.

'I should imagine you are pretty darn hungry?' Landon said, excitedly picking up the quilted menu from the specially designed ornate holder. 'I'm famished. Please, order whatever you like, Uncle Sam picks up the tab tonight,' he added, waving his arm in the air to catch the waiter's attention.

As Ron gazed down at the other padded menu, he came to the conclusion he wasn't going to be eating burger and fries tonight. He glanced over at the table next to them. A gentleman in a very expensive looking suit had just been served a dish that looked smaller than a child's portion. A small piece of fish, chaperoned by a few dangerous looking mushrooms, and a dribble of white sauce, described as "foam" on top, occupied the centre of a very large plate. It wasn't the quality of the food that concerned Ron; it was more the unoccupied space surrounding it.

A waitress approached the table, offered a rehearsed smile, then waited expectantly. Her rose water perfume touched Ron's senses briefly, bringing home his own unique aroma. Hastily he ordered random food from the menu.

'Smoked eel with flowers, for the starter, then the mutton and artichoke main please,' he said confidently, trying to sound as if he ate that sort of food every day. Truth was, he had never eaten either artichoke or eel, let alone flowers, and may never get another chance again. 'Can I add a plate of fries with that?' he involuntarily blurted out.

The waitress offered him a knowing smile, as if a child had just asked for crayons. 'With fries,' she said, writing on her pad in bigger letters than usual.

After Landon ordered his Foie gras, turbot and a bottle of Château Musar, the waitress dashed off to the kitchens to spread the mirth.

For a short while, they sat in an uncomfortable silence. Ron knew he was being fattened up in order to sell his soul to the devil, so he may as well do it on a full stomach.

'I'm going to use the rest rooms,' Ron said, suddenly standing. A look of concern flashed across Landon's face. 'Relax, I'll be right back,' he added before walking off.

Agent Landon watched Ron briefly speak to a waiter before being ushered through a doorway, at the far corner of the restaurant.

Ron stood in the centre of the marble shod rest-room, casting his eyes around at the decor. A man dressed in a tuxedo and white gloves hovered next to the sink, carrying a tray with toiletries upon it.

'Good evening, sir,' he offered Ron, as if standing in a lavatory wearing white gloves was the most natural thing in the world.

'Good evening,' Ron replied, a little wrong footed by the oddity of the situation. 'Just need to freshen up a little,' he added, unsure of the correct protocol.

'Of course, sir,' the attendant said. Placing the tray down, he started to fill the ornate basin with warm water. He laid a clean face cloth on the counter, along with a freshly opened bar of soap in a silver dish, then stepped back as his guest removed his shirt.

*

Landon looked a little relieved as Ron returned to the table. A newly acquired aroma of sandalwood emanated from his guest as he sat back down at the table. The food hadn't yet arrived, but two crystal wine glasses had appeared on the table, next to an opened bottle of red. According to the padded wine list, a bottle of Château Musar was going to set the tax payer back two hundred and nine dollars. Landon had half drained the glass in front of him already, so Ron took a sip to see what a two hundred dollar wine tasted like. He had to admit, it wasn't at all bad. He doubted it was worth the price, but it was nice.

'So, without beating around the bush any longer, I expect you want to know what all this is about?' Landon asked.

If this was not beating around the bush, he would hate to see the long version, Ron thought.

'Yes, please,' Ron replied amiably, gulping down another forty dollars worth of wine.

'Well, as you are probably aware, we have been developing an ever increasing vigilante problem.' Landon paused as the waitress re-filled the wine glasses, then waited a little longer until she had retreated out of ear shot before continuing. 'What am I saying? Of course you know about our vigilante problem,' Frank Landon seemed to find his own words highly amusing, causing him to chuckle like a schoolboy witnessing a nude picture for the first time. Ron's lack of response quickly brought him back to the subject. 'The incident with the "Pink Lady" and yourself, on the other side of town, is just one of the growing number of unfortunate attacks that we would like to see stopped.'

'We?' Ron asked.

'I am a member of the Federal Bureau for the Prevention of Interactive Services team,' Landon said, beaming with genuine pride.

'Never heard of them,' Ron drained his glass quickly, just in case the meal was suddenly withdrawn.

'That's because we are a covert operation, working discreetly within the shadows, making sure our country works within its proper channels. The police do the policing, lawyers take care of legal matters and judges hand out the punishment. That sort of thing.'

'How does that involve me?' Ron asked, warily.

'We want to employ you to take care of a few more vigilantes, the same way you did with the "Pink Lady",' Agent Landon leaned back in his chair.

'Like some sort of hit-man. I'm not a killer,' Ron protested, louder than he should have.

'That's not what the security tape shows from earlier today,' the Fed said, nonchalantly looking at his manicured finger nails once more.

'Hey, if you have that tape, you will also know it was her who attacked me! Her death was an accident, or at least, self defence,' Ron replied, through gritted teeth.

'Calm down, calm down. I'm not bothered in the slightest how it happened. We just want you to come and work for us. We need to get more of these self appointed judge, jury and executioners off our streets. If they are involved in more of your *accidents,* then so be it,' Landon attempted to sound sympathetic.

Before Ron could reply, their waitress arrived at the table and began setting down large, almost empty, plates in front of them. Ron's plate came with a couple of cylindrical shapes, decorated with some sort of colourful foliage on top.

'Bon appetite,' the waitress exclaimed proudly as she backed away. Landon laid a large napkin across his lap and made a start on his food.

'If you don't want the job, we will simply appoint someone else who is willing to do it, and then you will miss out on all the benefits of working for us.' Landon spread an innocuous blob of pâté onto a dry piece of toast.

Ron looked at Landon's toast and regretted ordering the eel, but he persevered nonetheless.

'Relax, we have been following the pink lady for quite some time now, and her growing popularity was starting to give us a little cause for concern. Until recently, she had undeniably been performing a public service by apprehending wanton criminals. I use the word recently though because she was beginning to overstep a line where we are unable to let her methods go unnoticed, so to speak. Her last two victims had received rather serious stab wounds from those pointy knives she carried. Had she not run into you, we would have had to arrest her through the proper channels, and I must say *that* wouldn't have gone down too well with the voters,' Landon smiled at his explanation.

'What are you expecting from me?' Ron asked, cautiously. Listening to the Fed's words, he suspected there may be scope for an alternative interpretation.

'We want your help to rid our country of these pesky "Min-heroes". I'm all for reducing crime but these vigilantes are starting to cause more harm than good,' Frank Landon hissed.

Ron watched the agent bite into another piece of heavily laden toast as he spoke. One of the corners broke off and landed Foie gras down on the crisp, opulent table cloth. Landon paid no attention to the fallout on the table as he talked on. Ron popped the last piece of eel into his mouth, chewed a little and swallowed; the oyster sauce did little to enhance the bland fish.

'So, providing they stop their vigilante activities, you would consider the task complete?' he asked, casually.

Landon pushed his empty plate away, revealing a crumb free circle of table cloth and looked directly at the ex-con opposite him.

'As long as they cease all vigilante activities and they are never seen again,' he let the last part of his sentence hang a little, 'we will consider the task complete,' he said, nodding at the idea.

Their waitress re-appeared at the table to clear the empty plates away. She frowned at the carnage in front of agent Landon, but on seeing the foliage still on Ron's plate, offered him a sort of "Well done for not eating the decorations," look.

'Why not just arrest them?' Ron suggested. He suspected what the reason was but he still wanted the Fed's interpretation.

'Every time we arrest one of them, the city goes nuts. We end up with protests, police ratings drop and riots break out all over the place. Last time, protesters attacked police officers and two civilians ended up getting themselves shot. That's two fatalities and a whole lot more damage than if the vigilante had just “disappeared”,' Landon justified. 'Crime is down and most of the people love them, so why not let them roam the streets unchecked, I hear you ask? Well it's not that simple. If we let them wander the streets, dishing out punishment without consequences, we lose control of our laws. We need to be the authority. Simple,' Landon said, ignoring the waitress as she set down more partially filled plates of food in front of them.

Ron thanked the waitress then paused for her to move out of ear shot again before replying.

'So you want *me* to roam the streets taking the law into my own hands by killing off vigilantes. Doesn't that make me a vigilante too?' Ron asked, watching Landon chew a mouthful of food he had just sliced from a whole red fish. He wondered if they charged extra to remove the fish's head.

'No, we want you,' he said, pointing his fork at him, trying to swallow the piece of red snapper before continuing, 'to find a way to remove these people from our streets within the boundaries of the law.' Landon smiled, revealing partially chewed fish in his teeth.

Ron knew he was not the sharpest tool in the box by any standards but he was failing to grasp how he was going to achieve such a task.

'And if I ask them to stop their illegal crime fighting and they refuse?' Ron asked.

'If you ask them like you asked the lady in pink, you will have the finest lawyers in the world to take care of the paperwork,' Landon suddenly went serious.

'You want me to bait them!' Ron suddenly realised his role. 'If they suffer some sort of accident attacking me, the court screams self defence, I walk free and we have one less Min-hero on the streets,' he added.

'You catch on quickly,' Frank Landon said pointing his fork again at Ron before returning to his snapper.

The idea sucked. Ron wasn't cut out to be a hit man, and that was exactly what this was, no matter how much it was sugar coated. He was a carpenter, up until the bar room incident at least.

'What if I say no?' He knew there would be consequences but he asked anyway.

'Then I will pay the bill for our meal and simply walk away,' Landon said, laying his knife and fork across the fishy skeleton on his plate.

Ron gulped down the last of his wine as he thought about his future. The fruity rich taste and pleasant warmth was a far cry from the lingering taste of lady ointment that prison life had to offer.

'OK,' Ron said, in resignation.

He had nothing to lose. If he walked away now, he would be on the run for the rest of his life or end up back in prison. He figured, if you were drowning and someone throws you a rope, you don't wait for a better looking boat.

Landon took a thick envelope from his inside pocket and slid it across the table to Ron. 'Inside is a key to an apartment not too far from here. The address is on the back of the envelope. It will be your new home for a while and you will find yourself quite comfortable there. The envelope also contains a little pocket money should you need anything else.'

Ron lifted the flap of the envelope and fanned through the thick wad of hundred dollar bills. The blasé way in which Landon spoke and pushed the years worth of cash across the table left no doubt that morals were not part of the job. Ron hated himself for slipping the bulging wad into his pocket and he hated being in the Fed's pocket.

'How will I contact you?'

'Inside your new apartment, you will find a mobile phone. It will have one number stored on it,' Landon said, laying a thousand dollars on the table and catching the waitress's eye. 'We will contact you soon. In the meantime, relax, make yourself comfortable.' Landon stood, brushing the crumbs from his lap.

Ron suddenly felt like a hooker, owned by a sugar daddy.

*

Mavis Oswald was due to celebrate her eighty-fifth birthday next month. She was a pillar of the community and the folk down at the church downright loved the little old dear. For almost forty years she had lived in the three bedroomed house in the up market Cherry Tree district. Sadly, she had lived there alone for the last twenty years, since poor old George mysteriously died in his sleep. Well that was what everyone believed, and she had no intention of disclosing any further details. Mavis just couldn't face the embarrassment if the truth ever got out.

Mavis and George, in their younger years, had enjoyed what some may call a rather energetic lifestyle. At the age of sixty six, and on heart tablets, doctors had advised him not to over exert himself too much. But George was a passionate man and when the urge took him there was just no quenching the fire inside him. It wasn't until the morning after that fateful night that Mavis realised something was wrong with her husband.

Usually, after their vigorous activity they would cuddle a short while before George turned over and went to sleep. On that occasion, Mavis had been the one to fall asleep first, only to find George still smiling at her when she woke.

The coroner personally drove out to Cherry Tree that morning to ask Mavis a few delicate questions. Mavis broke down, utterly distraught, and started blaming herself for killing George, but the coroner had simply patted her on the hand and said, "No man could wish to go a better way." Although it did comfort her a little, she still kept the finer details to herself.

These days, without the distraction of her husband, she turned to helping others. Right now, she was in the process of making sponge cakes for the church raffle. All proceeds from the church fete went towards the Help the Children fund. People seemed to love her sponge cakes more than anything else for some reason and folks quickly snapped up all raffle tickets in order to get one. Of course, people could buy ready made sponges down at the local store much cheaper, but they never tasted the same as hers. She used the same flour, caster sugar and eggs as anyone else, but Mavis's contained her very own home made jam and clotted cream for the filling. She also added a small measure of ground medicinal cannabis, just to ease away people's aches and pains, but she figured that should remain her little secret. Regardless of what made them so popular, she had just found out she was low on caster sugar, and that meant a trip to the store. She briefly considered popping round to Marie next door to see if she had some but she didn't like to bother her. Besides, she knew it would do her good to get out for a while.

*

By the time Ron found the recently built Cedar View residential apartments, it had gone midnight. Set back a good way from the road, stylish ambient lighting lit up three separate two story buildings laid out in a giant "H" arrangement. Heavy looking ornate gates and CCTV cameras overlooking the parking lot gave the impression of a safe haven.

Ron had been standing at the pedestrian access a short while, looking for a key hole within the door, when two giggling teenage girls approached. Clearly sneaking back from somewhere they shouldn't have been, they eyed Ron suspiciously and waved a little plastic key fob over a small sensor on the corner of the door frame. The lock clicked and the automatic doors slowly swung open. The party goers silently entered the complex and veered off to the right, cautiously looking back at the big man they had just passed.

The wooden signpost at the edge of the pathway, similar to those at a holiday complex, directed Ron towards the correct block. Scouring the numbers on the doors in search of number twenty-two, he was fully aware that his activities looked extremely suspicious. Eventually, he found the apartment, on the first floor, accessed via an external stairway to a balcony serving four other dwellings. Once inside, he quickly drew the blinds before switching the lights on.

The place was far larger inside than it had appeared from the outside. Soft, deep pile carpets ran throughout, and a large flat screen TV sat in the corner of the lounge. The open plan, modern kitchen was fully decked out with all the appliances needed to make a happy home. He made a thorough search of the place, opening doors and cupboards to see what he had adopted. Whoever had prepared the place had done a good job within a very short time. Kitchen cupboards had been well stocked with fresh food and the refrigerator looked as if it had just been filled. Walking into the bedroom, he browsed the wardrobes and dresser to find he had an assortment of tee shirts, jeans, and even underwear, in his size, ready for him.

Now, within the quiet sanctuary of his new apartment, a sudden weariness washed over him. The combination of working through the previous night shift at the abattoir, the long walk and the fancy wine with so little food was beginning to take effect.

Running the shower, he undressed and kicked his offensive clothes into the corner, ready to sort out in the morning. It had been a bizarre day, even by his usual standards, but the jets of hot water eased some of the tension away. As he lathered soap over his stubbled face, he cast his eye around the modern bathroom for a razor. Had he not been so tired, he would have checked the bathroom cabinets, instead he just rinsed the soap away. A shave could wait until tomorrow.

TWO

Thirty one years ago

Little Peter Ellison idolised his father and loved spending every minute he could with him, especially as the children of his own age tended to avoid him whenever possible, calling him "weird," and other names to his face. They said he was too bossy and accused him of trying to take over all the time but Peter Ellison denied their accusations. Their name calling didn't bother him too much, but what really did annoy him, was their total lack of order when he wasn't around.

The older boys would ride their bikes across the grass in the park when clearly written signs forbade it, others would play ball games with total disregard to all the notices stating not to. When he strongly protested, the bigger children simply laughed at him and pushed him over. Peter's father was a union representative at a packing plant and his love of rules and regulations clearly had an influence on his son.

Like any other inquisitive child, Peter was full of questions about the world he was growing up in, "Where does the sun go at night? How many little people live inside the television? Because mummy paints her face, does that make her an Amazon princess?" were just some of the questions he would ask. The one question that really changed little Peter Ellison's direction in life was the seemingly innocent question of "Why do we have laws?"

Like most responsible parents, his father tried to answer the questions as honestly as possible, except for questions on the reproduction process of course.

'You see son, it's like this,' he started, folding his newspaper up and setting it down on the table in order to give the question his full attention. 'If we didn't have laws, the world would turn into chaos. For example....,' he paused, as he thought of an appropriate example his nine year old son would understand. 'The law tells us all to drive on the right hand side of the road. If we ignored it and simply drove on whichever side we chose, we would all bump into each other and get hurt.' He watched his son's puzzled expression a moment before adding another example he might understand a little better. 'If someone took your nice, shiny red bicycle from the yard, they would be bad people and they would be breaking the law,' his father added, hoping for a spark of understanding.

Little Peter thought this over for a while but a worried expression crossed his face for the safety of his bicycle.

'But what if they took it anyway?' Peter asked.

'Then the police would punish them and make them give it back,' he replied, trying to alleviate some of the worry he had just heaped on his son.

'What if a policeman isn't there when the bad man takes it? Billy Watts had his bike pinched last year and a policeman still hasn't brought it back to him. His father said there is never a policeman when you want them as they are all too busy eating doughnuts,' young Peter stated, clearly concerned with the loophole in the law he had just discovered.

Peter's father started to regret not forwarding his son's original question to his wife to explain.

'Bad people will always go punished one way or another. If the police don't manage to find them, then God will judge them later,' he said, hoping it would close the matter.

'What if God is too busy eating doughnuts like the policemen?' Peter wasn't going to let this go without a satisfactory answer to his dilemma.

'God sees everything, everywhere. He looks through the eyes of his people and dishes out punishment in whichever way he chooses,' he answered, picking his newspaper back up in the hope his son would now go away and drop the subject.

Peter Ellison had indeed gone away but he hadn't dropped the subject. In fact, from that point on, he became obsessed with the concept of crime and punishment.

*

Present day

There was an awful din just outside the store as Mavis stood at the till, waiting to pay for her caster sugar. Mrs Richards had let her go first as she had a large trolley piled high with groceries and wasn't in any great rush to get back home anyway. Mrs Richards always did her shopping on a Saturday morning because her husband was at home on the weekends and could look after their five children. Mavis noticed she was looking a little worn these days but was far too polite to say anything.

After paying the young checkout girl for the sugar, she headed to the door to find out what all the commotion was about. Her walking frame made it slow going but she was advised not to risk going out in public without it, just in case her hip gave way. The doctors had told her that she really needed a replacement as the old one had completely worn out, but stressed, at her age the operation could be quite risky. After talking it over with her eldest daughter, they had agreed it might be best to use the walker for now unless it got really bad, then she would have to risk it. Clattering the frame against the automatic sliding doors as she exited the store, Mavis spotted a large crowd gathered on the sidewalk. On spotting Mavis approaching, they slowly parted to allow her a clear view of what had been causing all the noise. She stood, horrified.

Back in the day, when George worked at the power plant, he had worked extremely hard to gain a promotion. He always said that if people set their mind to it, anything was achievable. His new found role of assistant manager had brought them a substantial pay increase and an opportunity to buy the only other love of his life, a 1955 Chevrolet Bel air convertible. It was the same car his father had lent him all those years ago when he took Mavis on their first date. In the age before the internet, they had to spend months of searching car lots and scrolling through classified ads to locate the one they really wanted. Eventually, after a lot of hard work and months of looking, they found the red convertible, with white rear wings and a white soft top. Mavis christened it "Charley" and the two of them used it to travel the country, visiting different shows and sights.

When George passed, Mavis just couldn't bare the idea of selling it, even though, admittedly, it was a bit too big for her to drive. The nice man at the garage who serviced it each year, once made her a very nice offer to buy Charley, but there were too many fond memories to part with him. Besides, it was so easy just to lay her walker across the back seat when the roof was down.

Now, Mavis stood in shock, as a crazed man dressed in a parking warden's suit with a large cravat covering his face, attacked her late husband's pride and joy with a chain saw. Plumes of sparks flew in all directions as the screaming sound of a two stroke engine and tortured metal rang out. A pool of what seemed like Charlie's life blood began to run across the road, just as the Chevy folded in half.

'STOP!' Mavis tried to scream out in her frail voice.

'You have parked in a disabled bay without displaying a permit,' he stated authoritatively, without a shred of remorse in his voice.

'I left it on the dash board, the wind may have blown it down,' Mavis sobbed.

Forty year old Peter Ellison, or the "Meter Master" as he called himself, peered inside the wreck and spotted the permit lying on the floor.

'I'm bad,' he said, shrugging his shoulders. He then jumped into his highly modified, three wheel parking attendant buggy and roared away.

Gasps grew amongst the crowd as little Mavis stared in horror at her late husband's pride and joy as its fluids bled onto the ground. She had never sworn in her life, even through child birth, and she believed such vulgarities were totally unnecessary. Now, however, as she watched the mad man roar away in a cloud of tyre smoke, she shook her fist in the air at him.

'FUCKER!' was all she could manage before her hip gave way, sending her crashing to the floor.

Crumpled on the ground, in a pool of spilt caster sugar, she lay there sobbing. Her only consolation was, on this occasion, she believed her use of the profanity had been appropriate.

*

Ron woke to the sounds of grass cutting, just below his bedroom window. Even though the room was still dark, the red neon digits on the bedside clock told him it was now mid morning. He found himself lying on top of the bed, a damp towel still wrapped around him from his shower the night before. He couldn't remember going to sleep and he hadn't woken in the night for the first time in years.

He swung his legs over the side of the bed and planted his feet into the deep pile carpet for a moment, trying to rationalise the bizarre situation he had found himself in. Both his job at the slaughter house and his accommodation had been conditions for his parole. Neither would be missed, but that still didn't solve the dilemma he now had to contend with.

Landon had promised he would take care of everything but did he mean also with his parole officer? Somehow, he didn't feel a lot of trust towards the guy but when you're lying face down in the gutter, options were few. If Landon didn't act fast though, Ron knew there would soon be a warrant out for his arrest.

His parole officer had well and truly shafted him in order to line his own pockets. What could be more dodgy about an abattoir full of parolees on the pay roll and each crammed into a twelve by twelve bedsit, with just one communal bathroom above the premises?

Well, at least he had an apartment for now but he could hardly explain to anyone what he did for a living. What would he say? "Hi, I'm Ron. I eliminate small time wanna be super heroes that have become a nuisance." Not an ideal ice breaker at a dinner party.

He cast an eye around his new home. He knew he had sold his soul to the devil, plain and simple, but if he couldn't find a way to take care of the "problems" his way then he would have to return to being just another bum. There were certain lines he wouldn't cross.

Ron looked at the box containing what he presumed to be his new mobile phone, lying on the centre of coffee table, but he resisted the temptation to pick it up. Instead, he pulled on a new pair of jeans, donned a plain white tee shirt and a new pair of Converse from the wardrobe, then left the apartment.

Goose bumps instantly sprouted up on his arms from the cool, chill air as he walked down the staircase, prompting him to consider going back for a sweat shirt. Although the morning clouds had started to break up, it was a strong reminder that autumn would soon be here. The warmth of his new apartment had begun to soften him already. Had he been back in his old cell, the drafts would have gone unnoticed.

Pressing a button next to the glass exit doors, Ron stepped outside the Cedar View complex. What he failed to notice, was a black sedan, parked just down the road.

*

Sixteen years ago

Rachael Gordon appeared to be like other students her age. She studied hard, liked to hang out with other kids her age and was fond of lying in on a weekend. To the casual observer, she didn't stand out in any way. Average build, brown, long hair and a retainer to straighten out a slightly crooked front tooth.

Only by watching Rachael carefully, would you discover her slightly odd behaviour. If she was out with her friends at the diner, she would be inadvertently straightening out the salt and pepper pots, or re-stacking the paper napkins neatly. Of course, occasionally people would notice her foibles, but being good friends, they merely made light of the affliction. There were many other things they didn't see, however. She would place her school books in her bag in alphabetical order, coloured pencils were sharpened to a uniform length and the bookshelves in her bedroom were in strict colour order. No one could pin it down to a precise moment when Rachael's OCD started, but she began to realise herself that she was different from other people.

Her parents did their utmost to accommodate Rachael's eccentricities but, like most families, there was an element of natural chaos within the home. Although her younger sister wasn't excessively untidy, Rachael always felt the urge to close her sibling's door when she walked across the landing, in case the chaos escaped. On the few occasions her little sister ventured into her bedroom, she would begin to palpitate and sweat until she left.

In the lounge, if a coffee cup was left on the table, or a newspaper lay on the arm of a chair, Rachael would try to ignore it by escaping to the sanctuary of her own room. Eventually though, the image in her mind of the offending items would become so bad that she couldn't rest until she had tidied them away.

She lessened the problem to some extent by remaining in her room and immersing herself into her studying. The by-product of locking herself away in her bedroom was that it aided her studies in chemistry, eventually leading her to a first class degree in Medicine at a Pennsylvanian university.

By the age of twenty-two, Rachael had secured herself a good job at Drug-U-Like, a leading pharmaceutical company, helping to develop new medicines. Although well paid and amongst friendly people, she still couldn't find happiness. Her affliction was quickly becoming out of hand. All day at work, she found herself following people around, tidying up after them, rearranging their desks and generally working herself into an anxious wreck. Rachael's boss, Mr Richard Morris, was a very understanding man. He had spotted her affliction shortly after hiring her, but had hoped she might grow out of it in time. He was wrong.

The situation came to a head one afternoon, at a particularly busy time. Alex, Rachael's co worker, occupied a desk just a few yards away from her own. He was around the same age as Rachael and a pleasant man to talk with. She didn't know it, but he had almost asked her out on a date then had decided against it at the last moment due to her odd behaviour. Because of the high workload and lack of space on his desk, he had casually gathered the pile of files and dropped them on the floor next to him.

Rachael saw the incident and something inside her snapped, setting her off like a bomb. Screaming and shouting at the flustered Alex, she had snatched up the pile of discarded files and run off down the corridor towards the shredding room. By the time they caught up with her, poor Alex's files were completely shredded, and word was spreading throughout the building of her outburst.

Staff from all over the building began turning up to see what all the commotion was about, only to discover poor Rachael slumped on the floor of the shredding room, sobbing her heart out. It was the kindly Mr Morris who eventually convinced her to unlock the door after sending everyone back to their stations. He pulled the blinds down, sat on the floor next to the inconsolable young woman and talked with her for almost an hour.

A few phone calls later, and with total agreement from Rachael, he secured her an in-patient place at the Coften Rehabilitation Centre, under the care of Doctor Susan Willoughby. Dr Willoughby had identified and helped his wife get over the little known Scopophobia, after giving birth to their beautiful daughter ten years ago. Morris even arranged for the pharmaceutical company to pick up the bill under the guise of industrial stress.

Dr Willoughby specialised in obsessive disorders and knew only too well that the mind was a strange place. Every man, woman and child on the planet owned a unique set of thought processes and no two people react alike to the same sort of counselling. Even though she was known and respected for her results in treating people with obsessive compulsive disorders and phobias alike, Susan still felt as though she was just pushing random buttons. Diagnosing Rachael's problem was the easy part, she simply couldn't stand disorder to the point that she was compelled to act against it. It was finding out how to treat her that was the tricky part.

Each therapy session, when dealing with conditions of Rachael's severity, had to be approached meticulously. Doctor Willoughby almost had to become OCD herself in order to deliver the correct therapy. For the first session with Rachael, she had prepared the consulting room with the finest attention to detail. There were no papers on her desk, pencils and pens were stored out of sight and the waste paper basket was emptied and cleaned. Blinds were fully drawn, the desk arranged in perfect symmetry to the room and the white board polished to remove any traces of previous writing. Every little detail had to be thought of so as not to distract her patient from the initial interview. Dr Willoughby even took time over her own appearance, making sure her hair was tidy and her plain clothes were clean and ironed correctly.

When the time came for Rachael's first interview, the orderly led her into Dr Willoughby's consulting room then left without a word.

'Ah, Rachael, please come in and sit down.' Susan spoke in a friendly informal tone while all the time scanning her new patient intensely for any tell tale signs that would give her thoughts away. Rachael's body language spoke volumes but it was her eyes that told even more. Rachael nervously twisted her fingers together in front of her, indicating an initial reluctance to open herself up to scrutiny. It was a typical reaction but what pleased Susan the most was when her patient scanned every detail of the room, including herself, only to finish with her eyes cast downwards. To the untrained eye, they would have thought nothing of it, but Dr Willoughby knew Rachael could find nothing out of place that would cause further anxiety.

Their first therapy session had been short and sweet. They shook hands, introduced themselves formally, then spoke a little about Rachael's childhood, all nice and friendly. Then, just as Rachael started to relax, Susan Willoughby brought their session to an end. Rachael had been disappointed the session was over. She had found Dr Willoughby to be likeable and wanted to talk some more but now she found herself looking forward to their next session.

It was all part of a carefully planned session by Dr Willoughby, of course. One of the primary rules of treating a patient was to encourage them to feel comfortable and to have them looking forward to the next meeting. Although patients generally wanted to discuss what was on their minds, they would always procrastinate. The time was never quite right to share their feelings or what was on their mind. By keeping sessions short, patients soon learnt to open up quickly.

Over the next few sessions, Dr Willoughby started to introduce small items to see what it took to agitate Rachael. At first, she simply laid a pen at an angle on her desk and said nothing. The session had been strained throughout as they talked. Susan had carefully watched Rachael's eyes dart back and forth to the crooked pen as they talked about early school years. Weeks of testing Rachael's reactions to different levels of disruption proved fruitless until one day, Dr Willoughby introduced a scent into the room. The experiment yielded remarkable results. Just a few drops of concentrated lavender oil on a napkin, hidden inside her desk, filled the room with a powerful aroma.

The session started as usual, with an orderly showing Rachael into the room and Susan greeting her in the same friendly manner. Rachael immediately commented on the lovely smell of lavender as she took the usual seat opposite Doctor Willoughby. What she didn't comment on, to Dr Willoughby's delight, was the pile of untidy papers on the desk. The average person wouldn't have given the papers a second thought, but to Rachael Gordon, it should have sent her crazy.

Over the next few months, Susan Willoughby experimented with various different fragrances and different degrees of untidiness, always searching for different reactions in her patient. As time went by, they worked out that when Rachael became anxious, a handkerchief with a few drops of lavender oil, held to her nose, calmed her down.

It was a little under three months by the time Rachael was discharged from Coften Rehabilitation Centre and allowed back to Drug-U-Like. Mr Morris and all her co workers warmly welcomed her back with open arms, all be it with very tidy desks. She was also given her very own enclosed office at the far end of the building and a long way from the photo copying and shredding room. There was never a reoccurring incident like the one that led to her breakdown and life at the pharmaceutical company quickly returned to normal. Occasionally, if she stumbled across a particularly messy workstation on her travels, Rachael would discretely slip back to her office, where a strong aroma of lavender would slowly emanate from her closed door.

*

Present day

By the time Ron returned to his apartment the early afternoon sun had burnt away the chill. The gang of gardeners were still merrily busying themselves, pruning bushes and sweeping away leaves in preparation for the coming winter. None of them paid him the slightest attention as he stepped through the security door that had been wedged open with a five gallon steel gas can. He envied their simple life and would have swapped with them in a heartbeat but he knew that wasn't an option.

As he climbed the stairs to the upper apartments he could hear sounds of teenage screams and laughter coming from the far end of the complex. Through the smoked glass shield, serving as a wind break and noise buffer, he could just make out the shape of kids playing at the poolside. Even though it had warmed up a fraction, Ron was still a little surprised that anyone would brave the pool at this time of year.

Turning his key in the lock, Ron pushed the door open and was initially hit with a welcome blast of heat. As he stepped inside his apartment though he suddenly froze, senses on high alert as he detected a new faint smell of stale cigarette smoke. Cautiously, he checked all the doors along the hall. The bedroom, bathroom and closet were all clear but when he reached his living room, two thick brown envelopes now lay across the coffee table.

Ron eyed them suspiciously but made no move to seek out their contents. Instead, he went to the kitchen, ripped open a couple of pop tarts and shoved them into the toaster. In prison he was afforded little in the way of privacy, but he was surprised at just how much this invasion of his new space had irked him. He made a mental note to buy a new barrel for his lock the next time he was near a hardware store. He had no doubt both himself and the apartment was under surveillance, but for how long would most likely depend on his progress.

With a pot of fresh coffee brewing and the jam from a pop tart burning the roof of his mouth, he finally slumped down on his sofa and picked up the first of the brown envelopes. It felt hypocritical to now be the one looking through reports on the criminal activities of these mini heroes, or whatever they liked to be known as. Were they really criminals, Ron mused? They were only trying to do what the police couldn't, or possibly wouldn't, do. Half the time the courts would let the offender walk within twenty-four hours anyway. Then again, some of these vigilantes were pretty heavy handed when it came to a lot of petty offences. Ron could see how things could easily get out of hand.

A lot of the problems came from social media. It was easy to whip up outrage at the lack of law enforcement and when one of these vigilantes popped up, they received notoriety overnight. Each clip uploaded to the internet of one of them caught in the process of handing out punishment made their popularity increase. During the five years Ron had been locked away in prison, he realised the world had gone completely crazy. The boom in surveillance technology meant there was now a bloody camera on almost every street corner, just waiting to capture vigilante activity.

He spread the contents of the folder across the table and began sifting through the various newspaper clippings reporting on some mad man calling himself the “Meter Master”, going around sawing illegally parked cars in half. It seemed the police had regularly turned a blind eye to his crazy activities due to the guy's popularity, not to mention a steep reduction in parking offences. People seemed to love the clips of him sawing cars in half with his industrial, diamond tipped chainsaw. There were endless newspaper cuttings showing Cadillacs, Mercedes, and even Porsches, lying in the streets with crowds of onlookers cheering.

It was one local newspaper clipping with a picture of a classic Chevy Bel air in two halves that caught his eye the most though. As he read down the clip, he found a story on a little old lady, loved and respected by the community, who'd had her late husband's pride and joy destroyed by this maniac. The crowd, who had previously loved the Meter Master, had obviously turned against him for carrying out this particular act. Ron knew it would only be a temporary glitch in his popularity, so he needed to act fast before he regained his followers.

According to most of the reports, the majority of his activity had been carried out down south, mainly around Georgia. If he was going to investigate, he would need some sort of transport, so he turned to the box with his new phone in.

Although he wasn't new to mobile phones it was immediately obvious that during his five years of absence, they had come on a long way. After a brief investigation of the phone's functions, he found the thin touchscreen device was brimming with all sorts of technology from internet access to emails. Hell, it even had the ability to stream movies if he wanted. He opened up the digital phone book to see the single stored entry of "Office". No names, no departments just the single word.

He pressed the green dial button and listened. It rang twice then a female voice at the other end answered,

'Charlotte speaking, how may I help?'

Ron hadn't thought the conversation through very much before he dialled but he reckoned whoever Charlotte was, she would know all about him.

'Er, can I speak to Mr Landon please?' he asked.

'I'm sorry, but Mr Landon is unavailable. All requests and communication will go through me from now on,' she said, in a business like tone.

Ron wondered if she recorded automated messages in her spare time, the ones that always put you on hold for ten minutes when you needed to complain about something. He half expected Charlotte to start telling him that his call was important but they were experiencing an unusually high number of calls at this time, blah, blah.

'I need transport.' Ron didn't feel the urge to tell her why or where he was going, he figured they would find out one way or another anyway.

'You have transport. Grey truck in the parking lot, keys are in the small draw next to the cutlery draw,' she chirped.

He slid the suggested draw open and fished the keys out as she spoke. He was certain they hadn't been there yesterday though.

'Thanks.' Ron tossed them in the air and caught them again.

'Is that all?' she asked.

'Thanks very much,' he added, knowing he had

sounded a little short with her.

'I meant, is there anything else I can help you with?' Charlotte said.

Ron suddenly felt a little foolish and was just about to decline the offer, then suddenly remembered, 'I was supposed to meet up with my parole officer tomorrow, but clearly things have changed,' he said, hoping Charlotte would understand the obvious implications.

'Ah, yes. Mr Andrew Soul. We all know why he doesn't sign his cheques with just an initial don't we?' she said, cheerfully. 'It seems that Mr A Soul,' she emphasised the name, 'has been suspended recently for dodgy dealings regarding a certain abattoir owner and the misappropriation of accommodation funds. Your new parole officer is a Mr Landon,' she said.

Ron could almost hear her smiling. 'That *is* a coincidence,' Ron uttered sarcastically. He had to give them their due; they pretty much had everything covered.

'There is also a credit card in the box that you took the phone from. The pin is your date of birth and it has a daily limit of $400 to be used for alternative accommodation and gas,' she added. Ron figured, A Soul got just what he deserved for skimming off the backs of ex-cons. He also knew that anything he spent on the card would come from retrieved criminal assets.

'Thank you very much, Charlotte. That will be all,' Ron replied, in a much better tone.

'Good luck,' she added, then hung up before Ron could reply.

He stood in the kitchen, looking at the keys in one hand, the phone in his other, then decided to pack.

*

Jason was young and hadn't been gifted the highest level of intelligence, but he was an extremely hard working brick layer. Like most building workers his age, he liked to clown about and live life as best as he could. Throughout the week his only goal in life was to reach the weekend, because the weekend meant pay day, and pay day meant beer. With the Friday shift coming to an end he began cleaning up the pointing to his newly laid brickwork on the second floor of an office block they were constructing in Richmond Square.

There used to be an old library on the site, but with the development of technology, books were becoming a thing of the past. When the aged building was torn down, the locals went mad and protested at the town hall, even though most hadn't even set foot in the library. When the new offices were finished, they would at least provide around fifty new jobs in the area for a parcel company.

As Jason began to clean the tools and pack away ready for a new shift on Monday, a pretty girl, walking along the opposite side of the street, caught his eye. The sight was too much for his adolescent hormones. Standing at the edge of the scaffolding, he let out a loud wolf whistle, hoping to attract the pretty girl's attention. Gasps of horror rang out amongst his fellow workers as they all scrambled to get themselves out of sight.

'Fool,' old Bob hissed. 'You know what happens to wolf whistlers these days,' he warned. Old Bob had been around long enough to remember the days when wolf whistling was part of the dating game. It had been the usual method of attracting the attention of the young ladies, in the hope of starting up a conversation. Sometimes the woman smiled back and other times she would ignore you or offer a scowl in return. The latter would have all your mates ribbing you for the rest of the day.

Things were so much simpler in those days, Bob reckoned. Nowadays, you had do all the flirting on computers by posting out of date pictures of yourself and lying about what you did in your spare time. Bob missed the old days, when people actually spoke to other people, rather than typing.

One thing was for sure, he knew it was dangerous to wolf whistle at stray women these days. Not only was it a sure fire way of losing your job through a sexual harassment case, far more serious consequences lurked in the shadows. Bob had heard stories of fellow workers beaten to within an inch of their lives after being dragged down dark alleyways by some feminist group or another. They had eyes and ears everywhere and here was this young fool, standing at the edge of the scaffold in plain sight like a strutting peacock. Bob picked up his tool bag and quietly slipped away, as did the others.

Monday morning, just as old Bob was loading out his tools for the day, the scaffolding collapsed. At first, the health and safety squad suspected the scaffolders had done a shoddy job, but on closer inspection they found out that all of the clamps along one side had been tampered with. Old Bob, and one of the other workers, suffered broken bones in the fall. Ironically young Jason had not been there that morning, he had thrown a sickie. In truth, he was just nursing a hangover from drinking too much over the weekend.

*

As expected, there was very little traffic on the

road at six thirty on a Saturday morning but Ron knew it wouldn't stay that way. Soon, the highways would start to fill up with all the weekend warriors, seeking a break from the tedium of the working week. He had allowed a couple of days to reach Georgia, but he was in no rush. He even considered a stop off somewhere just to drag the journey out a little. Still, without any sort of plan, he would need time to think about what he was going to do to stop this parking nut job once he found him. Although Landon hadn't indicated a time scale on these little tasks, he guessed they would soon let him know if they thought he was taking the piss.

The truck they had supplied him with was newer than anything he had ever owned or driven in the past and it had so much high tech gadgetry it wouldn't have looked out of place flying to the moon. Equipped with a mini flat screen TV and voice controlled satellite navigation, it was the furthest you could get from the old GMC he had owned working as a carpenter.

Once on the freeway, he flipped the cruise control on and relaxed for a while. Eventually, the expected weekend traffic increased and forced him to slow it right down. Ron was amazed by the amount of folk dragging their trailers with speed boats to the coast or lakes, even though the weather had cooled. Just normal people taking their families away for a weekend in the pursuit of fun and happiness he thought, bitterly. He wondered if there would ever be a time he would get another chance of a normal life?

Eight years ago, he had begun to settle into a normal life with his girlfriend, Laura, but then it gradually turned sour before she eventually ran off with her gym instructor. They had shared an apartment for three years prior to the split. Looking back, he should have guessed it had started to fall apart when he was getting home from work to notes that simply said, “gone out”.

Ron and Laura first met at a pool party of a mutual friend. He had already drunk way too much when he had approached Laura and asked her for a dance. She had turned him down immediately of course but that didn't stop her secretly watching him throughout the night. She had instantly fallen for his boyish charms and his devil may care attitude to life. If the truth be told, she was also a little hurt that he hadn't pursued her further after her initial refusal. There had been plenty of other women at the party who were ready to jump in and flirt with him but she wasn't going to give in.

By the end of the night, Laura made a bold move and slipped a piece of paper with her phone number on it into Ron's hand before quickly getting into a taxi. She had expected a call the very next day but after hearing nothing for a week she managed to work herself into a fury. Laura eventually vowed to herself that if he called after such a long time she would ignore him. Not in a million years would she have considered going out with the Neanderthal after a whole week of no contact but he did call, and she buckled.

'Hi, this is Ron. We met at the party last weekend and you gave me your number,' he had said.

'Who?' Laura had asked, nonchalantly.

'Ron. Remember? I asked you to dance, but I'm afraid I was a little drunk at the time,' he laughed, nervously.

'Oh, yes, I remember you. I was a little worse for wear too. I can't remember giving you my number though,' she lied.

She listened to Ron as he laughed on the other end of the phone. In truth, she remembered everything about him. He had been dressed casually, in blue jeans and a white tee shirt that revealed his massive frame. Although clearly not a gym freak, his powerful build and square jaw cried out alpha male.

'Look, I, er, understand if it was a mistake, what with all the alcohol talking, but I just wondered if you fancied meeting up for a drink sometime?' he asked, slightly hesitantly.

It was immediately obvious to Laura that underneath his brutish looks and his over indulgence at the party, he was still a gentleman at heart.

'That would be great,' she said, a little too eager for her own liking, then quickly added, 'I can't make it this weekend though. How about next Saturday?'

It wasn't as if she was doing anything that weekend but she wasn't going to let him have things all his own way.

The following Saturday, Ron took her bowling for their first date. Although not the most romantic of venues, Laura had bowled many times previously so she genuinely enjoyed herself. Laura had a highly competitive side to her but Ron had been a whole different level. At three games down, Ron suddenly began to lose form, even dropping the occasional ball into the gutters. It was clumsily obvious that he was throwing a game but she happily took the win anyway. The whole night had been a success. After the bowling, they went for a nice meal then Ron drove her home in his old pick up. Laura had her own apartment at that time and was just about to ask Ron in for a coffee when, like a gentleman, he just kissed her and said goodnight.

After six months of steady dating, Ron moved into Laura's apartment. It was lucky that he didn't own a lot of stuff, as things became really cramped, but they managed.

Each week, Ron worked over a little on the nights and did a lot of weekends in order to save enough money to buy a bigger place. Twelve months later, they had enough money to secure a loan on an ageing run down property in a nicer part of town. They had plenty of fun doing up the old place, but things would occasionally become strained from time to time.

Ron's love of bowling became a real irritation to Laura so she would occasionally get theatre tickets for a Thursday or Sunday night so that he would miss his league nights. In fact, she did it so often that eventually, Thursday night, soon became "their" night. The other guys in the team eventually dropped him because of his constant absences. Ironically, shortly after being dropped, "their" night fizzled out and it became just another night in front of the telly.

As a result of her sedentary lifestyle, Laura started to lose her figure. She decided to join a gymnasium close to her office so she could call into it before going home. She quickly regained her stunning body, along with a desire for new conquests, this time in the form of the gym instructor.

Ron received the bombshell late one night after coming home to a letter saying she had left him because he had changed. She had written that he was no longer the person she had once loved and all he seemed to want to do was stay in and watch television. Her lawyers really went to town on him, leaving him with nothing except his clothes, his old pick up and his tools. After ending up renting a shit hole of an apartment, Ron vowed he would never fall for that again.

*

Sophie Parker refused to class herself as a vigilante. She didn't roam the streets attacking petty criminals but she did administer justice, in a way. Moral justice that is. Many years ago, she had been betrayed by the man she had loved and fully trusted. To make matters worse, she later discovered that it was her own sister who had been the other woman. Sophie never really recovered from that betrayal, and she still refused to speak to her sister. Sophie felt absolute trust could never happen again.

Now, as a result of her own past, she had become obsessed with uncovering and exposing all the lying and cheating adulterers. By day she was Sophie Parker, writer of computer code used to create small detail within popular games, but by night she went by the name Red Renarde. She carried a unique understanding of all things digital, so when her suspicions were aroused, Red Renarde found herself hacking into computers or phones to see what they were up to. It wasn't as if she spied on people indiscriminately but she did have a knack of sensing those who were up to no good. Because she wore neither a costume or a mask, unlike the Min-heroes, Red Renarde simply went about unnoticed.

She didn't target the younger generation flitting from one partner to another, she was more interested in exposing the home wreckers. Those who had long time partners, or had children and a family home. The ones willing to shatter their children's lives by searching out either a bit on the side, or a younger person. Those were the type who were the easiest to spot because they stood out like a sore thumb.

Red Renarde would sometimes sit alone in a bar, just watching those around her, looking for signs of deceit. Every so often a guilty suspect would enter the bar, suspiciously looking over their shoulder, making sure no one was about who might recognise them before sitting at a table with a spare seat opposite. Nine times out of ten, they would whip out a mobile phone and start texting their secret date. Red Renarde would quickly hack into their phone to see an affair unfolding. Plenty of times she would come across pictures of happy smiling spouses and their children, the very same family who were now being cheated on.

Sophie was fully aware she also carried the emotional scars of her parents breaking up when she was a young teenager. Not only did she have to watch them argue night after night about trivial stuff, but she had carried a secret guilt throughout her life. She found out about her mother's affair long before her father ever did but she could never find the courage to tell him. She had begged her mother time and time again to end the affair or at least tell her father, but all she ever got was broken promises that things would change. Trust was just a dirty word to Sophie these days.

Now, as she sat in the dimly lit bar called "Rendezvous," she spotted a well dressed man in his early forties enter the bar and look around nervously. The peaked cap on his head combined with the expensive suit couldn't have brought him any more attention even if he tried. Red Renarde watched him sit down in a vacant booth at the far end of the bar and call a waitress over. He whispered something into the waitress's ear, then pushed a twenty into her hand as payment for some sort of errand.

After nervously looking around, he predictably took his phone out of his jacket pocket and start punching the keys. Red Renarde discretely took out her own phone and opened a trace program she had written herself. Not only would it accurately detect every Bluetooth signal within the bar, it would also identify those that were in the process of a call or sending texts. She watched him finish the short text then he hit send. Immediately a cell phone number flashed up on her phone but strangely, no further information accompanied it. Her program was designed to search the data bases and pick up any previous cookies sent to that phone and it should also display previous numbers linked to it.

To have such a high level of security on a phone meant the guy was clearly of some importance. Now curious as to who he was, she watched him carefully to see who he was meeting.

A few moments later, a new Bluetooth phone signal appeared on her screen, indicating someone else had just entered the bar. Sophie casually looked up and saw the new arrival talking to the waitress who had been slipped the tip by the well dressed man. As the waitress led the young woman over to the secluded booth it was obvious to Red that this was the woman he had been nervously waiting for.

Sophie immediately highlighted the new signal on her screen and pressed search. There was little in the way of security this time, and within moments she had discovered that the phone belonged to a Janet Beacham, secretary to a large law firm dealing with high profile clients. Casually, she browsed Janet's social media activities until she came to her recent entries. Although mentioning no names, Janet had posted an entry, telling her friends that she was going on a date today with a guy she had met through work. A few of her friends had wished her good luck and predictably, a few had posted lewd comments accompanied with smiley emojis next to them.

Red watched the well dressed man stand and greet Janet with an awkward hug and a peck to the cheek, then they both sat back down.

According to Janet's social media, she was thirty-one a week ago and had suffered a string of failed relationships, some lasting mere weeks. Sophie found herself involuntarily shaking her head as she browsed Janet's history. For a legal secretary, she was clearly gullible if she was expecting a fairy tale ending to this relationship too.

Sudden movement from across the room brought Red back from her browsing. The two had abandoned the privacy of the booth and were now walking towards the exit. No doubt, using the *Rendezvous* had been Janet's choice of a first date meeting point, after all it wasn't far from her offices. The chances were, the place was mostly used for works parties and get togethers, such as birthdays or other special occasions. It was definitely not a comfortable experience for the well dressed man though and it showed as he led Janet towards the exit, trying to force a smile.

Red Renarde suspected they would head to some discrete, expensive restaurant where he could flash some cash to impress Miss Beacham, then who knows what later that evening. She discreetly angled her mobile phone up and recorded the happy couple as they passed her table. The facial recognition program on her laptop back at home would clear up who the mystery man was. Whoever he was, he looked overly nervous. If she found out he was cheating on his family, she would compile a file of evidence against him and expose the slime publicly.

*

'Charlotte speaking, how may I help?' came the familiar voice, over the Ford's speaker phone.

Ron momentarily wondered if the phone that Charlotte was using had any caller ID from the way she answered. He was under no illusion that his whereabouts were being monitored, so it would be inconceivable that she wouldn't know who was calling, yet she made no attempt to deviate from the formalities.

'This is Ron here,' he said, in a half hearted attempt at playing her own game. 'I was wondering if you could find me the names and addresses of all the suspected victims of the "Meter Master," please?' He figured that as long as he had a government agency looking over his shoulder, he may as well make use of them.

'Is there anything else?' Charlotte asked.

The question took Ron back a little and he wasn't sure if she was being sarcastic, but after a short pause he realised she was just being professional.

'No, thank you, that's all for now,' he said.

'I will send them over right away.' Charlotte hung up.

As the phone clicked off, he made himself a small wager that sooner or later, he would get her to crack a smile.

Almost instantly his phone buzzed and a little paper clip symbol appeared at the top of his screen, indicating his file had arrived. No doubt, there was a multitude of files on each of the vigilantes should he request them.

By the time he pulled off the road and onto the parking lot of "Sally's Eat n Sleep" motel, dusk had arrived. With only a handful of other motors scattered about the place he knew getting a room wouldn't be a problem tonight. He pulled up close to the red neon sign indicating the reception area then went in search of Sally. It wasn't a high class establishment by any stretch of the imagination. It was more the sort of place where you would expect to find chalk outlines on the floors, but Ron didn't let those sorts of details worry him.

The broken glass panel at the bottom of the reception door had been replaced by plywood, maybe as a temporary measure at the time, but it was now clearly showing serious signs of age. Ron pressed the flimsy handle down but the door remained stubbornly closed, forcing him to put his shoulder against it. As he burst in, a voice from the other side of the counter announced, 'Don't mind that door my dear, I've been meaning to get it fixed.'

A large, middle aged receptionist wearing a well worn red tee shirt with "Sally's" printed across the stretched fabric sat behind the counter. A smell of stale cigarette smoke hit him as he stepped down the few steps into the reception area and approached the tall counter. Partially obscured, was a small TV set in the process of showing some sort of soap opera. He knew it was a soap because the characters were always in the middle of a blazing row. No wonder so many people were on Prozac he thought.

'A room for the night please,' Ron asked, pleasantly.

The receptionist eyed Ron a moment then dragged out a big, tatty, vinyl bound register and started to thumb through the pages.

'Have you travelled very far?' she asked, in an attempt to strike up some degree of small talk, probably suffering from the effects of prolonged solitary confinement behind the desk.

'Not too far,' Ron replied, non committally.

The receptionist paused, waiting for her client to elaborate, but when she realised nothing else was forthcoming, she carried on thumbing through the pages.

'Would you like a ground floor or first floor room?' she asked, her finger poised over an entry in the book.

'First please,' Ron replied, giving her no time to strike a conversation up.

She scribbled something illegible in the book then turned it around and placed it in front of her new guest.

'It's fifty dollars up front, per night and I'll need you to fill the book in please.' She half watched Ron fill the ledger in whilst still watching the quarrelling couple on the TV.

Ron flipped the book back around and slid it over, along with his new credit card, offering the faintest of smiles. Without even looking at the entry, the receptionist popped the card into the reader, punched a few buttons and handed the device wordlessly back to Ron. He doubted the room was worth the fifty dollars but as it was being funded from the pockets of drug barons, it was a steal, so to speak.

'Checkout is at ten thirty. If you leave early there is a key box you can post your key through at the front of reception,' she said, pointing to an area just outside. Then she handed Ron a key with an oversized fob, along with his card and receipt.

Ron cast his eyes about for the room numbers as he walked across the almost empty parking lot, savouring the fresh air once more. At the top of the first set of stairs, all the rooms had adopted a one in front of their numbers in an attempt to indicate they belonged to the first floor. As he walked along the balcony, he pointed his key fob towards his truck and clicked the lock button once again, just to be on the safe side. The lights flashed briefly to reassure him that it was already locked. Double checking your property's security was a prison habit that everyone learnt quickly if they ever wanted to keep it.

It was evident by the musky smell that room one-o-seven hadn't been used in a long while, but it was still a little better than he had expected. For starters, there had been no chalk outline on the floor. Ron pulled the curtains closed then switched the light on. The majority of the small room was occupied by the large bed but at least it had a few homely touches. A small flat screen TV was bolted to the wall and a kettle, along with little sachets of instant coffee and powdered milk, sat in a dish on the dressing table below.

He flicked the switch on the panelled electric heater and was quickly rewarded with the smell of burning dust filling the room. The window at the back of room looked out onto the pool area and beyond that was "Sally's Bar". The dimly lit pool had been severely neglected and the dark liquid that filled it, topped with leaves, offered a stark reminder that anyone entering without their jabs being up to date would do so at their own risk. He pulled the remaining curtains shut, filled the kettle from the bathroom sink, then slumped down on the bed.

*

By the time Red Renarde managed to exit *Rendezvous*, the odd couple had already jumped into a waiting black car and were just driving off. She quickly tried to snap a picture of the car's licence plate as it drove off but another car was too close behind. With nothing more she could do about it for now, she turned and calmly walked away in the opposite direction. Although her Toyota was only parked two blocks down, she knew they would be long gone before she could get to it. She wasn't too worried about it though, she knew she could pinpoint their exact location from Janet's phone later.

That was the wonderful thing about technology. Designed to make our day to day lives easier and fun but in the wrong hands it could also be misused to seriously invade a person's privacy. She regularly told herself that what she did wasn't about invading the privacy of everyday people, it was about bringing justice for them.

On her phone screen, she watched the blue location dot indicating Janet's position as she headed out of town. They were obviously heading off to a remote location, no doubt a place where they wouldn't be spotted by prying eyes.

If it was going to be another long night of surveillance she would need to grab a burger before heading out after them. She would have at least an hour before Mr and Miss happy left the restaurant, no doubt in search of some sleazy hotel room for the evening. She considered taking the drive through but at the last minute decided to go inside as the foot-well of her passenger seat was already strewn with litter from her previous stake outs.

After grabbing her food, Sophie found a quiet seat away from others. As she sat there, all alone, she started to ask herself questions. What the hell was she doing this for? She knew this was becoming an unhealthy obsession, spiralling out of control. Sophie was all too aware that she was damaged goods and she hated herself for not being able to stop. It wasn't even as if she was really making a difference. Half the people she had previously exposed were still with their partners anyway. No doubt, they had shed tears and given hollow promises of never going to do it again but once a cheat, always a cheat. Half of all adulterers actually did it for the thrill of being caught.

As she sat, eating her burger, Sophie watched the people going about their business. Some looked as if they had been working late and either couldn't wait till they got home or maybe they figured it wasn't worth cooking when they did. Young couples still living with their parents used the place for a moment of privacy, and families used it to add an extra treat after a show for their young children. She realised, most folk had their own problems to contend with but at least they also had moments of happiness. Being hooked on other people's problems was just dragging her down into a pit of depression.

Without thinking, she took out her phone to see Janet's location and immediately hated herself for doing so. The blue dot indicated that they had settled on the outskirts of town. Taking another bite of her burger, she opened the street view and found the location was a small motel. According to the motel's out of date web site, it had forty luxurious rooms, surrounding a state of the art pool, and a first class restaurant and bar adjoining. Motels were ten a penny just outside large towns. The land was cheaper, and those passing through usually sought accommodation quickly after a long journey. Most likely Miss Beacham would see inside one of those luxury rooms tonight, but Sophie doubted that she would ever see inside Mr Well Dressed Man's home.

Putting her phone down, she absently watched a young couple a few tables away talking. Obviously truly in love, neither took their eyes from each other as they ate their food. Sophie bitterly wondered if either of them would end up in a sleazy hotel room trying to get intimate with a stranger in twenty years time. She berated herself for the dark thought.

Could she ever learn to trust someone again, she asked herself? Maybe her standards were just too high. Maybe she should have expected her ex would have been banging her sluttily dressed sister. Sophie realised she had serious issues and the more she dwelled on them, the more it began to eat at her. She finished off her fries and coffee then sat for a moment longer, looking at the flashing blue locator dot on her phone. Closing the app, she stood up then went home.

*

Ron woke to a darkened room. He could hear the muffled sounds of music coming from the rear of the building but it took him a few moments to remember where he was. Rubbing his hand across the stubble on his chin, he eased himself upright. He hadn't intended to sleep, but after the long day's drive he had needed to just rest his eyes a moment. Light creeping out from the bathroom cast long shadows across the darkened bedroom, giving the illusion of others in the room. He couldn't remember leaving the light on, but as his eyes adjusted to the room, he soon came to terms with his solitude. He flicked the light switch by the bedside on, took another gaze around the room then went for a shower.

It was almost eight thirty by the time he found the way down to "Sally's" front door, so to speak. The bouncer on the door, who looked like a heart attack waiting to happen, demanded a ticket as Ron approached. His aggressive, rehearsed tone changed immediately as soon as Ron flashed his residents giant key fob that had promised free entry in the brochure.

'Welcome to Sally's', he stuttered, completely out of character and stood aside as if Ron was the new president.

Inside, the place was clearly a very popular venue for both town locals and fellow transients alike. A low level stage had a Kenny Rogers tribute singer blasting out country and western tunes to his heart's desire. Ron chose himself a quiet table at the back of the room. A waitress, dressed in hot pants and looking almost young enough to be his daughter, quickly approached.

'Good evening, my name's Judy and I'll be looking after you tonight. What can I get you?' she asked, with a sixty four thousand dollar smile.

'I'll have a large Jack Daniels and ice please,' he

said, trying to avert his eyes from her short supply of clothing. 'Are you still serving food?'

'We sure are hun, I'll fetch you a menu,' Judy said, before dashing off.

Ron leant back against the squeaky, vinyl buttoned, bench seat and relaxed a little. On the low level stage the Kenny Rogers clone was now singing about a woman heading towards the cheating side of town. That was the defining thing about country and western music, they always told it how it was, he figured. Rock music usually waffled on about always loving someone, which was comical if you gave it any real thought. It's hard to imagine carrying on loving someone when they are banging your boss, have their hand in your pocket, then take away your house. Rock music was for dreamers who had never been on the receiving end of a shit storm; country music was for those who had experienced real life.

Young Judy returned, laid down a small paper napkin and set his drink down in front of him, along with a laminated menu card.

'I'll be back in just a moment to take your order, hun,' she said, then dashed off towards a whooping and cheering melee, sitting close to the stage.

Ron watched her taking drink orders, all the time receiving lewd comments and slaps to her backside from the drunken clientele. He felt sorry for the kid, and hoped she was just doing this job to help fund her college education. Maybe one day, she could come back as a lawyer and sue some of these low lives for harassment. In reality, he guessed things may not turn out to be so rosy for her.

He took a sip of the whiskey and savoured the

fiery liquid. The last time he touched strong liquor was in prison, at the hands of the "Still". Shuddering at the memory, he wondered what sort of damage he must have done to his lifespan by drinking that moonshine.

Judy reappeared, looking none the worse for her molestation and took Ron's order. The food turned out to be good and the portions even filled the plate, unlike the swanky place that Landon had taken him to.

By eleven, he decided the constant stream of depressive songs was enough to wear even the happiest of optimists down. He settled his bill with a fifty, telling Judy to keep the change, then headed to the door. The fat bouncer was now sitting on a plastic chair in the entrance hall, his head tilted forward and his eyes closed. For a moment, Ron considered calling a medic until he heard faint snoring sounds coming from the guy. Relieved, he stepped outside and savoured the cool night air and relative peace as the door closed softly behind him. He could hear a couple, just around the corner arguing about something. No doubt, the combination of alcohol and depressing music had fuelled the need to get things off their chests.

Although he needed to walk past them to get to his room, he figured it best to leave them alone to figure things out. He sat on the low wall and listened to the quarrelling as it grew louder and louder. Ron managed to gather from the occasional non profanity, that the guy had been unfaithful, and now she wanted him out of the house. Even though the argument was hotting up around the corner, the cold night air was starting to bite.

Ron was just about to take a long walk around the block when he heard an almighty slap that echoed across the complex. Things usually go one of two ways when an argument gets physical. Either it abruptly draws a line under matters, or it quickly spirals into a full on fight where one person ends up losing out dramatically. Ron paused a few heartbeats, then realised it was going down the violent route.

'Woah, buddy. I think it's gone far enough don't you?' he said, stepping around the corner and into sight for the first time.

If this wasn't déjà-vu, nothing was, he thought. He knew getting involved only brought him trouble, except this time, he had friends in high places ready to bail him out.

Ron edged himself between the couple, in the hope that he could calm the situation down. The guy was bigger than Ron by half a head but towered over the petite woman who was now desperately trying to stem the flow of blood from her nose. Without warning, the big guy swung a punch that might have felled a donkey had it made contact, but it was so telegraphed Ron leant back and avoided it then drove a punch into the guy's ribs. The delayed action of a punch to the floating ribs was a sight to see. Instinctively, the big man first squared back up to Ron, then collapsed to his knees, gasping for air from his folded lung. Ron knew the damage was only going to be temporary so he turned to the woman before the guy could recover. Although she had just managed to stem the flow of blood from her nose, he suspected she would look like a panda bear come the morning.

'Have you somewhere to go to tonight, other than home of course?' he asked.

She nodded, still pinching the bridge of her nose.

'I suggest you go there now and contact the police.'

Ron watched her as she slowly weighed up her options before she finally spat a large wad of blood at the kneeling man, then walked off. The big guy was just looking as if he was getting his breath back a little so Ron decided it was a good time for him to go too.

Locking the door behind him, Ron dropped the oversized key fob onto the dressing table and sat down on the edge of the bed. The all but brief skirmish with the big guy outside the restaurant had raised his heart rate and he knew sleep would be impossible. It wasn't just the woman getting knocked about that played on his mind, it was the young waitress getting abused that also troubled him. Caring just seemed to get him in trouble time and time again.

He picked up his phone and opened the file that Charlotte had sent him earlier, concerning the car cutting nut job. As he browsed through more pictures of severed cars, an idea came to him. He shuddered at the potential outcome if it went as planned but the guy had it coming. First, he would have to visit some of the victims to see what they had to say.

THREE

It was almost ten o'clock by the time Sophie crawled out of bed, her eyes fighting tooth and nail to remain closed. The image looking back from the bathroom mirror was shocking. On her way back from the burger joint last night, she had stopped off at the all night store to pick some milk up. On impulse, she had ended up buying a bottle of whiskey to drown out the demons. Very little of the spirit remained in the bottle this morning.

Bitter sweet childhood memories of her father were the reason behind the impulse buy. Although originally not a big drinker, he used to keep a wide collection of fine whiskies in a locked cabinet in his study. From a very young age, she would eagerly run to him and sit on his lap whenever he poured himself a glass of the golden liquor. He would offer the glass to her so she could take a deep breath of the fumes to see if she could identify the mixture of smells. The very first time, she had baulked at the smell, but natural curiosity had driven her to persevere. As time went by, she began to acquire a fondness for the smells and learnt to accurately identify some of the different ingredients. Even though her father would never allow her to sip the whiskies, he still felt the sting of her mother's tongue for playing their games. Occasionally, when her mother was out, he would allow Sophie to dip a finger into his glass on the condition she would swear to secrecy.

When her mother and father eventually divorced, he fell apart quickly and drank the entire contents of the cabinet within weeks of finding out about her affair. It broke Sophie's heart to see her father spiralling down, out of control, and just eighteen months later he died of liver failure. Now, as Sophie poured herself a cup of strong coffee, she realised just how her father must have suffered day after day. Buying the bottle had been a stupid idea, born from feeling trapped on a downward slope. Hell, it wasn't even a good whiskey.

She knew her life was at a pivotal point. If she carried on the path she was walking, it would only end in self destruction. From now on she needed to sort her own life out first. No more spying on others she thought. She noticed her phone was still lying on the coffee table, obviously discarded the night before. Reluctantly, she picked it up and unlocked the screen. Janet was still at the motel!

*

A heavy clunk echoed around the complex as Ron dropped the key through the slot in the top of the empty metal departure box. Although it was already eight thirty, there still wasn't a soul in sight. It had been around one AM when he turned his light off to go to sleep, as the faint hum of country music still filled his room. Maybe this *was* the cheating side of town and all other occupants were sleeping off the effects of a good night out, he couldn't help thinking.

The good night's sleep had left him in a positive frame of mind and determined to track down the Meter Master. Rather than systematically go through every name on the list of victims, he decided to head to a few of the more remote locations. Ron figured any nut job could find a parking offence in a city but the more remote incidents were surely the result of passing opportunities. There was one place he wanted to stop off at first that might reveal a few answers.

He took the eighty five, towards Atlanta, switched the radio on and settled down for another long drive. It was just after lunchtime when he pulled up onto a large commercial forecourt, containing every type of police vehicle you could think of. Most of the motors that were parked up had suffered some sort of damage to the front or side, probably from contact with the bad guys. He knew the police down here didn't take any shit from the criminals and if they failed to stop when ordered, they made them stop. This was the place where mechanics patched up all the broken cars before shipping them out again in a bid to stop more bad guys.

Ron pressed the key fob and the lights on the truck flashed as he headed off towards the building. A big sign on the edge of the parking lot directed all visitors towards a shiny fronted reception block. He knew, inside would be a young girl with one of those new fangled telephone headsets with a stick mouthpiece to talk into, just like the ones they used in Captain Scarlet back in the sixties. Receptionists usually lived in a world of isolation. If you didn't have an appointment, a printed form of some sort, or even a laminated ID pass, you were automatically turned away.

Ron figured Reception would get him nowhere so he walked straight past the empty security hut and towards the workshop entrance with an air of belonging.

'Got to really know what ya doing with all these

different motors, eh? Bet you can't learn all this in a college classroom?' Ron said to the old guy, leaning over the front of a partially dismantled Dodge.

A big pile of engine components sat on a steel trolley close by. The mechanic leaning over the motor eyed Ron suspiciously a moment, then figured the he must have been allowed in or something. Either way it wasn't his concern.

'Hell mister, half the young kids they send me couldn't even change a wheel. Don't know what they will do when us old folk are gone. We live in a throw-away society these days. If someone can't fix it, they just send it away and crush it, then buy a new one. No wonder my taxes are so God damn high,' he said.

Ron certainly knew how to get folk talking.

'Are these standard or souped-up motors?' Ron asked, casually.

'Nah, most of these units are kept pretty much standard, all to do with the emissions and stuff. We can tweak them a bit by altering the fuel mapping a little, or change the air filters for freer flowing ones, but the manufacturers like to build them tamper proof now. Not like the old days when we used to skim the heads, change the valve gear and throw a big carburettor on them. Them were the good old days.' The old mechanic was in his nostalgic element now.

'I bet you've modified a few strange motors in your time then?' Ron suggested.

'You name it, I've probably done something to it to make it better,' the mechanic said, with a mischievous grin.

'What about one of those three wheel things they use for the parking wardens?' Ron joked.

The old mechanic stopped his tinkering and looked at Ron as if he had just asked about his sister.

'What in God's name would anyone want to modify one of those death traps for?'

'You know, for one of those crazy TV shows where they race lawn mowers and such like,' Ron suggested.

'It would all depend on what you wanted the thing to look like I suppose,' he said, rubbing a greasy thumb across his white stubbled chin. 'I mean, with an unlimited budget you could do just about anything.' The old mechanic's eyes had lit up at the mention of a TV show.

'What about if you wanted to keep the thing looking standard, but with the ability to go really fast?' Ron asked, eagerly.

'Now, you're talking about a sleeper. Those things take a bit of extra thought. You can't just drop a "V" eight in it because the motor will stick out the top. You'd need something like a sports bike engine to give it the speed you're talking about,' he said, with disappointment on his face.

'Is that something you could do?' Ron asked, suggestively.

'Mister, I work on cars. What you want is a custom bike shop. Besides I've got too much work to do here,' he said, defensively.

'Thanks for your time anyway. Great to see a real mechanic in action by the way,' Ron said, turning to leave.

'You could try Rick and Ralph's down in Jacksonville. They're probably the best custom bike builders around. Don't come cheap mind.'

Ron's flattery had spurred the old mechanic into being a little more helpful.

'Don't suppose you know where I could buy one of those old three wheelers do you?' Ron asked.

'Police auctions, last Wednesday of every month. They sell off all the old vehicles that have supposedly outlived their life. There are some real bargains for someone who knows how to fix them. Good luck my friend,' the old mechanic said, before leaning back over the dismantled engine.

As Ron made his way back towards his truck, a young security officer poked his head out of the little wooden hut.

'Hey mister, you're not supposed to be in there,' he called out.

'Just been visiting an old friend,' Ron said, as he walked on.

The young security guard didn't bother pursuing the matter further.

For the remainder of the afternoon, Ron went to speak to some of the Meter Master's victims and by the end of the day he could understand why people had made this nut job out to be a super hero. The first three so called victims turned out to be real ass-holes. He had knocked on their doors under the pretence of writing an article for "Public Action", a new and exciting weekly magazine, coming soon. Some of them had been suspicious and reluctant to speak to him at first. One had just gone on and on about his insurance refusing to pay out on his Acura because it was parked in a dangerous zone.

The guy obviously had a light bulb moment half way through the interview because he suddenly said, 'Hey, I'm going to get paid for this article ain't I?'

Ron tried to look sorry as he closed his little note book, 'I'm afraid we don't have the funds to pay for the stories yet,' he explained.

'You print anything that I've just said and you'll hear from my lawyers in that case,' he said, aggressively.

Ron didn't retaliate in any way. Instead he simply thanked the guy for his time as he stood up and towered over him. The owner of the dissected Acura had flinched, worried that he was also about to became a victim of a violent crime.

The two other "victims" also turned out to be arrogant and self centred successful business men. The typical type who saw an opportunity and took it, regardless of the trail of bodies they had to step over to get there. One of them had claimed the store parking lot wasn't big enough and had therefore left him no choice but to park in the disabled space. He was in the process of suing the store for the price of a new Enclave and personal compensation for the distress caused by the devastating scene he had to endure. As Ron took notes, he tried to feign sympathy.

Ron's last call of the afternoon was at a young lady's home, just north of Albany. The address led him to a small rundown apartment block on the outskirts of town. Like all towns, they are arranged into the "have" and the "have nots", and this was definitely a have not side of town. Inside the rundown apartment block, graffiti covered the staircase that smelt as if it had doubled up as a urinal. Stepping out onto the first floor landing, a gang of lurking youths eyed him menacingly, but they obviously didn't fancy their chances against the big man and nonchalantly stepped aside for him to pass.

He found the apartment at the far end of the balcony and knocked the door. After a short while, he heard a faint scuffling from the other side, then a young voice called out, 'Who is it?'

'Miss Watkins? Sorry to bother you mam, I'm from a small up and coming magazine called Public Action. We are writing an article on the vigilante who calls himself "The Meter Master". I was wondering if you could share your story?' Ron asked, through the closed door.

He heard a faint click as the latch was unfastened, then seconds later a face appeared between the small gap that the flimsy security chain allowed. Ron stood back a little to allow the young woman to assess him. He realised he didn't look the most homely of visitors but offered what he thought would be his most welcoming smile. Miss Watkins' eyes darted along the balcony briefly, then back to the big man standing in front of her.

Ron couldn't help feeling a pang of disappointment at her lack of caution when she eventually unhooked the chain, but offered her another friendly smile none the less. As soon as he'd entered the little apartment, Miss Watkins rapidly re-chained the door behind them. Ron realised that the sad reality of the situation was she felt safer inside her home, with what could potentially be a homicidal maniac, than with the threatening gangs outside. A similar thought must have just occurred to her because she suddenly hesitated at the sight of the big man she had just invited into her lounge.

'Please, have a seat,' she said, indicating the armchair that had been stylishly covered with a floral throw. 'Can I get you some coffee?' she asked nervously, now keeping a little space between the big man and the door, just in case she had invited the big bad wolf into her house of bricks.

'That would be great, just a dash of milk thanks,' Ron replied, sitting down on the floral chair.

As Miss Watkins went off into the kitchen, he cast his eyes around the apartment. Although it was better suited to an older person he guessed it must have been rented that way. There was a framed picture on top of the television of Miss Watkins holding a small child. In the corner of the room sat a large wicker basket, neatly stacked with numerous toys that would probably suit a six or seven year old boy.

'It is Miss Watkins, isn't it?' Ron asked, holding his note book in front of him.

She had just walked back into the room carrying a tray, containing two coffee mugs and a half opened packet of digestives.

'Please, call me Emma,' she said, setting the tray down on the small table between herself and her visitor. Although still wary, she had visibly relaxed a little. 'You're a reporter then?' Emma asked.

'Only small time. To be truthful, this is my first article for them. They've asked me to write a piece about this crazy man who rides around cutting illegally parked cars in half,' he replied, picking up his coffee.

Emma's face reddened. 'I hadn't parked illegally,' she said, angrily. 'I had run out of gas on the way to work. After five minutes of honking and shouting at me, some men decided the only way they were going to get past me was to push me to the corner of the road. Unfortunately it meant I was left blocking a fire hydrant. I had to walk over a mile to get a can of gas and when I got back that low life had sawn my Honda in half.' Emma looked close to tears. 'It wasn't much, but I needed that car to get to work,' she added.

'I take it the insurance company wouldn't pay out?' Ron asked.

Emma looked a little sheepish. 'Truth is, the insurance had not long run out. I was waiting for pay day before I could renew it,' she sighed.

Life was a real bitch sometimes but it always seemed to be a bitch to the wrong people.

'I'm sorry I can't tell you any more than that. This so called, "Meter Master" had long gone by the time I got back to my two pieces of Honda.'

'Not a problem. You've given me plenty to write about,' Ron said, scribbling a few extra notes into the little book. 'Is that your son in the picture?' he asked, trying to ease the tension.

'Yea, that's little Bobby. He's with his father this weekend,' she replied, with an air of pride.
'You have any kids?' she asked

'Never met the right woman,' Ron replied, truthfully. There was a moment of silence as Ron downed the last of the instant coffee then stood. 'Much obliged to you for the coffee and the story, mam,' he said, holding out his hand.

Emma shook it without hesitation, all apprehension of her visitor long gone.

'Oops, nearly forgot,' Ron said, taking his wallet from his back pocket and pulling five hundred bucks from it. 'This is for your contribution to the magazine.'

He dropped the cash on the coffee table and offered a warm smile. He would pull some more of the dirty money from a hole in the wall later, but for now, he couldn't think of a better use for it.

*

Janet awoke to total darkness and a throbbing pain inside her head. A hazy recollection of going out to a bar the night before swam around in her mind but she couldn't recall the details. Slowly she forced herself to trace the events leading up to the present moment. What was the present moment and where was she, she asked herself? Her legs felt cold and numb. Instinctively, she went to reach for a blanket to pull over her legs. Panic engulfed her as she began to realise her hands and legs were tied. No, not tied, taped together. She tried to scream for help but her mouth had also been covered with tape, and the adhesive tugged at the hairs on the nape of her neck as she struggled to move her jaw. Frantically, she began thrashing about, kicking and forcing her body to and fro until eventually she had to pause to try to snort some restricted air back into her lungs.

Her arms had been tethered behind her back and to something, preventing her from standing upright. Adrenaline fuelled her senses enough to now realise that the darkness was the result of having a thick hood tied over her head. Through her sweat and tears, she could just make out tiny pin pricks of light filtering through the fabric. Although the hood was only loosely secured around her neck to allow air to flow, there would be no chance of pulling it free.

She tried to calm down a little, not because of any sort of escape plan but because she had no other choice. Her heart was hammering inside her chest and she felt

a desperate need to urinate.
She could hear sounds of distant traffic and the slight movement of the floor led her to believe she might be in some sort of vehicle, but she could sense no other people. If she could just free her hands, maybe she could get out and run for help. She strained her wrists against the tape, first twisting then trying to reach her fingers around in the vain hope of discovering the tape's end. It was useless. With her arms behind her back there wasn't going be any chance of freeing herself.

Having time to think a little more clearly now, she shuffled her bum over her hands and tried to bring her legs back. If she could just get her hands in front of her, maybe she could lift the hood and use her teeth to unwrap the tape. A tether stopped her from sliding her hands forward under her legs, so instead she lay on her back with her feet in the air. It was tough going, as the tape went high up her forearms, leaving little room to move, but she eventually pulled her legs through. As she lay panting for breath, she heard a key turn in the door.

*

Sophie glanced at her phone yet again as she walked past the breakfast bar. Although she had firmly decided to leave the life of Red Renarde behind and get on with her own, she couldn't help feeling a sense of responsibility for Miss Beacham. After all, she had witnessed her leave the bar with the well dressed man, arrive at a motel on the outskirts of town, but no movement since. If the blue location dot on her screen had indicated a return to Janet's home address, she would have dismissed all concerns. Janet Beacham's social network would have lit up with more stories of being used and discarded and Sophie could have got on with rebuilding her new life.

No one stayed in a motel past mid day, especially if they lived just an hour's drive away. There could be any number of reasons why Janet's phone was still at the same location. Janet could simply have lost the device, getting in and out of the car, or it could have slipped down the side of a chair. After all, it wasn't that unusual to lose a phone. Sophie knew she may be fussing over nothing but a nagging suspicion that something wasn't quite right lingered at the back of her mind.

It wasn't inconceivable that Janet had enrolled in another night of passion but Sophie figured no self respecting woman would stay a second night without an overnight bag. Then again, perhaps Janet wasn't as self respecting as she first appeared. After all, she had allowed herself to be whisked away to some seedy motel in the first place. Sophie chided herself for such poor thoughts. There was no saying that Janet hadn't been taken there against her will. Admittedly, she had looked a willing partner when she left the bar last night but that wasn't to say things hadn't turned ugly later. It was no good. Her imagination was starting to tie her thoughts up in knots and the only way to stop it was to witness Janet Beacham safe and sound. Only *then* could she close the chapter on the part of her life that was Red Renarde.

Up until now, Sophie had resisted the urge to trace the identity of the mystery man. His phone had carried a highly advanced encryption program, used to block any potential hackers from tracing his identity.

Only someone with a need for absolute secrecy would take such precautions, usually a government official. Facial recognition, on the other hand, was almost impossible to avoid. Sophie transferred the images that she had discreetly taken in the bar onto her laptop.

Although the advanced programming on her smart phone ran better software than most computers, it was still hampered by the smaller screen. Sophie's fingers nimbly danced across the keys, spelling out words faster than most people could speak them. After highlighting a square around the man's face and removing all remaining background from the picture, she entered it into a program. It wasn't quite a full frontal shot but she knew, somewhere in the system, there would be a picture that would prove compatible.

The program automatically took age differences, facial hair and hairstyles into consideration. It would focus on the things no one ever noticed beyond the superficial. The shape of the forehead, the size of the nose, cheekbones, or eye position in relation to ear position. They were the basic things that most people overlooked but the computer program was designed to flag up similarities. Airport security staff were trained to look for similar things when checking passports. It was amazing just how few passport pictures ever looked the same as the person's current image.

Sophie let the program run while she went off to make herself a cup of tea. With the ugly taste of last night still in her mouth, she vowed to lay off the alcohol for a while. Standing, waiting for the kettle to boil, out of curiosity, she held out her hand in front of her and watched her fingertips tremble. If she drove now, she would still be classed as intoxicated.

Her laptop pinged, indicating the search program had finished. Usually it would take just seconds but this had taken almost five minutes to come back with a positive match. Whoever he was, he must have worked hard to remain incognito.

Sophie sat back down on the settee and curled her legs up under herself, the mug of hot tea warming her hands.

'So, Mr Well Dressed Man, who are you?' she asked the laptop screen. The search revealed just two matches from the facial recognition program. The first, unsurprisingly, was a high-school graduation picture. Sophie couldn't help being proud at her software for picking out the young boy on the second row, standing behind others in a graduation photo. Now that the figure had been highlighted, she could see the subtle similarities to the images taken in the bar. Her software named the boy as Sam Young. Apart from the usual basic stuff that could be retrieved from the government births and deaths department, there was very little information. Usually, when she ran a search on someone, she would have to trawl through page after page of junk.

Sam had one sister, named Margot Dewsbury. She was married to a lighting technician who had worked at the Hollywood studios for the last ten years. Both of Sam's parents were deceased. Their father had died from a cardiac arrest aged thirty seven and his mother had been killed in a car crash on a rainy freeway, four years later. News pictures had shown an unrecognisable wreck, sandwiched between two trucks. The only other highlighted picture of Sam was at the funeral of their mother, standing next to his sister. This time, the picture was clearly the same man she had last seen guiding Janet out of *Rendezvous'* door. The same newspaper had used the tragedy in an article, campaigning for trucks to be limited to lower speeds. The remainder of the file revealed he had enlisted in the army for six years after leaving high school, then he had transferred into government security, where he has remained to date.

Sam Young wasn't a married man, so he wasn't cheating on his wife, but Sophie still held suspicions that he was up to no good.

'Shit!' Sophie suddenly said aloud. Whilst flicking through Sam's files, she had failed to spot Janet's blue location dot disappear from her phone. Most likely, the battery had just run out and shut itself down. Phone manufacturers loved to boast their batteries lasted days between charges but in reality, with all the technology they carried, you would be lucky to get twenty four hours out of them.

Sophie finished off the last of her lukewarm tea, put her coat on, then headed out the door. An icy blast of cold air hit her full on as she made her way across the complex, prompting her to zip up the flimsy summer jacket she was wearing in a futile attempt to keep the chill out. Quickly, she jumped inside her Toyota and slammed the door shut, blocking out the wintry elements.

Even though the engine started at the first turn of the key, she couldn't help feeling a little ashamed for the neglect she had shown towards her faithful little car. She hadn't had it serviced in over two years and, thinking back, she hadn't even checked the oil in all that time either. She made another promise to herself, that once she had found Janet, she would treat her little chariot to a little TLC.

She sat, waiting impatiently as the security gates slowly slid open until there was just enough room for the Toyota to squeeze through. Then she stamped on the gas pedal, pausing only for the briefest of moments at the road junction, before she tore up the road.

*

The Flintlock was just another out of town destination, designed to be close enough to get home after a good night out, but also far enough to protect local residents from all the noise associated with that good time. Like most red neck venues, the single story diner had billboards outside claiming to offer the best of everything. The best steaks, the best beer and the best music, all until late. The big gravel parking lot had no more than a dozen vehicles in it but Sophie knew, come midnight, there would be all sorts of drunken activity going on here.

She parked up at the far end of the lot and slid her mobile from her jacket. She knew it would come up blank but it was still worth a long shot. As expected, there was still no blue dot but that meant nothing other than it had run out of battery.

The cold wind hit her once again as she stepped from the car, a stark reminder her that winter was coming. With her jacket zipped right up to her chin, she slowly walked the perimeter of the vast parking area, moving the odd beer can to one side with her foot in the vain hope of spotting a phone. The more she thought about it, the more things didn't add up. If the bar in the city was too loud and busy, why in the world would he bring her out here?

She gave up searching after twenty minutes of kicking beer cans and headed around the corner of the building to the motel reception. Sophie doubted that the single, ancient security camera covering the entire diners parking area was even working, but it was worth a try. Drunken, illegal activity was the norm in these sorts of places and having surveillance was bad for business. The motel accommodation blocks, on the other hand, had little round globes containing modern CCTV cameras on every corner.

Sophie once again slipped into the Red Renarde persona, slid the large reception door to one side and stepped into the reception.

A woman in her late forties, sporting long, curly, blond hair and a plastic name badge with Jolene, looked up at the new arrival and smiled.

'Welcome to the Flintlock Motel. How can I help you?'

'Haay, 'am a wonderin' if you could help me. Ah bin a lookin' for ma sister. She didn't come home last night and our dear mamma is going plumb crazy with worry. She mentioned that she was comin' out here last night with her fella. The dirty hussy may have checked into one of your rooms with him. We just wanna know that she's okay, that's all,' Sophie said, laying down a thick southern drawl that she had used many times previously.

Sophie had found, face to face, the friendly accent managed to get folk talking, but over the phone, concise, clear English yielded better results.

The concerned look on Sophie's face must have triggered the motherly instinct in the receptionist.

'Oh you poor thing,' Jolene said, as she instinctively reached for the register. 'I was here from five o'clock up until midnight yesterday but I think we only had two check-ins in that time. There was an elderly couple, driving up to New York for a surprise fiftieth birthday party, and a young man, working out of town for a phone company and needed a place to stay for the night,' she said, turning the almost empty page back and forth as if miraculously, other entries might appear.

Sophie stood a while, deep in thought, a genuine look of concern written on her face now.

'Ah don't suppose you've had a mobile phone handed in bah chance do you? We've tried calling it all day but it seems to be switched off. She could have dropped it or summat,' she asked.

The receptionist didn't hesitate. She quickly bent down and brought up an old dusty shoe box with “Lost Property” written on the lid in thick marker pen and dropped it on the counter. She lifted the lid in clear view for Sophie to see. Apart from a couple of sets of keys, an old hairbrush and a half full shampoo bottle, there was clearly no phone.

'Sorry hun. I wouldn't hold your breath on a mobile phone being handed in around these parts,' the receptionist said, apologetically.

Sophie nodded her understanding and thanked Jolene for her time. Turning to leave, Sophie paused, hand on the sliding door lever.

'Ah don't suppose you have cameras on the front of the building do yah?' she asked, with pleading eyes.

'We do, but it's really not very good. The ones around the motel were updated last year but they haven't gotten around to doing in front of the diner yet,' Jolene replied. 'You're welcome to have a look if you want though,' she quickly added, seeing the crest fallen expression on the young southern girl's face.

Sophie thanked her profusely and sat down on the plastic chair offered, as the receptionist clumsily fumbled about with the CCTV controls. Eventually, after pressing every wrong button, Jolene managed to bring up yesterday's images of the diner's gravel lot.

'It records on a seven day loop,' the receptionist explained, pressing the backwards arrow at the bottom of the screen with the little cursor. The image rewound quickly until the recording indicated noon, then she took her finger off the computer mouse. 'Do you understand how it works?' she asked Sophie, as if she was teaching a child.

'Ah think so. This way to rewind and that way to go forward. And this button to freeze it?' she asked. 'It's very similar to mammy's VCR,' she added, keeping up the pretence.

The receptionist looked impressed. 'In that case, I'll go make us a couple of coffees while you look. Just shout if you need me,' she said, stepping through a side door into a little kitchenette.

Sophie knew the exact time Janet had arrived at the motel, so she quickly moved to around ten minutes prior. The recording showed that even though the parking lot was only half full, everyone had parked as close as possible to the entrance. No doubt, half the drivers exiting would be so drunk they would struggle to cross the large expanse of ground without a vehicle. An expensive looking RV sat close to the road, almost in the same position her Toyota now occupied. She watched the grainy image a while longer, her finger fast forwarding the recording at a speed where she could still see people arriving. She let the recording play at normal speed when a pick-up pulled onto the dusty gravel lot, four men hung onto the back as it raced around a little before parking at an angle in front of the fire doors. As the dust finally settled, she was just about to continue fast forwarding when she saw the black Sedan pull up alongside the RV. The image was very poor but she had no doubt the car was the same one they had got into, outside the bar. Sophie stared intently at the grainy screen, waiting for figures to appear but none did. Eventually the black car reversed up and drove off.

Jolene broke her thoughts as she came in from the kitchen holding two cups of coffee.

'Any luck there, hun?' she asked, setting a cup down in front of Sophie and looking over her shoulder at the grainy image on the screen.

'A'hm afraid not mam,' she replied, taking her finger of the fast forward button and picking up her coffee.

'Just call me Jolene,' the receptionist replied, indicating her obvious name tag.

'Susan,' Sophie replied, holding out a hand for a delayed formal introduction.

*

Rachael's fingers trembled as she held the letter. She had read it three times already but was still struggling to accept the words. A thin trickle of sweat ran between her shoulder blades and down her back. "Dear Rachael" the letter had begun. Why did all letters bringing impossible news start in that manner? She understood what it must have been like during war time when some poor woman would get a letter telling them that their husband or son had been killed in action. It probably went, "Dear Mrs Smith, I'm sorry but all your loved ones are dead. Have a nice day, signed, The War Office". Rachael read the letter once again, hoping that she had somehow read it incorrectly.

Dear Rachael,

I know it is another two weeks to your next session but I am writing to share some exciting developments with you. In two weeks time I will be getting married to my fiancé of two years, at last. As I will be relocating to Ontario shortly after, Dr Robin Morgan will be taking over your monthly sessions, which will continue as normal. I am sure you will find him to be a wonderful doctor, but please don't hesitate to call me if you have any questions.

Yours sincerely,
Dr Susan Willoughby

Rachael could feel her jaw involuntary clench as she held the letter in front of her. Why had she just been abandoned this way when everything had been going so well? It was as if she was some old piece of clothing, discarded and sent to a charity shop. She took a deep breath in, then slowly let it out again as Dr Willoughby had coached her to do in times of stress. She was strong and she could get through this, she told herself. Maybe Dr Morgan might be better than Susan Willoughby. What if he abandons her too though? Rachael felt her pulse quicken as she tried to rationalise her fears.

Her monthly therapy sessions with Susan had taught her to control her OCD just enough to get on with life. Their meetings had stopped revealing new issues long ago but Dr Willoughby had left the decision on when to stop the sessions altogether in Rachael's hands. The trouble was, the sessions had become so routine now, they were slipping into Rachael's OCD. She read the letter one more time before neatly filing it away in a small cabinet under the correct heading of "Dr Susan Willoughby" then reached for a small bottle of concentrated lavender oil.

*

Sophie checked Janet's social media once more, just in case she had logged on from an alternative source. With still no activity, she was becoming really concerned that something bad had happened. There was little the police would do at this point as they wouldn't be concerned until Janet didn't turn up for work tomorrow. Sophie knew she was getting sucked into something she didn't want to be in. Whatever she decided to do, she would need to keep her identity concealed. There were more than a few disgruntled people out there looking to take Red Renarde to court for exposing their extra marital activities.

She sipped her tea, then slid deeper into her hot bath, causing the bubbles to slip over the edge and soak the floor. Sophie could do no more today and once again the weekend had slipped away from her. She closed her eyes and basked in the warmth of the water as the sounds of a chilled wind picked up outside.

Suddenly, Sophie sat bolt upright, causing water to flood the bathroom floor even more. How could she have been so stupid? The RV in the parking lot! She had just taken it as being parked up but someone could easily have transferred Janet from the black car into the camper, undetected. The grainy CCTV picture had been poor and there would be no hope of picking up a license plate number but she distinctly remembered it being blue and white.

Stepping out from the bath onto the flooded floor, Sophie wrapped a bath robe around herself and tied the cord in order to keep the chill out. She noticed it had just begun to turn dark outside as she pulled the blinds shut and switched her laptop on.

If she could locate working traffic cameras close by, she may still be able to track down the RV as it drove off from the late night diner. It was a long shot as the area probably only had only a few traffic cameras but she had nothing to lose.

Sophie logged into the highways agency camera network and discovered there were only five cameras within a ten mile radius of the diner. It wasn't guaranteed they would pick up the RV and the odds that it would even pass one of the cameras were low. She sat, patiently rewinding images from each of the five cameras. It was painfully slow going and just as she was about to give it up as a bad idea, a clear image of a blue and white RV passed across her screen as it turned onto a busy freeway. There was too much traffic to get a good look at the license plate but now that Sophie had a time on the screen, it was simply a case of scanning along the freeway cameras until she could get the number.

Eventually, Sophie folded down her laptop lid and rubbed her eyes. She had spent hours of scrolling through traffic camera footage before eventually coming up with a clear image of the plate on the blue and white RV. However, after checking the number through the national data base, it came back as belonging to a 1998 Camaro, now registered as scrap. Sophie knew she was no longer just being paranoid. Something serious was happening.

*

Ron threw himself out of bed after waking to sounds of screaming coming from somewhere across the street. Half asleep, he peered out the hotel window expecting to see a woman being assaulted in some sort of way. As he stared intently, looking for potential victims and muggers alike, his focus drifted over to the skate park just across the street. A bunch of youths were happily showing off their skateboard moves on a graffiti covered half pipe. They were attempting increasingly difficult moves, in a vain hope of impressing a group of teenage girls nearby. One of the taller youths, probably not suited to balancing on a skate board, looked to have taken a fall and was sitting on a bench cradling his wrist. Ironically, it was his lack of abilities on a board that had led to a pretty young girl now fussing over him. Ron smiled at the scene.

Ron spent the next few days knocking on the doors of the Meter Master's victims, trying to gain as much knowledge as possible. One of his victims turned out to be a vociferous Italian man, who owned a restaurant, typically named *Mario's.* Although he had no time for Ron or his fictional story, he did let it slip that if he ever came across the culprit again, his friends in high places would make him disappear. It was exactly the kind of response Ron was looking for.

He could see why half the population loved this vigilante and the other half hated him. Folk had become fed up with the arrogance of rich people parking anywhere they wanted. Tickets, when they did happen, meant nothing to them and their deep pockets. With the Meter Master about, they had begun to think twice about where they left their prized auto-mobiles. The trouble was, too many innocents were suffering along the way too. The Italian hadn't been alone in expressing his desire for revenge. As soon as Ron found out who was behind the auto-mobile attacks he would share the knowledge and let nature take its course. First, he had one more victim to visit.

*

Even though leaves constantly fell like giant flakes of snow, it was clear the folks in this little area had been busy raking them up. The whole neighbourhood was like stepping back in time. Each single story house had a long garden at the front and a neat privet hedge on the boundaries to offer a modicum of privacy from their neighbour.

Most of the houses had large, open porch areas with some sort of seating area for dining or just whiling away the evenings in the warmer months. They were a good way of bringing the community together as folk sitting out on their porches would wave and talk to other folk as they passed by. It was good old fashioned communication, not like some of the youth of today who spent all their time inside their bedrooms texting. Half would claim to have hundreds of *friends* on their social media without ever meeting them, let alone talk to them in person.

Ron pulled up alongside the high kerbside. Like all the rest of the properties along the road, Mavis Oswald's house was well kept and the lawn immaculate. An elderly neighbour eyed Ron suspiciously as he raked the day's leaf fall from his lawn.

'If yer looking for Mavis, she's not home,' the old

man said, leaning on his rake.

'I don't suppose you'd know when she will be back do you?' Ron asked, in a polite, unthreatening manner.

'Dun't rightly know what time she will be back but if you want to speak to her you'll find her up at the church Halloween fete, end of the road, turn left.' The old man must have considered that was the end of the conversation because he carried on his raking, then paused and added, 'Only, the priest don't like you calling it a Halloween fete on accounts it can be associated with devil worshipping or something. He prefers it to be called the early winter festival, or something like that.' He went back to slowly drawing his leaves together.

Ron thanked the old man and climbed back into his truck, smiling to himself as he imagined the priest fighting a losing battle with the title of the fete. As he turned into the short road leading up to the church, parked cars lined the kerb. Pulling up in a space, he checked that he wasn't illegally parked. The threat of having his truck sawn in half hovered fresh in his mind.

The short walk up the hill led him to a set of the church's wrought iron entrance gates, already heavily decorated with all the usual items associated with devil worshipping. Just inside the church ground, a group of teenagers were still in the process of hanging bed linen over a mannequin in an attempt to make it look like a ghost. Pumpkins with hideous faces carved into them sat on top of random grave stones, waiting to be lit when darkness came. Ron marvelled at the artistry that had gone into them. A plastic skeleton had been wired into such a pose that it looked as if it was in the act of climbing over the church railings. The whole *Late Win-*

ter Festival looked great and Ron could sense the real feel of community spirit about the place.

A little old lady sat behind a large trestle, just inside the church gates, with a sign saying, "Adults $5 Children $2" next to her.

'Good morning mam,' Ron said, as he handed over a crisp five dollar note. 'I don't suppose you know where I can find Mrs Oswald do you?' he asked, cheerily.

The little old lady's wrinkled top lip gave her the impression of spitefulness.

'You can find her down the left side of the church, behind her cake stall,' she said, emphasizing the word "her".

Although he didn't know why, Ron immediately sensed friction going on between the two old dears. Maybe Mavis Oswald and the gatekeeper to hell were undergoing a popularity contest. Whatever the reason, Ron thanked her and set off in search of Mavis.

He wandered past an assortment of stalls selling all types of homemade crafts, books and bric-a-brac. Although it was still early for the Halloween activities, he guessed there would be no shortage of buyers ready to part with their money for a good cause around these parts. The cake stall was the only one that had a queue formed in front of it. A little old lady with white hair, who he assumed was Mavis, sat in a wheelchair, chatting away merrily to those waiting to be served. She wore a genuine smile and those around her were laughing at something she had just said. A woman in her mid thirties was in the process of carefully bagging slices of cake into paper bags for their line of customers.

The community was obviously very close knit, so it was no surprise when the laughter dried up as Ron approached the cake stall. Mavis Oswald, being the perfect host however, threw the newcomer a warm welcome.

'Hello stranger,' she said, with a mild southern accent.

Her smile was warm and genuine and Ron could see why the tight lipped gate keeper could be jealous of her popularity.

'I don't recall seeing you around these parts before.'

It was said as more of a question rather than a statement, so all eyes turned towards their new arrival.

'That is correct mam, I am a writer from a small New York magazine. I am writing an article on the man who calls himself "The Meter Master" and the effects his actions have on his victims.'

Any idle chatter between those in the queue suddenly stopped once more and all eyes turned towards Mavis.

'Mah Grandma has spoken in depth to the police men, mister. All that seems to happen is she gets upset and no action gets taken to find that mad man,' the young woman dishing out the cakes said, obviously angry at the lack of action being taken.

Mavis put a hand on her granddaughter's arm to comfort her rising anger.

'Don't mind Lucille. She is just trying to protect me from getting upset, Mr..?' Mavis let the question hang.

'Ron. Please, just call me Ron, mam.' He tried to offer his most apologetic look but he suspected it probably looked as though he just had wind.

'Well "Ron", if you would be so kind as to pass me my walking sticks and help this old woman to her feet, I can exercise my new hip while I tell you my story. My doctors have been so kind by fixing me up, but they made me promise I would walk as much as I could every day,' she laughed.

Lucille looked on in horror as the stranger stepped behind the big wooden table and approached Mavis. She relaxed a little when the stranger tenderly offered his arm to assist her frail old grandmother up.

'Don't wait up dear, I'm off for a romantic walk with my new man,' she winked at her audience, who all seemed a little more relaxed now.

Ron found himself flushing a little as all eyes fell on him. He could imagine that in her youth, Mavis Oswald would have been the life and soul of any party, pretty much as she was today.

The slow lap of the church grounds with Mavis turned out to be quite pleasant. As they walked, she explained the sentimental reasons for being so upset at losing her late husband's car to the vile, self appointed, parking warden. Even though her insurance paid out, they were only willing to offer her a measly payout for the car, saying it matched the current valuation. The nice man from the garage had brought the two halves of the Bel-air back and left them on the drive until she decided what to do with them. As Mavis talked, she became a little upset and dabbed a clean hanky to her eyes.

Even though it was only a short walk around the church grounds, Mavis managed to take full advantage of wearing her chaperone like a medal, stopping to talk to everyone. Each time she would introduce Ron as her new "Toy Boy" to the squeals of delight of all.

By the time they eventually returned to the stall, the queue had gone and Lucille was sitting down, reading a book. Ron gently helped Mavis back into her seat, under the watchful eye of her granddaughter.

'I can't thank you enough for your time, Mrs Oswald,' Ron said, stepping back around the table.

'You just call me Mavis,' she ordered, with mock scorn.

'Mavis,' Ron repeated, with a smile. 'Could I buy a slice of that carrot cake while I'm here then please, Mavis?' he asked.

'Ah, that's also my favourite,' she said, as Lucille popped a slice into a brown paper bag. 'Give our Mr Ron a slice of the special ginger cake as well, on the house,' she smiled mischievously at her granddaughter.

'Much obliged to you Mavis,' Ron said, handing a ten dollar bill to Lucille. 'Please put the change to your good cause,' he added.

As he walked back to his truck, he found his spirits lifted by the short time with Mavis. The old dear had been genuinely charming. It was sad that old people were often taken on face value. No one ever looked past the frail, wrinkly exterior to see the character inside that had also lived a younger life.

After climbing back into his truck, he opened the paper bag and took a bite of his ginger cake. The moist cake was perfectly cooked but he also detected one rouge ingredient that he had tasted many a time before, usually when his fellow inmates had shared stuff that their wives baked for them. He took a second bite, then wrapped the cake back up for later. Ron pulled away from the kerb with a smile on his face.

*

“Rick and Ralph's” was just like all the other factory units on the large industrial estate. It consisted of a small compound with a strong security fence all around it, allowing a reasonable level of security for stored vehicles awaiting repair or modification. As Ron walked through the open gates, he cast his eyes around at a few of the partial projects within the compound.

An old Dodge pick-up, with a fancy blower intake poking through the hood, stood in the far corner of the compound. Its doors were still in primer and the grill was missing, probably awaiting the body shop for some deep lacquered paint job. A few spaces along was a mangled wreck of a drag bike. Its missing handle bars and a bent anti wheelie frame were most likely the consequence of trying too hard when the lights went green.

What caught Ron's eye the most though, was the quad bike, sitting on a trailer close to the shuttered entrance. It looked pretty much a stock machine at first but on closer inspection Ron could see the powerful "K" series BMW engine had got a super charger unit bolted to the side. He stood admiring it for a moment, then his eyes became drawn to a smooth surface where the engine serial number used to be. It was immediately obvious this place didn't care where its replacement parts originated from, Ron figured.

He headed towards a green door next to the corrugated shutter and tried the handle. Ron half expected just a few people to be there on a Saturday afternoon but instead, he found a hive of activity going on inside. At first, no one spotted him as he stood, just inside the doorway. A radio was playing loudly and someone was grinding away at a piece of box steel that was fixed firmly in a vice. The shower of sparks from the grinder flew half way across the shop floor but no one paid them the slightest bit of attention. Another guy was working away under an old Chevy Nova, sitting high up on a car lift.

'Hello sir, can I help you?'

A young lad, holding two mugs of coffee, had just appeared from a little room on the side of the building, which must have been a canteen. Ron smiled at the lad.

'Yes, I'm looking for someone who could do a rather odd modification on a traffic buggy for me,' Ron lied.

The lad grinned like a Cheshire cat.

'That's not odd mister, we've already done one of those,' he proudly announced.

'Can I help you mister?'

The guy who had been working under the car, fixed Ron with a suspicious look as he wiped his greasy hands on a cloth.

'He wants us to do another traffic buggy,' the young lad beamed.

'Go take Joe his coffee,' the mechanic cut the lad off sharply.

The youngster looked offended by the curt instruction, then it suddenly dawned on him that he may have said too much already.

They watched the boy walk away before Ron dropped all pretence.

'I'm looking for the owner of that modified traffic buggy,' he said simply.

'I can't give out confidential information just like that,' the mechanic said, nervously carrying on with wiping his hands. The cloth was doing nothing to remove the black oil from his fingers but it served as a distraction.

'Aiding and abetting a criminal is a serious offence, you know.' Ron let the message sink in a moment or two before adding, 'Is the boss about?'

'He won't be in until Monday,' the young mechanic replied defensively, knowing he could be on shaky ground now.

'OK, I'll come back on Monday and have a talk with him. I might even bring a few of my FBI friends to have a chat about some motorcycle parts that have gone missing.'

Ron could see the young lad was starting to get flustered now.

'I honestly don't know where he lives mister. He just came in one weekend, laid down a wad of cash and asked us to make the fastest traffic buggy possible. Rick allows use the workshop on the weekends but he would go crazy if he found out we had done something illegal.'

It was an unwritten agreement that a lot of garage owners had with their workforce and it usually worked well for both parties. The junior mechanics could work on their friends and families motors on the weekend to earn a little extra cash and the garage owners had the comfort of knowing the building was safely occupied.

'You mean to tell me you didn't have an address for this guy?' Ron asked, calmly.

It was like a game of chess and he knew he had mate in two moves.

'That's right mister, he just came in one weekend and paid up front with cash,' the mechanic confirmed, nervously clutching his oily rag.

'How can you make out the invoice without an address?' Ron asked, knowing full well there would be no invoice.

The guy suddenly realised he was in a deep hole. If the IRS were set upon him, life could become very difficult.

'I do have a cell phone number,' he offered, weakly.

'And maybe a description of this customer and the vehicle he was driving?' Ron prompted. The young mechanic knew he was beat, so just nodded.

The net was starting to close in on the Meter Master.

Once back in his truck, Ron pressed “Office” on his cell phone as he drove away from the industrial estate. The radio automatically went silent, then the ring tone filled the truck's cab. It rang twice then, 'Charlotte speaking, how may I help you?' came the opening reply. Ron smiled at the predictable response.

'Hi Charlotte. I am not sure if this is possible at all but if I give you a cell phone number, could you trace its location?' he spoke towards the little screen in his truck.

'Sure, send me the number,' Charlotte said, without hesitation.

Ron slowly read the number off the oily scrap of paper that the mechanic had torn from a note pad.

'Just one moment,' Charlotte replied. The music burst back into life for a few moments while she was obviously working some sort of magic on the other end of the line, then just as abruptly, she came back over the speaker.' You should have the cell phone's location on your sat nav screen now. The current location is the address that the phone is registered to under the name of a Peter Ellison. I will compile a file on him and send it to your phone in a moment,' she added.

Ron shook his head in amazement at her efficiency.

'Thank you, Charlotte, you have been most helpful yet again,' he replied, with a beaming smile on his face.

'Yes I have, haven't I?' Charlotte replied, then hung up.

Ron knew, he would have to meet up with this assistant one day. The little blue flashing dot on his screen indicted it would be too far to travel tonight, so he went in search of another motel.

FOUR

'Peter!' the pitiful sounding voice called out from upstairs once more.

It was the fourth time within the hour that his mother had called down for him but rather than respond, Peter Ellison just turned the television up. After all, it wasn't his responsibility to care for his mother. That should have been his father's job, he thought bitterly. If his father hadn't been so self centred, maybe he wouldn't have left them both all those years ago.

As a child, he had idolised his father but at some point, things had quickly turned sour. Even at a young age Peter knew that his parent's constant arguing had something to do with him. Amidst their blazing rows he would often hear his name called out just before one of them stormed out from the room.

The last trip he could remember taking with his father had been to see the White Sox play. Even though he wasn't a huge baseball fan, it had been worth going just to be with his father. As it had been the last game of the season, the parking lot had been crammed full so, in desperation, they had parked down a residential side street. At the time, Peter had loudly expressed his objection to partially blocking a fire hydrant.

'No one will notice. Besides, if I drive around anymore, looking for alternative spaces, we will miss the start,' his father had replied, angrily.

'But it's the law!' Peter protested, again.

'I'll take my chances,' had been the blunt reply, drawing an end to the discussion.

Later, while standing in the long queue for the turnstiles, Peter's father suddenly realised his son was no longer at his side. The moment of panic was only brief, as little Peter eventually shuffled back up to his side.

The game had turned out to be great, with the Sox winning by some considerable margin, and the atmosphere had been electric. That atmosphere, took a drastic turn for the worse when they returned to the side street, only to find their car was missing. Peter's father had been livid after discovering his car had been towed away to the pound.

Although the cab ride home had only been short, his father's swearing and aggressive behaviour delayed Peter's decision to confess that it was himself who had alerted a policeman to the parking offence.

Peter waited a whole week before he considered it was safe to tell the truth about the parking infringement. His parents had always stressed that honesty was the best policy so when he did tell, the reaction caught him completely by surprise.

His father had picked him up and shaken him violently, all the time shouting at him through gritted teeth. Peter became so scared that he thought he was about to hit him, a thing that had never happened before. His mother had come running into the room to see what all the shouting was about and began screaming at his father to stop. From that point on, his parents began arguing more and more until eventually, his father up and left.

'Peter,' came another call from upstairs.

'Coming mother,' he sighed.

He couldn't wait to get back to work to do the job he so loved.

*

As Ron sat on the edge of the bed, scrolling through Peter Ellison's history, the hum of traffic outside buzzed the thin, single pane of glass in his motel window. The file that Charlotte had compiled was quite extensive, especially considering she had only been given a cell phone number to work from. Name, address, the fact that he was still living with his mother, and every other piece of information that had ever been filled in electronically, was right there for Ron to see. Hell, it even revealed his blood type and national insurance number.

According to the new information in front of him, Ellison was employed as a parking enforcement agent. Ron read that a second time. This guy was damaged goods for sure. A driving licence picture of the man appeared as he scrolled further down. There was clear evidence Peter Ellison was fond of his food by his additional chins but it was the wild comb over that gave him a comical sketch show look. His hair had gone from the top of his head, leaving just a few long, unruly strands on either side that was fooling no one.

Ron decided that with this new tracking ability, he could probably just arrive at Ellison's location tomorrow and covertly monitor him for a while. Throughout the week Ron's investigations had already revealed the extent of misery that this one man parking crusader had created. The ninety seconds of delight he may have brought to his internet viewers was vastly overshadowed by the long lasting impact on his victims.

*

The canvas canopy at the front of the street cafe offered little in the way of protection from the horizontal, fine rain that blew against Ron's face. The staff inside, occasionally glanced his way but none took the big man seriously as wanting to be served.

Ron stood, shielding his phone as much as possible as he watched the small blue dot indicating Ellison's movements. According to the little map on his screen, the ticket man would appear around the corner any minute.

Ron had been watching the lunch time traffic and although it looked chaotic, it flowed well without any interference. Cars would park illegally for a few minutes while their passenger would quickly nip into the shop to pick up a pre-ordered pile of sandwiches then drive off. It harmed no one and Ron suspected whoever had sanctioned the parking restrictions in the first place, was the sort of person who had pulled the legs off spiders as a child.

The moment Peter Ellison appeared around the corner Ron could see that he had one of those unmistakable identities that made him stand out from others. Even with a flat cap on his head, Ron could visualise the lone strands of hair, laid flat across Ellison's head. There was a natural sneer to the warden's face, even before he spotted the abandoned vehicles in the restricted parking areas.

In a blink of an eye, he had whipped his citation

pad out and frantically began filling in new tickets. Ron had to admit, the guy had ticketing down to an art. Within the first few minutes he had managed to ticket four vehicles. Even as angry drivers began to surround him, waving their new fines and shouting their protests, he continued to shuffle along, writing more tickets. Within ten minutes of his arrival, word had spread, giving others enough time to drive off unscathed. The feeding frenzy was over but a look of triumph filled Peter's face as he stood, guarding his territory, like a raptor awaiting his next prey.

*

'Good morning, is Janet about please?' Sophie asked in a cheery familiar sort of tone. She knew that only the most disciplined of receptionists would play hard ball when faced with the possibility they were dealing with a co-worker's friend.

'I'm sorry, but Janet isn't in today, she has phoned in sick. Maybe you could try her at home,' the receptionist for Fletcher Rosworth Solicitors answered.

The answer caught Sophie a little off guard, causing her to pause longer than she wanted. She suppressed the desire to ask for her home number, as that would just give the game away. Besides, no office would give out a home phone number.

'Oh dear, she seemed a little off colour last week but I didn't say anything,' Sophie said, reciprocating the receptionist's concerned tone. 'I'll give her a call later but I'll let her sleep for now,' she added.

Sophie ended the call and stared, deep in thought at the phone lying on the coffee table. Could she have read the whole situation so terribly wrong? She quickly flicked through all the data she had hacked on Janet's home address. According to the phone company's records, Janet didn't have an active land line so she must have called from another phone. Things just didn't add up. She didn't believe Janet was sick for one minute but she also didn't doubt she had called in. Sophie decided it might be worth ringing Janet's door bell, just to be certain.

*

Janet's strained tones had made the telephone call even more convincing. Her kidnappers had dialled the number for her, then pressed the receiver hard against her ear. The vicious looking knife at her throat left her with no doubts to the authenticity of their threat. "Convince them you are too ill to come into work," one of her captors had instructed. Tears had rolled down Janet's face as the familiar voice at the end of the phone had wished her well before hanging up.

'What do you want from me?' Janet sobbed, as all sorts of thoughts jumped around in her head, none of them pleasant.

Without answering, they clumsily replaced the hood over her head then led her to a couch of some sorts. As she sat there, Janet realised no one would be coming for her now. She needed to get away from being a door mat and begin to stand up for herself.

She had always suffered from lack of confidence, even as a child. Kids are naturally cruel and any sign of weakness is immediately exploited. At school, she had been the wounded deer, walking amongst the wolves, looking for pity. Only the timely intervention of Marie Wilks had stopped her life becoming a grand shit show.

During one break time, Janet had been at her locker when a group of bullies had ambushed her and started to turn out her stuff onto the floor. At first, Marie Wilks took no notice of the trio of bullies as they brought down their quarry. It was only when she noticed one particular girl that she had previous issues with, that she decided to intervene.

'Leave her alone,' Marie demanded, confronting the biggest girl in the group.

The confidence in her tone left no illusions there would be consequences if there was a failure to comply. The tallest of the bullies squared up to Marie Wilks and Janet feared there was going to be a fight on her behalf. A few moments of eye contact convinced the tall girl that there was going to be no healthy resolution and she turned away, the other two following closely at her heels.

'Why do you let them walk all over you?' Marie had asked her.

At the time, Janet believed it was a stupid question. Of course she couldn't fight all three of them.

Now, only as Janet sat with the hood over her head did she start to understand, Marie Wilks didn't take the pack on, she merely targeted the alpha dog. Without a leader, the pack is nothing. She quenched her sobs and tried to put herself in Marie Wilks' shoes.

'Hey limp dicks, I want to talk to someone in charge,' she demanded, in what she thought was her most confident tone.

She received no answer but she heard people in the room shuffling chairs.

'I don't know exactly what you want but I do know, you need me to cooperate. If you don't want me screaming the next time you put a phone to my ear, you had better talk to me.'

She started to feel a genuine rage as the adrenaline built up inside her.

A short while later, Janet heard the soft click of a door latch, followed by the scraping of chairs as several people all stood at once. She sensed a sudden change in atmosphere within the room and realised someone of importance must have entered. A moment of satisfaction washed over her for the deduction worthy of Sherlock Holmes. Janet flinched at the sudden sound of a chair being placed just in front of her.

'Ah, Janet. Poor, poor Janet. You must be feeling very frightened right now.'

The deep voice, carried a sort of eastern accent she imagined to be Egyptian. A strong smell of stale cigarettes radiated from whoever was sitting opposite her.

'Why have you kidnapped me?' She asked, in a pleading tone that she immediately regretted.

'It seems, Janet, that you are the key to our..,' he paused a moment while he searched for the right word, 'investigations,' he continued.

Under the hood, Janet's brow furrowed. What the hell was he talking about? Maybe he thought she was a lawyer or someone else of great importance.

'You do realise, I'm just a secretary?' she asked, genuinely puzzled.

The reply came in the form of a thick laugh, which just angered her more.

'Dear Janet, you underestimate your importance,' he mocked.

Every time he used her name, it fuelled the hatred she was developing for this man.

'You have the key to all the information we desire,' he laughed again, clearly pleased by his words.

The suck ups within the room also laughed with him.

Then it suddenly dawned on her, they were talking about the iris recognition security device that was used to access all the high profile files at work. Fletcher Rosworth was renowned as one of the most secure legal organisations around, dealing with all the rich and famous alike. Although she regarded herself as being low down within the company, she still had access to the secure filing systems. All she had to do to access files was type the file code into a computer then offer her eye up to the scanner at the selected station within the office.

'You're wasting your time if you are thinking of getting into the secure files. You can't access them outside of the building,' Janet said, defiantly.

'Dear Janet, please, let us worry about that.'

*

Sophie firmly held her finger on buzzer again. She had tried it several times already, gradually increasing the ring's duration with each press. Even if someone was sick, they would have at least answered and told her to shove off by now. Each of the six buttons had an adjacent, clear typeset label, identifying the occupants, so she knew she had the right apartment. She was just about to leave, when a woman appeared in the hallway. She put her key in the mailbox and began retrieving its contents before noticing Sophie standing out in the street. With a pile of junk post in her hands, she opened the outer door and propped it with her foot.

'Who you looking for sweetie?' she asked.

At first, Sophie had taken the woman as being Janet before she opened the door but now, face to face, she could see the differences. Although the woman's face was similar, she was a little taller and of a bigger build.

'Hi, I'm Marcy. Do you know if Janet's home?' Sophie played the thick southern accent again.

'How do you know Janet?' the woman asked, cautiously.

'Just a friend,' Sophie replied, realising she was under suspicion.

'Listen, do you know where she is? She hasn't yet come back from a date that she went on Saturday night. I've phoned all her friends and have even called the police, who won't do anything for forty eight hours. If you know something, please tell me,' she said, with a hint of desperation in her voice.

'I'm sorry, I don't know any more than you do at the moment.' Sophie decided to drop the fake accent.

'Who are you, really?'

'Like I said, just a friend.'

Sophie stepped back out onto the sidewalk and turned to go.

'I'm her sister, I know all her friends,' she said, in an accusatory tone.

'We don't always know who our friends are,' Sophie replied, then walked away.

*

Set back behind an overgrown privet hedge, Peter Ellison's house looked in need of some serious attention. The peeling paintwork revealed large areas of unprotected timber and if it was not already rotten, it would soon fall victim to the elements. The small yard to the side, by contrast, stood uncluttered and a shiny new lock on the garage door indicated that there may be precious contents behind it.

Ron craned his neck around the side of the unkempt hedge to see if there were any signs of activity within the house. He knew Peter was busy satisfying his ticketing lust, but Charlotte's file said his mother still resided at this address. Ron couldn't imagine anyone still living inside the derelict looking old shack but, cautiously, he pushed the old wrought iron side gate open and slipped into the back yard. He knew the unkempt hedges would keep him hidden from the neighbour's view as he edged himself alongside the old garage.

The garden beyond looked as if it hadn't seen a lawnmower in at least a decade and an apple tree halfway down still bore unpicked rotten fruit. Maybe, once upon a time, this may have been a happy garden, but the here and now was a very different story.

A small wooden door at the rear of the garage also showed no signs of recent use and by the look of the weeds, probably not since the lawnmower last passed through it. An antique looking padlock hung on the rusting staple, just begging to be levered off. Ron cast his eyes around for something sturdy to jam behind the lock. Ironically, he spotted a pair of old decaying garden shears poking from the brambles close by and after a few scratches, managed to drag them free. He took another quick glance for signs of activity from the house, then jammed the blades of the shears behind the lock's hasp. The rusted lock held fast but the rotten wood of the door jamb gave up its hold on the fixing screws without a fight. Ron tugged the handle and the door opened a fraction, offering a teasing glimpse of what was inside. Although he could only just make out the shape of a covered vehicle sitting on a car transporting trailer, Ron immediately knew what it was.

The brambles put up far more resistance than the padlock did, but after a lot of effort he managed to open the door enough to squeeze inside.

Pulling back the tarpaulin, the traffic buggy looked unremarkable in every way. He pulled the canvas back further so he could lift the hood, just to be certain he wasn't mistaken. He had to admit, the engine looked like a piece of art in itself, with a turbo charger and lots of chrome parts tucked neatly away, for only the privileged to see. Ron walked to the back of the cart and opened the little aluminium trunk. Inside, wrapped within a foam moulding, like the type they use for keeping jewellery in place, was a diamond belted chain saw. Ron knew, this was also a custom design and would have cost a small fortune. There was easily enough evidence here to put Peter Ellison away for criminal damage, should he alert the police. That wasn't the name of the game however.

Peter Ellison's secret identity was his greatest form of defence against his angry victims. As soon as Ron leaked Peter's identity to the media, a witch hunt would follow and the Meter Master would be no more. There had been a lot of people who expressed a desire to catch up with Ellison and dish out punishment, either physically or through the courts.

After covering the buggy back up, he left the way he came and made his way back to the front of the house.

On the way back to his truck, a thought suddenly occurred to Ron. Where was Peter's mother? The last thing he wanted to do was to expose an old lady to an angry mob. Returning to the house, he knocked the big brass door knocker twice, then stood back and waited for any signs of activity. As he predicted, there was no answer but he knocked once more, just loud enough to be classed as aggressive. He pressed his face close to the grimy glass panel in the door, shielding out the remnants of the sun with his cupped hand. Nothing.

Convinced the house was empty, he turned and started to walk away, then stopped. He stood silently, straining his ears for something he may or may not have heard. He stepped down off the porch and looked up towards the upstairs windows. Dirty net curtains behind an old sash window flickered in the cold breeze.

'Mrs Elliot?' Ron called up, in a sympathetic tone. He paused a moment then called out again. 'Mrs Elliot, are you up there?' he asked, a little louder.

'Peter? Is that you Peter?'

The voice sounded frail.

'Are you all right, Mrs Elliot?' Ron called, suddenly concerned.

'I can't get up,' came a weak response.

Had she fallen, he wondered? He hadn't figured for this but there was no way that he was going to leave her in trouble. He tried the handle on the front door but it was locked. Things were becoming messy now but he couldn't walk away. He gave the door a trial shove with his shoulder and it yielded instantly, causing him to stumble a few paces into the hallway.

'Mrs Elliot?' he called out, more as a way to announce himself than anything else, as he climbed a few steps towards the first floor.

He knew a total stranger bursting into a bedroom might come as a bit of a shock. Cautiously, he made his way along the landing towards the only closed door.

'Mrs Elliot?' he called out again, softly.

'I'm in here,' came the frail reply.

Ron edged the door open carefully, just in case she had fallen behind the door.

The image took his breath away. Prison life had prepared him for all kinds of horrors but nothing like this.

As he entered the room, his feet began to lift the sticky carpet with every step. Horrified, he cast his eyes on the rancid pile of old takeaway cartons and empty bottles, scattered randomly around the room. In the middle of the room, on a double bed, lay a gaunt figure of a little old lady, her sheets brown with excrement.

Ron immediately stepped back from the room, unable to speak for the dread of emptying his stomach, and went in search of fresh air.

'Charlotte, I need a paramedic, social services and the news at Peter Ellison's house, ASAP please,' he interrupted her usual announcement. 'I'll explain all later,' he added, before hanging up.

He stood on the open porch a moment, fighting back a tear, then returned to the bedroom, pushed the newspapers off a chair next to the bed and held Mrs Ellison's hand until the medics arrived.

*

'It's an off-line security system. You can't just hack into it,' Janet said, defiantly.

'It can still be accessed via the internet,' the Egyptian voice argued, as the strong smell of his cigarette breath filtered through her hood.

'Not unless someone at the other end sanctions the request...'

Janet suddenly understood. They had someone on the inside. As long as they had the right code, her authentication would access it.

'The files will still appear red on the security management log,' she added, in desperation.

'You let us worry about that, Janet,' the Egyptian argued once more.

Janet sat, contemplating her predicament for a moment. What could she do to resist? No one at Fletcher Rosworth would expect her to put her life on the line, even for such sensitive information. But would her captors let her go afterwards, she asked herself?

They had kept a hood over her head so that she couldn't see where she was. No, it was so she couldn't identify her captors. A wave of relief washed over her as she realised, they must be intending to let her go. The warnings of grave consequences if she lifted her hood all made sense now. They had allowed her to use the toilet, but even though her bonds were temporarily cut, they had insisted she must not remove the hood. It had been humiliating at the time when her captor guided her to the seat, but now she felt glad that she hadn't seen a face.

'I will come back later, Janet, to begin our little task. It will be best for both of us if you simply cooperate,' the Egyptian warned.

She said nothing, but the scrape of chair legs across a hard floor indicated her captor was leaving.

*

'I'd like to speak to Sam Young please.'

Sophie knew only too well her request would trigger a trace program but that was just what she wanted. National Security didn't take too kindly to having strangers calling them on their secure, internal switchboard. Obviously the number wasn't listed but any reasonable hacker could get it if they tried hard enough. The tricky bit though, was not getting caught in the process. Her voice coming out of the speaker at the other end would sound very different after going through the modulator. She knew the blasé way in which she had requested the deputy chief of security by name would also trigger alarm bells.

As predicted, Sophie watched a trace program start up on her computer screen within thirty seconds.

'Who shall I say is calling?' the secretary on the other end of the line enquired.

They were good, Sophie thought. Then again, they should be. There were no confrontational questions such as, "Where did you get this number?" etc. They would just keep Sophie talking until they finished their trace, then send a team round in large SUVs with blacked out windows to ask some questions, or so they thought.

Sophie watched their trace program bounce around her ghost servers, edging closer and closer to her real location.

'Just a friend of Janet Beacham. I was wondering if he has seen her since their date on Saturday night?' she said.

Eight ghost servers down, by now they would have realised that their caller's line had been protected but they would still believe their trace program would prevail.

'Just one moment, I will try to locate him for you.'

The friendly female voice on the switchboard concealed any sign of suspicion well. She was definitely not one to play poker against.

Ten ghost servers down. Sophie knew she had well and truly piqued their interest by now. She could imagine the group of agents all gathered around a computer screen, waiting for the complex trace program to come to a location. Twelve ghosts, and then the phone suddenly went dead. Sophie's program was designed to cut off once twelve servers had been traced.

The call had served its purpose though. It had suspiciously linked Sam Young and Janet Beacham together and was now etched in a digital recording. If any harm came to Janet after that, he would need to explain it away exceptionally well.

Sophie would really stir up the hornets nest later by sending an email to Sam's work account, routed via an internet cafe in Taiwan of course.

*

Even though the paramedics had arrived within ten minutes of Ron's call, Mrs Ellison had closed her eyes on several occasions, causing Ron to fear the worst. Now, as he stood to one side watching the medics move about her like a well rehearsed dance, he was relieved to see her eyes flicker open again.

'Are you family?' one of the medics asked Ron.

Neither had even acknowledged his presence in the room up to this point. They had immediately set about administering IV lines and hooking up monitoring equipment on their entry.

'I was just passing by and heard a faint call for help,' Ron said, speaking a half truth.

'Well mister, lucky that you did. Another couple of hours and we might have had a very different situation.'

With that, the two medics gently transferred the extremely frail Mrs Ellison onto a gurney and fastened a series of straps across her. The stench of faeces from the vacated bed filled the room, causing the second medic to cast his eyes around as if only just noticing his surroundings. He shook his head in disgust.

'Someone needs to be held accountable for this,' he said.

In another choreographed motion, the two medics lifted the gurney down the stairs to their waiting ambulance.

'The police are on their way. If you could hang about I'm sure they would like a statement off you,' the driver of the ambulance said, as he started the motor.

'Sure thing,' Ron replied.

He watched the ambulance roar off up the road, only putting its flashing lights and sirens on as it neared the junction.

Ron walked back into the hallway and spotted a note pad on a small table at the foot of the stairs. He scribbled the words “Check the garage” then pinned the page to the front door, and left. He had no intention of being there when the police arrived.

He could already hear the sound of approaching sirens as he climbed into his truck. He knew, one look inside that bedroom and they would turn it into a crime scene. A charge of wilful neglect would be minimal, but his note to check the garage would lead them straight to the Meter Master's identity. The press would also be all over the scene when they arrived.

Ron drove almost to the end of the road, pulled alongside the kerb, and waited. Sure enough, two squad cars pulled up outside the house, instantly followed by a black van with a satellite dish fixed to the roof. The press would have a field day with this. It would probably even end up on the six o'clock news.

Ron was just about to pull away when he saw the familiar, chubby features of Peter Ellison, behind the wheel of a silver Sedan, drive past him. Ron watched him stop, just short of his home, oblivious to the shit storm he was just about to walk into.

Inside Peter Ellison's head, something must have suddenly dawned on him that things were beginning to look a little shaky because he didn't get out. His obvious hesitation caused an officer to become suspicious of him as he rushed over to investigate. Within moments, Peter Ellison was face down on the hood of his car being cuffed, as a film crew recorded the spectacular arrest.

Ron watched Ellison get bundled into the back of a squad car before he quietly drove away. The following morning, headlines read, "The Meter Monster caught". There would be no coming back from that.

Before Ron made his way back home, armed with copies of the morning papers, he revisited "Rick and Ralph's" body shop to convince the owner to take up a suggestion that would benefit all. Four weeks later, all the local newspapers were filled with pictures of a little old lady being presented with the keys to a fully restored Chevy Bel Air. Apparently, the owners of a body shop had taken it upon themselves to perform the charitable act when they heard of what the despicable

"Meter Monster" had done to poor Mavis.

Emma Watkins, much to her surprise, also found herself with a tidy nine year old Honda Civic. Admittedly it wasn't on as grand a scale as Mavis's Chevy, but it was welcomed just as much.

Had the garage been linked with aiding such a monster, things would surely have turned out very differently, but the positive publicity did wonders for the body shop, bringing orders in that would last throughout the following year.

*

Janet had absolutely no idea of what time of day it was but she felt totally exhausted. They constantly refused her requests for them to untie her hands from behind her back, probably suspecting she would secretly lift the hood. However, even the pain in her shoulders and wrists didn't stop her from dozing off now that she had convinced herself that they would let her go. She had decided to cooperate fully and couldn't imagine, had the tables been reversed, the president sacrificing himself to cover up any information on her behalf.

She woke with a start; her bonds were cutting off the blood supply yet again and had made her arms go to sleep. Janet was just about to plead with her captives if they would consider bonding her hands in front of her instead, when she heard the door open.

Chairs suddenly scraped back as her jailers leapt to their feet, no doubt to greet the important Egyptian. She could make out a lot of different voices in the room now, and someone was giving instructions on how to set up some sort of equipment.

As she sat, straining her ears to see if she could

pick up on what they were saying, dark thoughts started to creep into her head once more. Earlier, she had believed that if she cooperated, they would let her walk free, but what if they figured it would be better without any loose ends? Would they have bothered to keep her hooded if they were just going to kill her though? The questions kept bouncing back and forth inside her head and it was driving her crazy.

The sound of wooden chair legs scraping across the floor just in front of her brought her back to the moment.

'Hello Janet. I hope they have kept you comfortable?' the Egyptian asked.

She said nothing. His over familiarity still grated on her nerves.

'We are going to lift the hood now, Janet. All we want you to do, is look into the iris recognition device, just as you would do at work. Please do not attempt to start looking around, it would not be good for your health. Do you understand, Janet?'

He allowed her time to acknowledge her understanding. She had no doubts as to what “not good for your health meant”. Janet nodded, feeling reluctant to speak in case her voice betrayed her fear.

A pair of hands started tugging at the cord around her neck, causing her to flinch away. Even though the cord had been tied loose enough to allow a clear air flow into the hood, it gave her a terrible feeling of vulnerability. As soon as the dark cloth was lifted, the bright artificial light flooded in, sending a pain to the back of her head. She fought down the temptation to look around, as her eyes tried to adjust to the new light. In her peripheral vision, she could see that she was in an old office with worn and tatty booth dividers, but very little else. With the earlier threat to not look around still fresh in her mind, she focused on a faded square on the blue panel, just in front of her.

The Egyptian placed a hand firmly on her right shoulder and spoke, close to her ear.

'Look into the machine please, Janet,' he instructed, firmly.

Although he spoke politely, Janet could easily imagine him using the same tone, as he ran a sharp knife across someone's neck.

The optic identifier that sat in front of her looked like a laboratory microscope viewfinder, minus the tray which usually carried the subject matter. Hesitantly, she leaned forward and placed her eyes over the scanner. There was a short pause as the machine cast a red line of light across Janet's iris, then a low bleep sounded to confirm the action had been approved. Even though she had no alternative, Janet still felt a pang of guilt wash over her for breaching the company's security system, a system they had built their reputation on. Their reputation was not worth her life though.

'Thank you, Janet. This will be all over for you soon, I promise. My men will now find you a place where you can sleep a while. It is getting late and I suspect you are tired,' the Egyptian said.

Without another word, they replaced the hood and led her back to the couch.

*

Sam Young sat at his desk, drumming his pencil against his brow. He had been forced to do a lot of amateurish lying in order to cover up the phone call to the secure line. He had also been forced to confess to taking Janet out on a date, but he had stressed he had returned her safely to her apartment later that night. What he couldn't explain though, was who had made the untraceable call. Only his senior position stopped any additional, awkward questions, but he knew it all looked suspicious.

Amon had promised him they would let Janet live, providing she cooperated of course. If all went well, the Egyptian was to leave her close to home with a firm understanding that family "accidents" would happen if she decided to talk.

Sam just hoped she didn't do anything stupid. What concerned him more right now was who did make that phone call? Someone must be watching him and he needed to find out who, before things got too messy. Politics was, by its very own definition, messy. Presidential candidates standing at the podium, promising the world or going round kissing babies was just a front. No one really witnessed the corruption and back handers going on behind closed doors as they fought to find dirt on their opponents. Bribes, blackmailing and just plain threats of violence were very much the name of the game but the average American citizen refused to believe it went on.

Information was worth more than gold to the right buyer and Janet just happened to be a key to a vault. The most important thing, was making sure the dirty paper trail didn't lead back to any future president.

Sam Young had already received a substantial payment into his offshore account for delivering Janet. The whole event was supposed to be over within seventy-two hours with no loose ends, but now he needed to find out who had seen him. He could only assume that someone had seen him leave the bar with Janet. The caller had gone out of her way to link him and Janet together that night, and that meant she had the advantage over him. He knew he needed to tie up this loose end and find her fast. Luckily, this was what he was trained to do.

*

Sophie switched her laptop on and quickly hacked into Janet's email account. Although it was doubtful, she was curious to see if Janet had logged on recently. From there she planned to add a simple program onto her system that would immediately alert her if someone else tried to view Janet's mail. The moment she logged into Janet's account, a red warning flashed onto Sophie's computer screen then it automatically logged off.

It took Sophie a moment or two to realise, a similar program to the one she was just about to add was already running and monitoring for any activity. Luckily, her fire wall had instantly shut the program down but she was still annoyed with herself for being careless. Whoever was monitoring Janet's account already would be able to see someone logging in. Sophie had alternative software that was far more secure but it was slow and she hadn't expected someone to have got there before her.

She knew the whole thing was starting to get out of hand. It was one thing to expose low life cheats but now Sophie had suddenly found herself up against government security services. She regretted ever getting involved in this stuff but she felt responsible for Janet now and wasn't going to let it go.

The cursor continued to flash in the corner of the blank screen as her fingers hovered over the keyboard. If she took this further it was becoming clear that Sophie was going to have to go up against National Security.

*

Ron waited patiently as the secure, steel gates to the parking lot rattled slowly open, bringing his journey to an end. It had been a long, tedious drive home and apart from catching a few hours sleep in an all night diner's car park, he had chosen to drive throughout the night. He now just needed to get home and grab some sleep.

Slamming the door shut on his truck, he clicked the button on the key fob and slung his back pack over his shoulders. Although it was just after mid day, he was weary enough to sleep standing up.

Heading toward the apartment blocks, he heard cursing coming from the far side of a light blue Toyota. A woman's voice filled the air with the sort of profanities that would make even the hardiest of inmates blush. Ron continued walking for the briefest of moments, then paused. Every cell in his body screamed at him to keep on walking but something inside him over ruled the warning. Casually, he walked over to the source of profanities.

'Need a little help?' he offered.

A woman, sporting a mass of tangled red hair, popped her head up into view, obviously startled by his sudden appearance. Her thick woollen jumper hung down, several sizes too big, as she walked to the front of her car and stood facing him. She held a wheel brace defensively in her hand as if he was just about to mug her. Ron could see her tightening her grip on the wrench so he held his hands up in mock surrender,

'Sorry, I didn't mean to startle you,' he smiled.

'So, you see a poor, defenceless woman trying to change a flat tyre and you thought you'd come rescue her, right? Is that how you see us, eh? Poor, defenceless creatures?' the red haired woman ranted, as a smear of dirt on her brow moved around with her facial expressions.

The outburst immediately took Ron by surprise. 'Jeez lady, I was only trying to be neighbourly,' he said, backing away and holding up his hands once more, this time in earnest. 'My mistake.' Ron angrily emphasised the word, "Mistake", before he turned and walked away.

Sophie stood there, panting, partially from the struggle of trying to undo the wheel nuts and equally, because the big man had made her jump. She had already been on edge since the disappearance of Janet but since stumbling across the trace program, she had become even more jittery. Every stranger was now a potential enemy.

Her pulse began to slow as she watched the stranger walk towards the residential complex, the adrenaline from the initial shock subsiding. She cringed inwardly from her reaction of the offer of help. The first guy to show her any sort of decency and she had gone all mad dog on him.

*

Ron threw the keys down onto the coffee table, sank back into the soft chair, and took a deep breath. The anger was still bubbling up inside him. What was it with him and women? All he had done was offer her a hand to fix a tyre. Hell, he'd have probably offered a hand even if it was a guy struggling with the damn tyre. Maybe that was his problem. There was no place in the world for nice guys these days. Taking another deep breath, he closed his eyes and breathed out again, slowly. He felt the anger subside a little. As he sat quietly, he made a mental note to avoid the crazy red head in future, at all cost.

The warmth of the apartment started to wash over him and he knew sleep would quickly take him if he didn't move. Although the temptation to close his eyes was great, he also knew he wouldn't be able to sleep tonight if he did. Easing himself from the comfort of the soft chair, he went to the kitchen to make a drink. Filling the kettle, he slowly cast his eyes around the apartment. Since coming home, he had taken no notice of the room but now, as he scanned for signs of intrusion, he was pleased to find there was none.

Ron took a mug from the kitchen draining board and spooned a rich measure of instant coffee into it. Whoever had stocked the kitchen originally clearly hadn't scrimped on quality when it came to the coffee.

The second of the folders still lay unopened on the kitchen worktop where he had left it. He had been tempted to ignore the folder for a day or two, but the confrontation in the parking lot had fuelled a need to let off steam. After pushing the kitchen window wide open to get some cool air in, he took his coffee, along with the file, and sat down. He ripped the seal from the top of the folder and spread the contents across the small coffee table then took a sip from his mug.

The first page said, "The Man Eaters". He leant

back in his chair and rubbed his face with the palms of his hands.

'Seriously?' he asked out loud. Surely someone was playing a sick joke on him. Everyone had heard of the *Man Eaters.* They were likened to being an all female mafia, founded originally by five women. The only difference between them and the mafia, was the *Man Eaters* were untouchable. No one had ever dared go up against them for fear of being labelled sexist. Politicians knew that one wrong comment would lose them fifty percent of their vote overnight, and the police were governed by the politicians.

The trouble with turning a blind eye to the Man Eaters overzealous activities was it had encouraged them to push the boundaries further. Currently, they mainly operated within the eastern states, but their heavy handed activities were slowly drifting towards the west.

Ron flicked through a few pages of the thick file, reading about some of the casualties who had stood in the way of their ideals. There were no pictures of the ring leaders, only A4 maps with little numbered circles around areas where their recent so called retaliation incidents had happened.

Thankfully, the brief was clear on this one. He wasn't being asked to take them down, he was just being commissioned to locate and identify their ring leaders. From there, others would be responsible for concluding the “desired outcome”. The way the brief had been worded didn't leave much to the imagination.

Although his part sounded safe in theory he still knew this task was akin to dangling his testicles over a hornets nest. It wasn't going to end well. Ron took another gulp of his coffee and began to study the rest of the files. He was going to have to use stealth and every bit of cunning to expose the ring leaders, without putting himself in harm's way.

*

'Can I speak to the man in charge please?' Ron asked the receptionist. He had spent half the night wracking his mind to come up with some sort of clever covert operation but had drawn a blank. He figured that attempting to join a women's only gym, then kicking up a fuss for the obvious refusal, was going to be a sure fire way to provoke a response.

The women only fitness centre was located dead centre of where the first incidents occurred on the A4 map. The gym itself hadn't any recorded cases of attacks within its premises but Ron suspected that could easily change today. Seventeen severe beatings had, however, been recorded within the large parking lot that served the shopping mall across the road.

A dozen or so women, waiting for a "Mpower" class, turned to watch the Neanderthal make a fool of himself. Mpower was a combination of martial arts and gymnastics, performed to upbeat music and specifically designed for women.

The receptionist, who was in her early thirties with cropped dark hair, stared at him incredulously. With horror and loathing written across her face, she gritted her teeth, then offered the big guy on the other side of her counter a menacing smile.

'Mister, I suggest you turn around and leave while you are still able to,' she said, slowly. 'We run a women only gym, managed by women and owned by women,' she added, emphasising each word for the simpleton to understand.

'Ah, but who changes the light bulbs for you?' Ron offered, with a cheeky wink.

'OUT!'

The sexist comment was too much for the receptionist. She leapt to her feet, knocking her chair backwards and thrust her finger in the direction of the door.

Ron held up his hands, 'OK, OK, I get the message. You know it's sexist to have an all female gym don't you?' he muttered, as he backed away.

'OUT!' she repeated, thrusting out her finger towards the exit once more.

'Don't come crying to me when you want the top off your pickles then,' he said, walking away. A staple gun flew across the reception towards Ron but it was well wide of its mark.

As Ron walked down the stairs he glanced nervously over his shoulder to see if he was being followed. He had well and truly kicked the hornets nest. If that didn't gain the attention of the *Eaters* nothing would. He headed across the road to a little coffee shop, where he could sit and monitor all the activity around the gym. Inside, he made his way over to a vacant window seat and waited for the waitress.

He could just imagine the hot talk inside the gymnasium right now about how a Neanderthal had just tried to join a women only gym. Ironically, regardless of the show he had just put on, he thought single sex fitness centres were a great idea. All too often, a good workout was spoilt by the opposite sex. Guys would immediately try to impress the women by lifting weights far above their usual limits. It wasn't just a male thing either. He had witnessed the female of the species, shuffling slower than an ageing granny on a treadmill so as not to smudge their meticulous make up.

A waitress came over and took Ron's order of coffee and a piece of apple pie. He wasn't really sure what sort of reaction to expect, but he may as well eat while he waited. If the hornets were coming, he would expect to see increased activity outside the fitness centre soon. The waitress placed his plate of apple pie on the table in front of him, along with a fresh cup of coffee.

'Eat it up while it's still warm, hun,' she said, with a genuine smile.

Ron thanked her and relaxed a little. There was no way of knowing who was part of the organisation, but the waitress seemed genuine enough.

FIVE

Under the name of National Security, Sam Young had obtained copies of all the CCTV recordings of the *Rendezvous* bar. He had sat through hours of grainy images of people coming and going throughout the night. With countless possibilities as to who might have seen him, and no guarantee they were even inside the bar, it was useless. He cringed as he plainly identified himself exit the bar and get into the car with Janet. Should things go wrong and Janet was to disappear, he would need to take care of the original recordings at the bar.

Because this was personal, Sam couldn't use the unlimited department resources available to him had it been a genuine national security threat. There was a lot at stake here but he would need to take care of this discretely. No longer a small time player in the game of double dealing and espionage, he had firmly placed both feet on the wrong side of the line. The stakes were high but crime definitely paid, and it paid well. His senior role in National Security gave him access to all sorts of sensitive information and if he didn't have access to other departments, he knew those who did.

Whoever had tried to access Janet's email account had taken precautions to avoid discovery but they had not been thorough enough. They were within the state of New York somewhere and that most likely pointed to either a friend or member of Janet's family.

He would sit down later and go through all of Janet's social media contacts to see if any of them possessed the computer skills necessary to evade detection.

The Egyptians were releasing Janet later this evening at an undisclosed location. A strong threat to her family's welfare would stop her going to the police of course, but he would need to monitor her closely for a while, just in case.

'Everything OK, Sam?'

He had been so engrossed in his own little world that the sudden enquiry made him jump. Sam quickly composed himself and tried to appear nonchalant.

'Not much happening to be honest, Brian. Just flicking through the social to see if anything's being flagged up,' Sam said.

Brian Walters was an enigma that could easily be overlooked due to his gangly appearance. Standing at six foot six, and no more than one hundred and ninety pounds, he gave the impression of being fragile. The thick rimmed spectacles added to the illusion of being far from the typical alpha male candidate. Only a fool or the unsuspecting would dismiss this man as a threat. Although his appearance screamed "office nerd", those who knew Brian, knew he also sported a second dan in Taekwondo. His long legs and light frame gave him the perfect mix of speed and agility for the high kicking Korean martial art.

Brian was no pushover intellectually either. He had pipped Sam to the post of Chief of Security when the new president took office, even though he had fewer years behind him. Sam had been magnanimous in defeat, openly pledging to support Brian throughout his time at the top. Everyone applauded his sporting behaviour, but deep down Sam harvested a bitter resentment towards his rival, vowing his allegiance would only be to himself from there on.

If Brian suspected Sam was searching for something specific, he would immediately throw all available resources at the problem. Were that to happen, Sam would lose control of the situation.

'Keep up the good work then, Sam. I'll be at home if you need me,' Brian said, buttoning up his long winter coat. He had already been in since five AM that morning and only now, twelve hours later, was he handing over to the evening shift. No wonder they had given him the top job. Sam watched him leave the office from the corner of his eye, then continued with his search.

*

Janet woke with a start. The pain in her shoulders confirmed she was still living the nightmare of being kidnapped. Her hands were still taped behind her back and although care had been taken not to bind them too tight, the positioning had taken its toll on her shoulders. They had led her off to another room after the iris recognition and gently laid her down on a couch. One of them had even tenderly lifted her head and placed a cushion under it before leaving the room.

Surprisingly, it hadn't taken her very long to drop off to sleep. It may have been that she had accepted that she was powerless to do anything about it or maybe, deep down, she believed that they were going to free her soon.

Now, as the harsh fluorescent lights filtered through the fabric of her hood, Janet's senses slowly returned. A tinge of fear crept over her as she realised this was going to be the end of her ordeal one way or another. She had played out different scenarios inside her head as to what would happen if she was released. Janet couldn't identify her captors to the police but she could lead them to Sam Young, the slime who had asked her out for a drink then drugged her. They must know, if they released her she would instantly report him. If they tried to pay her off to remain silent, she had already decided that she would accept the money as if agreeing but still go to the police. Surely they would anticipate that move. If she had, then they must have thought about it too.

'Ah, good morning, Janet. I do hope you have managed to get some sleep.' The familiar, heavily accented voice, spoke in a tone that would have been more at home in an expensive hotel foyer, rather than coming from a kidnapper.

Janet just nodded once towards the voice. She had already managed to sit herself upright on the couch, even though her bonds painfully forced her arms back.

'Please forgive us for treating you so badly, Janet, but this is not personal towards you. As you may or may not be aware, your employers hold some sensitive information that we are interested in. Unfortunately, their security measures left us no choice but to inconvenience you a little. We now have that information, thanks to your cooperation, and we are going to let you go.'

He spoke as if explaining something to a young child, but Janet bit back any sharp response. She was fully aware; no good would come of venting her anger at this point.

So far there had been no threats or bribes for her

silence, but she knew they were coming. Even though she had lost track of all time she suspected that it was most likely to be around early Tuesday morning. Work would expect her to either show up later or at least phone in sick at some point soon. If not, they would want a serious explanation.

'Moores Terrace, Seattle, is a lovely place at this time of year, Janet.'

His words immediately sent a shiver down her spine. So, this was to be the threat, was it? He was making a point, that no member of her family was going to be beyond his reach. Although her older sister, Diana, lived in the same building as she did, her younger sister, Marie, had moved away to Seattle two years ago in order to be closer to her husband's workplace. Being really close to her sisters meant Janet was devastated when Marie had announced that she was moving away. Marie had been heavily pregnant during the move and shortly after, gave birth to Rebecca, a healthy baby girl. Janet understood exactly what this slime ball was referring to when he mentioned her sister's address.

'Do you understand what I am saying to you, Janet?'

His constant over-familiarisation made her want to scream at him, but she was beaten. She nodded.

'I understand you are threatening my family,' she answered, through clenched teeth.

'A most unfortunate situation, Janet, but we are all pieces on a giant chess board,' he replied.

A pair of hands either side lifted her slowly to her feet causing the pain in her shoulders to become almost unbearable.

'Goodbye, Janet. Remember, not a word to anyone

about our little adventure,' he added.

Janet said nothing.

*

Sam Young read the email in horror. By passing through his work's email address, he had well and truly been incriminated in a kidnapping case.

“We know you are involved in the kidnapping of Janet Beacham. Should any harm come to her, we will release evidence of your involvement in her abduction to the press. You have been warned”.

Sam knew just deleting it would still leave a copy on the backup systems, and obviously the person who had sent it knew it too. He felt a touch of panic pass over him for the first time in years. His overconfidence may have led him to become sloppy, but he wasn't some kid who could be blackmailed. His finger hovered over the delete button a moment as his mind raced through all his options. Instead, he left the email in his inbox and shut the system down.

*

Ron loosened his belt a little. After sitting in the street side cafe for over two hours, he had ended up ordering over half the menu. At first, he had only ordered the apple pie so as not to look too suspicious while he sat in the window watching the gym. The pie had turned out to be genuinely the best he had ever tasted, and he had tasted more than his fair share in his time.

Doreen, the waitress, had been overjoyed by Ron's praise of her apple pie. 'If you like that, honey, you should try our spiced rack of ribs,' the chirpy waitress had said.

Ron had resisted the temptation for almost ten seconds before caving in. From there on, he had ordered the spicy chicken wings and a bowl of curly fries. He couldn't remember the last time he was physically unable to eat another bite but he had well and truly hit the wall now.

In prison, his mighty appetite had made him a bit of a celebrity amongst the other cons by wining various eating challenges. Like most prisons, boredom encouraged the onset of ridiculous challenges, and challenges meant secret betting. The screws would either look away or even sometimes encourage the activity. It was good for morale. If they were entertaining themselves, they were usually staying out of trouble. Ron had once taken on a challenge of eating ten loaves worth of toast within the hour. That had drawn a large crowd from all over the prison; even the governor had bet his fellow officers that it wasn't possible. He had ended up losing his five dollar stake.

Ron began to realise his low key surveillance operation was in danger of rapidly falling into another eating freak show. Throughout his feast he had, however, managed to keep vigilance on the activity across the road. Apart from a few average looking members coming and going with their gym bags slung over their shoulders, there seemed to be no suspicious activity. He suspected he had wasted his time by trying to stir up trouble at the gym. There had been no clear evidence that the Man Eaters were based at the fitness centre anyway. Ron asked Doreen for the bill, left a big tip, and vacated the little diner.

It was going to take a lot more planning to uncover the organisation but he hadn't a clue how he was going to go about it yet. He stood outside the cafe a moment, taking in the fresh cold chill. The sky had begun to take on a slight yellowish tinge, the sort of tinge that warned snow could be on its way. His now distended stomach screamed out for him to go home and lie down. Tomorrow was another day.

The wind blew savagely across the parking lot, biting into any exposed flesh as he walked back towards his truck, prompting him to pull his hoodie over his head. Still suffering from his epic meal, he pulled the truck's key fob from his pocket and clicked the button, eager to escape the elements. Reaching out for the door handle, a shadow momentarily caught his eye but it was too late to react.

A loud crack rang out across the lot as a baseball bat connected with Ron's temple. His world suddenly went dark as he keeled over like a giant redwood. As he fell forward, his head bounced off the door mirror of his truck, offering him the slightest delay in hitting the ground directly. Once on the ground, he became vaguely aware of a group of assailants gathering around him, each willing to offer their own interpretation of pain on him. With a head still full of clouds, all he could do was curl up into a ball and bring his arms up to protect his head.

Although the blows rained down painfully on his arms, legs and ribs, they lacked a certain conviction usually associated with hardened criminals. That was not to say the beating was pleasurable, by any standards, but the initial blow that caught Ron on the side of the head should have killed him had it been administered with serious intent. Instead, the strike had merely knocked him senseless, which by Ron's own admission wasn't too far from his natural state. The narrow space between the parked cars hampered his assailants' ability to surround him completely but they were determined to swing their clubs none the less. Another blow caught him square on the back of the head and the lights went out completely.

Ron had no idea how long he had been unconscious but when he did start to come around, thankfully the beating had stopped. As the fog began to fade, he could still sense a crowd around him, but there was some sort of argument breaking out. He tried to pick himself up off the floor but a hand firmly pressed down on his shoulder and a familiar woman's voice spoke close to his ear.

'If you know what's good for you, stay down,' she hissed.

As the hostilities directed towards his head had stopped at that moment, Ron felt it was worth going with the advice.

He felt a sharp pain in his hip so tried to establish a more comfortable position, but the hand on his shoulder kept him still. He could just make out heated exchanges between two women but with his ears still ringing from the clubbing, he was only able to pick out a few words.

'I will deal with him personally,' the woman pinning him to the ground said.

'Maria will hear about this,' the other woman argued.

'No one stops a code red,' a different voice chirped in.

A trickle of blood ran down Ron's brow and

across his swollen eyelid, prompting him to close his eye to stop the blood getting in.

With the concussion still hanging over him, the next thing he remembered was a pair of hands on his arm and waist. Their vice like grip managed eventually to roll him over onto his back, bringing him back into consciousness. He groaned and felt a desperate urge to vomit as he pushed himself up into a sitting position and leant his back against his truck's wheel.

Ron folded his arms across the tops of his knees and rested his head on them for a few moments, trying to ward off the nausea. Experimentally, he lifted his head a little. The mother of all hangovers would have been preferable to how his head felt at that point, but at least the urge to empty the contents of his stomach was subsiding.

'Mister, I don't know where you went to get your degree in stupid but you had best find somewhere else to use it in future,' the familiar voice spoke again.

He lifted his head a little and saw it was his red haired neighbour, the one who had blown up at him in their parking lot. She was wearing a blue tracksuit with the hoodie pulled up over her head but the unmistakable strands of red hair were desperately trying to escape.

Anger immediately touched Ron and he tried to spurn her assistance, just as she had done to him the previous day. He tried to stand by turning onto his side and pulling himself up by the door handle. It was a slow, clumsy manoeuvre, but pure stubbornness saw him eventually get to his feet, where he stood, precariously rocking back and forth. Once more, he snatched his arm away from the woman's offered assistance.

'I can manage, thank you,' he grunted, patting his pockets in search for his keys. They weren't in any of them but he carried on patting nonetheless in the hope that they would miraculously appear.

Eventually, he spotted them lying on the floor where he had just taken his punishment. If he wasn't mistaken, he guessed there would be a key shaped indent in his hip. The effort of standing had awoken the nausea once more but his pride wouldn't let him ask for help to retrieve them. The red haired woman just stood, watching, her arms folded in front of her in an equally defiant stance. Ron took a deep breath, exhaled slowly then bent forward to pick his keys up.

*

Sophie had been shocked and disappointed to hear the sexist outburst from her neighbour inside the gym. She had been sitting in the waiting area, waiting for her "Mpower" class when all the fuss kicked off. Something didn't quite feel right about his actions though. The guy had been genuine when he had offered to help her change the flat tyre, so why all of a sudden turn asshole? She had felt ashamed by her outburst at him and had even been tempted to knock on his door to apologise but now she was glad she didn't.

She tried to attend the modern day craze of martial arts and aerobics set to music whenever possible. Not only was it a good workout, it was also fun and it provided a good level of self defence. The stupidity of her neighbour trying to join a women's only gym had caused all those waiting to roll about in stitches. Sophie had kept the fact that she knew him quiet, partly because she didn't know what to say and partly because she felt disappointed with herself for starting to like the guy. It didn't matter, she wasn't involved and that was the way she intended to keep it.

Mpower classes only lasted an hour but they were one of the most high intensity workouts possible. Only those looking for the next step up from advanced aerobic classes would attempt them. A while back the press had made a big thing about Mpower after a group of marines had failed to keep up with the high intensity workout. In truth, the typical marine's body just wasn't suited to high intensity aerobics, but the press had loved it. The trial had reaped tons of free publicity for the Mpower creators and classes had really taken off.

The two women who instructed the classes at the gym were at a level of fitness others could only dream of. They both had advanced martial arts training, gymnastics, and a desire to create moves that were suited to Hollywood. Throughout the day, they each took two, one hour classes that would have seen most athletes dropping. The classes weren't just about sweat and tears though. Occasionally a session would end in fits of laughter as they tried to master some crazy move, resulting in heaps of bodies sprawled all across the floor.

The workout had managed to distract Sophie from her neighbour's stupidity for a while but it couldn't completely take her mind from Janet's well being. Powerful and dangerous people were involved in her abduction and those types didn't usually take kindly to strangers poking their noses into their business. If they were to discover her identity, she would probably be at just as much risk as Janet, maybe more. Hopefully, now they suspected someone was watching them, Janet would be a little bit safer.

As always after the hard workout, the shower afterwards invigorated her and left her feeling good. She resolved to go straight home and find out what had happened to Janet, no matter what the risk. Just as she was cramming the last of her sweaty workout stuff into her bag, a little red triangle popped up in the corner of her phone. Sophie knew exactly what the alert signified, she had designed it. She hadn't designed the app for the purpose it was being used for though.

Four years ago, Sophie had presented an idea of creating a women's danger alarm in the form of an app, to the fitness centre. The idea was, if anyone found themselves in trouble or felt threatened, all they had to do was press the alert symbol on their phone and it would transmit a distress to all others within the immediate vicinity. It was a simple idea. All phones within a ten mile radius would bleep an alert, then the GPS map would guide them to the source of the distress. It worked very well for the first year, saving several vulnerable women who had found themselves in tricky situations. Unfortunately though, the *Man Eaters* got hold of the app and decided to use it as a beacon to bring together those eager to dish out punishment to any male who seemed to cross their line.

It was plainly obvious to Sophie who it was that had attracted the attention of the women only vigilante group. Phone in hand, she stood staring at the flashing distress signal a while, undecided what she was going to do about it. Part of her wanted to ignore it totally because the fool probably deserved a good kicking, but another part wanted the fox to escape the hounds. At first, the alert looked to be coming from the fitness centre itself but on closer inspection Sophie could see it was originating from the internet cafe, next door.

Slipping her coat on, she headed down the stairs and out onto the sidewalk. Sophie cast a discreet glance around to see if there were any large gatherings, or maybe her neighbour lying somewhere, bruised and battered on the floor. With no obvious signs, she turned left and walked towards the parking lot.

With her hood pulled up over her head, she casually walked in front of the internet cafe. The window was littered with advertising posters designed to lure customers into the world of cheap internet access. As she passed by, she noticed a group of faces back away from the exposed parts of the glass. Sophie crossed the road still trying to figure out why there were code reds gathered in the internet cafe, when she spotted her neighbour sitting in the little diner across the street. Why choose that diner and why had he been there for so long, she thought?

Without looking around, she strode across to her Toyota, got in and drove off. She was fully aware eyes from within the internet cafe would have been watching her. She drove towards the exit at the far side of the parking lot but just before she reached it, she turned quickly and parked alongside a large panel van, out of sight.

What the hell was he up to? Was he trying to get himself killed, she asked herself? The low brick wall in front of her obscured the internet cafe but she could plainly see the entrance of the diner where the idiot sat, stuffing his face.

The cold weather had plainly encouraged most shoppers to park closer to the entrance of the mall, but her neighbour's truck was amongst a small cluster of vehicles at the far corner of the lot. Sophie couldn't quite make out his licence plate from where she sat. If she could have, she would have started to find out the background on this guy.

As time slowly passed by, the temperature began to drop, heightening Sophie's urge to drive off even more. She didn't owe her neighbour anything and besides, it was all down to his own stupidity that he had booked himself a beating. Several times, she had held the key, ready to start the engine and drive off but each time she took her hand away again, exasperated by her own indecision.

Finally, movement from the diner caught her eye as his unmistakable figure stepped out onto the pavement. He stood a moment, looking around and clutching at his stomach, before eventually walking towards his truck. Sophie cussed him to hurry up. The longer he dawdled, the more likely he was of getting spotted by the Eaters. With her view of the internet cafe obscured, there was no way of noticing if his predators had already seen him. If they had, they would either dish out the punishment here, or try following him home and do it there.

A number of crouching figures moving along the wall to her right confirmed the action was about to start, here and now. Sophie watched the pack close in on their quarry. She counted at least six of them, all carrying baseball bats, weaving in-between the wall and parked cars, stalking their prey, like lionesses stalking a sick wildebeest.

Still unsure whether to intervene, Sophie waited a while. Maybe, if she let the girls dish out a bit of well deserved punishment first, they would get fed up and go home. After, she could go over, check he didn't need a lift down to the emergency room, and it would all be over. She didn't want to stir up trouble at the fitness centre because, after all, she enjoyed her classes.

Sophie heard the first sickening blow from where she sat. She immediately felt bad for letting the ambush happen. The surprise attack had quickly brought their wildebeest down with a continuous rain of blows that showed no sign of letting up. If they didn't stop soon, it was going to end up being a homicide investigation.

Sophie leapt from her car and ran over. By the time she reached the scene, the guy was lying curled up on the floor like a middle aged foetus.

'Stop!' she shouted over the melee. The blows continued. 'I said STOP!' Sophie grabbed a bat that was just about to bury itself into the side of Ron's temple. The girl wielding it instantly turned on Sophie, a feral look in her eyes, before she slowly recognised the owner of the restraining hand.

'He had it coming,' the girl hissed.

Behind her eyes, Sophie could see the pent up feelings that desperately needed to be released on some-one, anyone.

'He's unconscious, and besides, I know him,' So-phie appealed to the group of assailants, as the big man started to groan and try to get up. She pressed down on his shoulder and brought her mouth close to his ear, 'If you know what's good for you, stay down,' she hissed.

'Maria will hear about this,' said the butch, blond haired woman who Sophie had just stopped mid swing. The savagery on her face had dulled a little now and she reluctantly turned away.

Sophie knew she would have to do some explaining later, but she carried more sway than most because of her app development.

She watched the lionesses slink away, angry at being deprived of their wounded quarry. The big guy groaned and slowly got up onto his hands and knees, a trickle of blood ran down his face from a cut on his forehead. Sophie watched the battered man stubbornly pull himself to his feet. A sudden recognition appeared on his face as she offered a hand.

'I don't need your help,' he slurred and pushed her hand away.

She rolled her eyes at him, fully aware he was still bitter from her refusal of his help yesterday. She watched him with both amusement and pity, as he finally got to his feet and started looking for his keys. After a few extra moments of pocket patting, he spotted them lying on the floor. The prospect of having to bend down again and retrieve them in his current state was clearly not one he relished. Involuntarily, he cast his eyes towards Sophie, but his male pride firmly stamped on the idea of asking for help. Sophie, in return, folded her arms and mirrored his defiance, damned if she was going to pick the keys up for him now. The big oaf bent down to retrieve his keys, and collapsed.

*

It was still the early hours of the morning by the time Janet finally stepped into her apartment. Although she knew her sister would have gone frantic with worry, she just couldn't bring herself to knock on her door yet. What was she going to say to her? Diana was the most assertive and confident one out of the three of them and if she knew what had happened, she would insist on going straight to the police regardless of the consequences. Janet knew they couldn't protect their little sister all the time, at best the police would only appoint some random officer to perform an occasional drive by.

Loud knocking on the door made her jump. There was only one person who knocked on her apartment door. Apart from Diana, everyone else had to press the buzzer to gain access into the building. Janet knew she had to face her sister some time and delaying it would only make things more difficult later. She paused at the door and peered through the little spy hole. She couldn't ever recall looking through it before and was surprised to see the fish eye view of the hall. Not only could she see the full view of her sister, patiently waiting, she could also see down the hall towards the stairway.

Doing her best to compose herself, Janet undid the security chain and opened the door. She was going to try and play things cool and act as if nothing had happened but as she stood facing her sister, she crumbled and broke into tears.

For the last few days, the only company Janet had been in was that of her kidnappers. It was no surprise her emotional state had been pushed to the limit. The initial look of relief on Diana's face immediately switched to one of concern for her sister's distress.

'What's happened?' Diana asked, wrapping her arms around her younger sibling.

Janet began sobbing, then stepped back and gestured Diana to enter the apartment. Inside her lounge Janet hesitated, trying to find the right way of starting the conversation.

'Before I start, you need to make a promise to me that you are not going to go straight to the police,' Janet said.

'You have to be kidding me!' Diana stepped back a little, displaying her anger at being forced to agree to the condition.

'The safety of Marie and Becci depend on it.' Janet was determined not to talk until she had a promise.

Diana was clearly shocked at the mention of a threat to their sister and niece's welfare. 'I promise I won't go to the police, for now, but you had better have a damn good explanation.'

Janet knew it was going to be the best she would get from her sister.

After making a couple of mugs of instant coffee Janet sat her sister down and began to tell her the whole story. For most of it, Diana sat quietly, a horrified expression etched across her face. Occasionally she would ask Janet questions such as, did she hear what language the men in the room talked in? Or, how long did the journey take to drop her off at the bus depot?

Diana burst out with a tirade of foul language when she heard about the threat to their little sister and family.

'You have to go to the police,' Diana said, shaking her head in disbelief.

'You promised,' Janet immediately protested. 'If they find out I've talked, something bad will happen to Marie and Becci,' she pleaded with her sister.

'The police will protect them. They will post a patrol car there to keep watch.' As soon as Diana said it, she realised it wasn't a great idea.

Janet just looked at her elder sister and shook her head.

'Just how long do you think they will keep up the surveillance on the house? Weeks? Months? A year? These people are used to getting what they want. I didn't even think they could get past the security system, but they did. These are ruthless professionals,' Janet tried to reason with her sister.

'They can't just get away with it,' Diana said, frustrated but beginning to realise her sister was right.

'No one must ever know what's happened,' Janet warned, taking Diana and looking her squarely in her face.

Reluctantly, Diana nodded her understanding.

A thought suddenly occurred to Diana. 'A woman came looking for you while you were away.' She looked to Janet for any sort of explanation.

'What did she look like?' Janet asked, furrowing her brow.

'Slim, but not skinny. About our height with medium length red hair. She was pressing the intercom, so I asked if I could help her. When I asked her who she was looking for, she answered in a thick southern accent that she was looking for you. You hadn't come home and I was really worried about you so I challenged her as to who she was. She said "just a friend". She obviously didn't know that I was your sister, so when I told her that I knew all your friends, she dropped the phony accent and just said, "We don't always know who all our friends are," or something like that and walked off.' Diana shrugged her shoulders.

Janet thought long and hard, none of her work colleagues fitted that description at all. Most were old men, apart from the odd few women who didn't even come close to what her sister had just described.

'I have no idea who it could be. I just hope she doesn't jeopardise Marie's safety.'

*

Ron partially opened his one working eye as consciousness gradually returned. Never being one to jump to rash conclusions, he began to slowly absorb his surroundings and assess his physical state. It took a few more moments before he realised he was slumped in the passenger seat of his own truck, with the stroppy red head driving. He felt an urge to kick her out of his truck but he doubted he could even muster up a stern voice in his present condition.

It was his own fault he was in this situation. He had been stupid to let his guard down in the parking lot right at the moment he should have been on high alert. He had walked into the lionesses den, underestimating their ferocity. The full sequence of events was sketchy at best but he remembered the beating. He also remembered the red haired woman stopping his attackers somehow, then offering him a hand to stand up. Ron cringed at himself as he also remembered shunning away her help. The last thing he vaguely remembered was bending down once more to pick up his keys. The part Ron had no recollection of, was losing consciousness as he bent over and head butting the side of someone's Honda.

He knew he had to thank this red haired woman but both pride and the uncertainty that his tongue would allow him to speak delayed the attempt. Ron slid himself into a more comfortable position, one that said, hey, I've restored consciousness. His driver cast a quick glance in his direction, then swiftly returned her stern gaze back towards the road.

'Thanks,' he blurted out, through a swollen jaw. In prison, if you had to thank someone, you owed them and no one wanted to be in debt in prison. It irked him a little that she didn't acknowledge him but he said nothing more.

The remainder of the journey passed quickly and in silence. Ron resisted the urge to turn the radio on, in much the same way a scolded child wouldn't dare ask its mother for sweets.

It was only as they sat waiting for the big steel security gates to their complex to slide back that Ron realised his rescuer must have left her car back at the fitness centre.

'Where's your car?' he asked the obvious question.

'I'll pick it up later,' the red haired woman said, dropping the truck into the lot and opening her door. She was clearly not prepared to discuss the matter further.

'I'll drive you back over,' Ron said, frantically getting out of the truck in a bid to catch up with her. He already owed her for saving his neck, so the last thing he wanted was to be in her pocket again for forcing her to take a bus ride.

His sudden movement of getting out of the truck made his legs momentarily buckle, creating the need to cling to the door mirror. A moment of nausea washed over him again as he fought to control his senses and a thumping in his temple started up. The red haired woman lifted his arm and placed it around her shoulders in an attempt to steady him. Ron's initial urge was to snatch his arm back and crawl back to his apartment on his own, just as his earliest ancestors would have done as they emerged from the primordial soup. However, her sweet, rose smelling scent and wild strands of red hair immediately intoxicated him, convincing him to take up the offer of assistance.

Ron realised from an early age that beauty was a double edged sword. Those who had it and preened it, often ended up the ugliest. With a mass of tangled red hair escaping from under her hoodie it was clear, even in his concussed state, that this woman spent very little time in front of a mirror. She didn't need to.

He suddenly realised he was staring directly into her eyes and she was looking back at him with a puzzled look on her face.

'I should have taken you straight to hospital. That bat must have cracked that thick skull of yours. You can't even stand, let alone drive,' she said, supporting him like a lean rod of steel. She may have been slight in build, but every muscle and every sinew of this woman meant business.

The pair made their way across the complex and up the stairs to his landing as if they were a drunken couple, returning from a night out on the town. His initial reluctance to accept her help was now firmly replaced by a dread of being discarded on his doorstep like a daily newspaper.

Ron began patting the pockets to his jeans and jacket in search for his keys once more, when the red haired woman held them up in front of him. He smiled at her through his swollen lip before taking the offered keys and mustering just enough composure to stand unaided. Ron had spent all his adult life fending for his own welfare, choosing never to rely on others for anything. Now, as he stood unaided outside his own front door, he felt a sense of loss as the residual heat from this stranger began to ebb away.

'Do you want to come in for a drink or something?' he asked, clumsily.

'No, I'm good thanks,' she said, suddenly aware of their awkwardness. 'I'm going to get something to eat,' she added, backing away.

'Thanks again,' he repeated.

'No worries. I might knock on your door later to see if you are still alive. They have strict rules here on bodies stinking up the complex,' she said, deadpan.

Ron smiled again, his swollen lip made the act painful but it felt worth it. He watched her retreat along the balcony to the top of the stairs, then stop.

After a few moments of indecision, she turned around and walked back to him. Ron watched her return, hopeful she had changed her mind about the drink but she stopped just in front of him. The parking lot fury had returned to her face.

'What the fuck did you mean by shouting all that sexist stuff off at the fitness centre?' she growled at him.

Ron opened his mouth to speak but was quickly cut off.

'Yesterday, in the parking lot, when you asked if you could help, I felt bad for snapping at you. I thought you were a genuine, decent guy trying to be nice, and then this?' she gestured with her right hand towards his beaten face. 'Just another chauvinistic pig as it turns out.' She shook her head and turned away once more. It was clear that the rage was still coiled tightly within her.

'I can explain,' Ron heard himself pleading in a pathetic tone. 'If you'll let me?' he quickly added, before she went off on one again.

She remained facing him, wanting to vent her anger some more, but his pathetic pleas poured water on her fire. 'I'll check in on you later,' she repeated, before walking away as if she had never returned for the rant.

'It's Ron, by the way,' he called after her, realising he didn't even know her name.

'Sophie,' she replied, pausing momentarily on the last step, before heading off to her own apartment.

*

Janet picked up a jar of bolognaise sauce and dropped it into her basket. Diana had phoned in sick on her behalf to give her a little more time to get some proper sleep and compose herself. As a way of a thank you, Janet offered to cook them both dinner but her culinary skills were limited to say the least. That meant spaghetti bolognaise, the choice of single people throughout the globe. She also added a ten dollar bottle of wine to the basket. Janet hadn't a clue whether it was a good or bad wine but at ten dollars it had to be better than paint brush cleaning standard.

The five minute walk to the supermarket did her good. It was a way of restoring a little confidence and taking another stab at normality. The cold drizzle blowing onto her face was a welcome feeling after the long ordeal of being forced to wear the hood. Pulling up the collar on her coat to stop the cold wind blowing onto her exposed neck, she headed home.

The route back to the apartment took her down several narrow residential streets, all lined with parked cars. With her head down and collar up, she failed to spot the same black sedan that had whisked her away a few nights ago.

'Get in Janet,' the familiar voice made her jump.

The car door had swung open just as she passed. Janet backed away instinctively.

'We need to talk.' Sam Young made no pretence of remorse; instead he talked as if securing a business deal.

'Just get the fuck away from me. You've had what you wanted, now leave me alone,' she said, turning her back to him and walking on. Tears began to well up in the corner of her eyes as her heart thumped wildly. Why couldn't he just leave her alone?

'Janet, you need to get into the car, for the sake of your sister,' the voice within the car added. She stopped dead. Every cell in her head was urging her to scream and her heart threatened to leap from her chest. Instead of screaming, she slowly turned, looked up and down the quiet street, then walked towards the car. Screaming would achieve nothing.

'What?' she demanded, standing two paces from the open door. She could clearly see Sam Young sitting in the back of the car. So, this is how they work she thought. Sitting in the darkness, hidden away from prying eyes, never willing to expose their dirty hands.

'Get in,' he repeated.

'No, you come out.' The last glimmer of the old meek and mild Janet Beacham was disappearing completely.

'We need to talk,' he repeated, as if that was reason enough for her to comply.

'Then talk. Just say what you need to say or we can bring this whole damn business out in the open. Your choice,' Janet stood defiantly. The bag of groceries in front of her felt like a small shield.

Sam remained in the back of the car, the darkened glass continued to guard his dirty identity. 'I'm really sorry that you got dragged into all of this,' he said, his tone softening.

Had Janet not learnt what this vermin was capable of, she might have felt sorry for him, instead she just stood, waiting for him to get to the point.

When he eventually realised he wasn't going to get a response, Sam asked. 'Who was the woman who contacted me?'

'What the hell you are talking about?' Janet replied, genuinely puzzled by his question. A fraction after her response, she remembered the woman who had been looking for her, but she said nothing.

'Some people will probably come to see you soon. They will want to know what happened the other night,' he said.

Janet sensed an uncertainty in his voice.

'Who is coming to see me?' she asked.

'It doesn't matter who. We had a drink, then left our separate ways. That's all you need to tell them,' he snapped.

'It couldn't have been a very good night then could it?' Janet replied. For once, she felt she was not the vulnerable one anymore.

'Eh? What are you talking about?' Sam Young looked puzzled.

'I mean, you invited me out for a drink, then we left our own separate ways? Was it because we didn't hit it off? Maybe you were a Sagittarius and I was a Capricorn? Or maybe your charm just dried up towards the end of the night?' she said, bitterly.

'I don't give a fuck why we left separately,' he hissed. Sam was unused to being on the defensive and it irked him. 'Remember, we know where your sister and niece live.'

The expression on Janet's face told him he had regained control.

She turned and walked away, now shaking inside with rage from the sudden encounter. As she neared the end of the road, Janet heard the black car approach. Determined not to give him the satisfaction of showing fear, she focused on the sidewalk. Although she couldn't see in, Janet knew the slime ball was staring at her through the darkened glass.

As soon as she stepped through the door to her apartment, she broke out into floods of tears. Maybe Diana had been right after all, maybe they should go to the police. As a department manager, Diana was used to dealing with awkward people in difficult situations. Janet didn't like phoning her sister at work but she needed to tell her what had just happened.

*

As Diana stood in the shower, the hot spray did nothing to wash away the tensions of the day. The phone-call from Janet this morning to tell her of the new confrontation, along with a day full of argumentative customers, had left her head swimming. Although she had initially agreed not to go to the police, she knew it was the wrong decision. Tonight, she would gently try to convince her sister to change her mind but ultimately, she would leave the final say in Janet's hands.

As she was stepping from the shower the phone in the lounge began to ring. Hurriedly, Diana wrapped a towel around herself and leaving a trail of drips along her hallway floor, rushed to answer it.

'Hello,' she snapped, then instantly regretted her tone. She was so used to forcing politeness she had little time for cold callers and utilities salesmen. Friends and family members, like most people these days, used cell phones to stay in touch.

'Is Janet back safe?' came the voice on the other end of the line.

Diana sat back on the arm of the couch, instantly taken back. 'Who is this? How did you get my number?' she asked, anger rising inside her.

'We met on your doorstep.'

'Who are you?' Diana demanded once more. She wanted some answers and clearly this caller knew more than she did.

'You can call me Red Renarde if you want. Janet is under surveillance at the moment but I just want to know if she has been returned safely.'

Diana was used to listening to irate customers on the end of the phone but this voice oozed calm and confidence.

'Red Renarde, the investigator?' Diana asked, suddenly taken back.

Red Renarde was becoming a modern day Robin Hood sort of character and the media loved her. Her services couldn't be bought, and she only took the fight up for those who needed her the most.

'I just wanted to know if she's safe,' Red persisted.

'In the lobby the other day, you said you were a friend. If you are a friend, we really need your help,' Diana challenged. The line remained quiet as Diana waited for a response. 'Did you hear me? We need your help!' she repeated, angrily.

'Do you know who the people are that took your sister?' Red asked.

'It was someone from the government. They were after some information Janet had access to,' Diana answered. She realised she didn't know much more than that, other than he was someone pretty high up.

'Sam Young, works for National Security. That means he has access to almost unlimited intelligence resources. Daily, he rubs shoulders with the type of people who will inform the press your granny was once a mass murderer working for Hitler and that you eat babies for breakfast. Should you alert the police, they will most likely smear your name really badly, or alter records to show you never existed, and then one day you'll find you really don't. If they have let Janet go I would suggest you fade back into the shadows and forget about them,' Red subtly pointed out.

'That's just it though. Sam Young caught up with Janet again today,' Diana said, bitterly.

'He's kidnapped her again?' Red asked.

'No, he wanted her to get into his car but she refused. Said something about someone coming to see her soon. Said she has to deny that they kidnapped her. Can you believe the nerve of him?' Diana said.

Red remained silent for a while. Did she really want to get drawn into something she would probably lose? She knew she had already pushed her luck with the phone call and email. The chances were, they had every resource tied up looking for her right now. What she had said to Diana was true. Governments may act as if they played by a set of rules but in truth, they lied to the world on a regular basis.

'Will you help us, please?' Diana asked, again. Sophie lifted her arms in exasperation, a fruitless gesture on the end of a phone but it needed to be done none the less. The conversation stalled a while longer.

'I'll look into it and phone you again tomorrow. I can't promise anything though,' she heard herself say. Quickly, she hung up to prevent herself from volunteering to do anything else she didn't want to do.

Sophie could feel the whole situation coming down on her like an unwanted landslide. Why had a member of National Security kidnapped Janet Beacham and was it on official business? The demand for Janet to deny that she had been abducted, clearly pointed towards not being official. She knew that the company Janet worked for had access to highly sensitive information. The type of information that was valuable to either a president or a president's enemies. It was the sort of information that ultimately would win or lose an election. In 1974 the leaking of such information even led to the downfall of Nixon.

Sophie leant back in the chair and cupped her face. So much for getting her life back. She glanced at the clock on the wall and realised time was running away. Pulling her coat on she stepped from her apartment to go and rescue her car, then maybe afterwards she might knock on the big oaf's door to see if he was still alive. Out of curiosity, she took a detour through the parking lot and out of the big sliding gates. In passing, she took her phone from her pocket and snapped a picture of Ron's truck licence plate. The bus ride would give her enough time to carry out some background checks on her mystery neighbour.

*

The bag of frozen peas Ron had found in his freezer was now rapidly turning to mush as he held the unopened plastic bag against his forehead. He was grateful to whoever had stocked his freezer for him, maybe they had anticipated his medical need, who knows.

He couldn't push the encounter with his neighbour from his mind. She had definitely saved him from a further beating, that's for sure, but she must have held some sort of influence over the gang. Maybe she was one of them but just didn't want a neighbour targeted in case of repercussions. The beating wasn't anything worse than he had suffered before but the first blow had caught him totally off guard. If his head had been a baseball, it would have cleared the way for a home run. If she did look in on him later it would be a good opportunity to question her and find out if she was involved with the women vigilantes, he thought. First, he needed to get his head clear.

*

Sam Young softly closed the door behind him as he stepped from Brian Walters' office. He had taken a big risk by showing him the email threatening to expose him as a kidnapper. The story that he had just presented to Brian would have been worthy of an Oscar. He had revealed his initial hesitance in accepting this woman's request to go on a date because of his dedication to his career. Sam told how the night had been filled with plenty of uncomfortable silences between the two of them before she eventually made a feeble excuse and left without him. Sam had pretended to be embarrassed for not dating in such a long time and joked to Brian that it was just as well because he probably would have forgotten what to do if it had gone any further.

He also confessed that because he was concerned that something might have actually happened to Janet, he had set out to see for himself. Fortunately, he had bumped into her as she was walking back from her local shop. The reunion had been awkward, Sam said, but there was no doubt that she was quite alright, he even urged Brian to go and check for himself.

Brian had listened to Sam's story without interruption or any sign of suspicion on his face. Either he had taken the bullshit, hook, line and sinker or he was a good poker player. He had even tried to ease Sam's embarrassment by making light of the botched date.

'Don't worry Sam, we've all been there at some stage or another,' he reassured.

Brian had also agreed it would be best to send someone round to Janet's apartment, just to confirm for the official records that she was in fact safe. Brian's biggest concern though, had been with the breach of their security measures and the way this person had managed to avoid a trace. Brian wanted a team put on the case in order to track down whoever was responsible for the email.

Sam figured that he couldn't have played it better. Now he could utilise whatever resources were necessary in the name of hunting down his observer. Whoever it was that thought they could blackmail and intimidate him, was just about to find out they had messed with the wrong person.

*

After Sam left, Brian just stared at the closed door for a while. Although he had initially tried to console him, there was something not quite right about the whole situation. Of course, he had done the right thing to come to him with the email, it would have been highly suspicious had he not. Sam's awkwardness had seemed genuine when he had talked about his lack of dating but Brian still sensed there was more to this.

Although Brian had confessed that he had been in the same situation as Sam, it was not entirely accurate. Yes, of course he had encountered relationships which didn't work out but he had never had a date go so badly wrong that she had left alone. He knew there would be no point looking through Sam's emails for something suspicious. Only a complete fool would be stupid enough to present evidence that would incriminate himself. No, the real reason alarm bells were ringing inside Brian's head was, why had someone with such obvious hacking skills bypassed their security in order to leave a fake message? If it was a hoax they would know it was a risky one. They would probably also know that the message couldn't be completely erased by just deleting it.

The National Security technology and surveillance department would usually make short work of tracking down whoever had sent the email but Brian had doubts this person was going to be anything but easy to catch. His instincts screamed at him that something was going on but for now, he would just let the wheels turn.

*

Sam had only given Ryan the lightest of touches on his shoulder but the young technician had leapt with surprise. Ryan Powell, at just twenty three, still had very little concept of real life. He had been warned time and time again about playing games on the computer during work time. Three written warnings and daily verbal warnings still hadn't managed to stem Ryan's need to alleviate the boredom.

The truth of the matter was, the kid was just too good to sack. If you could pool the knowledge of the whole IT department it still wouldn't spill over Ryan's shoes. He had flown through university scoring straight "A"s in anything computer related. With so few tasks worthy of his talents he all too often ended up playing computer games all day. Occasionally, his supervisors would hand him some sort of menial task but he would complete it in no time at all then drop straight back into his little fantasy world.

Ryan was just about to enter an enemy space craft when Sam had touched him on the shoulder. His headphones had blocked out all external sound and the little mirror that he had strategically placed against the partition wall in order to spot anyone coming, had been obscured by an empty KFC bag. The shock had made him jump like a startled cat, causing his knees to bang on the underside of his desk, scattering a jar of pens all over the floor.

'Christ, you scared the shit out of me,' Ryan said. A broad grin started to creep across his face as he desperately tried to regain his composure. He stooped down to gather the jar of pens and coloured pencils, most of which had been broken or out of ink as long as he had been there.

'Didn't they give you a written warning for playing computer games not long ago?' Sam asked. He had known Ryan since the day he had joined the security team eighteen months ago and genuinely liked the lad. With Ryan, there were no ulterior motives and the kid hadn't a bad bone in his body. In fact, all he was interested in was computer games, pizza, hanging out with his mates and work, pretty much in that order.

'Yeh, three. Ol' Whitey said the third one was normally a sacking offence and I was on borrowed time now,' Ryan grinned.

'I don't know how you get away with it. The rest of us would be in the job centre queue if we had done that. You're not giving Whitey sexual favours are you?' Sam laughed.

'Nah, they just love my natural charm don't they?' Ryan replied. His beaming smile made it hard to argue the point.

'OK, I believe you. Listen, if I can drag you away from shooting zombies for a moment, I need this email analysed for clues and I need this phone call's origin,' Sam said, handing Ryan a printout of the details.

'No probs, will get the results back to you in an hour or so.'

Ryan's confidence was genuine but Sam doubted it would be that simple. He knew the young wizz would relish the challenge though, maybe even more than the games.

Sam smiled at Ryan's over confidence, 'We'll see,' he said, patting him on the shoulder and walking away.

'They weren't Zombies, they were elite soldiers,' Ryan called, as he watched Sam walk away.

Without turning, Sam simply raised his hand in acknowledgement. He envied Ryan's simple world.

*

Sophie didn't head directly to her car once she got off the bus; instead she took the long way around the edge of the shopping mall. Most of the day time shoppers had dwindled away, now replaced by couples, out for the evening at any one of the restaurants and bars conveniently spliced between the high priced fashion stores. She felt a little edgy by the recent events but she also felt a slight air of excitement.

Even though Sophie had made no promises, she had more or less agreed to help Janet and her sisters. God only knew how, but she knew it was the right thing to do. It was as far into another league as it got and Sophie knew there was a very real chance she could get burnt.

Her neighbour was also turning out to be a bit of a mystery. During the bus ride over, she had traced his licence plate to see who his truck was registered to. It turned out that it was a long term rental and, after delving a bit deeper by hacking into the rental company's computers, she found out the truck had no named driver assigned to it. The registered agreement had been drawn up under the name of "Mortan Maintenance, contractors," specialists in pest control. The short bus ride hadn't given her enough time to search for more but she promised herself to check it out further at a later date.

The main lights in the fitness centre had been

turned off and the minimal background security lighting sent ghostly silhouettes of the gym equipment against the plate glass windows. On the other hand, the cyber cafe below remained brightly lit but Sophie doubted any member of the vigilante squad would still be hanging around.

She made her way across the lot, constantly scanning for movement but also avoiding heading straight towards her Toyota. At the last minute she changed direction and clicked the key fob. Once inside, she quickly started the engine and roared off, narrowly missing a woman walking to her car. Sophie cursed herself for being so on edge.

The prevention of Ron's beating wasn't the problem. She would just explain that her neighbour had recently lost his wife and was drunk, or something like that. No, what had really set her on edge was the uncertainty of whether she was clever enough to beat National Security. Hacking into their secure server had been arrogant, stupid and careless.

As she sat waiting for the gates to the complex to roll open, Sophie toyed with the idea of just going straight to her own apartment. If she did, the weight of not knowing if the big man had collapsed into a coma or suchlike would play on her mind all night, and besides, he owed her an explanation.

Sophie pulled the Toyota into her usual space and sat quietly with the engine off for a few moments. The whole crazy series of events had happened in such a short space of time. Taking a deep breath, she sighed it out forcibly then pulled on the chrome door release.

She took a non committal detour around the far block to see if there were lights on in Ron's apartment.

At first, she couldn't quite tell from the ground floor but as she closed in, a faint glow of light just crept around the edges of the curtains.

Still unsure if it was the right move, she knocked on his door. It was loud enough to be heard but not too hard as to sound aggressive. If he didn't answer straight away, she wouldn't knock again, not until tomorrow that was, she decided. Within seconds, a security chain rattled, followed by the sound of a bolt sliding back on the other side of the door. His security measures took her a little by surprise. After all, it wasn't as though he was small and vulnerable.

The door opened and immediately the big guy almost filled the opening. He still had the same pair of Levi's on but now he sported a clean white tee-shirt which, along with his bare feet, indicated he had recently had a shower.

'Still amongst the living then,' she observed dryly.

His left eye had almost swollen shut and the lump on the edge of his hairline made him resemble John Merrick, but it didn't stop him beaming a broad smile at the sight of her.

'I wasn't sure you would still come. Please, come inside,' Ron said, stepping to one side to allow his visitor room to pass him.

'I won't stop. Just making sure you hadn't passed out or something,' Sophie said, backing away a step. She had so much she wanted to ask but she knew, each question was just another step towards more mess in her life.

Ron looked crestfallen by her refusal but he knew the score. 'I just wanted to say thanks again for saving my hide back there.' He rubbed his swollen head to confirm his point.

'Forget it. You were just another damson in distress,' she said, turning away.

'Isn't that supposed to be a "damsel" in distress, at the bare minimum,' he laughed. 'I think a damson is a type of plum, or something alike,' he added.

'Like I said, just another damson in distress,' she carried on walking.

Ron smiled at the jibe. Stepping out onto the edge of the balcony, he called down after her, 'Can I at least buy you dinner one night, in a way of thanks?'

'Maybe,' she said, before disappearing from sight.

Ron stood, looking over the balcony, breathing in the faint smell of rose water hanging in the still, damp air.

SIX

Mark splashed cold water against his face in the futile hope it would wash some of the weariness away. It hadn't been the ideal time for a sleepless night but the only predictable thing about children was their ability to be unpredictable.

Starting a new multimillion dollar project, under the spotlight of the town planners and health and safety alike, was going to keep him on his toes. The first shovel of earth was going to be witnessed by the press as some sort of ceremonial occasion. Constructing the first new museum in thirty years had been a controversial decision, one which many had objected to. A large percentage of the locals wanted the money to be spent on yet another school in the area but ultimately, the vote had gone to the museum. The town planners said it would enhance the area's cultural status and generate pride amongst future generations.

It had just been unfortunate that little Rebecca had chosen last night to come down with a high temperature. Marie had given Becci some medicine and lay, cramped, alongside her daughter most of the night, in an attempt to allow her husband a little sleep before his big day. It was a heartfelt gesture but it hadn't worked. Becci had managed to cry, on and off, right through to the early hours of the morning. Only at five AM did she eventually fall asleep from sheer exhaustion. Thirty minutes later, the alarm clock rang. Mark had managed to put a brave face on and he assured Marie that he would be fine but deep inside he was almost falling asleep as he left the house.

Marie woke with a start, disorientated by the fact that she hadn't realised she had fallen asleep on the sofa. The clock on the fireplace still only said nine-thirty so she hadn't slept that long. She knew a noise had brought her from her nap but she couldn't recall what it was. She suspected it was probably Beccie's monitor but just as she was rubbing the sleep from her eyes, the door bell rang.

Still half asleep, she staggered to her feet, desperate to reach the door before the visitor woke Becci.

'Good morning,' the slightly annoying delivery man chirped. 'Special delivery for a Marie Beacham,' the guy held out a rather large bouquet of flowers. The use of her maiden name took Marie a little by surprise, but rather than make a fuss about it, she simply signed the little digital pad thrust in front of her then thanked the courier. She watched the man walk away, whistling happily to himself, before retreating back into the house.

Becci had, thankfully, remained quiet so she made her way into the kitchen to make herself a coffee and see who had sent her the beautiful bouquet. After putting the kettle on, she sat at the breakfast bar to read the little card attached at the base of plastic wrapper.

"To my dearest sister, Your welfare is always at the front of my mind. Janet".

Marie read the card again. What the hell was that about, she thought? It was a strange message to put on such beautiful flowers. Once she had finished putting them in a vase, she would ring her sister to thank her and catch up on the recent gossip. Becci began to cry.

*

By the time Janet put the phone down from talking to her sister, she was left feeling physically sick. The message couldn't have been any clearer. Marie had caught her off guard when she called and thanked her for the bouquet. "What bouquet?" she had asked, genuinely at a loss as to what her sister was babbling on about. It was only after Marie had read the cryptic card back to her that it sank in. Had there not been a chair to sit down upon quickly, she would surely have fainted. Janet tried, unconvincingly, to laugh it off, saying she had forgotten all about it, but she knew Marie suspected something was wrong. Rage and fear boiled up inside Janet but she was aware there was nothing she could do about it. The only choice she had, was to comply with her kidnapper's demands. Maybe if she did, they might leave her alone. Janet knew she was kidding herself though.

*

Brian's sat nav led him to two medium sized apartment blocks in a fairly respectable residential street. They were of a sixties style, with mosaic floors in the reception hall and coloured glass panels above the entrance door. The small details distinguished them from the mundane looking buildings of the modern era that surrounded them. From the road he gauged there could be no more than six or seven apartments to each of the blocks.

He was unsure if Janet Beacham would be home

yet but if she wasn't he could easily call again later. Normally, he would have assigned one of his agents for a welfare check but his instincts screamed at him to do this personally.

Stepping up the few steps from the street, he pressed the last button on the intercom panel and waited. Seconds later, he heard a click from the speaker, then a faint voice answered, 'Hello.'

At first, Brian wasn't sure if the metallic voice coming from the box on the wall belonged to a little girl and so nearly asked to speak to her mummy. 'Can I speak to Janet Beacham please?' he asked, erring on the side of caution. There was a long pause, almost to the point he suspected the little girl may have gone.

'I am Janet Beacham,' came the reply.

'I'm sorry to bother you, Miss Beacham. My name is Brian Walters, I work for National Security and I'd like to ask you a few questions, if I may?' he said. There was another long pause, then the security lock buzzed open.

Janet's heart felt like it was going to jump out of her chest as she pressed the door unlocking button. She half hoped Diana would come back early but her sister's fiery personality would have blown the whole situation.

Janet opened her apartment door, stepped across the threshold onto the landing and waited for her visitor. A small elevator divided the three story building, but none of the residents ever used it. Occasionally, visitors or people carrying heavy objects would use it to get up to the top floor but most occupants used the stairs. Now, Janet looked towards the silver door, unsure if her unwelcome visitor would use it.

Almost predictably, the heavy, stairway fire door swung open and a tall man appeared onto the landing. Dressed in a dark two piece suit and white shirt, he looked every inch the government official that he claimed to be. He wasn't built like typical government muscle, without a neck, but Janet did notice his shoulders were quite broad. He flashed a warm smile as he walked towards her, the sort of smile that a week ago might have convinced her that he was kind hearted and trust worthy. Not today though. Especially as Sam Young had used a similar smile.

As the tall figure approached, Janet felt the urge to back away, but she defiantly resisted and stood her ground. He stopped a few feet away and produced his identification badge, plainly trying to avoid encroaching into her space.

'Look, I'm really sorry to disturb you like this but I could do with asking you a few questions,' he explained, not quite sure how he was going to tackle the sensitive subject. Brian could see that the woman in front of him also felt awkward.

It was likely that Sam had told her that he also worked for National Security, so she must have guessed the reason he was there but it did feel as if she had been expecting him.

Although the landing that they stood upon was a fairly long space, even with the lift and the fire escape door separating the two apartments, it was far from private.

'Would it be better if we went inside where it's more private?' Brian suggested, looking towards her neighbour's door.

'Of course, please come in,' Janet offered, grudgingly. She stepped back into her apartment, allowing him to follow and close the door behind.

As the long hallway opened into a deceptively large lounge, Brian realised the old building was far deeper than he first thought. Inside the room, the decor was clean and fresh with thick carpets and a large three-seater settee piled with scatter cushions. The stylish pictures of Disney characters, hanging in heavy frames, suggested a childhood theme of memories and innocent, uncomplicated times.

Janet positioned herself in the middle of the room plainly reluctant to offer her guest a seat, indicating this was to be a brief meeting. Brian understood her gesture all too clearly. He figured it would be best for both if he just dealt with the facts rather than trying to break down the barriers between them.

'As I said, I work for National Security and Sam Young is one of my staff. We recently received an anonymous email declaring that you had been kidnapped. Whoever wrote that email indicated that Sam had been responsible. We are aware, by Sam's own admission, that the two of you went on a date and, for whatever reason, you left separately on the night,' Brian shook his hand in a dismissive gesture. 'We are not interested in why, that's between the two of you and it's none of our business. We are interested in two other things though. First, I wanted to see with my own eyes that you are safe and well. Secondly, I want to hear from your own mouth that you have not been kidnapped or taken somewhere against your will. Has anything like that happened to you Miss Beacham?' Brian asked.

He looked intently at the young woman in front of him for signs of distress. As security, he had been trained in interrogation methods and body language. The effectiveness of such behavioural signals was largely dependent on knowing a bit about the person being observed beforehand. Most people used their observational lie detector naturally without even knowing it.

Brian watched Janet's eyes cast downwards and to her left. A lie. She inadvertently brought her hands together in front of her, grasping her wrist occasionally. She didn't trust him and long pauses in her answers told Brian, within her mind she was writing a story on a blank page.

'No. I decided to come home as I was not feeling well. I think it was something that I had eaten. It may have been the sushi I had at lunch time. I haven't had a problem before with it. I just needed to get home,' she repeated.

'Janet, I know something is wrong. Something has happened, hasn't it? Please, you can talk to me in the strictest confidence,' Brian said.

Janet had constantly added detail to her alibi, in a vain attempt to convince him, and maybe herself, that this was the correct version of events.

'Nothing's wrong. That's what happened,' she snapped. 'As you can see, I'm here, safe and sound,' she said, forcing a smile.

Brian could see the smile was nothing more than a plea to let matters drop.

Janet edged towards the doorway, a gesture hovering on rudeness and a desire to show she had nothing more to add.

Brian realised, whatever was going on inside this young woman's head, further harassment wasn't going to help. He nodded his understanding and allowed himself to be ushered towards the door. 'Look, I can't force you to talk to me but if you ever change your mind please call me, any time.' With that, he pulled a card from his pocket and handed it to Janet.

As he walked down the stairs and out of the front door he realised something big was going on.

*

All thoughts of gaming forgotten, Ryan rubbed the back of his head in frustration. Whoever had made the phone call knew exactly what they were doing. The technology available to the National Security team made all the other cyber intelligence look stone age. It wasn't like the movies where the police would gather round in a smokey room, keeping the suspect talking right up to the point that a team of feds burst through his front door, shouting for him to get down on the floor. The idea of live traces may have been exciting for the viewers but live tracing was old tech. What Ryan had at his disposal was record tracing. An electronic record of global telecom data exchange. It had taken a lot of negotiating and more than a fair share of dodgy deals to secure but the American government had set up one of the best global telecommunication trace networks in the world. Regularly, foreign telecommunication companies stepped in with massive investment packages in order to run a country's network, and the host governments usually let them. They weren't arrogant enough to believe that they held the only monitoring system, but they did believe it was the best.

Every network kept a detailed log of its customer's outgoing, incoming, texting and data transfers, in order for billing. Even the smarter criminals who bounced a signal around the world in order to prevent detection were now finding themselves outwitted. None of this was legal, of course, and any evidence found couldn't be used in court, but that was just small detail.

With the technology at hand, Ryan's trace should have been simple, but each time he ran it, the results came back different. It shouldn't have been possible but it was as if the person making the call had simultaneously dialled from every inactive number around the world. The same results came back when he tried to trace the email. He knew Sam was going to be pissed when he told him that he couldn't find the sender but there was nothing he could do about it. Ryan wasted the whole day applying complex algorithms and trying to understand what was happening in a vain attempt to descramble the mess.

*

As Sophie pulled into the parking lot, she noticed Ron's pick-up was still in the same spot she had parked it in yesterday. She wasn't overly concerned that the big oaf maybe lying on the floor suffering from delayed brain damage but a seed of doubt had been sown. She immediately chided herself for caring but rather than walk straight to her apartment, she found herself walking the long path that circled the other blocks. She would just walk straight past the building, maybe take a glance up at his window, nothing more. After all, he wasn't her responsibility and he brought his troubles upon himself, anyway. Seeing his heavy drapes pulled back, Sophie kept walking.

Dropping her keys down on the edge of the kitchen table she pulled the cork from the half drunk bottle of red wine from the night before and sniffed. The smell made her wince. She wasn't sure if the wine had gone bad or if it was just poor quality. Being no expert on red wine, she had picked it up at a supermarket on a whim. At $7.95 it should have at least been drinkable. Sophie had been tempted to buy a bottle of single malt but the scarring from the last one led her to compromise. Now, as she tipped the remainder of the wine down the sink she regretted the purchase.

Slumping down on the settee, she automatically reached for her laptop. Most would have been forgiven for thinking that after a long day of computer coding she would have wanted to distance herself from another keyboard. Although her job required a high degree of technical knowledge, it also allowed her to shut herself off from the outside world.

She opened up Fletcher Rosworth's web site and browsed through the usual sales pitch. All the services offered were advertised under the guise of "specialists". Specialists in family law, specialists in unfair dismissal, specialists in accident claims, etc. What did catch Sophie's eye, however, was the line "Serving high profile clientele since 1900".

Highly sensitive information was usually isolated from the internet in places like these. As with the FBI, certain files were only exposed to the internet under the strictest of precautions. Very secure information access would need someone with security clearance to first request a file and then someone else within the building to sanction the request. This would mean the files Janet had been forced to access would also have needed someone on the inside too.

Sophie picked up her phone and dialled Diana's

mobile number. It was answered on the third ring.

'Hello,' Diana cautiously answered. Caller ID would have come up with "private" written across her screen and that always made people wary when answering a phone.

'If you still need my help, we need to meet up,' Sophie said, without introduction.

'OK. When? Where?' Diana asked. The abrupt offer had caught her a little by surprise.

'I'll let you know soon. Speak to no one about this though.'

'You have my word. Thanks for helping us,' Diana quickly added.

'Listen, I will try to help you but we are up against the major league on this one,' Sophie replied, then hung up.

She couldn't afford to underestimate her opponents on this one. Wild stories of people crossing swords with governments then meeting with coincidental accidents were not all media hype. First, she needed to find out which files had been accessed and by whom.

*

Although the swelling on the side of his head and jaw had gone down to manageable levels, the bruising from various strikes had started to shine. Rather than venture outside and traumatise the local population, Ron decided to study all the information the Man Eaters file had to offer.

Witness statements and police reports gave a lot of conflicting information about what had happened at each of the events. One thing all the reports managed to agree upon, however, was the attack response time.

All retaliatory action occurred usually no later than two hours after the so called catalyst event.

If he'd gone straight to his pick-up after causing the disturbance in the fitness reception, he would most likely have missed his introduction to the game of crack the skull. It would be easy to assume the receptionist had ordered the hit, but the waiting room had been full. Any one of the women watching could have pushed the button.

A soft knock at his door brought Ron back from his thoughts. He quickly scooped all the loose papers together, pushed them back into the file, then dropped it neatly down by the side of his chair. As he stood, a purple boot shaped bruise around his ribs cried out in pain.

'Hi, just come to see if you are all right,' Sophie said, standing a short way back from the open door. She had a dark hoodie pulled over her head but her unruly hair was putting up a good fight for freedom none the less.

'Hey, my favourite rescuer. Come on in, I'll put some coffee on,' Ron said, stepping to one side, once again hoping she would accept his invitation this time.

Sophie held up a brown paper bag with a bottle of some sorts in it. 'Just a couple of glasses,' she replied, stepping past him.

He closed the door and followed the faint scent of rose oil into his lounge.

Suddenly aware of his untidiness, he began bouncing about the apartment, picking up cups and pushing papers into disorganised piles. Sophie, either seemed not to notice the mess, or genuinely didn't care.

'I hope you like a single malt,' she said, pulling an

eighteen year old scotch whisky from the brown paper bag and placing it on the kitchen counter. Ron grinned, as if the cat had just been offered the cream.

'A woman who first rescues me then brings round a bottle of scotch, my life has just taken a turn,' Ron replied, discovering two heavy based whisky tumblers lurking at the back of a kitchen cupboard. 'Take a seat,' he nodded his head towards the couch in the middle of the room.

Ron carefully peeled the soft foil away from the neck of the high end whisky. He felt a spirit of this quality almost deserved a ceremony of some sort, or at the very least, a small jig. Easing the cork stopper from the bottle he sniffed at the fumes, capturing their first outing for nearly two decades.

Sophie paid no attention to Ron as he faffed about over the bottle. Instead, she just stood, looking out of the gap in the drapes, as if expecting someone to come.

Now, with a glass in each hand, Ron stood and watched Sophie staring out of the window lost in thought. He knew her decision of whether to stay or go was on a knife's edge.

'Grab a seat,' he repeated, trying to make it not sound like an order.

Taking the half filled whisky tumbler from him, she perched herself on the single hard backed chair by the small table. Ron tried to hide his disappointment at her decision to keep the distance.

'I just wanted to say sorry for the other day,' she said, taking a large gulp from her glass.

She took Ron aback a little. Not by the apology but by the way she didn't even flinch as the strong spirit poured down her throat.

'You know, in the parking lot, when you offered to help,' she continued, mistaking his silence for misunderstanding.

'No sweat, we all have bad days,' Ron said, rubbing the bruise on the side of his face to emphasise his point.

He lifted his own glass to his mouth. Before the amber liquid had even touched his lips the well crafted aroma had already made its way through his nose to prepare his taste buds for the treat.

He sat awkwardly on the edge of the couch while his guest perched higher on the wooden chair at the end of the room. Ron tried to break the lingering silence with a clumsy stab at small talk. 'Have you lived here long?'

'What was all that about, back at the fitness centre?' Sophie clearly wasn't there for small talk.

Her direct approach immediately put Ron on the spot.

'It's complicated. I'll tell you about it another time,' he said dismissively. He wanted to get to know her, not be interrogated.

Sophie stared at him, a blank expression on her face. Clearly the cogs were turning inside her head. She slowly downed the rest of her drink, without deflecting the icy stare.

'What do you do for a living?' she eventually asked.

Her ability to keep constant eye contact made him feel as if he was being toyed with. This was a question he had prepared himself for though. 'I'm just a maintenance guy. You know, just going around fixing stuff.'

He tried to sound casual about it. Ron didn't like having to lie; he wasn't very good at it. Lying needed lots of imagination and a good memory, both traits he seemed to lack. 'How about you? What do you do?' he asked, in the hope she would cut him a little slack. Nervously, he took a large gulp from his glass and realised he was starting to match Sophie's pace.

'I am part of a game writing team called V.P Flinch, they specialise in creating virtual reality horror games.'

Her detailed reply sounded like a challenge for Ron to put his cards on the table. Without another word, Sophie stood and walked to the kitchen counter and picked up the bottle of scotch. 'So, who do you work for?' she said, topping up their glasses.

Ron suddenly realised he was a mouse, trapped between the paws of an alley cat.

'Oh, I am just a one man set up really. I go anywhere where I'm needed.' He tried desperately to sound casual about it.

'And is that your own pick-up out there?' she enquired.

Ron just nodded. He was so far backed up against the wall; a nod seemed less of a lie. He figured that if you stood in front of another person and lied directly to their face, you were no better than a politician.

'So you don't work for Mortan Maintenance then?' Sophie asked in a casual tone.

Ron looked puzzled.

'Who?' he replied, knowing he was now on the ropes.

'The company who has leased the truck on your

behalf.'

Sophie's stare was now clearly a challenge to see if he would stop digging the hole he had found himself in.

Ron sighed deeply. 'Look, I can't actually tell you what I do because I'm not allowed to and I really don't want to lie to you because I like you, so can we just talk about something else?' he asked, getting agitated now.

'OK, what were you doing at the fitness centre then?' Sophie wasn't just going to be fobbed off.

'That was to do with my work,' he replied. 'Why did those women listen to you in the parking lot? Are you part of their gang?'

The night had suddenly turned to rat shit, so he figured he might as well get something out of it.

'Whoa there, big boy. You're the one with all the cloak and dagger secrets. Don't go pointing the finger at me in order to deflect your issues. Yes, I did know some of them as it happens, but I'm damn sure I'm *not* part of their gang, as you put it.' Sophie became louder as her anger rose.

Ron held his hands up in a gesture of surrender. 'Look, you're right. I do have secrets but they are genuinely to do with the work that I'm involved in. I hate not being able to talk about it and *that's* the truth. I wouldn't blame you if you walked out that door and never spoke to me again. I'd prefer it if you didn't though.' Ron gave her what he judged to be his most wounded puppy dog look.

Sophie's suspicious nature screamed at her to turn and leave. It would be the cleanest solution, but something about him made her hesitate.

'So, is "Ron" even your real name?' she asked.

Ron nodded, sensing there was a chance he might miss the storm. 'Ronald Sebastian Hawley,' he offered, 'but my friends just call me Ron. Well they would if I had any,' he added, shrugging his shoulders.

'I can see why you don't have friends, Ronald,' Sophie replied, emphasising his full name.

Without thinking, Ron reached out and touched her hand. It felt the natural thing to do, a gesture of friendship between couples. She didn't pull away, but the moment lingered a little too long and became clumsy.

'Another drink?' Sophie took another gulp then moved away to break the tension. Ron had hardly touched what was in his hand but it created an opportunity to exit the intimate situation.

'I'm OK for now, thanks.'

Ron noticed Sophie sway a little as she walked to the kitchen, the alcohol flooding into her system. It was obvious, even to a dinosaur such as himself, that this woman had deep seated issues, but underneath her steely exterior lurked a vulnerability.

She paused, ready to pick up the bottle, then changed her mind. 'I'd better go. It's getting late,' she said.

Whatever thoughts were milling around inside her head, she had concluded it was time to cut and run. The old battery operated clock hanging on Ron's kitchen wall indicated it was only just before nine but he let it go.

Without another word, Sophie walked towards the door.

'Maybe I can buy you that dinner sometime?' Ron offered, following at a safe distance so as not to crowd her.

She paused at the threshold of the open door, the fresh, cold air that flooded in erased any intimacy shared mere moments ago. Sophie realised her behaviour had started to become erratic as she looked at the big guy standing like an anxious schoolboy, asking for a prom date.

'How about next Saturday night, at eight?' she suggested, calmly.

'Next Saturday, at eight. It's a date,' he repeated, stepping in a little closer.

Still unprepared for her space to be invaded, Sophie stepped away onto the landing, and went.

*

The only light still shining on the fifth floor was that of Sam Young's. At just ten thirty, the Thursday night life in the street below had already started to fizzle out as people rushed off to get a few hours sleep, ready for the following day of work. Ryan had been beside himself at his failure to come up with a result on the task he had been given. “It must have come via the Commies,” he had pleaded. Although he was mainly referring to China, he also included Russia, regardless of the fact the Soviet Union had collapsed in the early nineties.

Even though Ryan was a technical wizz, he was still wet behind the ears when it came to the idea of dirty backhand dealings. Technology was cold and sterile. It never lied and the ones and zeros did exactly what they were programmed to do. Sam could pick up a phone right now and have one of his non declared Russian friends arrange a phone call in the same way that the hacker most likely had. He could exchange a piece of delicate information for a favour, but nothing was just black or white. Sam almost felt sorry for Ryan. The lad would take it as a personal failure, forever playing on his mind. Maybe a few more setbacks would do the kid good.

Janet's apartment was now being monitored around the clock along with any online activities. If the mystery hacker made contact, they would soon know.

Minor cyber security breaches were incredibly common, especially against the FBI system. Hackers, or in most cases wannabe hackers, viewed it as some sort of rite of passage to at least breach the outer shell of security of one of the government departments. Ninety percent of the time breaches were carried out by grad' students pitting themselves up against the big boys. They usually underestimated the government's willingness to step outside the law in their surveillance methods though.

The dumb-ass majority of hackers just blundered in and ended up getting arrested, charged with attempting to breach national security, then sent on their way with a criminal record. The cleverer ones were secretly monitored in case they fell into some sort of criminal activity at a later date, but the really smart ones were hired. That's how Ryan came to work for them.

Like Ryan, Sam knew he was beginning to take things personally but this *was* personal. Someone was watching him and to make it worse, they had caught him with his hand in the cookie jar. If he didn't find this person soon it could come back to bite him at a later date. Although he now had permission to utilise full department resources in order to find her, he would still use one of his private contacts to make her disappear.

He picked up his jacket, switched off his table lamp and headed for the elevators. The winter was really beginning to bite now and he knew it would be cold out there, even though he could see the last of the weekday party goers waiting for taxies in their flimsy summer clothes.

Sam briefly considered popping down to the surveillance department on the second floor, but decided against it. Besides, it was too early yet, and anyway, they had strict instructions to ring him straight away if anything came up.

*

Sophie cursed herself for being weak. The feeling of being lonely and miserable after work, combined with the knowledge that it would have been her father's birthday, had been too much. Because it didn't seem right not to raise a glass in his memory she had found herself once again in the liquor store. That was what she told herself anyway. The expensive single malt had stirred up fond memories and a strong reminder of her father's downfall but she had gone past caring.

As she had walked back from the store, clutching her brown paper bag, she knew she was looking over the edge of a black hole. She hadn't meant to go to Ron's apartment but, like a moth drawn to a flame, she had found herself standing at the foot of the steps looking up at his window. She had stood there asking herself questions. What if she got burnt again? What if he turned her away? The barriers she had put up to prevent herself from getting hurt were also bringing her to the brink of depression. Unlike the moth, she had lived within the shadows for fear of getting burnt, but at least the moth would have lived its life.

Sophie had fully intended to keep things non confrontational, even though he clearly had secrets, but the alcohol had loosened her tongue. The brief night had almost turned sour from the start, but there was an honesty in the guy. He had been awkward in trying to conceal the truth from her, then she backed him into a corner, forcing him to confess that his job had sworn him to secrecy. His confession now posed a moral dilemma for her. Did she respect Ron's need for secrecy or should she, now armed with his full name, find out all there was to know about him? She surprised herself for even considering not looking into his background. As she trawled through Ron's history, she felt shocked to find out that he had recently done time for assaulting two police officers. The reports said he had instigated a fight with some guy who was having a peaceful drink and when officers went in to break it up he went wild and attacked them too. Sophie berated herself for accepting the reports at face value. She knew how the system worked. Stories were written by the victors of wars and when it came down to the law, the police wrote most of the stories. Nonetheless, she would have to confront him about it.

His prison release forms revealed he had been assigned work at a meat processing plant, with accommodation included. That much figured, most parolees ended up assigned to dead end jobs that no one else wanted. Some stroke of good luck must have happened to him shortly after starting work at the meat factory though because not only did he change jobs, he also changed his address and his parole officer.

His first parole officer, Andrew Soul (Sophie

smiled as she read the name), had filled out his rehabilitation forms meticulously, in typical bureaucratic style. Addresses past and present, full name, insurance number, possible people he might contact if things turned bad. It was all there. Frank Landon, his current parole officer, had been the extreme opposite. The new forms were vague, and only partially updated. It was as if he was encouraging Ron to drop off the radar to some extent.

It was only after she had done a search on Frank Landon that the penny dropped. Sophie sat there, open mouthed and in shock at what she had just stumbled onto. Landon was head of The Federal Bureau for the Prevention of Interactive Services. The department had recently been established to keep all public services working within their own parameters rather than intermingling with others. In simple terms, all those engaged in unofficial policing, ran the risk of coming face to face with a heavy handed member of their organisation, ready to stop them at any cost. They were called Reapers.

The government completely denied Reapers existed of course, but it all made perfect sense as to why they had recruited Ron. Reapers usually consisted of violent ex-offenders who suddenly find themselves being thrown a lifeline in the form of becoming an unofficial hit man. It was a win win situation for the feds. If the ex-cons did their job well, it meant the end of another vigilante, but if they screwed up and got caught, they just went back to prison for a very long time.

They were only set loose on the Min-heroes of course, never the big hitters because that would be counterproductive.

The big boys were still regarded as almost an official crime fighting department in their own right as they brought serious resources to the table. Those who didn't have the multimillion dollar budgets, just going after the small offenders, were seen to be more of a nuisance rather than a benefit.

Was there a chance Ron was here for her, Sophie asked herself? That question would have to wait for later. Red Renarde had work to do first.

*

The idea of being forced to change jobs angered Janet but that was exactly what she felt was happening. If she stayed at Fletcher Rosworth's it would just invite her kidnappers to put her through the whole ordeal again at any time. She would never be able to stop looking over her shoulder and even if she did, the guilt of betraying her employers would gnaw away at her conscience. What made her feel worse, was her friends and colleagues had welcomed her back with open arms and genuine concern for her health. She had used the feeble excuse of some sort of food poisoning, but that lie also burnt into her soul.

The intercom buzzed, drawing Janet's attention away from the job vacancies section of the local paper. Crossing the hall to the small panel on the wall, she pressed the answer button.

'Hello,' she answered, cautiously. The easily identifiable image of a courier dressed in a brown uniform appeared on the little screen.

'I have a small package for a Miss Beacham.' The delivery man's nose filled the whole image of the screen, as he leant in close to the speaker in a futile attempt to block out the traffic noise.

Janet buzzed the release button to enable the courier to enter the building. By the time she had removed her door chain and stepped out onto the landing to meet him, the courier had already stepped through the doorway at the top of the stairs. No doubt, his heavy delivery schedule encouraged the two at a time stair climbing technique.

He approached, carrying a jiffy bag in one hand and a little hand held organiser, complete with a plastic pen hanging off a curly wire, in the other.

'Good afternoon,' he beamed, handing over the digital organiser.

Janet offered a token smile, then squiggled a shape that resembled nothing like her normal signature onto the digital screen.

Without a second glance at the child like squiggle, the courier handed over the jiffy bag, 'Have a nice day,' he beamed, safe in the knowledge he was another step closer to the end of his round.

Janet watched the delivery guy disappear through the stairway exit, then went back inside her apartment.

Standing in her kitchen, she curiously turned the padded brown envelope over to see if the sender had written a return address on it - they hadn't. After a few moments of uncertainty, she ripped the top off the package and slid out a budget Nokia into her hand. She shook the bag a little and a used charger followed, but nothing more. The entry level phone looked more suited to propping a door open rather than every day use. Only yesterday, had the phone company agreed to send out a replacement under her insurance but this wasn't what she had been expecting. Janet didn't in any way regard herself as a technology chaser but her old phone by comparison looked futuristic. This one didn't even come with a box.

The brick like phone buzzed in her hands and the words "Text received" filled the little blue display window. Instinctively, she opened up the file and read the message, "You are being monitored. Be outside Pascal's restaurant at eight tonight. Do not talk to anyone about this and do not bring any other cell phone with you. Tell Diana to do the same. Red." Janet stared at the little blue screen a moment longer, until eventually the battery saver faded it out. She wanted to call her sister but resisted the urge.

Sophie knew she was beginning to play with fire. It wasn't as if she didn't have enough of her own issues to contend with, but walking away from this was no longer an option for her. If she didn't stand up to the corrupt bullies willing to step on the weak and vulnerable, who would? Maybe after helping Janet, Red Renarde could disappear for good. Maybe.

*

Ron waited patiently inside the portable site office as two men in bright fluorescent jackets, sporting matching plastic hats, argued over a detail on a drawing. The one who had his back to Ron kept arguing about a lack of room to route a soil pipe between two joists. The other kept on repeating that the joists were the correct distance, according to the drawing.

'Well, Mack, that makes it all better then, doesn't it? We'll just hand the customer a bucket and tell them, "That's your bathroom because the drawing said the joists were in the right place",' the plumber laughed.

'Jeez, okay, okay, I get what you're saying. I'll give planning a call in a bit and see what they have to say about it,' said the taller and rather more distressed looking man. A little hand stitched label on his left shoulder, with the word "Manager", indicated that everyone's problems were unfortunately his problems.

Even though the plastic clock on the wall indicated half past two, Ron noticed the manager's lunch lay barely touched. The cold coffee had grown a film of white stuff over the top and the sandwich had now attracted the attention of an enthusiastic fly.

As the worker left the office, his copy of the drawings tucked firmly under his arm, Mack's attention slowly returned to Ron. It had already been a day of problem after problem and the last thing he needed was the health and safety team showing up again asking about the scaffolding. Ron hadn't announced himself as a safety inspector but he rolled with the assumption.

'Look, I'll tell you the same as I've told the other dozen or so of your inspectors. That scaffolding was secure. The lads that put it up were good lads and they've worked on my jobs before. I'm telling you, someone sabotaged that scaffolding.' The manager slumped down in his chair and cast a sideways glance towards his cold coffee and hardening sandwich.

'I take it Robert Smith, the guy that got hurt when it collapsed, won't be back for a while,' Ron said, looking down at his note pad.

'Old Bob probably won't ever come back now. What with his age and a broken hip, it'll take him ages to recover. No doubt, he'll get a big pay out from our insurance that will see him out until he retires. It's a shame, he was one of the best brick layers I've ever known, even for an old guy. It's a big black mark on my record though. Health and safety violations tend to hang over your career these days,' Mack replied, miserably.

'Well, I won't take up any more of your time. I can see you're pretty busy here,' Ron said, as yet another fluorescent vest and plastic hat shaped figure appeared at the doorway. Mack raised a hand in acknowledgement as Ron left. The new arrival entered the site office and began to unroll another set of drawings across Mack's desk, obscuring his sandwich once more. So far, Ron could see nothing suggesting a link to the man hating vigilante group.

Rather than head straight back to his truck though, Ron decided to take a stroll around the immediate vicinity. The new community hall construction site sat quite a long way back from the road. The city planners described the vast expanse of sidewalk as urban space. In reality, it was just a clever way of utilising the old road, made obsolete when the new highway had been built. The "urban space" did look kind of nice though Ron conceded, with its big stone planters and stylish looking benches.

A selection of modern stone artwork had been randomly positioned around the walkways. They were the sort of pieces that only art critics understood but to Ron they just looked as if a four year old had been undecided on a dog or a fish. It wasn't that he didn't appreciate art, it was more, he just didn't get it. Rather like a group of drunks only finding a joke funny when under the influence, an artist only gets art when they've mislaid all their marbles. Ron remembered seeing a Picasso painting in a Chicago museum, of an old blue zombie playing a guitar.

After strolling around for twenty minutes, he found nothing of significance so headed back to his truck. The small street he had parked in had obviously fallen victim to the new road system because it had now turned into a dead end. The lack of traffic passing through had also meant a lack of trade for most of the old stores.

Ron lifted the key fob, ready to unlock the truck, then noticed something out of the corner of his eye. High above a closed down Spanish restaurant, a little pink sign had been painted on a second floor window identifying a women's only fitness centre. The glow of fluorescent tube lighting and the thick condensation on the windows indicated the place was in full swing. The tenderness around his bruised ribs convinced him to resist any temptation to investigate the coincidence further. After safely climbing into his truck, he tapped an address into his sat-nav. Maybe old Bob could shine a little more light onto what had happened instead.

*

Pascal's restaurant was no more than a five minute walk from Janet and Diana's apartment block. A mixture of good quality food and reasonable prices had become a winning formula over the years for the small family run place. Unless you made a reservation at least a week in advance, it was almost impossible to get a table.

The idea of having Red Renarde on their side was both thrilling and scary at the same time. Red was a kind of modern day Zorro mixed with a pinch of Robin Hood, fighting for the greater good. She had exposed countless moralistic corrupt figures over the years, regardless of their status. The press tripped over themselves to be the first to print one of her comprehensive reports, exposing the rich and famous or the average person, man or woman alike.

The anonymous fact based stories never failed to double a paper's sales figures. The more the press sensationalised a "Red Renarde" story, the more people loved her. To have her fighting for your cause was the same as winning the lottery.

The brick shaped phone in Janet's pocket buzzed.

'Hello,' she answered, pressing the phone firmly against her right ear whilst covering her left in an attempt to block out the traffic.

'There's a bus approaching, get on it and I'll call you again shortly.' The phone went dead.

'We have to get on the next bus,' Janet spoke close into her sister's ear.

Diana just nodded her understanding. They had suspected there would be a few cautions taken.

Within fifteen seconds, a big, silver bus rounded the corner and pulled up at the stop. Apart from a lone man sitting halfway up the bus and a group of cackling women taking up the whole of the rear seat, the bus was empty. The man was probably on his way home from a late shift, and the group of women appeared to be on their way to a party. No one paid any attention as the new passengers got on.

Diana sat next to the window and fixed her eyes on the door to see if anyone else tried to follow them on at the last minute. No one did, but then again, if anyone wanted to follow them they would probably have been sitting inside a warm car a short way back anyway. The phone buzzed again.

'As soon as the bus takes the next right, get off then quickly walk straight into the mall, then take a table inside the little diner, four stores in on the left. I'll meet you there.' The caller hung up once more.

'Quick, we have to get off now,' Janet stood and tugged at her sister's sleeve.

Diana, once more, followed without question. The bus doors had hardly finished opening before Janet stepped off, still leading her elder sister by the sleeve. It took no more than six steps to cross the sidewalk and enter the familiar mall entrance opposite the bus stop. As Diana was led by her sister, she cast a quick glance behind to see if anyone was following. She half expected a black sedan, containing two men in trilby hats and smoking woodbines to pull up, like in the movies.

It had been a clever tactic to take a bus just for one stop. Any tail would have stayed far enough behind so as not to get spotted, so getting off after turning a corner would also hide them momentarily.

Diana allowed her sister to lead her through the mall's automatic sliding doors and into the late night shopping complex. Most of the activity had died down now and no doubt, staff were eagerly awaiting closing time.

The little diner on the left was still half full and waitresses were still walking about taking orders and delivering food to tables. As they entered, Janet pulled her sister towards a window seat so they could be spotted by Red but Diana pulled back.

'She knows where we are going to be. I suspect she will want a little more privacy.'

Janet nodded at Diana's logic and headed towards

a booth at the rear of the shop. With a clear view, they sat and watched the entrance for a good ten minutes or so, waiting for Red to arrive. With the evening coming to an end, new customers were becoming less and less frequent. A man and woman entered and sat at the window seat Janet had first been drawn to. Then a group of four women, who looked as if they had already been somewhere, entered, but no red haired woman.

A moment or two later, a woman with long blond hair and broad rim spectacles sat down at their table. Janet said nothing but gave her sister a questioning look. Diana prided herself for thinking she had a good memory for faces but she just stared at the new arrival, full of uncertainty.

'Hello again, Diana. It's nice to see I'm not that obvious,' the blond haired woman said.

'Red?' Diana asked, cautiously. Her eyes focusing on the newcomer's painted lips and the heavy eye make up behind her glasses. Red Renarde returned a slight tilt of the head in acknowledgement.

'Hello Janet.' The blond haired woman held out her hand.

Janet looked to her sister for confirmation that it was indeed the right woman. Diana smiled and nodded at her sister.

'Pleased to meet you,' Janet shook the stranger's hand.

'Thank you for helping us,' Diana offered.

'I'm not sure what I can do yet about these people but I'll try my best,' Red replied.

'Why *are* you helping us?' Janet asked.

The simple question seemed to take Red back a little. It was as if no one had ever asked that question before.

Red gave a little shrug of her shoulders, 'Maybe because I know what it's like to suffer injustice. Maybe it's because I loathe bullies, or maybe it's just because I'm in a position that I can help.'

The sisters could see the question stirred a lot of thought in Red.

'Were you waiting here before us? We've watched the door since we got here but we didn't see you enter,' Janet said, trying to break the tension.

Red smiled at the innocent question. It was a Sherlock Holmes moment if ever there was one. 'You looked, but you didn't see.' The famous quote was lost on the sisters. 'I slipped in close to the group of women who came in earlier. You were looking for a single woman, so naturally you paid no attention to a group of four women.'

'Why are we are under surveillance and who are they?' Janet asked, still finding it hard to comprehend that someone was watching them.

'Yeh, well I'm afraid that's mainly down to me. You see, I broke into their security and let them know that I had proof you had left the bar with Sam Young. I made it clear on their record, that if anything happened to you, he had been the last person seen with you. I should imagine he had to do some serious covering up,' Red explained. She could see that Diana now understood the ramifications of what could have happened to her sister.

'So, once it became common knowledge that he had been seen, he had to release her,' Diana said, fully understanding Red had probably saved her sister's life.

'National Security will most likely continue to

monitor your activity for the next few months in an attempt to find me, then eventually pull their surveillance,' Red assured.

'What happens then?' Janet asked.

'That depends on how much your kidnappers dislike loose ends. Because you are under government surveillance, they will most likely leave you alone for now,' Red replied.

'So we are safe until they pull the plug on surveillance?' Diana asked.

'Don't be too sure. This is where it all gets messy. Sam Young is dirty. I suspect he is selling incriminating information about senators to anyone willing to buy it. Being high up in security, I imagine he is also pulling most of the strings and they have a ways of covering up "incidents" quickly,' Red warned. 'You said he contacted you again so you would confirm an alibi?' Red questioned.

'Yes, that's right. The slime ball followed me back from the store the other day and threatened that if I didn't cooperate fully something bad would happen to Marie. That's our younger sister,' Janet explained. 'They even threatened my niece, little Rebecca,' she added, with moisture in her eyes.

'And did anyone contact you to ask where you had been? Red asked.

'Yes, some guy came around. I just had to tell him I was okay and nothing had happened,' Janet said. 'I don't think he believed me though,' she added.

'What was he like? Red asked.

Janet shrugged her shoulders a little, 'He seemed genuine enough but then again, so did Sam until he kidnapped me.' Janet rolled her eyes for being so gullible.

'I think you did the right thing by not talking at this stage. There is no telling who's dirty and who isn't.'

Sophie felt sorry for Janet. Until recently, she had lived in a world of rainbows and pink fluffy animals. In Janet's world, people were who they said they were and altruism was the default setting. To the likes of Sam Young though, the Janets of the world were no more than keys to vaults containing the most coveted secrets to some of the most powerful men in the country. Information was the currency of the corrupt and Janet, whether she liked it or not, was now in their pockets. To go to the police would put loved ones in danger but to do nothing would allow these people to win. Even if she did leave Fletcher Rosworth's, someone else would be coerced into taking up the role of the puppet.

Red listened carefully to Janet's detailed account of the abduction, occasionally stopping her to cross reference her when she talked about the security measures.

'How many security staff remain within the building when it closes for the night?' she queried.

Janet couldn't give an accurate answer as she was never the last to leave. On many an occasion she had witnessed the security officer, dressed in the usual blue shirt and tie, enter the building and take over the reception desk but there were still others around at that time. Once he did arrive the main entrance was locked, meaning anyone working late would have to be let out, Janet explained.

During their meeting, it became obvious to Red that the main concern of the sisters was that of the well being of their younger sibling and her little family. The trouble was, the people who had kidnapped Janet also knew how much her family meant to her.

It was only when the coffee shop staff began wiping down tables that the three women realised it was nearly closing time at the mall. Red was satisfied that she had gained enough information for now. If she needed more, she would arrange another meeting.

'Can I have the phone back please?' Red asked, holding out her hand. Janet suddenly looked concerned.

'Don't worry, I'm not abandoning you but if you keep it, it may become compromised,' Red tried to re-assure them.

'Have they got our apartments bugged?' Diana asked.

'Your social media and email accounts are under surveillance and a couple of goons were sitting in a blue panel van watching your apartment block as you left earlier. I'm not sure if they have been inside your apartment, but your cell phone is now being monitored too,' Red nodded her head towards Diana.

'I should be thankful my replacement hasn't come yet then,' Janet said, miserably.

'It will be bugged as soon as it does come,' Red warned.

'How can they even be allowed to do that?' Diana asked, incredulous.

'Allowed has nothing to do with it. Besides, they can just claim it's a matter of national security,' Red replied, with a shrug.

If you do need to contact me, just go onto this website and request a free sample.' Red handed each of them a business card. The writing on the front said, "For all your sewing needs". It was so innocuous Diana would have dropped it straight in the trash had it been posted through her mailbox.

Red Renarde had set up the false website years ago when she had first started helping out people. Once logged onto the web address, it just looked like a sewing site. There were various articles about thread thicknesses, needle sizes and fabric swatches. In fact everything you would find on a high quality needlework website. The main difference with this site, was that it wasn't visible to the public domain. It could only be accessed by typing in the exact address as you would an email address.

By clicking on the free sample request, it would achieve two things. First it would alert Red to the need to contact her and second, it would automatically accept a Trojan computer program, allowing her access to the sender's web cam. The web cam access could come in useful if her client was held against their will.

Because the walk back to their apartment block was less than a mile, it wasn't worth the sisters waiting for a bus. Instead they took a slow walk back, each churning their thoughts over as they walked. Janet couldn't help feeling a sense of loss by the absence of Red's phone in her pocket.

As they turned the last corner to their apartment block, a parked blue panel van at the kerbside suddenly stood out. Normally, neither would give it a second glance but now it became blindingly obvious. A strong smell of stale tobacco smoke leaked through the gap in the side window, alerting them to the presence within. The sisters looked at each other to see if each had clocked the obvious surveillance. The van's occupants, momentarily caught off guard by the two women approaching from their blind spot, quickly slid the tinted window closed.

SEVEN

Things were starting to get way too messy for Sam Young's liking. He couldn't stand loose ends at the best of times, but right now, a ball of string was unravelling before his very eyes. The sisters were obviously not taking his threats seriously and he was convinced the woman hacker must be behind their defiance, but he still needed to find out for sure. If he wasn't managing to get his message across, maybe it was time he stopped being the nice guy.

The two idiots who were supposed to be watching the girls had just left his office under a threat of becoming department store watchmen. They had sworn blind that they had tailed the bus all the way back to the depot, carefully watching each stop just in case the girls got off and yet, at the final stop, no one was left. Sam spent the next hour or so combing the footage from their dash cam's memory card, to confirm his agents' story. As he watched the playback several times over, he could clearly see the sisters standing on the pavement, waiting for the bus. Although the bus momentarily obscured the pair as it pulled alongside the kerb, he could still make out the sisters walking up the bus isle in search of a seat.

He patiently forwarded the surveillance video to each stop, carefully scrutinising every passenger getting off or on, right up until it reached the depot. He even watched the image of the stationary bus for five minutes before one of the agents went to search inside the bus. It was only after the third time of watching the footage, that Sam realised the bus had been obscured from sight, just long enough for passengers to get off outside a shopping mall. It had been the very next stop, less than a mile from where they'd got on. No one would have anticipated them getting straight back off the bus.

'Son of a bitch,' Sam said, leaning back in his leather swivel chair. He sat there a moment, holding his forehead, deep in thought. Eventually he picked up the phone, 'Ryan, get me all footage from the security cameras inside the Swan shopping mall from yesterday, around eight PM to closing last night.' Sam waited for Ryan to read the request back to him before adding. 'I need it as soon as possible please.'

Ryan knew that meant drop everything else. 'Right on it,' he replied, knowing this was his chance to redeem himself from his earlier failure.

*

Jack Wilks thought of himself as being a fairly smart sort of guy. He was under no illusion of having the academic skills needed to do the same job his bosses did in the court room, but he did consider himself street smart. As far as he was concerned, fancy lawyers wouldn't last five minutes out on the streets in the rough part of the neighbourhood. Inside the courtroom they smugly hid behind objections and overruling but out on the streets objecting would probably just get them a knife in the eye.

In Jack's mind, all those at Fletcher Rosworth saw him as nothing more than a night watchman, guarding their precious building. What they didn't appreciate, was he was so much more. While they were out enjoying themselves at the theatre or some swanky restaurant at night, he was the one guarding their precious secrets. That was why he decided to take the opportunity to make a whole load of extra cash.

A few weeks ago, a well dressed man had approached him in the underground car park, just as he was getting into his car to go home. It had all been cloak and dagger sort of stuff. At first, Jack had dismissed the guy as some sort of nut. The man had asked him if he would like to earn a substantial amount of money just for letting someone inside to access one of their computers. He promised no one would even know they had been there. Jack had angrily waved the guy away, started his engine and begun to pull away when a large brown envelope, crammed with hundred dollar bills dropped into his lap through his open window. He had immediately switched his engine off and flicked through the contents. There was fifty thousand dollars in unmarked bills in that envelope.

Mr "Smith," as he called himself, promised another fifty once the job was complete, if he was willing. All he needed to do, was open the door, point out the location of the mainframe computer, then go back to watching the ball game. Even his highly paid bosses couldn't bring in that sort of cash for so little work. Jack went home that morning fifty thousand dollars better off.

*

Data theft is nothing new. Since the dawn of time, spies have been used in one way or another to steal secrets. It's what makes the world turn. From finding out how the next village grew bigger cabbages to understanding the guidance system on a nuclear missile, all the rest sat firmly between the two.

Safeguarding such secrets had moved along too. Written files became too cumbersome and took up a lot of storage space, so everything was transferred to digital. At first, that seemed to work well but eventually clever computer people discovered how to bypass security protocols and still steal the secrets. It became a battle of computer nerds. One side fighting to keep information safe, the other doing their best to steal it. Eventually, drastic security measures were introduced that were slightly inconvenient but a whole step safer.

Fletcher Rosworth was one of the few that isolated its data from the internet. Rather like pulling the lead out from the back of the computer. Any request for information to be transferred over the internet by lawyers would have to be sanctioned from the Fletcher Rosworth building. Metaphorically speaking, someone needed to push the lead back in before they got their information. That couldn't be done outside office hours, unless some fool was willing to let a stranger into the building during the night that was.

*

It was becoming obvious to Sophie that Sam Young was just a middle man in his position of power, willing to sell secrets to the highest bidder. She wasn't crazy enough to believe she could stop the legions of the corrupt, ready to sell the nation out, but she could expose a few of them. If she brought Young down and exposed whoever it was who was pulling his strings, she would class it as a victory. The tricky bit was working out who else was involved.

Even though Janet was needed for the retina scan, it still required someone on the inside at Fletcher Rosworth's to sanction access to the server. According to Janet, the cleaners came in around five pm for a quick dust and Hoover but most of the time other staff stayed late and were around while they worked. That only left the security guard. Either he knew considerably more about computers than his pay grade suggested or he was being paid to look the other way while someone else did the technical stuff.

Sophie went through the Rosworth's personnel file and found out that the regular security guard was a man by the name of Jack Wilks. After a little bit of digging around in Wilks' bank statements she found what she was looking for. She hadn't expected him to be so stupid as to deposit a large sum of money but it did seem he had learnt to live without touching his balance of $72 for the last two weeks. Sophie smiled at his stupidity.

She knew, if she dug a little deeper, there would be enough evidence somewhere that would incriminate him. The trouble was, Wilks was just another puppet in the game. The puppet masters would never leave such an obvious trail. If she could find out who Janet's kidnappers were, they might just lead her to those pulling the strings.

*

The CCTV cameras within the Swan shopping mall were not what you'd call state of the art security. Just six out of the eight cameras were currently operational and the image resolution was poor compared to the high definition of today's modern technology. Ryan had been forced to wave his National Security warrant under the nose of the officer in charge, after he started asking for requisite forms to be filled in. It was amazing how the threat of standing in the way of government business always changed the attitude of the obstinate, Ryan thought. The security guard immediately started stumbling over himself, quickly adding all footage of the previous night's surveillance onto a memory stick, in a new bid to appear helpful.

Now, as Sam sat at his computer screen reviewing the low quality footage, he tracked Janet and another woman, who he assumed was her sister, enter the mall. He watched the sisters walk purposely along the atrium and straight into a coffee shop. They must have known that they were being tailed because Janet could clearly be seen looking over her shoulder before going inside the shop. No one catches a bus just to travel a few blocks, enter a shopping mall then go straight into a coffee shop unless they are planning on meeting someone, Sam figured.

With just the main atrium camera and one other showing the coffee shop entrance from afar to work with, he spent the whole morning examining every other person using the shopping complex. By lunch time, he had printed off a pile of pictures, one of which had to be his suspect. The sisters may have given them the slip this time but next time, he would have an agent positioned inside that coffee shop. Sam felt smug. Whoever thought they could get the better of him would have a shock coming.

*

Sophie looked at the GT500 on the driveway of Jack Wilks' property and smiled. At least the guy had good taste if nothing else. The '67 Mustang was probably twice the value of his house and stood out like a sore thumb in the neighbourhood. A quick check on the police database showed that it had been in Jack's possession for all of three days now. According to records, it had come from Golden Classical Autos, who had owned it for the last twelve months, no doubt busy restoring it.

Money had clearly burnt a hole in Jack's pocket, resulting in him chasing his dreams. Sophie knew only too well, if she dug a little deeper she would discover the Mustang had either been brought with cash or paid for through an anonymous buyer. It didn't matter either way. At least now, she had proof he had been bought.

*

The help desk had been unusually quiet throughout the morning, for a change. The lull in activity meant Diana could at last catch up on the mundane task of filling in the product return forms. A dreaded task her colleagues always seemed too busy to undertake.

Reaching for another form, she spotted a young man in the corner of her eye, heading in her direction. He was dressed in scruffy blue jeans, a white baggy tee shirt with the Diesel logo printed across it and a black textile jacket with the hood pulled up. She tried not to stare too long as the lad approached but there was something familiar about his face.

'Excuse me please, I'd like to return this item,' he said, smiling as he stepped up to the desk. Diana's face was a picture of surprise as she suddenly recognised Red. She quickly composed herself, took the offered bag with the store's logo printed on it and peered inside. She immediately recognised the budget phone, then cast her eyes quickly about the store to see if they were being watched. The few shoppers browsing garments on the racks appeared to pay no attention to them.

'Of course, sir. Is there anything else I can help you with?' Diana asked, maintaining the pretence.

'No thank you, but I'll be in touch soon.' Her last words left no doubt as to what she meant.

Diana watched as Red nonchalantly drift away towards the exit, occasionally lifting tags as if to check out the price on the odd garment. Diana cast her eyes around the store again to see if anyone else was watching but when she looked back, Red had gone. Without another glance, Diana routinely placed the bag under the counter.

It wasn't until lunch time that Diana had a chance to take the phone to the staff room and read the text message already on it. It read, "Need to meet at your apartment. Have an idea but involves risk. Press the door unlock button at exactly 19:45 tonight by this phone's clock. Leave any other cell phones inside Janet's apartment."

By the time Diana left work, it was dark and it had just started to rain. She normally regarded herself as a calm, rational sort of person but during the ride home she realised the whole situation was getting to her. Caught between knowing she should go to the police and fearing for her sisters' welfare, she felt trapped.

As the bus pulled up close to home, she cast her eye across the street to see if the blue panel van was still there. It wasn't. Although the van was nowhere to be seen, she did spot a dark sedan, with misted windows, further down the road. It may easily have been a coincidence but Diana had become too sceptical for that now.

*

At a quarter to eight, the two agents in the black sedan across the street witnessed a young man approach the apartment building and let himself in. Although he appeared to be a resident and was the wrong gender, the new arrival was automatically recorded on camera and logged in nonetheless. What they didn't see from their location, however, was the assumed resident only offered a key up to the lock before the door opened.

Red Renarde had easily spotted the two goons sitting in the sedan but she walked past it as if oblivious of her surroundings. As she made her way up the steps to the apartments, she scolded herself for becoming too sure of herself. If they ever caught her they would, at the very least, put her in prison. Sam Young would no doubt do his best to make her to disappear though.

Stepping onto the first floor landing, Red heard a door unlock, then Diana appeared. Red held a finger to her lips in a gesture for silence as she stepped from the landing and into Diana's hallway. Once inside, she pulled a little silver device from her pocket and moved it back and forth, slowly moving through the apartment, checking each room. In the lounge, she unplugged the Alexa AI device before speaking.

'Cell phones upstairs?' Red asked. Janet and Diana both nodded, unsure if it was now safe to speak. 'Sorry about that, you can't be too careful,' she continued.

'Did you spot the dark sedan across the road?' Diana asked, concerned.

'Yeh, they've been there all day. They're waiting for you to try and sneak out again. They will stick to you like glue after losing you the other night,' Red smiled. 'I have a plan, but it will involve me getting into Fletcher Rosworth's,' she added.

*

Even though the project manager had confirmed his suspicion that the scaffolding had been tampered with, Ron decided it wouldn't hurt to go and visit Bob, the only casualty of the incident. "Old Bob" turned out to be the sort of guy anyone would warm to. He was the type who would stop and offer help if he saw you bent over the hood of your car, with steam bellowing out from the motor. He had been there, done that, and would tell you everything you needed to know about life and a lot of stuff you didn't. There wasn't an ounce of malice in the guy. His wife, though just as charming, was the flip side to the chalk and cheese pair. As soon as Bob started to go off on another of his stories, she rolled her eyes, gave Ron a sympathetic look, then got up to make some coffee and fetch some cookies.

'That young Jason has a lot to answer for though,' Bob said, eventually coming back to the topic in hand. 'Still, can't blame the lad too much. He's bin hanging around us old folk far too long. Ye see, we keep mocking the younger generation for using those damn computers to find love. Keep on telling him that in our day, we'd just go up to a young lady and start a conversation, or, if she didn't look our way, we'd just give a little whistle.' Old Bob was amongst happy memories as he spoke. 'I guess we must have put the idea into his head,' the old brick layer added.

'You're certain it wasn't faulty scaffolding then?' Ron asked. He didn't doubt the site manager but it didn't hurt to double check.

'Hell no. Them boys are good lads. They were genuinely devastated when they heard of the incident. They even came around the other day and brought me a nice little present,' Bob nodded towards the crate of beer sitting in the corner of the room.

Ron sat and listened to a few more of Old Bob's stories, while feasting on his wife's home baked cookies, for a little longer. Eventually, he politely thanked them for their hospitality and left. It had been a pleasant afternoon talking to Bob. Although he wasn't the same age as the old brick layer, he could still relate to the way society seemed to be heading in the wrong direction. Courtship used to be an art-form in itself, built from the desire to communicate. It was an opportunity for the males of our species to go out and do stupid things. It gave them a chance flex their muscles to the ladies then hurt themselves by showing off.

Rejection was just a sign of a bad performance. Ron had lost count the amount of times he had offered to buy a pretty girl a drink at the bar, only to be brutally rejected. You had to take that with a pinch of salt and walk away. These days, people seemed to go out of their way to be offended.

Poor Bob had almost been killed by a vigilante group overreacting to an innocent wolf whistle, a whistle he hadn't even carried out. The health and safety people were putting the accident down to faulty scaffolding but Ron now knew, it was clearly sabotage. Whatever their motives behind the attack, the ring leaders needed to be identified and stopped before someone got killed.

He decided to stop off for a burger on the way back to the apartment. The cookies Bob's wife had made were genuinely tasty but Ron had been on his best behaviour by not eating them all.

Taking the drive through, he ordered himself more than enough food for two, then drove to a remote space in the parking lot and switched off the motor. It felt like a little piece of sanctuary as he sat inside his truck, away from all the other diners. Plus, no interaction with others meant there was less chance he was likely to get caught up doing the right thing, again.

Ron sat quietly, reflecting on the situation he had found himsef in as he ate his family size meal. He knew he wasn't cut out to do this sort of thing, whatever this thing was, and maybe the time to cut and run was here. With a bit of money stashed away, it might be possible to go back to the simple life of a carpenter. As he chewed his food, he did a quick tally up in his head of the amount of money he would need to set up again but the figures fell short. He would still need to squirrel some more away first. Then again, would anyone want to employ an ex con to work for them, he wondered. For now, he was trapped.

Braving the heavy rain, he dashed across the parking lot, binned his food wrappers then ran back again, slamming the truck's door to keep the elements out. Ron sat there a moment longer, still deep in thought, then fired up the engine and headed home.

It was only a short hop on the freeway and thankfully the traffic was fairly light. Even though the rain had begun to ease off, any heavier traffic would have made conditions dangerous. With a lot of brake lights suddenly appearing in the distance, he decided to take the next junction just in case he got stranded. It wasn't much out of his way and it was far better to take to the back streets than be stuck for hours in a possible wreck.

As Ron carefully wound his way through the streets, something in the corner of his eye caught his attention. Slowing down, he wound down his window for a clearer view. It was a fight on the other side of the road between a couple of burly looking men and .....Sophie. He screeched to a stop, jumped out and ran back to help.

One of the heavyweight guys had a copious stream of blood pouring from his nose but the other had managed to pin Sophie's arms behind her back. Ron winced as he watched Sophie run her heel down the guy's shin then throw her head back, catching him square on the jaw. Although she was fighting like a hell-cat, it was apparent the sheer size of the two heavies was beginning to wear her down. The guy with the broken nose had recovered his senses a little and was just about to bring the little she devil to account when he suddenly realised more trouble had arrived. Ron hammered a full on shoulder charge into the guy, causing a sickening, rib breaking crunch. Sophie momentarily paused her wild thrashing as she recognised her rescuer, but the brute holding her also realised he was facing a new threat. It was no good. His buddy wasn't getting up any time soon and things were getting out of hand.

Releasing the hell-cat, he went for the gun that was tucked away in his shoulder holster. He would have no hesitation in putting a couple of rounds into this stranger if he needed to. The guy had made a grave error of judgement by releasing the tiger's tail when it was at its most ferocious. Instead of running away as he had anticipated, the woman spun around and executed a perfectly aimed kick, square on the target his wife had affectionately named, "the love spuds". His gun clattered to the floor as he doubled over in pain, then something else hit him on the side of the head, sending the lights out completely.

Ron winced again as he watched Sophie plant her foot square onto the man's groin, then spin around and connect another kick to his head, knocking him out cold. He also watched the gun slide across the ground and realised, things had been just about to turn ugly.

'Come on, let's get out of here,' he said, pulling Sophie towards his truck. The door was still wide open and the engine running.

She let him guide her away at first then stopped, 'Wait.' She effortlessly twisted her arm free of Ron's grip and ran over to a black sedan just across the street. She opened the door and grabbed something from the dash.

'Go!' she ordered, climbing into Ron's truck and throwing the stolen dash cam into the foot-well.

'What the hell. Who were those guys?' Ron blurted out, as he took off through the town.

Sophie said nothing, as her eyes cast a lingering glance behind her.

'Well?' Ron persisted.

'Drop it.' She wasn't in any mood to explain herself.

'Drop it! Seriously? I happen to drive by and see you getting mauled by two gorillas and you tell me to drop it?' he said, incredulously.

'Why were you driving past at this time anyway?'

Sophie asked, aggressively.

'What? Now I'm the one under suspicion? If you must know I've just been over to visit an old friend.' In Ron's mind it was as near as possible to the truth so he said it with an air of confidence.

'Girlfriend?'

Ron shook his head and smiled. 'Funny, I can't imagine dating someone who lays bricks for a living.' His adrenaline rush was dying down now and besides, he was past caring what she thought.

Sophie looked a little puzzled by his cryptic answer but let it go. She knew he had just saved her neck tonight.

Pulling into their parking lot, Sophie noticed the security lights had already been triggered by recent activity. She cast a cautious eye around for anything untoward but there was nothing. They had abandoned any attempt at conversation during the drive across town but once Ron switched the engine off, the silence rang out. Sophie was the first to break that silence.

'Thank you for helping me out tonight.' She stared at the dash as she spoke.

'Look, if you're in trouble maybe I can help,' he said, with sincerity. A tone which immediately struck a chord with her.

'It looks like trouble follows us both around,' Sophie replied, and offered a look that dared him to deny it.

Ron paused. 'I'm a regular trouble magnet all right,' he agreed.

'So how did you go from prison, to becoming a Reaper?' Sophie saw no point in beating about the bush.

'A what?' He furrowed his head, genuinely confused by the question.

Sophie looked hard at Ron for any hint of deception, but saw none.

'You seriously don't know what you are, do you?' she asked, faintly amused.

'I get crazy vigilantes off the street, that's all. Not all of them mind, just the ones who have overstepped the law,' he said, defensively.

Even though the explanation sounded justifiable to him, he had a feeling he was about to discover just how stupid he'd been.

Sophie shook her head, 'You're what they call a "Reaper". Someone paid by the government to go around knocking off anyone who steps on their toes. They usually choose ex-cons, homeless, or other down on their luck low life because you're expendable. They don't care how you work but if you get caught doing something illegal they will deny any involvement and leave you at the mercy of the wolves. They promise you a home, money and a bright future in exchange for knocking off anyone who tries to do what the law won't. You're just another puppet.' It was clear Sophie wasn't a big fan of the so called "Reapers".

Ron shook his head defiantly. 'Hey, that's unfair. There are people out there doing more harm than good.'

'So they employ a vigilante to kill other vigilantes?' Sophie lifted an eyebrow.

'I don't kill them, I just make sure they stop.' He considered owning up about the accident with the woman in pink but now probably wasn't the right moment.

'Why were those men after you?' He'd been honest, now it was time to see if she would come clean too.

'I suspect they were from the government, trying to catch me for hacking into their national security computers,' Sophie said, taking another glance behind to make sure they hadn't followed.

'You're wanted by the government?' Ron asked, totally aghast.

Sophie shrugged her shoulders, 'They have a corrupt senior official who had arranged the kidnapping of a law firm secretary in order to get their hands onto sensitive files and he now knows I'm onto him. I suspect he's the one who set that goon trap for me just now.' Sophie spoke in the sort of casual tone that suggested it was an everyday occurrence but Ron couldn't believe his ears.

'What can you hope to do against the government?' he asked, suddenly realising anything he had ever done, spiralled into insignificance.

'No, you're not listening to me. It's just one official as far as I can tell.' Sophie tried to explain but she knew Ron wasn't taking it in.

Sophie shivered as the truck interior began to cool down. 'Look, I'll try and explain it all to you over a cup of coffee if you want. It's getting cold in here.' She pulled the handle, causing the door to click open slightly and paused to see if Ron acknowledged the offer. He nodded his assent, then they both got out.

'Drop your phone off at your apartment first.' Sophie instructed, without offering an explanation. Ron paused momentarily to see if she was joking but realised she had been deadly serious.

*

The moment Ron stepped through his front door,

he knew someone had been inside his apartment again. The new invasion into his privacy angered him and served as a reminder that although he was no longer behind bars, he wasn't free.

The afternoon with Old Bob and his wife had been genuinely pleasant, and taking a glimpse into Sophie's life had taken him by surprise. Now, as he made his way through the stale smell of cigarettes, he realised Sophie had been right by labelling him a puppet.

Flicking the light on in the lounge, he instinctively glanced towards the coffee table. Two more sealed folders lay there like unwanted tax demands. In fact, Ron would have preferred tax demands. If he had a normal life, at least he could have worked an honest day's work and paid them off.

The time to walk away was drawing closer but he knew he had to be patient. Besides, if he walked now, he would never find out what Sophie had to say. He dropped his cell phone on the top of the brown folders, picked up the bottle of scotch Sophie had brought over the other night, and left the apartment.

Standing back a little, Ron heard the security chain rattle briefly before the door to Sophie's apartment opened.

'Thought you might like this back,' Ron said, holding up the half bottle of single malt. Sophie said nothing but gave a quick glance past his shoulder before stepping to one side for him to enter.

Although the layout to Sophie's place was identical to his own, the contents took him completely by surprise. At the far end of the living area was a rather expensive looking couch but at the other was a large computer work station with three screens squeezed together. Electronic equipment, some with information displays on the front of them, littered the floor next to the table. The numerous connecting wires trailing across the floor looked like someone had upturned a pan of spaghetti.

'Did you expect furry pink animals and fluffy cushions?' Sophie said, noticing the big man's gaze.

'I'm guessing all this stuff ain't for making computer games?'

Ron walked over to the stack of technology and cast his eyes slowly over each piece, trying to establish if he could understand any of it. He couldn't. Sophie watched him with an element of amusement and also a little apprehension. She had never allowed anyone into her apartment and share in her secrets before. Now, for the first time, she had found herself opening up, to a reaper of all things.

'So, what happens when you get a folder with my name on it?' she asked, with a touch of a challenge in her tone.

Ron laughed, 'I think you're safe. I'm on the verge of cutting and running as it is.' He looked towards Sophie and noticed she was waiting for him to elaborate. 'I'm just not cut out for this sort of stuff. I'm just a casualty of being in the wrong place at the wrong time,' he shrugged his shoulders.

'So, what made them recruit you?' she asked, handing him a glass of scotch then flopping down on the expensive looking sofa.

Ron sighed. His greatest regret was the Pink Lady's death. It wasn't possible to tell just one part of his story in isolation so he started from the bar room brawl incident. He turned a dark crimson and protested his innocence as he recapped on how he had come by the nickname of the "Pig sticker" while in prison. Sophie burst out laughing. It wasn't just his story that tickled her, it was his obvious discomfort too. After he explained how his parole officer had got him fired by revealing the nick name to the abattoir boss, which also cost him his bedsit above the same place, Sophie understood why he described himself as a magnet for trouble. He confessed, even though he was at rock bottom, he had stolen the cheapest bottle of whiskey just in case the young assistant was made to pay for it. She could see Ron was visibly upset when he admitted being the cause of the Pink Lady's death, but it was also clear it was not intentional.

'So that's what really happened to her then. The police report said she had fallen from a fire escape and broken her neck,' Sophie said, sitting back.

'You knew her?' Ron said, in horror.

'Knew of her,' she corrected. 'You were right when you said some of the vigilantes were doing more harm than good. The Pink Lady had already skewered several people for minor offences and they found her husband pierced through the heart when they searched her home. You would have probably been next,' she reassured.

It was a relief to Ron that she had seen his side. He continued with his story, telling her about how he had fled to the soup kitchen but Landon had somehow tracked him down. It felt good to talk about things openly to Sophie. For the next hour or so he had talked about the things he had done since reluctantly accepting the job, right up to the night she had rescued him from his beating. He laughed at the memory of that night.

Sophie stood up and walked over to Ron. Without warning she put her hand around the back of his neck and kissed him passionately. The kiss took him completely by surprise and when Sophie eventually pulled away, he looked bemused.

'What was that for?' he asked, looking like the cat who had just got the cream.

'That was for not being the total ass hole I first took you for.' She took Ron's glass and refilled it, then sat back down.

Ron resisted any temptation to quiz Sophie further on what she had been up to. He figured she was already on the verge of opening up to him. He took another sip from his glass.

*

News of his two goons being overpowered by a skinny woman and a passer-by had sent Sam Young ballistic. To top it all off, they had even allowed their surveillance camera to be stolen from their vehicle. He was left with nothing more than a woefully vague description of a woman dressed as a man and a burley guy. The only consolation in Sam's mind was at least the pair had done a right number on his men. One had suffered broken ribs and a concussion, the other a broken nose, two black eyes and the unlikelihood that he would be extending his family any time soon.

It was obvious to him that the woman must have visited the sisters. To what end, he didn't know, but he dare not be seen harassing them. It was also obvious he needed them to start taking his threat seriously.

Picking up his briefcase from the side of his desk,

he unlocked it and removed his personal cell phone. He wrote a short message, "Have a small job for you if you're not too busy" then scrolled through the short list of contacts, highlighted the name "John" and hit send. It took less than a minute for a reply to come back, which read, "Full or partial service?" Sam knew exactly what the question referred to. The full service meant a fatal hit on a target, partial would mean just broken bones. The fee remained the same whichever option he selected from the gruesome menu, at twenty thousand dollars. Either option required the same amount of effort but broken bones left witnesses. Sam texted back, "Partial. Will wire details and transfer usual fee". He knew there would be no further reply so he deleted the texts and put the phone back in the briefcase. There was no shortage of low life out there he could call upon if he wanted someone maimed or killed. The trick was finding the ones who didn't leave a trail. He would send the target's name and address, along with half the fee via an overseas transfer later. How bones became broken was not his concern but he knew it would get his message across to the sisters. The fee would be paid without question by his clients.

To come so tantalisingly close to catching the suspected hacker was frustrating but her ferocious assault on his men had now allowed him to sanction a use of deadly force if he needed. Sam wondered if it had just been a coincidence that the mysterious passer-by had waded into the two heavies during the process of arrest. It was feasible he was just a Good Samaritan but he didn't trust in coincidence. After spending so much time and effort in trying to snare this woman, he now felt as though he hadn't slept in days.

A pile of neglected files waited on his desk for his attention. The majority of national security threats were usually aimed specifically towards the president but they never came to much. If they were to pursue every threat on the president's life, they would need to arrest half the population of the United States. Sam looked at the darkness outside and realised it was late again. He picked up the files, stuffed them into his briefcase and promised himself he would take a look at them later at home and then left.

Brian stood on the balcony, unobserved, as he watched Sam Young walk across the foyer and out of the building. He knew something was not right with his man but he couldn't quite put his finger on it. Protocol meant he should take him off the Beacham case but he needed to see where this obsession was leading. Sam's disproportionate use of resources just to watch Janet Beacham was a sure sign he was getting desperate. Even though Janet wasn't talking, Brian knew she was somehow linked to whoever had sent the mystery email.

If he could find the hacker first, he would surely find out what Sam was involved in. The trouble was, after the assault on two of his agents, she had moved herself firmly into the dangerous category. It also meant she could pay a very high price if she resisted again, and that might prove somewhat convenient for Sam.

*

Ron was under no illusion of his tendency to be big and clumsy in most aspects but after unleashing his life's story on Sophie, he could sense she was ready to tell him about hers. Clearly, opening up her feelings was going to be a big issue to her and underneath the fiery red headed shell, stood a fragile soul. To make small talk at this point might push her back from the edge.

Although Sophie wanted to talk, she still found it difficult to start the conversation. Throughout her whole life she had discovered talking had never achieved anything so to do it now felt alien to her. Leaning back on her sofa, she took a sip of her whisky, closed her eyes and smiled. The first memory that came to her was one of her early childhood and the summer holidays shared with both her parents.

'I guess my childhood memories are pretty typical up to the age of eight and even after that, a lot of kids go through worse.' Sophie shrugged her shoulders. 'At the age of eight, my father decided to buy me a puppy to cheer me up after I went down with measles. I named him Mario, after the little Italian plumber off the computer game.' Sophie smiled at the thought.

Ron smiled back, even though he had no idea who Mario was.

'The trouble was, dad didn't consult mum and they ended up in a blazing row. Even though I got to keep Mario, the atmosphere between my parents took a turn for the worse from that point. There was never any doubt they loved me but it broke my heart to see them drift apart.' Sophie took another sip of her whisky and hesitated, as if unsure whether to continue. After a few moments of thought, she sighed, and then continued. 'In my mid teens, while studying for exams, I came home during a spare study period and found my mother in bed with a friend of the family.' Sophie's eyes moistened at the painful memory. 'That changed my life completely,' she confessed.

'What did you do?' Ron realised, as soon as he spoke that perhaps the question was a bit insensitive.

'What would you expect from me? I blew up. I screamed at her and called her a whore and a tramp before storming out of the house in a fit of rage.' She rolled her eyes, fully aware of her own fiery temperament. 'By midnight, ravaged by cold and hunger, I was forced to return home. My mother broke down in tears and apologised to me. She said she had become so distant from my father that she felt so lonely.'

'Did they split up?' Ron asked.

'I wish it had been as simple as that. I brought her sob story about being lonely but I also insisted she must tell my father things were over or end the affair. She never did end the affair and I never found the courage to tell dad either.' A tear ran down Sophie's cheek at the guilt of not being strong enough. 'He eventually learnt of the affair through someone else and it broke him,' she concluded.

As Sophie carried on with her story, Ron got up and re-filled their glasses. She told him about her father's death and how she still felt guilt for not warning him of her mother's infidelity. Ron sat down beside her and placed his arm around her shoulder. Sophie buried her head into his shoulder and sobbed openly about it for the first time.

After a short while, Sophie composed herself, wiped her eyes with the cuffs of her sleeves and sat back once more.

'At least you had a father. It bankrupts me every year, sending father's day cards to all potential candidates,' Ron said, trying to lighten the atmosphere.

Sophie laughed. 'At least you weren't weaned off

your mother's milk straight onto a single malt,' she retorted.

'Single Malt! You don't know how lucky you were to have only the best. I had to do with left over dregs at the local bar and the occasional amphetamine that I found stuck to the carpet.'

'You had amphetamines,' Sophie said, in mock scorn at his over indulgence.

Ron just smiled.

'Help me,' Sophie suddenly exclaimed. 'You can help me and I can help you,' she added, for clarity. The machinery inside Sophie's head suddenly came alive, as if someone had flicked a switch.

'Sure, I'll happily help you but I still don't think I'm cut out for my sort of work,' he replied.

'You were right when you said some of the Min-heroes weren't nice. If you continue, I can help you put the worst of them away.'

Sophie's enthusiasm was contagious.

Ron smiled at her sudden change of mood. He knew he would have followed her into the underworld with nothing more than a pair of Speedos and sun glasses at that point.

'When do we start?' he asked.

*

Marie was the type of person who flapped over her punctuality, especially when others were dependent upon her. This morning of all mornings Becci had chosen to throw a tantrum and had deliberately tipped juice all down the front of her clean clothes. It seemed that, at the age of two, Rebecca had somehow developed a sixth sense in knowing just how to stress her mother out.

Marie was due to pick up Lynn and Sarah at eight thirty in order to miss all the big queues at the Woodland Park Zoo but she was now late. Not used to driving further than the local store didn't help either. Although the zoo was only an hour's drive away, she usually preferred Mark to drive on the busy freeways, especially amongst all the big trucks.

After yet another complete change of clothes and a new outfit bundled into a day bag, she eventually strapped Rebecca into the child seat in their silver Volvo. Rebecca immediately started throwing another tantrum at having to conform to her mother's plans, whatever they were, as they backed off the drive. In a last act of defiance she kicked off a shoe but it raised no response from her mother. To Marie, a battle had been won and even though Becci was still screaming her protest from the back seat, she could now relax a little.

It was eight forty-five by the time she pulled up onto Lynn's driveway. The front door opened in anticipation as she got out of the car. Her friend Lynn stepped out onto the porch, little angelic Sarah stood at her side. Sarah was the ultimate contrast from the she devil strapped inside the back of the Volvo.

'I'm so sorry I'm late,' Marie apologised, rolling her eyes towards the rear of the car, in a gesture only another mother could understand.

'I know the feeling,' Lynn smiled, sympathetically.

Marie snorted at the notion, 'You must be kidding. This little angel hasn't got a tantrum in her body,' she said, picking up her friend's daughter and giving her a big hug. It was Lynn's time to snort a protest.

'Don't you fall for the, "I'm so sweet butter wouldn't melt in my mouth routine". Any other time, her head would be spinning around while vomiting green spew.'

They both laughed at the image. Marie loved Lynn's outlook on life. Nothing ever seemed to really faze her. They had met at an antenatal clinic and instantly struck up a good repartee.

Two weeks ago, Marie had suggested doing something to relieve the boredom while Mark was away ten hours a day.

'You need to get yourself a secret lover,' Lynn had joked.

'What about the other nine hours and fifty-nine minutes?' Marie replied.

They had fallen about in a schoolgirl style fit of giggles.

'How about a trip to Woodland Park Zoo?' Lynn had suggested in a brief moment of seriousness.

'Sounds good to me,' Marie had said, jumping at the idea.

Now here they were, two weeks later and on their way.

It didn't matter that the two girls were probably too young to fully appreciate the zoo because Marie and Lynn had never visited it before either. Once everyone was securely fastened inside the Volvo, Marie cautiously made her way towards the freeway. With all the excitement of their adventure, no one noticed the dirty black Dodge pickup following at a distance.

The instant Marie turned onto the I-5 she became caught in the busy morning traffic build up. Heavy trucks started to surround them and Marie's instincts screamed at her to pull off at the very next exit. After ten minutes of driving though, her panic inside started to subside a little. The big heavy trucks, for their part, remained in the inside lanes and those wanting to pass had another two lanes to do so. Even though Marie had travelled the same route many times, she had always done so as a passenger.

Lynn detected the tension in her friend. 'I have just the thing for long journeys. Do you mind?' she said, pointing to the CD player in the dash.

'Go ahead.' Marie's eyes flicked for the briefest of moments to the player, then back towards the truck on the right side of them.

Lynn ejected Fleetwood Mac from the player, re-cased it and dropped it back into the glove box. Then, she pulled a bundle of CD's from her bag, selected one, and slid the untitled disk into the machine. After a short moment of hiss, the speakers suddenly burst into life with a rendition of "Old MacDonald had a farm". Marie laughed out loud and relaxed a little. By the time they had reached the third track, they were all singing "Row your boat" completely out of tune.

As they approached Tukwila, Marie stopped singing and focused her attention once more on the increased volume of traffic. She had almost passed a slow moving truck, carrying large bundles of steel tubing when the dirty black pick up rammed into the left side of them. With no time to react, Marie was sent spinning across the front of the Semi, leaving the truck driver no chance of avoiding a collision. Even though he reacted instantly, the weight of his load carried him straight into the side of the silver Volvo, bouncing it across into the next lane. The driver of a green panel van pulling off the freeway, had no way of avoiding Marie's car. Although the impact was light, it was enough to send them both onto the intersection barrier, causing the Volvo to flip completely onto its roof.

The whole episode merely lasted seconds but to Marie and Lynn, the crash seemed to happen in slow motion. Only the initial impact with a black pickup, and the loud bangs as the air bags deployed all around them, remained vague. It had strangely felt like a fun fair ride as the Volvo pitched into the air but unlike the fun fair, they had finished the ride upside down. The engine revved loudly for a brief moment then went quiet. Ironically, "Hush, Little Baby" had just started on the player as the two girls in the back began to scream.

EIGHT

Janet immediately recognised the tall figure waiting for her as she entered the reception area. He was just another sickening reminder that things were not going to go back to normal of their own accord. Brian raised his hands a little, discreetly trying to placate her for his intrusion. He knew Sam had already leant on her but it was vital that he made contact with the hacker first.

As Janet made her way towards the lifts, she tried to avoid direct eye contact with him but he headed straight for her.

'I know you're busy, Miss Beacham, but I just need one moment,' Brian said, positioning himself between Janet and the lifts.

She knew it was futile to refuse. He would only come back again and again. She shrugged her shoulders in a gesture of resignation.

'I know you are caught up in something and you have suspicions of me for some reason. I suspect you don't know who to trust and quite frankly, I know exactly how you feel, but I need to contact your friend urgently,' he said, looking around to see if anyone else was within ear shot.

Janet looked at him, incredulously.

'Now why would I be suspicious of you?' She held her chin in a mocking gesture of being deep in thought.

'Maybe it could be the twenty-four hour surveillance team you have situated outside our apartment block? Or perhaps the fact that our phones and computers are bugged? You tell me. Of course I can trust you. Is there anything else I can help you with today, Sir?' she asked, heavy with sarcasm.

Brian didn't blame her for the mistrust. Hell, he couldn't even trust his own men at the moment.

'Listen, if you do see your friend, give her this.' He produced a business card from his pocket and offered it to her.

Janet made no move to take the card from him but simply stared at him.

'Look, hacking into National Security is a very serious offence on its own. Assaulting two agents and evading arrest puts things into a different category altogether. My department is slowly closing in on your friend and I have a hunch that someone within would rather see her resist again, that way they could justify silencing her permanently. I, on the other hand, would rather find out just what it is that someone in my department is trying to cover up.'

He offered the card once again. This time Janet eyed the card, unsure of what to do.

'She can phone me on her own terms and I promise there will be no attempt to try to trace her. I'm sure I couldn't even if I tried,' Brian added, as reassurance.

Janet slowly took the card from his fingers, desperately wanting to trust the guy. He seemed genuine but she knew, judgement of character wasn't her forte.

'I'm not sure if I'll see her again,' she said, taking the first step towards trusting the agent. It was the first time she had acknowledged knowing the woman they were hunting.

'I will order the surveillance dropped on your apartment but please, let me know if anyone troubles you, Miss Beacham.'

Brian stepped to one side and allowed Janet free passage to the lifts.

*

Ron closed the door to his apartment and slid the flimsy security chain in place. It was a futile gesture when it came to security but if his employers did decide to let themselves in during the night, at least he would hear them.

Even though the clock on the DVD player said 01:48 he knew sleep wouldn't come easily. Last night he had been on the point of walking away with nothing but the clothes on his back but now he felt he had a purpose in life. He knew he was acting like a pimple ridden teenager, but the feeling was good none the less. There would be no harm in embracing the good times while they lasted. After all, he had already used up twice the quota of bad times most would have suffered in their lifetime.

He flicked the TV on then went in search of food. It wasn't as if he wanted to watch anything, he just needed some sort of distraction. As the picture came to focus on the screen, a man and woman were desperately trying to sell a pressure cooker as if their lives depended upon it. It was the best time of night to relieve American, drunken insomniacs of their hard earned dollars.

Ripping open the foil wrapper, he shoved a couple of jam filled pop tarts into the toaster and pressed the lever down. He had spent the evening with Sophie, formulating a rough plan to expose whoever it was that was stealing information from Fletcher Rosworth's. Well, now he thought about it, Sophie had formulated the plan but somehow she had made him feel as if it was a joint scheme. He didn't mind though. The majority of the work was to do with computers and electronic surveillance stuff. His limited input was going to be more a role of heavy weight bruiser, which he had to admit, sort of came naturally. But more importantly, Sophie had vowed she would somehow help him escape from his life as a reaper.

She had also promised to supply him with the names of the ring leaders within the "men eaters". Sophie felt that they had it coming for taking her safety cell phone app and twisting it into a call for vengeance app. The four "Madams" as they liked to be called, were the female equivalent to the Mafia's "Don's". Each governed several large states and were now seen to be the largest aggressive feminist organisation to have ever been formed. There was even talk about eventually getting a member of their assembly into the Whitehouse as the first female President. After all, women did account for fifty percent of the voters.

Ron slumped down on his sofa and casually picked up one of the unopened brown folders. Holding his pop tart in his mouth he ran a thumb under the security seal to open the envelope. The napalm like jam oozed from the tart and dripped down his chin, causing a muffled curse. Inside the folder were the usual newspaper clippings, covering all the reports of the vigilantes' escapades. Grainy pictures within the cuttings showed someone dressed from head to toe in a light blue cat suit carrying the sort of spray bottle florists used. The report claimed the perpetrator was running around spraying lavender spray onto anyone who dropped litter. At first, it hardly seemed worth warranting his services but as Ron read on, he discovered the spray turned out to be so strong it was burning her victims' skin and causing blindness. It never ceased to amaze him, the number of crazy people out there trying to change the world, when all he wanted was a normal life. Normal was just subjective though. It sat somewhere on a scale between licking windows and rocket science. There was no doubt Sophie was screwed up just as much as he was but she too genuinely just wanted to help others.

The information she could give him on the Man Eaters would get Charlotte off his back for a while. Even though Charlotte didn't usually pester him, pressure from other government departments had pushed her into asking for regular progress reports on this one. Maybe the threat of an all female congress had got someone at the top sweating a little.

Ron looked up from the folder and noticed the duo on TV had comically stuffed a whole chicken, along with a few veg, into the cooker in a vain attempt to show how life changing their pot could be. He couldn't help but smile at the scene which wouldn't have looked out of place on the television show Jackass. He let out an involuntary yawn as the night finally started to catch up with him. This could all wait until the morning.

*

Ron instinctively reached for the baseball bat at the edge of his bed as the loud banging on the door pulled him from his sleep. Automatically, he leapt towards the bedroom door, momentarily pausing to try to shake off the effects of sleep. Still unsure whether someone was inside his apartment or not, he needed to be alert. The banging happened again. This time, he realised it was coming from the front door. Without switching a light on, he edged down the hallway and carefully peered through the security spy glass and immediately recognised the tangle of red hair.

'Those bastards have attacked Janet's sister,' Sophie said through gritted teeth, as she squeezed through the barely opened door.

Without waiting for an invite, she stormed into Ron's lounge and paced about. He closed the door and quickly followed. Sophie was standing in the kitchen, her hands firmly planted on the counter as if desperately trying to control the urge to throw something.

'Those bastards are hurting Janet's family because of me!' she raged.

'Slow down a moment. Tell me what's happened.' Ron tried to get a grip on the situation.

'They ran her younger sister's car off the freeway while they were on their way to the zoo. She had her daughter with her along with a friend and her daughter too.'

Ron could see Sophie was on the edge of tears.

'Was anyone hurt?'

Sophie shook her head. 'Just a few minor cuts and bruises,' she said, knowing it was some sort of consolation that they had escaped serious injury, but she also knew the consequences could have been much higher.

'Could it have just been an accident?' Ron knew it was a long shot and felt stupid as soon as he asked.

Sophie let out a snort of derision at the question.

'The black pick up was on false plates and it also failed to stop. What do you think?' she asked, clearly still fuming.

Ron held his hands up to indicate he realised it was a dumb question. Sophie instantly felt a pang of guilt for snapping at him. She had banged on his door in the early hours of the morning, barged into his home and snapped at him.

'I'm sorry, I didn't mean to snap at you. I'm just so pissed at them for targeting innocents in order to get to me,' she said.

Ron silently slid a mug of hot coffee across the counter towards Sophie and let her calm down a little before speaking again.

'They know you are on to them and you must be getting close to uncovering the truth,' he said. 'You either walk away and hope they leave Janet alone or you bring them to justice. I don't think you can go half measures on this,' Ron tried to simplify the situation.

Sophie's feelings were still running high and she wanted to explode with rage but she knew Ron was right. It was no use shouting and screaming. Emotions only led to mistakes. She took a sip of the hot coffee, absent mindedly burning her lip in the process but ignored the pain.

'We need to get Janet's family to safety before we do anything else,' Sophie spoke as if she was ticking off items from a shopping list. 'Next, we have to find out who is stealing information from Fletcher Rosworth.'

Ron nodded at her reasoning.

'Maybe they could go on vacation for a while?' he suggested, thinking about Janet's family.

Sophie paused, lost in thought, then eventually shook her head.

'They won't do anything else just yet. They will monitor the situation a while to see if I've understood their message. Besides, her husband has work commitments. I know some people who can look after them for now though, they owe me a few favours,' Sophie said, thinking about how she had helped various private investigators over the years.

*

Jack Wilks slid his little portable TV under the shelf, behind the reception desk. Officially, he wasn't supposed to watch TV but everyone sympathised with the tedium of the job so turned a blind eye. Everyone, except Mr Martin that was. He was Fletcher Rosworth's office manager and some may say self appointed douche bag, who wouldn't let anything go.

The game between the Rams and the Broncos was due to start at seven and Jack Wilks had fifty bucks riding on the Rams to win. Jack knew he would have to wait until Martin left the building before he could set his portable up. At ten past seven, the familiar sound of the bell chimed and the lift doors opened. Jack remained seated behind the reception desk, nonchalantly looking at some paperwork in front of him.

'Goodnight Mr Wilks,' Mr Martin chirped, as he pressed the exit button for the automatic doors to open.

'Goodnight Mr Martin,' Jack replied, as if noticing him for the first time.

He knew a lot of the staff here disliked Harold Martin. Everyone else was on first name terms with each other but oh, not Mr Martin. It was the likes of Harold Martin that gave Jack the reason to take the lucrative pay off. He carefully watched the immaculately dressed Harold Martin disappear out of sight before sliding his TV from the shelf.

Jack had just got the little TV set up when he spotted a guy in a brown uniform wheeling a sack truck full of boxes up to the glass doors. He swore out loud in exasperation. There was supposed to be no deliveries after six-thirty but still they came. No doubt pressurised by the delivery company's promise of next day delivery. Jack would be quite within his rights to send the guy away but he knew someone upstairs would only bitch at him for doing so.

He had already missed the start of the game so a few more minutes made no difference now. All he really had to do was wheel the boxes into the corner for the day staff to sort them out in the morning.

'You're working late tonight,' Jack said, after unlocking the glass doors from his desk and waiting for them to swing open. It was the usual "blame the management blur" most disgruntled employees used in order to strike up conversation.

'Tell me about it. Van broke down earlier but do you think they will let me off delivering this lot?' the delivery guy moaned, as he wheeled the boxes over to the corner that Jack had directed him to. Jack's animosity for being disturbed quickly melted away. He even felt sorry for the big guy, forced to deliver at this time of night. The courier placed the clip board that he had been carrying under his arm on top of the boxes and offered Jack a pen. It was a routine so common it needed no words, but as Jack bent over to sign, he realised the paper was completely blank. Jack was in the process of flicking the blank sheet of paper over to see if the delivery sheet was upside down, when things suddenly went black.

'You seem to have a natural talent for that,' Sophie said, stepping into the foyer and adopting her Red Renarde persona.

'You seem to bring out the beast in me,' Ron smiled back, as he dragged the unconscious guard towards a door labelled "Stores".

They bound the guard's wrists and ankles together with cable ties then stuffed a rag into his mouth. He would wake with a lump on his head but no permanent damage.

There was no way the guard's jacket was going to fit Ron and not look ridiculous, so he just took his hat instead. No one would pay any attention to him sitting behind a desk anyhow. Pushing the door open, Ron briefly stepped out onto the street. It was the signal Janet had been waiting for as she stood just a short way up the road. As Janet stepped into the all too familiar reception area she glanced up at the guard's hat, now perched snugly on Ron's head.

'He's going to be alright isn't he?' Janet asked, genuinely concerned.

'He'll have a headache, nothing more. Don't forget, this slime sold you out.' Red had no time or sympathy for the likes of Jack Wilks.

They had decided it was best to keep Janet back until Jack had been safely tucked away, just in case things went messy. Red could erase the security tapes before they left but if Jack saw Janet, it would be just another loose end.

Had someone reviewed the security tapes from

the previous morning, however, they might have noticed a blond haired woman talking to Janet just in front of the lift entrances. The meeting had been short notice and risky but Sophie had needed to contact Janet quickly in order to set up tonight's plan. Janet had agreed to Red Renarde's idea instantly. The news of her sister's crash had left her shaken but more determined that these people needed to be stopped.

'Want me to come up with you?' Ron asked, as the two women stood at the entrance to the lift.

'No, we should be alright. You just sit and watch the game,' Sophie said, pointing towards the security guard's TV.

'Just like being at home then. You know where I am if you need me,' Ron smiled, then went and sat down to play the part of a night watchman.

Janet's heart was jumping out of her chest as they stepped into the lift. Up until now, the most criminal thing she had ever done was play knock door, run, or smoked a joint behind the bike store. All pretty tame stuff compared to most of her school mates, she realised.

Unlike some, Janet had found study needed a lot of concentration and late nights in order to graduate. This career meant the world to her and she knew if they got caught, it would be the end to it all. Janet also knew, she was way in over her head and if it hadn't been for Diana's support, she would have given in by now. She knew the people they were up against were ruthless. Had Red Renarde not hacked into the National Security system and left a record that she had been seen with Sam Young, she might have become just another missing person statistic. On average, around fifty thousand missing person reports are filed every month in the states, some are found some are not. She wondered just how many had been in her situation.

The lift's bell tinged as they reached the all too familiar third floor. The eerily deserted office area looked like some sort of experimental maze for rats. Shoulder high partitions, divided up work areas in a half arsed attempt to offer privacy to the staff.

'Which one's the manager's office?' Sophie asked, pointing to the large glass fronted offices surrounding the rats maze.

Janet wondered why she wanted Mr Martin's office but pointed it out nonetheless.

'It's just one less thread to lead back to you,' Sophie answered Janet's puzzled look.

The off-line secure data storage system was untouchable to outside hackers, but like so many high tech ideas, operator error was often over-looked. Fletcher Rosworth took their security very seriously but at the end of the day they were still just a law firm. The main frame system would identify and log the terminal that had just been brought out of sleep mode as being that of Mr Martin's. What it wouldn't do, was detect the new USB lead connecting a small black box device Red had just plugged into it.

The screen lit up instantly and a prompt appeared, asking for a user optical scan. Red Renarde clicked a button on top of the device and moments later, a picture of a black and white moggy filled the screen in front of them. Sophie cast a questioning look towards Janet.

'Mr Martin is rather fond of his cat.' Janet gave a nervous laugh. She also felt a little guilty for invading her boss's privacy.

Without looking down, Sophie's hands drummed softly away on the keys and the cherished pet was replaced by the UEIF bios start up screen. She clicked the little black box twice more and a page of written coding appeared. Janet watched in awe as a screen full of gibberish altered a dozen times before Mr Martin's cat reappeared.

'We're done,' Sophie said, pushing her chair back. She unplugged the device and stuffed it back into her coat pocket.

Janet had expected them to be there a lot longer. 'Did you find out which files had been taken?' she asked, slightly puzzled.

'I'll look later. I've installed a sleeper program that will allow me to access the files on line without an optical scanner.'

Sophie walked to the door but Janet remained at the desk. Clearly uncomfortable at compromising her company's security system, she hesitated.

'I've just handed the complete contents of Fletcher Rosworth over to you.' Realisation at what she had just done suddenly dawned on Janet.

Sophie laughed, 'Seriously? You think this is the most sensitive information I have access to?'

'Why are you helping me?' Janet looked hurt at her own stupidity. She was in way over her head to know who to trust.

Sophie sighed and sat down opposite Janet. 'Look, I know this must all seem like a nightmare to you but I'm just trying to help. I can put your computers back as they were and walk away if you want me to but you know they will come back to you at some point.

Maybe they won't attack your sister again if you follow their instructions, who knows.'

Sophie sat, patiently waiting for Janet's decision. It was good that she had pulled her up about it because it also meant she was getting smart to the risks of data theft. The clock on the wall said it was just coming up to eight. They had plenty of time and Ron could handle anything down at the desk so she let Janet mull things over a bit longer.

The black and white pussy cat had long disappeared back into sleep mode before Janet spoke again.

'I'm sorry. Let's get this bastard.'

Ron stared out of the corner of his eye towards the lifts as the bell tinged. It was highly unlikely there had been others left in the building but he didn't want to draw attention to himself, just in case. His apprehension was short lived though as the familiar faces of the girls appeared. He stood up, walked towards the exit and pressed the electronic door opener.

'See you in a bit,' Sophie planted a kiss on Ron's cheek, then the two women left.

Ron just nodded and waited for the door to swing closed again. The powerful locking magnets would once more secure the door from unwanted intrusions. Turning, he walked back towards the janitor's room.

Even though Jack Wilks had regained consciousness, with his hands and feet cable tied together and tethered to the cast iron pipes within the janitor's room, he was powerless to escape. As the door opened, brightness flooded into the previously unlit room, causing him to squint. Jack's eyes bulged in terror as his towering assailant produced a butterfly knife from his pocket and stylishly flicked it open.

'Now, I'm guessing you're a little pissed at being bundled inside this cupboard.' The big man in front of Jack casually picked at a piece of dirt from under his finger nail with the knife as he spoke. 'This leaves me with a little dilemma. I don't want anyone to know I've been here you see. I want it to be our little secret. Rather like the time you let those other people in to play on your computers.'

The fire in Jack's eyes suddenly went out. He knew he had been backed up against a wall.

'I can't offer you a wad of money like the others did, but I'm sure we can still keep each other's little secrets can't we?' Ron paused and stared menacingly at Jack, knife still in hand.

With an air of defeat, Jack simply nodded.

'I have to hand it to you though Jack, that's one helluva car you've brought,' Ron added, as he slid the razor sharp blade through the ties around the security guard's wrists and dropped the hat back on his head. Jack allowed a wry smile at the compliment.

'Don't get up, I'll let myself out.' Without another word, Ron walked from the janitor's room and out onto the street.

*

On the inside, Sam Young was livid at Brian's decision to pull the surveillance from the girls apartment block but outwardly he brushed it off as if it wasn't an issue. The hit on Janet's sister had been perfect. Even though the local police put it down to a car thief, he was in no doubt Janet would have received the message, loud and clear. If he couldn't find the woman who was watching him, at least Janet would think twice before contacting her again. Brian's order to remove the surveillance didn't mean he was going to let this drop though. He still had plenty of his own contacts who could make troublesome people disappear.

One thing he didn't need right now though, was to have Brian on his back looking over his shoulder. With a little over twelve months to go before the next presidential elections, his contacts would be prepared to throw millions at him for the right information. Even junior politicians were worth having their backgrounds scrutinised just in case they became successful at a later date. The more dirt they found on a senator, the more they owned them, simple. With even just a little leverage, minor policies could be implemented, resulting in multimillion dollar windfalls. Maybe it was time for Brian to suffer an accident of his own. It would be risky, but it would be worth it to get him out of his way, Sam thought.

*

Brian flattened himself against the wall as he watched the big guy exit the front door of Fletcher Rosworth's. He would be prepared to put money on it being the same guy who downed one of his agents. There was an air of confidence in the way he stepped from the building and casually walked up the street in the same direction as Janet and the other woman. Brian felt a passing urge to check up on the security guard but his gut instinct told him these people were not all bad. They may be a little grubby when it came down to the law but Janet just wasn't the type to get involved in hurting people. Besides, if they had harmed the guard, or worse, it wouldn't make that much difference at this point.

He crossed the road, leaving enough distance to avoid detection just in case the big man should turn around. As he drew level with the smoked glass window of the solicitors, he peered in and noticed the security officer emerging from a doorway at the rear of the reception. Brian allowed himself a small smile, knowing his judgement hadn't let him down.

*

Janet looked up as Ron entered the almost empty McDonald's restaurant and sat down at their table. The booth at the back of the restaurant offered a small amount of privacy but more importantly, it also allowed access to the fast food chain's Wi-Fi. Sophie either failed to notice Ron, as he sat down or she just chose to ignore him, as she busily continued to tap away at the clip-on keyboard. Ron showed no sign of being offended by the snub.

'Is he alright?' Janet asked, referring to the security guard.

'He seemed a bit pissed that he wasn't going to get another car out of it but there was a hint of relief on his face when he found out he wasn't going to the Pen either,' Ron smiled.

Janet slid a lukewarm coffee and a burger that she had bought for him in his direction. The milk in the centre of the coffee had started to scale over but he gulped it down nonetheless.

'Any luck on the files yet?' he asked, taking a bite from his burger.

'Just downloading the last of the encrypted files that were opened on the night Janet was taken. We can take a better look when we get back to mine.' Sophie's eyes didn't move from the screen as she spoke.

They had agreed to use the late night fast food restaurant for two reasons. First, Sophie wanted to be certain she had access to the secure files before they got too far away. Second, they needed to be sure no one was following them.

Sophie separated the keyboard attachment from the small tablet and ruthlessly stuffed both halves into her bag.

'All done. Let's go,' she said, standing up. The coffee on the table that Janet had brought for her would go untouched. Without another word, the other two followed Sophie out of the door.

The cold, night time air was a stark contrast to the warmth of the restaurant, but even though she wore a thick coat, Janet seemed to be the only one to notice.

'Go on ahead. If I don't catch up before you reach the truck, leave without me,' Ron suddenly announced, handing the keys to Sophie. She gave him a look of concern, but didn't argue.

Shortly after they took a left at the end of the street, Ron slipped into an unlit entrance of a block of run down apartments. Months of windswept litter lay piled up against the entrance door and the cracked light covers indicated a serious lack of maintenance. He wasn't certain, but Ron could have sworn he had seen the same tall figure on leaving the restaurant as he had when exiting Fletcher Rosworth's.

*

Brian had considered going into McDonald's and confronting the three of them together but he knew, if it got messy, he would have his hands full. Besides, the only important one at this time was the red haired woman. She held the answers, that much he was sure of. All he needed to do for now was follow them and hope when they split, the muscle would go off on his own way.

Brian was in the process of edging his way around the outside of the restaurant in order to get a better look at the trio when suddenly, they had all stood up to leave, forcing him to dash for cover. With nothing else close by, Brian had to make do with the meagre cover of a few saplings, hoping that the darkness and shadows would do the rest. Undetected, he watched the three exit the restaurant and head up the street. Years of experience and covert training had taught him how to easily blend into the shadows. Unlike the movies where the cop stood out like a sore thumb in his dark mac, whilst carrying a newspaper, Brian figured he had surveillance down to an art.

*

Ron waited silently in the shadows for the tall man to walk past the unlit entrance. As soon as he did appear, he leapt out and dragged him into the darkness and slammed him up against the wall. Ron was in no doubt the guy had been following them and the only way to find out why, was to go all out mad dog on him.

Caught completely off guard and winded from his encounter with the wall, the man offered no resistance as Ron turned him around.

'Why...?' Ron started to speak but was cut short by a sharp blow to the side of his head. A brief moment of confusion passed over Ron, causing his eyes to flick around to see who else had joined the fracas. It didn't seem possible, but it slowly dawned on Ron that there was just the two of them at this party and his opponent had used some fancy footwork on him. Ron answered the high kick with a thundering punch into the man's ribs that would usually have dropped a bull. However, rather than falling to the ground, an open palmed strike came out of nowhere and connected with Ron's mouth. Just as Ron began to realise that this tall, skinny guy's speed could be a problem for him, the stranger suddenly dropped to his knees, gasping for air.

It had taken a while but Ron's ferocious punch had finally caught up with the man. Now, with all his fight gone, Ron dragged him back to his feet and pinned him against the wall, forearm across his throat. The metallic taste of blood trickled into Ron's mouth, firmly reminding him of his opponent's speed. He turned his head to one side and spat a wad of blood to the ground, but taking his eyes off the man had been a big mistake. Suddenly, a Glock pistol appeared and pressed hard against Ron's temple. There was no need for words. The fight was over and Ron wasn't the victor.

'It was a good body shot though wasn't it?' Ron smiled through his blooded lips, as he slowly released his forearm and let his opponent regain his feet.

He figured when your time was up, your time was up. No good complaining about things if you were willing to mix it with the bad guys. The tall man, still clearly in pain from the blow, nodded his assent at Ron's flippant remark.

'Please, don't shoot him,' Sophie called out, shocked at the sight of the gun pressed against Ron's head.

The brief fight had taken Brian completely by surprise. He had felt like a child ravaged by a fully grown bear. He was usually more than capable against opponents his size during sparring but this guy had walked through his best shots, and won. Only his government firearm training had seen him instinctively reach for his weapon.

Brian stood motionless, fighting the pain away before eventually easing the big man away from him, carefully ensuring the bear had stepped out of reach.

'Lady, I'm standing here, probably with half a dozen broken ribs that your boyfriend is responsible for, and you're asking me not to put a bullet though his head. That's a pretty tall ask if you don't mind me saying.'

Brian clutched at his side, as they all stood in silence. Then taking everyone by surprise, including himself, he made safe the Glock, spun it around and offered it to the guy who had just put him on the floor.

Ron eyed the weapon suspiciously.

'I just want to know what's been going on. Think of this as a token of trust,' Brian added, still surprised by his own actions.

Ron tentatively took the gun from the stranger. Up until that point he had never even held a gun, let alone used one. The majority of his fellow prison inmates had, at some stage, used guns to hold up liquor stores or threaten someone with, but not Ron. He had never gone looking for trouble; it always just seemed to find him.

The weapon felt dirty in his hands. At least with a good old fashioned punch up, the loser could always pick himself up and limp away. Maybe even shake hands, make up and laugh about how dumb the fight was in years to come. Guns were impersonal. They put holes where holes shouldn't be and the chances of shaking hands and laughing about it at a later date were slim.

'Why are you following us?' Sophie asked.

'I need to find the truth about what it is that's going on between a member of my staff and your friend.'

Brian's gaze flicked between the two of them.

Sophie gave Ron the briefest of nods in a gesture that meant she was prepared to trust this man. Without a word, Ron handed back the gun, relieved to be rid of its responsibility.

'We'll talk over a cup of coffee. I'll fetch Janet and meet you back at McDonald's.' Sophie didn't wait for an answer.

'That was one hell of a punch you have there,' Brian said, still holding his injured ribs.

'Yeh, sorry about that,' Ron said, 'but you did kick me in the head,' he added, as they walked back up the street.

*

Maybe it was because it was now coming from his own pocket, or maybe it was the severity of the consequences if things went wrong, but the usual sum of money Sam had just transferred suddenly seemed a large amount. If the hit went to plan he would need a water tight alibi. If something went wrong though, he would do time.

He pressed the button on the speaker phone, 'Hello Sally, can you book me a flight to LA for next Saturday morning, returning the following Monday afternoon please?' He could easily have booked his own flight but solid alibis were made in the detail. The surprise visit for his sister's birthday would kill two birds with one stone. He would have the perfect alibi as the hit was being carried out on Brian. There would be no turning back now.

The night's events had taken a toll on Sophie in a most peculiar way. She had invited Ron back to her apartment to formulate a plan but no sooner had she closed the door behind them, she found herself pouncing uncontrollably on the bewildered man.

Seeing the gun pressed against Ron's head earlier had stoked a panic in her but now it was over the adrenaline had been replaced with lust. Sophie's animal instincts took over and Ron suddenly found himself pinned against the hallway wall. Her hand made its way inside his tee shirt and began exploring the contours of his chest.

Unlike the boys in the glossy underwear magazines, Ron's physique wasn't ripped but his broad chest and natural muscle mass screamed of power. Reaching up, Sophie pulled his head down to meet hers until their lips met passionately. Ron winced slightly but resisted the urge to pull away as she reopened the wound on his lip. The new taste of Ron's blood only fired Sophie's lust further. Shuffling backwards, Sophie led Ron towards the lounge, stumbling over furniture and tugging at each other's clothing as if the world depended upon it. Eventually, they ended up on the sofa, Ron's tee shirt drawn tightly over his head and Sophie now naked from the waist upwards.

Passionately, they continued kissing, as Sophie's

right hand unsuccessfully fumbled at Ron's belt buckle. In an act of chivalry, Ron intervened and loosened the awkward belt buckle for her. Sophie took over again and pushed Ron's jeans and underpants down in one clean sweep with her foot, revealing his acquiescence to take things further. She ran her hand down low, then flicked her tongue across his nipple.

'In the bedroom now,' she suddenly commanded, standing and taking him by the hand. Ron didn't wait for a second invitation. Instead he let Sophie lead him away.

As with all sensual love making though, the wild lust has to end at some point. Tonight, it ended three short steps towards Sophie's bedroom as Ron fell to the floor, shackled at the ankles by his jeans. He desperately tried to force the jeans over his Timberland boots in an attempt to save the moment.

Sophie's display of burning lust quickly turned to one of raucous laughter as Ron lay struggling in a vain attempt to free himself. With his dignity flapping in the wind and his pride dented, he briefly lay on the hall floor, panting from his struggle. Combined with the absurdity of the situation and Sophie's contagious merriment, he too burst out laughing.

*

As soon as Brian Walters stepped out from the stately home style building, the giant, black gloss door gently swung closed on its automated mechanism. Even though the building hadn't been used as a residential dwelling since the late sixties, the exclusive offices still retained the building's prestigious characteristics. The place looked fit for a president, with its huge stone entrance and the detailed brickwork over the door and windows.

The autumn cascade of red leaves, falling from the overhanging maple branches that lined the long twisting gravel driveway, was keeping a team of gardeners busy. At the end of the drive, two eight foot high sandstone pillars stood, firmly setting a boundary between public and private property. Neatly embedded within the right hand pillar was a small brass plaque. Etched on it were the words, "Fletcher Rosworth, HQ".

Although still a family run business, the original founders, Henry Fletcher and Walter Rosworth, had long passed away. Morgan Fletcher and Gwendoline Saran now sat at the sharp end of this multinational law institute. Morgan, the son of Henry Fletcher, at the age of sixty four, could also be described as being in the throes of his very own autumn. Although he displayed a few grey hairs, his razor sharp intelligence and fiery temperament showed no sign of age. Gwendoline Saran, the granddaughter of Walter Rosworth, had inherited her fifty percent stake after her mother and father were killed when their plane was shot down over Israel. The incident was brushed off as a by-product of Middle Eastern tensions and as such, a regrettable occurrence. To date, there had been neither an official enquiry nor apology from either government.

Aged just thirty two and equipped with a Harvard law degree, many viewed Gwendoline as the future sole CEO of Fletcher Rosworth. It had ruffled a few feathers when she had chosen to use her husband's name within the family business, but she remained steadfast to matrimonial traditions.

It was only because of Brian's National Security

status that he been granted the privileged meeting with the pair but he knew this delicate situation needed a personal touch.

Morgan Fletcher had been beside himself as soon as he had been informed of their security breach. The very foundation of his father's empire had been built on the idea of discretion and privacy. If news leaked out about a confidentiality breach it could be a catastrophe, he had ranted.

Morgan was completely incensed at the news and had been reaching for the telephone in order to ring the police when Gwendoline intervened. It was the subtle way in which she went about the intervention that had impressed Brian most. Morgan's fiery temperament was obviously nothing new to her and she took no immediate steps to stand in the way of his phone call. She must have known, Morgan was not someone who could simply be told not to do something. So rather than tackling him head on, Gwendoline set about asking her senior mentor a few innocent child like questions.

'Won't the press find out if we go to the police?' she asked, with a look of concern on her face. 'After all, news always leaks out once it's in the public domain,' she added.

Morgan had paused, receiver still in hand but no number yet dialled. The machinery in his mind suddenly jolted into action and forced him to hang up.

Brian had sat and listened to Gwendoline present innocent sounding questions to Morgan, each leading to a similar conclusion. Each of her questions had carefully steered Morgan towards explanations and ideas as if they were his own. She had occasionally thrown the odd suggestion Brian's way, that too steered him to the only rational course of action.

By the end of their meeting, Morgan had somehow ended up a spectator, happily listening to Brian and Gwendoline formulating a plan to retrieve the stolen files.

'There has to be a third party within our company who is acting as an alert to any new sensitive information,' Gwendoline suggested.

'If that's the case, why don't they just steal the files directly?' Morgan questioned.

'Too risky. Your system would leave a trail back to the person accessing them. By connecting to the internet, remote access could be done by anyone. Janet means nothing to them, so if it all came to light, she's expendable,' Brian chipped in.

'We could bait these crooks into attempting the same thing again then?' Morgan suggested smugly, leaning back in his chair as if he'd just discovered the cure for cancer.

Brian shook his head. 'That could put Janet and her family at risk. They might try another kidnapping.'

'We will arrange the best private security money can buy for them. I'll be dammed if we are going to leave one of our employees, or their family, for the wolves!' Gwendoline said, furiously.

Brian didn't like the idea at all. 'I'll ask Janet, but if she says no, that's the end of it. She's been through enough already,' he warned.

'We'll still need some credible bait.' Gwendoline looked Morgan's way.

Morgan sat deep in thought for a moment then a sinister grin crept across his face.

'Leave that to me. I have someone who owes me a

few favours,' he said, keeping his cards close to his chest.

Brian was pleased with how well the meeting had gone. Although Morgan had a short fuse, he was ready to listen to the voice of reason. That voice came from Gwendoline's subtle way of manipulation. As he drove away, he couldn't help wondering her husband had ever made a decision that was truly of his own making.

Brian decided it was best to keep the minor detail of Sophie hacking into their computer systems quiet. He figured it would have been a step too far. Instead, he had convinced Morgan they would be better off letting him bring his own data specialist in to monitor any movement on the new file. When they had questioned him about this person, he had steadfastly vouched for her integrity and honesty. Now, he just hoped he had judged Sophie correctly.

*

Robert Holling could quite justifiably be described as someone who has come from an extremely privileged background. Both his father and mother were accountants, exclusively dealing with high profile customers whose wealth would appear as obscene to most. The bigger their client's income, the disproportionately small their tax payments became. His parent's specialised accounting skills meant they too became extremely wealthy. As a child, Robert grew up wanting for nothing that money could buy.

Because his parents usually spent so much time away from home, they hired expensive nannies and tutors to prepare Robert for life. For his sixteenth birthday his father brought him a brand new Porsche in preparation for when he moved away from home to study at Columbia University. The only thing he lacked, was a family life.

People envied Robert Holling for his seemingly privileged lifestyle, but what they failed to spot was the damage caused by a lifetime of emotional isolation and neglect. Even the school holidays were spent in a home just occupied by servants and gardeners. The rare occasions his parents were there, they were too busy entertaining clients with their fancy dinner parties to take an interest in him.

Robert's emotional isolation eventually guided him towards gambling as a means to finding an alternative stimulus. At first, it barely stirred an interest in him because money meant so little. Winning or losing made no difference. It was only when he drew two hundred thousand dollars as stake money from his college fund that he began to feel a buzz of excitement. Losing such a large sum of money would stir the wrath in his father. Inevitably, his college fund ran dry, he racked up some sizeable debts and the heavies came knocking on his parents' door demanding money.

Robert actually enjoyed the thunderous attention he received from his parents for blowing a cool half a million dollars. Even though he was labelled a disappointment by his parents, at least they had taken the time out to label him personally. The welcomed attention from his parents didn't last long though.

Determined to avoid any further scandal, as soon as Robert graduated, his father, through his contacts, secured him a well paid accountant's job at Fletcher Rosworth. It was close enough to keep tabs on his son but also situated far enough away to avoid regular home visits.

By relocating their embarrassment of a son, his parents inadvertently did the one good thing for him. They forced him to become responsible for himself and by doing so, made him learn to appreciate those less fortunate. His gambling habit didn't go away though.

Now, as Robert Holling stood in Mr Martin's office awaiting his next task, he couldn't help but notice a new brown folder with a high profile name sitting on the desk. All he had to do was make one simple phone call and he could instantly wipe away some sizeable gambling debts. In fact, the name he had just read could make it worth twice his usual fee.

*

Ron lay, staring at the trail of scattered clothes along Sophie's hallway floor. His left arm had gone dead from the weight of her head resting on it but he had no intentions of waking her.

Their love making had been full of laughter from the start. There had been no fake moaning or movie star performances, just pure animal lust. Sophie had sat on the edge of the bed teasing and laughing at him as he frantically pulled against his knotted boot laces in a desperate bid to free his jeans. Their kissing had been passionate and Sophie hadn't been shy in guiding Ron to her needs, but that too had resulted in laughter when she almost knocked herself out on the head board. The activities eventually came to an end when the squelching and farting noises became too loud to ignore. Exhausted, they had both collapsed back against the pillows, laughing once more.

Ron had vowed, after all he had endured previously, to never love another woman but here he was, once more out of control with his feelings. This time it felt different though. Behind her bad ass attitude, lurked a genuine woman who cared about others.

Even though he was a caveman when it came down to the technology scale, he knew enough to realise Sophie was right at the top. She possessed both the skills and nerve to take on the bad guys, no matter who they were.

Sophie stirred a little then moved onto her side, freeing up Ron to quickly slide his arm back to himself. Pins and needles surged into his finger tips as the blood gradually flowed back into them. Softly, he swung his legs onto the floor and eased himself from the warm bed to go in search of a glass of water from her kitchen.

'Nice ass,' Sophie called out in a sleepy voice as Ron's naked body silhouetted at the bedroom doorway before she stretched out to claim the newly vacated warm spot. Ron just smiled.

*

Brian knew he was entitled to drop Sam anytime on suspicion alone, but first he needed to find out who was at the head of this organisation. Technically, it was still only Janet's word against Sam's as far as the kidnapping was involved but he had no doubt she was telling the truth. What hurt Brian more was the fact that he hadn't for one moment suspected Sam of being dirty.

He had personally vetted every member of his staff to make sure they were trust worthy but he had misread Sam altogether. His deputy chief of security, even now, showed no signs of harbouring guilty secrets and had even genuinely appeared to be concerned after noticing him holding his side the other day. Brian had thanked him for his concern but laughed it off as being an overzealous sparring session the night before.

An additional problem for Brian was that Sam had become closer to his staff than he had. Even though he had a good working relationship with them, ultimately, Sam was the one who dealt with them the majority of the time. Brian couldn't be sure that Sam hadn't corrupted them, so for now, he would have to keep this to himself.

*

Morgan Fletcher delivered on his promise to supply some believable bait in order to lure the data thieves out again. The following week, a thick folder with the name "George Walker" printed in bold capitals across the front of it had appeared on the desk of Mr Martin, ready to be transferred to digital data.

Even though sensitive information about high profile clientele was a daily occurrence, news of receiving a presidential candidate quickly spread throughout the office. If the information was to fall into the wrong hands, there was a very real possibility it could have repercussions on the next election result. Every employee within Fletcher Rosworth had signed confidentiality agreements when joining but that didn't stop talk within. As soon as new files arrived, they were transferred into a digital format, then any hard copies were professionally shredded and incinerated. The only way to obtain the sensitive information after, would be through authorised security clearance. Not even personnel from the other branches of Fletcher Rosworth had open access to these files.

*

With the file now planted, the trap was set. All they could do was to sit back and hope the players took the bait. Brian knew he was taking huge risks to uncover the truth but Sophie was the only one he knew wasn't involved for certain. He had gone out on a limb by vouching for her integrity, even though she was a known hacker. It had taken time for her to eventually trust him enough to reveal her real identity. He knew, by doing so she had risked going to prison, he would reciprocate that trust now.

Brian had even offered her a job within cyber security if she wanted it. Sophie had shook her head, 'You lot have far too many rules and regulations for me. It wouldn't do to get caught breaking confidentiality laws now, would it?' she scoffed

'No. We mustn't get *caught* breaking confidentiality laws,' Brian had retorted, with a cheeky smile.

*

Janet had been so relieved that Morgan Fletcher and Gwendoline Saran had shown such understanding that she immediately welcomed their plan. Even though the whole operation needed to remain low key, Brian promised she would be kept under surveillance whenever she stepped out of her door. No one else within Fletcher Rosworth would be alerted to what was going on, just in case word got out.

Brian was still unhappy about exposing Janet to another potential kidnapping. The bait had already been planted at Fletcher Rosworth's and although he knew it was about a presidential candidate, he was still awaiting details. With such luring bait, they anticipated the hackers would get careless and try to access the information from within the building. Sophie had already hooked up remote access to all the security cameras, so even if these people got in again and tried to erase the tapes, she would still have her own copy. The security guard was going to do time after all but he didn't know it yet.

As an additional precaution, Brian slipped an innocent looking bracelet over Janet's wrist. There was little in the way of elegance to it but within the plain leather band, lay a GPS tracking device. Should the worse happen and they did manage to kidnap her again, they would never think to take such a worthless looking bracelet.

'I'll get the details of the folder to you as soon as I get them,' Brian said to Sophie, as he stood and slipped his arms through his jacket.

Sophie had acknowledged him with a simple nod of her head. Even though she disliked the plan, she had remained quiet while Brian spoke of his meeting with the Fletcher Rosworth CEOs but now that he had left the restaurant, she picked up Janet's jacket and laid it across the table. Without a word of explanation, she unfolded the blade from her small penknife and slid it into the corner of the jacket's collar. Then, she pulled out a roll of stiff looking ribbon from her pocket and began forcing it through the cut until it had completely disappeared. Just before handing the garment back to Janet, Sophie held her mobile close to the collar. The phone bleeped twice then a street view map appeared on the small screen, showing a little blue dot exactly at their current location.

'It will only work within a couple of miles radius

but it will be more accurate than that thing,' Sophie said, nodding towards the bracelet.

*

Sam Young pushed his chair back and clutched his stomach. 'I think I'm about to burst,' he laughed.

It had been a long time since he had sat down to any sort of family meal and his sister had excelled in her cooking. Sam's visit had meant to be just an alibi but in truth he was genuinely having a good time. His sister had been overjoyed by his surprise arrival and wouldn't hear of him staying at the hotel he had booked. Instead, she had insisted on making up the spare room rather than let him leave.

Sam casually cast a glance towards the clock on the wall. Anytime between now and tomorrow night the planned events would see his problems disappear completely. His heart beat loudly within his chest at the thought.

'What are you smiling at?' Margot, his sister, asked, noticing her brother's far away expression.

'Just happy to be here enjoying the occasion, Sis.'

He clutched his stomach once more to emphasise his contentment.

'Well, make sure you have space for pudding,' she replied, playfully.

NINE

Brian couldn't help but like Ron. Even after their little scrap the other night, he felt no animosity towards the big bruiser. The punch he had taken to his side had indeed cracked two of his ribs but he was certain, even if he hadn't managed to pull his gun in time, Ron wouldn't have taken things further. At the end of that night, Ron had even offered to take him to the hospital, genuinely concerned.

Without doubt, Ron was better to have as a friend rather than an enemy Brian mused as he placed the big square tray on the edge of the table. He began offloading the feast of fries and burgers onto the petite circular table top. As he placed a burger box in front of Ron, he discreetly laid a small, black plastic, memory stick next to it. Without a word, Ron palmed the stick as he pulled the food closer. The move was so slick that no one within the restaurant would have noticed had they been under surveillance.

Brian had set up the brief meeting with Ron, mainly to exchange the memory stick that he had promised Sophie but he also wanted to learn more about the people he was dealing with. Although he hadn't yet seen signs of a tail, he still had a feeling they were being watched and the last thing he wanted was to implicate the girls further. He placed the empty tray on a nearby shelf then sat down opposite Ron.

'That contains the details of the file we are using for bait,' Brian said, picking up a pinch of fries.

'Is it full of bullshit?' It made no difference to Ron either way what was on it but he was still curious.

'Hell no. We figured someone inside Rosworth's would probably be describing the contents to the buyer. For the sort of money they would be paying, they might want to check out some of the detail first,' Brian said.

'Has someone agreed to this?' Ron asked, slightly confused.

Brian carried on chewing his fries for a moment, then picked up his large coffee.

'Are you kidding? These presidential candidates are not as stupid as they look.' He took a sip of his drink before continuing. 'This situation is like winning the lottery to them. It's a get out of jail card,' he added.

Ron paused, his double cheese burger inches from his mouth. A puzzled look on his face told Brian he hadn't quite understood.

'You see, they *want* certain information to get out,' Brian said, trying to explain the workings of the political mind. 'Everyone has their skeletons in the closet, right? Believe me, every part of a future president's life will become public knowledge eventually. The trouble is, timing. Come election time, just as the voters are about to put their crosses in a box, the last thing they need is a fresh scandal to drive the voters to the other side. Candidates won't have time to smooth things over and fill the voter full of bullshit. If, whatever is on that stick,' Brian nodded towards the space he had discreetly dropped the memory stick, 'comes out now, he will still have the time to turn it around and come out of it smelling of roses.' Brian leant back on his small plastic chair, smiling.

'Sneaky bastards. So they know the dirt will inevitably come out, but this way they control the timing,' Ron said, grasping the concept now.

'It's not as if they can just come out and confess these things at random. I mean, can you imagine sitting on a late night chat show and confessing to doing the baby sitter ten years ago, or whatever,' Brian laughed.

Ron smiled, 'Probably not the worst some of these politicians have done.'

'I've heard tales that would make you puke,' Brian said, sombrely.

'Goes with the job I guess.' Ron tried to lighten the moment a little.

Brian acknowledged the gesture with a shrug of his shoulders, 'They're not all bad,' he said in defence.

'I imagine they all need to be a little thick skinned.' Ron gulped down the last of his coffee then stood and patted his pocket 'I'd best get this to Sophie then,' he added.

Following Ron's lead, Brian stood too. As he pulled his arm through his coat sleeve in preparation of facing the cold, wet night, he turned to Ron, 'You two suit each other.'

Ron paused a moment. He hadn't thought they had been so obvious with their feelings.

'She's had more than her fair share of shit, that's for sure, but her morals are unquestionable. Oh, and don't ever piss her off. You will suddenly find yourself on the wanted list of every government of every country including this one if you did.' Ron smiled at the thought, then left.

Although the meet up with Ron had been the safest way to get the file to Sophie, it had also given Brian another chance to assess the people he needed in order to flush out the rot from his own department. He only had himself to blame for becoming so detached from his own staff. If Sam was on the take, he couldn't know who else had been dragged into his shady dealings. Going down the path of trusting outsiders was a risky choice but he had a good feeling about these two.

As Brian stepped from the restaurant, freezing rain, with occasional flecks of snow, stung his face. He pulled his collar up tight in an attempt to protect his neck from the icy chill, then headed towards the subway. It had been both easier and less conspicuous to use public transport to meet up with Ron.

With the brutal weather, Brian failed to notice a black sedan in the middle of the parking lot, its engine running and the wipers intermittently clearing the darkened screen. It wasn't an unusual occurrence given the conditions but it was something he would have usually spotted. The two men inside the sedan said nothing as they watched the big man leave and get into his silver pick up and drive away. Once gone, their eyes immediately flicked back to the taller figure as he pulled his coat tight around his neck. They waited a few moments longer until their target reached the small pedestrian access to the parking lot then got out and followed.

*

The dash to reach his pickup had taken no more than a minute but the freezing rain had soaked Ron through. Without waiting for the truck to warm up, he had driven away, eager to get the file to Sophie, but by the time he had reached the exit his screen had fogged up completely. Ron pulled over to let the truck's demister catch up from the steam rising off his wet shoulders.

As he waited, he began to feel guilty for not offering Brian a lift. He knew they were supposed to avoid being seen together but there was little chance anyone would see them in this weather. He backed up a little, then swung the truck around and headed towards the other end of the lot, searching for Brian's tall figure.

Parking close to the pedestrian exit at the far end, he could make out the unmistakable silhouette of Brian in the distance. A short way behind him, two men suspiciously followed. Even though neither of the men were dressed for the poor weather, they made no effort to hurry.

Brian sensed an additional presence just before he heard the sounds of footsteps echoing from the roadside culvert. He had been arrogant to walk along a poorly lit road that he would have warned others against. He slowed, almost imperceptibly, to see what his followers would do. If they were just walking the same way, they would quickly catch up. If they meant him harm, they too would slow down.

The footsteps slowed. Without looking around, he reached inside his jacket, unclipped the strap across his pistol, and gently eased it from his holster. If they were just punk kids intent on grabbing an easy buck from him, they were going to be in for a nasty surprise. Nothing could be taken for granted though.

Another set of oncoming headlights approached. If they were going to strike, Brian knew they would wait until the car had gone by. He decided, as soon as the car had passed, he would quickly turn and confront his pursuers. If they were innocent, he could always apologise but somehow, he doubted they had his best interests at heart. Brian closed his eyes against the glare of the headlights, then, as soon as the car passed, he spun around and levelled his gun towards his followers.

He was too late. A shot rang out and took him clean in the left shoulder, knocking him onto his back. Screaming pain seared through his body but his survival instincts urged him to send as many rounds as possible towards his attackers while lying on the ground. With the blood pumping steadily through his shoulder wound, Brian eventually passed out, empty Glock still in his grip.

Sheer luck alone had guided one of Brian's rounds through the left eye socket of the guy who had shot him. Unfortunately, his luck had ran out there. The second of his assailants had hit the ground in a bid to avoid the hailstorm of bullets flying his way. Another one of the wild rounds had nicked the skin on his hip but it was nothing more than a graze. Carefully, he stood up and eyed his dead partner. Even under the dim light, he could make out blood oozing from the hole in the back of his head. Although they had been warned to be careful of this hit, the guy's speed had taken them both by surprise. Their target also now lay prone on the sidewalk, icy water running alongside his body. The man was most likely dead already but he couldn't rely on chance, not in this game. Two more rounds to the head and the job would be complete. He cautiously approached the figure, gun at the ready. Spider like trickles of blood emerged from underneath the body and joined the rivulets of rain as he took aim.

Out of nowhere, a ferocious blow suddenly hit

him in the side of the head, sending him sprawling to the ground. His gun flew from his hand and clattered into the pulpit, to be lost within the storm waters. Even with a head full of flashing lights, the assassin swiftly pulled out his knife but it was too late. Ron grabbed the dazed attacker's wrist and bent it sharply behind his back until he heard a sickening crack of bone and joints as they exceeded their limits. The knife fell harmlessly to the ground, then Ron drove the screaming attacker's face deep into the mud, close to the side of the road.

*

Sam Young's cell phone silently buzzed within his trouser pocket. The temptation to sneak a quick look at the message was immense but he managed to resist the urge. Although he was amongst his own family, he still didn't want to show any signs of excitement in front of witnesses.

He threw down the empty hand of cards he had been dealt, much to the cheers and hollering of the others at the table.

'At last!' Ralph, his brother in law, shouted, throwing his arms in the air in victory.

Sam had won the last six games in a row, much to everyone's despair. In fact he could have gone on winning all night had he not wanted the excuse to slip away for a moment.

'Even I can't win them all,' Sam said, grinning broadly as he stood up. 'You lot can practise amongst yourselves while I go powder my nose,' he mocked. 'I'll be back shortly to bankrupt the lot of you,' he added, with a serious face.

He walked away to playful jeers from all around

the table. Even though they were only playing to a large pot of quarters and dimes that would still probably come up short for a round of drinks, a competitive edge was still there.

Sam locked the bathroom door and perched himself on the on edge of the bath. Taking his phone from his pocket, he opened the message. These stakes were in another world compared to the card game downstairs and if something had gone wrong there was a possibility the trail could come back to him. Even though he had taken extreme precautions, nothing was infallible.

He opened the message and stared at it for a while. It was just a two word text, "Job complete". There was no name to the number and he knew the sender would have destroyed the SIM card straight away anyway. He also knew he had crossed a line he could never step back from but from now on, he wouldn't have anyone watching over him.

He wasn't interested in the details. That way, unless someone phoned him first, he could genuinely act surprised when he got back to the office on Monday. His pulse started to race at the thought of having Brian out of the way.

Sam opened a secure banking app on his phone, punched in a few numbers and transferred the rest of the fee over as agreed. Half up front, half on completion of the hit was the arrangement. He could have waited until Tuesday but he knew there would be a shit storm blowing by then.

Free from Brian's watchful eye, he would now devote all resources to finding the woman who was watching him. If Janet stepped out of line once more, she too would join the missing persons list. He composed himself, slipped his phone back into his pocket and headed back downstairs.

*

Ron slumped back onto his cold leather couch in just his boxer shorts. His blood stained clothes lay dumped in a pile in his bathroom, a stark reminder of the long night's drama. Still in shock from the shooting, he gazed absently at the clock on the wall. It had been almost six hours since the paramedics carried Brian away.

The medics had praised Ron's quick thinking for flagging down a passing taxi before he ran back to Brian. The driver had been frightened out of his wits and suspected he was being held up, so tried to drive off. Ron was having none of it and leapt on his hood shouting, "Call the paramedics and the police now!" before eventually running back to Brian.

As soon as he spotted figures lying on the ground, the driver realised it was indeed a genuine emergency and radioed for help. Ron had ripped his sweatshirt off and plugged the bullet hole in Brian's shoulder, then held him until help arrived. The wait had seemed agonisingly long but for the first time in his life he had been relieved to hear sirens heading his way.

The medics reached the scene and had instantly set about administering emergency aid to Brian moments before the law arrived. They showed no interest in who shot whom but the police, on the other hand, took Ron back to the station and questioned the life out of him. With one dead body and another in only a slightly better state, there had been a lot of questions. For four hours, Ron had gone over and over his story of just being in the wrong place at the wrong time, or the right place depending on their view of the situation. They suspected he wasn't telling them everything but there was nothing they could charge him with. His identification and address had checked out but the moment they found out he had done time for assaulting one of their fellow police officers, they had given him a hard time.

Eventually, unable to keep him any longer without charge, they let him go. Ron had politely asked for a lift back to retrieve his truck but predictably they had refused, citing they were far too busy, even though the station was full of officers sitting around eating doughnuts. To them, they had scored a moral victory by making the blood soaked ex-con get a cab.

Both Sophie and Ron agreed, it must have been a professional hit attempt on Brian and it didn't need a genius to know who had sanctioned it. Out of sheer anger, Sophie had sent a message to Sam Young's private cell phone to tell him that the job had been done. She knew it was playing with fire but she also knew it would spook him when he realised he hadn't gotten away with it cleanly.

Sophie folded down the lid of her laptop then slumped onto the couch next to Ron. 'No news yet,' she said, answering the obvious question on his mind.

'Just as I was just kinda getting to like the guy,' he replied.

Sophie slid closer and kissed him gently on the cheek. 'Didn't the medic say you may just have saved his life?' she asked as she repeated the words he had spoken earlier.

'That's what they said but I think they were just trying to humour me.'

He sat staring at nothing for a while, then got up. 'Coffee?' he asked, trying not to dwell on the night's events.

'Only if I can crash here tonight,' she smiled at him. 'I can keep you informed if there is any news that way,' she added, with a cheeky smile.

Ron smiled back. He still felt partially to blame for letting Brian walk away in such bad weather and not coming after him sooner. On the other hand, had he come sooner they may have both ended up being killed.

'Sure thing,' he replied, thinking there could be no better distraction.

*

Sam sank into the lush, business class seat and stretched his legs out. His privileged seating meant he could relax and take a drink while the rest of the passengers crammed themselves in. The cattle class were so intimately packed together that in any similar situation, they would have at least shared a dinner first.

He took his phone from his jacket pocket, that was hanging on a peg nearby. It was starting to concern him that there were still no messages or missed phone calls. Even if Brian had been lying at the bottom of a river, by now he would have expected a phone call to say he was missing. He toyed with the idea of phoning the office with a bogus reason but decided against it. By the morning, one way or another, he would know Brian's fate. He replaced the phone in his jacket pocket and hung it back up inside his private booth.

A few moments later, a stewardess brought the large glass of Bourbon he had requested and placed it in the cup holder set in the leather arm of the chair. Sitting back in his seat, Sam took a long sip of the fiery liquid. The next few days would undoubtedly be messy but once the dust settled, he would be left alone to run the show completely.

As the plane began to be pushed back, Sam's private phone buzzed, indicating he had a new message. With all the stuff going on, he knew it would play on his mind throughout the flight if he ignored it. Quickly, he retrieved the phone once more and opened up the message. He swore to himself quietly. It was from his contact at Fletcher Rosworth but the idiot had used his own cell phone to send it. The timing of the message couldn't have been any worse. Even if he deleted the message from his own phone, there would be records now leading back to him. With the damage already done, Sam read the message. It just read, "George Walker. Worth double?"

Every American knew Walker. He was loved by the majority of the people and hotly tipped to win the presidency. Indeed, it was well worth double. Taking another large gulp of his drink, Sam re-read the message and licked his lips.

He deleted the message and immediately put a block on the number. It was bolting the stable door after the horse had left but it gave him an element of an excuse. As soon as he landed, he would contact Robert Holling from a pay phone and agree his price. Things were becoming too disorganised for Sam's liking but information like this would easily earn him a six figure pay-out.

The sound of the engines whirring into life and the stewardess taking one last check of passengers brought him from his thoughts. He had genuinely hoped to avoid using Janet again but with Brian out of the way, he could afford to be a little more heavy handed if need be. In fact, it would be better for all if she disappeared once this job was complete.

*

Ron peered out of the little coffee shop window overlooking the busy mall entrance. Just across the way, the street entertainer who had perched himself on an old crate was happily murdering a rendition of Bob Dylan's "Mr Tambourine man" on an old guitar. A flat cap containing a few pre-emptive silver coins lay on the ground just in front of him in a desperate hope that his biggest fans would add to it.

As with all entertainers, the quality of their act is usually measured by the size of the crowd willing to attend their performance. On this particular busy afternoon, the flow of shoppers within the mall had been crammed together like sardines but somehow, the area in front of the busker had become empty.

Even though Dylan himself wouldn't have recognised his own tune, Ron was there today to protect this street performer. Ron had opened up another folder in order take his mind off the recent events. The file had described a pair of vigilantes, calling themselves "The Music Protection League" as unique. The vigilantes had taken it upon themselves to seek out amateur musicians and stop them playing by smashing their instruments up.

Yet again, the public were divided. Some were naturally outraged that the police were failing to protect these poor developing artists. Others felt that anyone prepared to rid the streets of such tortured instruments were doing a worthy service.

A tip off from Charlotte had led Ron to an area where the duo had last been sighted. Although there were still no photographs, the pair were reported to be dressed in full body Lycra, styled as piano keyboards. Even though Ron doubted they would show, he would welcome the distraction of chasing a pair of keyboards through the mall.

He took another sip of his coffee as he contemplated what was going to happen with Sophie and Janet. Things were getting heavy, even by his own standards, and he wanted out more than ever but he knew Sophie would never walk away. Brian's shooting had shaken him up more than he first thought.

A commotion just outside, by the mall's entrance, suddenly caught Ron's attention. As he scanned the sea of shoppers, he could just make out a pair of figures, dressed in white and black, slowly forging through the dense crowds. A constant gap in the crowd opened up like a ship's bow wave then immediately closed again as soon as the duo had passed. Swinging his jacket over his shoulders, Ron headed out.

A thought momentarily flicked across his mind. Maybe it wouldn't hurt to wait until these freaks took care of this guy's guitar. He shook the selfish thought from his mind. After all, where would Ed Sheeran be now if someone had stamped on his early ambitions?

The passage across the crowded mall was slow. Even with someone of Ron's size, the crowd were less than willing to allow him access to the imminent scene of carnage. By the time Ron did reach the melee, the two piano keyboards had begun swinging their bats.

Up close, Ron was surprised to see that the two figures setting about the busker were only of slight build. The costumes they had chosen to dress themselves in gave the impression they would be better suited for selling condoms. One of the bat wielding prophylactics was intent on destroying the busker's pride and joy, but he was having little success. Just like a mother running back into a burning building to retrieve her baby, the musician had shaken off all thoughts for his own safety and had opted to take the pain himself by shielding his instrument.

Ron grabbed the vigilante's bat mid swing.

'That's enough buddy. I'm sure his playing will get better one day,' he said, as the bemused Lycra clad pianist turned to face him.

'They must be stopped. They are ruining music,' the vigilante said, frantically tugging on his bat in a desperate attempt to carry on with his calling.

By now, the second guy had built up enough courage to come to his buddy's rescue and took a swipe at the big man daring to obstruct their musical cleansing.

The strike was slow and sloppy by anyone's standard and it allowed Ron the time to move the man still dangling from the bat, into his partner's strike. A sickening sound of a potential home run rang out across the mall, then the bat went light as the dangling guy crumpled to the floor.

'Look what you made me do,' the second keyboard screamed, through a muffled Lycra mask. Incensed, he took a second swing with his bat.

Ron decided he'd had enough of this pair. He swatted the feeble strike away, then rammed the end of his buddy's bat into the rough approximation of the keyboard's stomach.

Instantly, the black and white figure dropped to his knees and wretched. Well, Ron assumed he wretched. With the fabric mask covering the vigilante's mouth, all Ron could go by was the wet lumpy patch spreading across the masked man's chin.

Ron pulled a bag of zip ties from his jacket pocket, secured the vigilantes together and then tethered them against a kiddies plastic horse ride outside a nearby card shop. With a mall full of witnesses to testify to the attack on the busker, and the intervention of a Good Samaritan, the police would have no choice but to arrest the pair. Ron handed the bat to the bemused busker, then casually walked away to the sound of approaching sirens.

*

'Ah, Sam. Please come on in,' Brian said, as Sam peered through his office doorway. It was almost worth getting shot just to watch the colour drain from Sam's face. Shunning all the doctors advice, Brian had insisted on being back at work in time for Sam's return.

Although Sam looked ashen momentarily, Brian was amazed at how quickly he had regained his composure.

'Jeez, what happened to you, you look like shit?' Sam asked.

'Just an attempted mugging, would you believe?'

Brian forced a sinister smile that left Sam wondering if he was being played with.

'What sort of idiot tries to mug someone like you?' Sam tried playing to his boss's ego.

'We are not yet sure. There were two of them. One I managed to shoot dead, the other is in a secure hospital waiting for questioning,' Brian said, casually.

'Hell!' Sam said, blowing a low whistle. 'Is there anything I can do? Want me to question him?' he added, then quietly berated himself for seeming too eager to get to the prisoner.

Brian shook his head and immediately regretted the action as pain cursed through his shoulder.

'We're going to let him stew a bit longer. There's no ID on either of the guys and the live one is refusing a lawyer at the moment but I'm sure he'll talk eventually.' Brian watched Sam carefully for a reaction but there was none at all.

Sam sat at his desk for the rest of the morning, contemplating his next move. The hit had been carried out by a guy named Ramirez and his brother. He had never met either but word was, Ramirez could be trusted to hold his tongue if things became messy. Now, with a fifty percent chance that Ramirez was dead, the question was, if it was his brother who survived, would he keep quiet too?

Sam wished Brian had managed to get off two clean shots, instead of just the one. He could feel his whole operation becoming sloppier by the day. Even if the survivor didn't squeal, if it was suspected to be an assassination attempt, suspicion would surely fall Sam's way. If that was the case, at the very least, he would lose his job. He decided he needed to act fast and remove the file on Senator George Walker before someone else did.

*

Sophie took a sip of beer from her bottle, then almost snorted it back out through her nose as Ron described the two characters from the shopping mall. The vision of two giant black and white condoms jumping about with baseball bats was too much for her. She could somehow envisage it becoming some sort of high school sex education video in the vain attempt at stopping unwanted teenage pregnancies. It warmed her heart to see Ron genuinely laugh as he told the story. Since Brian's shooting, he had become withdrawn and lost to a deep place.

'What?' he asked, noticing the curious look on her face.

'I know this whole thing with Janet and that government creep is getting heavy, but I can't leave it now.' She knew Ron had been drawn into this whole situation against his will. 'No hard feelings and all that, if you want to walk away,' she added.

Ron smiled, as much to reassure himself as it was for Sophie.

'And miss all the gunfights and stabbings?' He gave a fake look of shock. 'You must be kidding.'

A moment of quiet passed between the two, each knowing nothing else needed to be said.

Sophie looked back down at her phone and absently tapped away at the keys. Eventually, she broke the silence.

'Brian says he owes you a beer or two.'

Ron suddenly realized she must have been messaging him. He knew, texting from her own phone would have compromised her security.

'Tell him he owes me a new pair of jeans too,' Ron chided.

'He said maybe next time,' Sophie laughed at the reply. Clearly there was an element of bromance forming between the two. 'Should I book you two a room?' she asked.

Ron just grunted and took a sip of his beer.

*

Janet felt nervous as she slipped unaccompanied from her apartment. Up until now, Diana had refused to let her out of her sight if the others weren't about. Now, with everyone busy at work, it was her one and only chance to buy a gift for Diana. They had all agreed she was never to leave the apartment alone, so she felt guilty for taking a chance. More so for knowing how much time each of them had sacrificed.

Janet was sick of being a prisoner in her own home and fully convinced no one had taken the bait. They had tried so many times to lure any potential kidnappers out over the last few weeks but to no avail. She had walked through unlit alley ways, crossed deserted parks late at night and even stood alone at the lakeside feeding the ducks for hours on end. All the time closely monitored by Brian, Sophie and of course Ron, whom she had secretly come to bear a crush on.

Although she liked Sophie, Janet couldn't help feeling a pang of envy towards her for seemingly having it all. The rough and ready look of jeans and unkempt hair only reinforced her superfluous attitude towards beauty. Combined with her obvious intelligence, Sophie could have been a right bitch, but she wasn't. Instead, she had been like a big sister to her, watching over her and most likely saving her life. It was also clear that Sophie and Ron complemented each other in the bizarre way that opposites attract.

The busy lead up to Christmas meant Diana had been called in to work all over the weekend. It was probably the only chance for Janet to slip out into the hustle and bustle of the busy crowds without detection, or so she thought. Not wanting to stray too far from her apartment block, Janet chose the same mall they had first met Sophie at. It was within walking distance, and the heavy crowds meant she would never be alone and vulnerable.

As she approached the mall's entrance, the festive crowds thickened, causing Janet to question her decision to leave the safety of the apartment. Physical contact with the other shoppers couldn't be avoided as everyone began squeezing through gaps and jostling to get to where they wanted to go.

Janet's mind began to race as she constantly imagined each stranger brushing against her was potentially someone waiting to abduct her. She stepped from the crowds and into the relatively quiet doorway of a book shop in order to steady herself. Taking a few calming deep breaths, she chided herself for being a victim of her own imagination. Not only had she been subject to a previous kidnapping but now she was a victim of her own fears. How could she be so frightened of shopping amongst crowds, when previously she had loved the melee of trying to grab a bargain? Janet knew she was in danger of becoming paranoid of her own shadow. Crowded places were safety, everyone knew that. She took another deep calming breath then stepped back into the stream of people. Even though the crowds were thickening, she began to gain a little more confidence now.

After an hour of browsing clothes shops, Janet's aching feet steered her back towards one of the first stores she had visited. There had been a nice winter coat with a fake fur collar she knew Diana would love. Had it not been so expensive, she would have even considered buying one for herself. Janet smiled as a devious thought crept into her head. She was sure Diana would let her borrow it at some point.

Although she had a passion for shopping, the thick crowds had started to wear her down. With her new purchase, she let out a sigh of relief then headed towards the mall's exit.

As Janet wove between the masses, she had no reason to suspect the dark haired woman standing in the doorway of a perfumery had been waiting for her. There was nothing unusual about the woman's appearance. She wore a thick, knee length, blue coat that was partially unbuttoned, revealing a multi coloured silk scarf around her neck, and she carried a branded store bag, just like many other shoppers.

Covertly, the woman slid a clear plastic cap from the top of a large onyx ring on her left index finger, revealing an inconspicuous needle tip. Once pressed against a body it would automatically inject a small quantity of sodium amytal, an anaesthetic drug commonly used during medical operations. Just as Janet approached, she stepped from the shop doorway.

'I'm so sorry,' apologised the woman in the blue coat, as she stepped right into Janet's path, causing something sharp to dig into her leg.

The sight of the woman in blue, frantically trying to rescue the contents of her bag from the busy mall floor immediately quenched Janet's anger. Absent mindedly, Janet rubbed her leg as she bent down and helped pick up the few remaining items for the other shopper.

'No harm done,' Janet uttered handing the items over with a sympathetic smile.

As she stood, her head suddenly felt light.

'Are you OK?' the lady in blue asked. 'You look awfully pale,' she added, with a look of concern.

'Yeah, I think so. I must have just stood up a bit too quickly,' Janet replied, trying to clear her head from a sudden overwhelming desire to sleep.

'You probably just need a little fresh air. Come, I'll walk you outside and you can sit on the bench for a while. I'm sure you'll feel better after you get away from these crowds,' said the helpful shopper.

Janet allowed herself to be led towards the mall's exit. She knew a breath of fresh air would surely help and the last thing she wanted to do was faint amongst so many people.

She began to feel guilty as she realised she was now leaning heavily onto the kindly shopper for support. Janet's mind screamed at her to shut her eyes, just momentarily, that way she would feel better when she opened them again. By the time she eventually stepped into the open air, Janet's eyes were fully closed. The last thing she remembered was an additional pair of hands coming to offer more support.

*

Sam sat in the light blue Kia mini-van, watching the crowds of shoppers as they poured in and out of the mall's entrance. He had already been there for half an hour and was now getting edgy. Although reluctant to lift Janet so soon after the screw up with the hit on Brian, the money was just too good to ignore.

Earlier in the morning, he had found out that it had been Ramirez's brother who had survived the botched assassination attempt. He had tried to plead that he was only trying to protect his brother after Brian had turned a gun on them. Such an alibi may have worked on anyone else but not against the head of National Security.

Sam figured, Ramirez probably hadn't even told his brother who the target was. Regardless, he would now be charged with attempted murder. Sam just hoped the two he had recruited to pick up Janet would fare better.

He had been right in the middle of a security meeting when the message pinged to say Janet had finally gone out unaccompanied. The staff meeting was just a mere formality about who was to be babysitting the President over the festive break, so he cut it short and left his team to decide amongst themselves. He allowed himself a wry smile, remembering their faces as he announced he was "just popping out for a while".

Just then, a man and woman suddenly appeared from the crowds, supporting what looked to be a drunken woman. Pressing a button on the van's fascia, Sam slid the automatic side door open to receive the trio.

*

Without even bothering to remove her coat, Diana slumped down in her chair. The day had been nothing short of non stop hell. The festive season had proven itself to be anything *but* festive. In all her years of dealing with customer satisfaction, she had never had a day with so many difficult people. She was used to people returning defective items, or at least imagined defective items, but it still amazed her just how many would attempt squeezing into garments two sizes too small, then come crawling back for refunds when the seams burst.

Today had seen whole new levels of idiotic complaints. One woman had tried to return a toasted cheese maker, claiming she had only just purchased it and it didn't work. Diana had calmly pointed to the melted cheese still at the back of the product then, after looking up the serial number, found out that the model was in fact three years old. The customer had gone hysterical, shouting and screaming at the top of her voice, prompting Diana to hit the panic button under the counter. It was the first time she had ever had to use it to call security over. The manager had also rushed over and comforted her for a while, then led her off to the staff room where he fixed her a hot cup of coffee with a shot of brandy in it to calm her nerves.

Diana took a deep breath then let it out. Slowly the day's tensions began to ebb away, only for a sense of tiredness to replace them. With a glance at the clock, she realised, even though it was almost seven o'clock, she hadn't yet heard from Janet today. Although her sister knew better than to pester her while she was at work, she had usually at least received a message or two by now. Since all the trouble started, there hadn't been a day pass without some sort of communication.

Still reluctant to move from the couch, she pulled her phone from her coat pocket and stared at the screen. There were no messages but to her surprise, especially after the day she had just endured, she found that Janet had been the last person to call. She hit the redial button. Instantly, Janet's voicemail leapt into action informing her that she wasn't available to take her call right now but she could leave a message. Diana hung up without uttering a word.

She stared at the phone in her hand a while, urging herself to keep calm. In her head, she sought to find reasons why Janet wouldn't answer. The most likely explanation was that she had forgotten to charge it or maybe she had dropped it down the toilet like she did at the festival two years ago. Whatever the reason, Diana felt a bad feeling creeping into the pit of her stomach.

Without hesitation, she picked up Janet's spare key from the top of the book shelf and headed for the door. They both had spare keys to each other's apartments just in case either one of them lost theirs. Until now, neither had cause to use it, but this time, Diana needed to find her sister, fast.

*

The incoming call sent Brian's phone dancing across the kitchen table. The vibration from the silent alert sounded like an amplified drum on the wooden surface. Brian craned his neck to see who was calling as he stood at the kitchen sink, hands still immersed in suds. He had a dishwasher of course, but like most single men, he seldom needed more than one plate or dish at a time. Wiping bubbles from his hands with a kitchen towel, he walked over to the table and picked up the phone.

'Diana?' he asked, cautiously.

It was the first time she had called since exchanging numbers.

'Is that Brian?' the shaky voice on the end of the line asked.

'Yes, what's wrong? Has something happened?' He knew this wasn't going to be a social call.

'Have you any idea where Janet is?' Diana tried to remain calm, but there was an unmistakable air of desperation in her voice. 'I've just been into her apartment but she's not there. Ron is away on business and Sophie hasn't heard from her all day,' she added, before Brian could ask the obvious questions.

'Give me five minutes and I'll get right back to you.' Brian abruptly hung up.

He was angry but it wasn't going to achieve anything by pointing out that they had all agreed Janet shouldn't be left alone.

Lifting the lid on his laptop, he quickly logged in to the National Security server. All high risk diplomats carried security trackers in case of a kidnap and each of the devices came with its own security signature. Within a few moments, a map of the United States of America filled Brian's screen. Little green dots with codes next to them represented the locations of each of the high tech tracking devices assigned to all important personnel. If the system was ever hacked, only the locations of the allocated devices could be seen, not who carried them.

It was common knowledge phones could be easily traced, so the first thing kidnappers did these days was to throw them away. Alternative locators were a little less conspicuous. Janet's discreet leather strap around her wrist, with the small battery powered SIM locator sewn in, looked to hold no value.

Brian pulled a piece of paper from his wallet and typed the six digit number into a drop down box on the screen. He had decided not to use Janet's name when he assigned the tracker, for extra security. Immediately one of the green dots on the map acquired an additional circle around it, identifying Janet's location.

*

Ron winced as he took a sip of the stone cold coffee he had long forgotten. He had sat in the parking lot for over an hour now, watching and waiting for the "Lavender Girl" to show up. Charlotte had directed him to the latest locations where Lavender Girl had last been seen, spraying her powerful scent. It seemed anyone daring to drop litter around fast food establishments had become a prime target for her.

At first, Ron couldn't see the down side to the woman's actions, but further down the reports he was reading, he noticed some of her victims had been burnt by the powerful, long lasting perfume. Up until now, her attacks had been focused around ill mannered youths, seen throwing food wrappers from open car windows. Sadly, it would only be a matter of time though until some innocent child got blinded.

Yet again, he found himself sitting in his truck watching out for some crazy vigilante to show but today he felt more at ease. Ron had spent last night with Sophie, talking about what their future would hold. He had already given a lot of thought to where his life was going and all outcomes had looked bleak. To get out of the reaping business, he would need Landon's consent; otherwise he would just become another ex-con who had skipped his parole. He didn't even have a passport, he confessed to Sophie.

She had draped her arms over his shoulders and kissed him, then whispered in his ear, "And if you had a new identity and a new passport?" He realised at that moment, there was a chance that he wasn't trapped doing this for the rest of his life after all.

The public were only interested in stories of vigilantes going around dishing out justice in ways that the police could not. If the cops intervened, they were accused of failing the people but if an innocent bystander got hurt, they were labelled neglectful.

No one seemed to care that half of these vigilantes were in need of some sort of psychiatric help themselves. Landon just wanted them to disappear in any way possible, as long as it was done discreetly.

Ron absent mindedly took a gulp of the coffee as he read through the file, causing him to screw his face up and spit it back into the cardboard cup. He was tempted to pour the remainder into the gutter but the last thing he needed was a face full of industrial perfume. Something suddenly occurred to him. Whoever this Lavender Girl was, she probably knew how to mix the right chemicals to get such a powerful scent. One of the earlier attacks had been reported by a member of Drug-U-Like, a large pharmaceutical developer. It was a long shot but Ron figured it may be worth investigating further.

He punched the address of Drug-U-Like into his sat-nav and realised he could be there within a couple of hours. It had to be better than sitting in random fast food parking lots. Stepping from his truck he placed his cold coffee into the nearest bin then, after one last look around for the Lavender Girl, got back into his truck and drove off.

TEN

The coffee that Ron had just poured himself from Drug-U-Like's reception area was in a whole different league to the cold, stale one he had discarded a few hours earlier. He had only managed to savour the first sip though when he spotted a young man bounding down the stairs to meet him.

'Mr Hawley?' the young office worker asked.

'Please, just call me Ron,' Ron said, offering his hand.

'Alex,' the fresh faced man shook Ron's hand, 'How can I help you?' he asked, a little bemused by his visitor.

'You reported an attack against a friend of yours a short while back?' Ron asked. 'Sprayed with some sort of strong scent I believe,' he prompted.

Alex suddenly looked a little uncomfortable and glanced around to see who was within earshot.

'Please, take a seat,' Alex indicated the small seating area away from the receptionist's desk. 'I might get into trouble for talking to you but I suspect the attacker used to work here.'

'Used to work here?' Ron echoed.

Alex took another look around. 'There was this woman who worked here, Rachael. She really knew her stuff but one day she completely flipped out. Ran off with a pile of my papers and put them through the shredder. A whole week's work gone in an instant. Turned out she had some sort of OCD about neatness. Mr Morris, our boss, managed to get her into a private clinic that deals with those sort of things. Well, the therapy must have worked, because a few months later she returned, right as rain.'

Ron gave Alex a bemused look, 'What makes you think this Rachael was the one who attacked your friend?'

'Because when Rachael came back from her therapy, if things started to get too much for her, she would hold a heavily scented handkerchief to her nose,' Alex replied.

'Let me guess, scented with lavender?' Ron could suddenly see the link. 'Why did she leave?'

Alex shrugged his shoulders. 'I really don't know. Rumour has it, her therapist moved away and she went off the rails again.'

Ron took a sip of his complimentary coffee as he thought.

'I don't suppose you have the name of this therapist do you?' Ron asked.

Alex shook his head. 'Sorry. I once overheard Mr Morris mention a Susan when he was talking about an appointment with Rachael but I don't know any more than that.'

'Can I speak to this Mr Morris?' Ron asked.

Suddenly, Alex looked very worried. 'Look, if you start asking for the name of Rachael's shrink, I'm going to get into very big trouble for talking to you,' he gave a pleading look towards Ron. 'Mr Morris was very protective of Rachael, sort of like a fatherly figure,' he added.

'Relax, I know the score. Maybe I'll come back

another time and go straight to Mr Morris. I'll make no mention of you if I do,' Ron said, getting to his feet.

'I'd appreciate that.'

Alex shook Ron's hand, as if he had just clinched a deal.

*

Ron fired up the truck and sat a while, waiting for the condensation to clear from the windscreen. Alex had risked getting into trouble by speaking to him but he had also filled in a big section of the puzzle. Ron knew Sophie would be able find out more on her laptop in an hour than he could in a lifetime of driving about.

He was just about to drive off when his phone rang. "Caller unknown" filled the screen where either a phone number or a name usually appeared but he immediately knew who it would be.

'Hello,' he answered casually, choosing not to use Sophie's name just in case he was wrong.

'Janet's gone missing. We have a location that's about an hour's drive from you. Can you meet us there as soon as possible?'

Sophie didn't bother wasting time on small talk. Her knowledge of computers, and such like, had taught her nothing was fully secure. Ron understood why some found her blunt and unapproachable but it didn't trouble him at all.

'On my way,' he replied, then hung up.

He momentarily felt good about reciprocating Sophie's curt approach to conversation, then immediately felt foolish for forgetting to ask for an address. Twenty seconds later, a bleep cut across Johnny Cash, indicating he had just received a text message. It read, "Thought this might come in handy". Underneath was an address. Ron just smiled, put the truck in drive and pulled off Drug-U-Like's parking lot.

*

As Brian pulled up onto the gas station's forecourt he switched his lights off and rolled into a parking bay. A silhouette of someone sitting in the driving seat of a blue Toyota three spaces down immediately caught his eye. Before he even managed to come to a complete stop, the familiar figure of Sophie, dressed in blue jeans, a dark jacket and a baseball cap, was already approaching. Without invite she pulled open his passenger door and climbed in.

'How the hell did you know where to come?' Brian asked.

Although Sophie had witnessed him give Janet the locator bracelet, he hadn't revealed any details needed to track it.

'Just call it women's intuition,' she replied, curtly.

Brian shook his head in despair.

'You know this thing will most likely get ugly,' he warned. 'Not only will these people probably be armed, they won't hesitate to put a hole in anyone getting in their way,' he added, fully aware that his words would have no impact on Sophie whatsoever.

Brian felt he was stuck between a rock and a hard place. Even though he desperately needed backup, he couldn't be sure his presence wouldn't leak out if he called for it.

'Don't worry, I'll make sure I'm well behind you.' Sophie offered him a rare smile.

Looking down at her phone screen she was pleased to see that Ron was just a few minutes away.

She had also given him the address of the gas station because it was close to Janet's indicated location.

Sophie hadn't been a bit surprised when Brian had pulled up. No one would be stupid enough to drive straight into a situation without stopping to prepare themselves first. When Diana had phoned earlier, enquiring about Janet's whereabouts, she had told her to contact him straight away.

Brian climbed from the Escalade and opened the rear tail gate. Inside, discreetly mounted in the floor of the trunk and covered with black carpet, was a flat steel box. He unlocked the heavy looking padlock and lifted the steel lid. Sophie let out a low whistle as an array of guns came into sight.

'All part of the Job,' Brian said, handing Sophie a heavily padded vest. 'Put this on.'

Sophie took the jacket and slipped her arms through it. It was deceptively heavy but also reassuring at the same time. The vest was guaranteed to stop anything short of a fifty cal round. The wearer may end up with a broken rib or two from the impact but that was better than holes. Brian would be the first to vouch for that.

'Have you ever fired a gun?' Brian asked Sophie, as he went about securing extra magazines into his own vest.

Sophie nodded her response but it was lost as he slid a Glock 19 into his shoulder holster. He looked across at her for the response.

'Yes,' she replied, audibly this time.

Brian took another pistol from the case, slid a 15 round magazine into it then cautiously offered it to Sophie. She went to take the gun but Brian momentarily held onto it.

'You stay back, keep watch for trouble from behind and the sides, and do exactly as I say. If I tell you to run, you run. Got that?' Brian was determined his instructions were non negotiable.

'Got it,' Sophie acknowledged.

Brian offered a piercing stare, trying to judge her sincerity, then eventually released the weapon. It was a bad situation and he seriously considered calling in the police. He had gone down a path he shouldn't have but it was too late to turn back. Just then, another set of headlights appeared in the distance.

Brian switched off the light in the back of the Escalade and guided Sophie to step out of sight. With a certain amount of suspicion, he watched a grey pickup slow, then turn into the gas station. Brian backed away from the driver's line of sight but to his horror, Sophie stepped out and waved the pickup over.

'What the hell are you doing?' he hissed.

'Relax, he's one of the good guys.' Sophie's smile was lit up by the headlights.

'Have I come at a bad time?' Ron asked, grinning at the suspicious scene.

Brian had been lurking behind the open tail gate of the Escalade as Sophie emerged into view.

'I'm sure glad to see you big man,' Brian said, emerging from the shadows and embracing Ron. It was the first time they had seen each other since the shooting.

'Figured someone needed to be here to plug the bullet holes again,' Ron joked.

Sophie just rolled her eyes.

'Brian's tracker is showing Janet's location about

a mile up the road but I'm not convinced she's still wearing it,' Sophie said to them both.

'What makes you think she's not wearing it?' Brian asked. Although he hadn't said anything out loud, he knew there was a very real chance they could be looking for just a body at this point.

'They wouldn't have killed her already. They haven't yet retrieved the file from Fletcher Rosworth's,' Sophie said, as if reading Brian's thoughts. 'I haven't picked up the additional tracker that I planted in her jacket either. Although the signal isn't as strong as the one you've planted, I would have had something by now,' she added.

'Maybe she's not wearing the jacket,' Brian suggested.

'I asked Diana to search the apartment for it. She was adamant it wasn't there,' Sophie confirmed.

'C'mon, just talking about it ain't going to help the girl. The only way we'll know for certain is if we go look,' Ron said. He didn't do high tech or sport a university education like the others but he was more than capable of stating the obvious. The obvious was usually what the highly educated over looked Ron found.

Brian nodded his agreement with Ron's logic. 'You'd best put this on first,' he said, handing Ron a vest.

The Armoury within the Escalade always carried four jackets just in case of emergencies, along with enough fire power and ammo for a small war. Brian waited patiently, trying to suppress a smile as he watched the big guy open up the strapping and wriggle into the tight fitting garment. The end result made him look like a Britney Spears drag artist but he knew at least it would offer him some protection.

'I don't suppose?' Brian asked, pulling one of the remaining hand guns from the secure case and offering it to Ron. He knew just how uncomfortable the big man had been when he had handed his gun over on that crazy night they had first met.

'Nah, I think I'll pass.' Ron eyed up the gun as if someone had fished a turd from a swimming pool. 'But I will take those if ya don't mind,' he pointed to a pair of night sticks recessed into the armoured lid.

'Be my guest,' Brian knew the night sticks would be more effective in Ron's hand than a gun anyway. 'OK, let's go then,' he said, climbing behind the wheel of the black Escalade.

Sophie climbed in the front passenger side, eyes remaining fixed on the locator while Ron perched himself in the middle of the back seat.

*

Janet woke, then immediately vomited. At first, she thought she may have collapsed outside the shopping mall. She moved to wipe her mouth but her arms failed to respond to her brain's request. It took a few moments more for the fog within her mind to clear enough to realise this wasn't the shopping mall. For one thing, the floor within a mall didn't move. Even through the darkness, the effort of opening her eyes sent pains shooting through her head.

'She's awake.'

Janet instantly recognised the voice of the woman shopper who had bumped into her. As she tried to move her face away from the rancid pool of vomit, Janet realised her arms weren't responding because they had been tied behind her back. All rationality disappeared as the thought, "They are really going to be mad at me for sneaking out alone now," jumped into her head.

A pair of strong hands hauled her up into a sitting position.

'You're a hard person to get alone these days.'

Sam Young's voice came from just behind her, sending her heart rate soaring. There was no mistaking the purpose of her second kidnapping now.

She realised they hadn't put a hood over her head this time and it frightened her. After her first ordeal, everyone had assured her that it was good that they had hooded her. It was an indication they would eventually let her go because she wasn't able to identify her kidnappers.

A lump of her vomit slid down the side of her face as she now sat awkwardly on the floor of the moving vehicle. Outside, it seemed darker than usual. Then it dawned on her, if there were no street lights, they must be driving out into the wilderness.

She flinched away as something suddenly brushed against her cheek.

'Don't worry. I mean you no harm,' Sam Young spoke tenderly into her ear.

The very same person who she had trusted in the beginning. The one who had been so charming that she had allowed herself to dream of a future with him. The one who may now decide if she even had a future.

'I am only trying to clean you up a little. I'm afraid the anaesthetic has that effect.'

He gently wiped the side of Janet's face with something soft. She didn't pull away this time. There was no benefit to sitting, bound, with her own stomach contents sliding down her face she reasoned.

Tilting her head up slightly, she tried to establish where about they were but the windows were too high to see from where she sat. Yet again, she felt utterly helpless and totally alone. Then panic gripped her again as she desperately felt around her wrists for Brian's bracelet. It had gone.

*

'Found it,' Ron held up the leather wrist strap.

Brian took the tracking device from Ron and examined it in the beam of the Escalade's headlamps. Although the strap had been cleanly cut with something sharp, there was no sign of blood on it.

He had parked close to the indicated satellite position then they had fanned out in their search. With no buildings close by they knew they would be looking for either a bracelet or a body. While it was some relief there was no body, they also knew Janet was in real trouble now.

'Shit, they could have taken her anywhere,' Brian swore. The situation had got just about as bad as it could.

'No,' Sophie stood, lit up by the headlights, shaking her head. 'They were clearly driving in this direction in order to throw the bracelet this side of the road, right?' She didn't bother waiting for an answer before continuing, 'They still haven't retrieved the file yet so they will need a place that has internet.' She looked towards Brian for his acknowledgement.

'A motel?' Ron suggested. He figured it was the obvious choice.

'Possibly, but there is the risk of being spotted

and will they want to rely on the shitty Wi-Fi they usually serve up in those joints?' Sophie said, working through her line of reasoning. 'They will need a fairly good connection in order to operate the optical reader. They can't afford to rely on an intermittent server. A better solution for them is something like an office or maybe even a library.' She looked towards Brian for suggestions.

'The nearest place I can think of along this road is a little town, about eighty miles south of here. It's set back, just off the main highway and it's called Locwood or something like that,' Brian shrugged. It was a long shot but it was also all they had.

'Let's go then.' Sophie climbed back into the passenger seat and shut the door - the decision was black and white in her mind.

He didn't like it but unless he could come up with an alternative idea, here and now, this was the one Brian would have to run with.

He briefly looked to Ron for alternatives but Ron just shrugged his shoulders before getting back into the Escalade too.

By the time Brian climbed behind the wheel, Sophie had already plugged her phone into the charge point and was intently studying her screen.

'What's the range on that thing?' Brian asked, nodding towards the device in Sophie's hands. 'A couple of miles out in the open,' she answered without looking up.

'And amongst buildings?' Brian pushed.

'Half that.' This time she looked directly at him. It was obvious what he was thinking. Their chances of picking up Janet's signal would be slim.

Brian stared out of the windscreen and into the wilderness, hand paused on the ignition key, contemplating his options. A moment of silence passed as his imaginary coin stopped spinning and landed on a winning side. He turned the key, prompting the powerful v8 to roar into life, then pushed the selector into drive. The four hundred horses under the hood frantically dragged the two and a half tonne SUV off the sandy shoulder and onto the black top in a bid to find their needle in a haystack. Even the plush refinement of the Cadillac's interior couldn't mask the urgency now being placed on the motor as the speedometer flicked to the naughty side of one hundred miles per hour. If they failed to pick up the signal, they would surely end up looking for a body.

*

Janet eased herself into a slightly less uncomfortable position. The hard floor of the people carrier was making her bum go numb and the bindings on her wrists offered no way of supporting herself. Sam hadn't invited her to sit up on the seat and her own stubborn pride was preventing her from asking. She had no real way of knowing just how far they had travelled but she guessed they must be out in the middle of nowhere as they hadn't taken a turn in ages.

'This one here,' the woman from the mall suddenly called out from the front seat. Janet made a mental note that if she came through this ordeal, she would need to punch the bitch, square in the face.

The people carrier slowed almost to a stop before turning a sharp left, causing Janet to lurch against Sam Young's knee. She realised their journey must be coming to an end and, like it or not, she would soon discover what fate had in store for her. After another five minutes of steady driving, she felt the van slow down and turn again. Even though it felt they were only moving slowly, Janet heard the tyres screech as if driving over a smooth surface. Through the floor, she felt the van dip down a steep slope just before bright, artificial lights flooded the interior. She realised they must have pulled into some sort of underground parking lot. A small glimmer of hope washed over her. If it was a public place, she might soon have a chance to scream for help.

Moments later, Janet felt the van come to a halt then the motor went quiet. The two in the front got out and shut the doors behind them, leaving her and Sam Young together. After a few minutes of silence, Janet spoke out.

'Not going to put a hood over my head this time?' she dared ask, fully knowing the repercussions of now being able to identify her captors. She wanted to make a point that she understood the implications of not being hooded.

Sam laughed. The act was so patronising that Janet was forced to put him on the face punching list.

'What good would that do? You already know my face.'

His arrogance grated on Janet further. Even though he had removed the tracker from her wrist, he must have known they were onto him.

'What about the others? I could identify them,' she pushed the issue further.

'Do you think we're amateurs? Get it into your pretty little head that should you testify about any of this, your sister and niece won't be so lucky next time,' he said, through clenched teeth.

The cold tone of his voice sent shivers down her spine but what he said also sent her mixed signals. On one hand it was a very real threat but on the other, it also gave her hope that he *would* let her go again. She knew she was clutching at straws and reminded herself that the slime-ball couldn't be trusted.

At least he had just described her head as being pretty. The thought couldn't have been any more inappropriate but it did made her smile a little. With all the recent things happening to her, Janet realised she was starting to develop a dark sense of humour.

The side door suddenly clicked and began to slide open automatically.

'All clear,' the bitch shopper uttered.

'OK, Janet, nice and easy now. Let's not try anything silly, there's no one around to hear you,' Sam said, reading her intentions. He stepped from the van, eased her feet onto the ground, then helped her to stand.

Either due to the side effects of the drug, or just cramp from sitting awkwardly, Janet felt her legs wobble a little as she stood. The reason made no difference. She would not be able to out-run her captors anyway.

The underground parking lot was completely deserted, bringing her to the conclusion that they weren't within residential premises. If they were, it would have been full at this time of night. As the woman led them to a door in the corner of the building Janet realised Sam was right, no one would hear her if she screamed.

*

The loud impact made Sophie yelp as she looked

up in time to see a sudden spray of blood and entrails fill her line of sight. The coyote had come out of nowhere, but at a hundred and ten, nowhere sort of hits you fast. Maybe it had thought the distant set of headlights posed no threat but unfortunately the creature had been proven wrong. It was of little consolation to the wild dog now but at least he had taken out the expensive Cadillac's headlamp. Either way, it's moon howling nights were well and truly over now. Maybe he would boast of the achievement when dining in the canine equivalent of Valhalla or wherever kamikaze coyotes went.

The loud bang had even been enough to bring Ron from his snoring. Brian was amazed that anyone could be relaxed enough to sleep during such break neck speeds, let alone on their way to a possible gun fight, armed with just night sticks. He couldn't help admiring the big guy's sense of calm.

'What the fuck?' Ron said, immediately alert to the possibility of action. His waking world turned out to be a stark contrast from the dream he was enjoying. Seconds ago, he had been writhing on a bed with the same red haired beauty now sitting in the front passenger seat. He realised, slightly embarrassed, that the evidence of his dream was still showing through the fabric of his jeans.

'Damn coyote, came out of nowhere. It took a lamp out but I think we're OK,' Brian said. He had slowed down to seventy and was frantically spraying water onto the wind-shield in a futile effort to clear the blood.

'Coyote OK?' Ron asked, leaning back in the plush seat once more.

Sophie just rolled her eyes at the question.

By the time Brian had washed enough remnants of the animal off the screen, they were just coming up on the turning to the little town of Locwood. Small pricks of light in the distance appeared through the trees as the only evidence of the town's existence.

Locwood had originally developed from a railroad stop, used for filling steam engines with water but now that everything ran on diesel, the once thriving town was slowly on the decline. The sign said it was home to a thousand people and Brian estimated at least nine hundred and ninety nine of them must have been tucked up in bed right now.

'Stop here,' Sophie pointed to the side of the kerb. After briefly messing around with the settings on her phone's screen, she absently waved Brian on, 'OK, but slowly.'

The Escalade now looked like a prop from an apocalyptic movie as it crawled along the street. The area where the headlamp used to be was now filled with flesh and fur and the grill and bumper hung down at an angle. Had they hit the animal in anything smaller than the big SUV at that speed they would surely have gone off the road. It took a whole ten minutes to crawl along to the end of the small town, pausing at anything that looked like an office, but there was nothing on Sophie's scanner.

'Go back down the other side,' she ordered, in desperation. As there was nothing much else to do, Brian complied.

Another ten minutes passed as they neared the end of the main street once more.

'STOP!' Sophie suddenly shouted.

The heavy Escalade lurched to a halt. There was

no activity on Sophie's screen now but she was adamant it had flashed green.

Without a word, she climbed from the motor and walked down the middle of the street, occasionally turning and pacing back and forth. Ron and Brian remained within the vehicle, waiting for the verdict. They watched her walk over to a large set of sliding gates securing some sort of underground parking lot, pause a moment, then turn and beckon them over.

'Show time,' Ron said, as he climbed from the rear seats, night sticks now tucked securely into his vest.

'She has to be in there,' Sophie said, holding out her smart phone for them both to see. They could see a little dot, blinking within the outline of the building. It was no wonder they had missed it on the first pass. The thick concrete and steel used within the building's construction would have masked most of the signal.

Although the gates were a little over six foot high and designed to prevent the theft of vehicles, they were not designed to stop people climbing over them. Planners had probably figured no thief would be stupid enough to corner themselves on the off chance of nicking the odd item.

Ron cupped his hands for Sophie to climb up. She stepped gracefully from Ron's hand to the top of the gate and sprang down the other side in one fluid motion. Even though the limited movement in Brian's shoulder made the climb painful, he made no mention about it. Ron passed the shot gun back to Brian then, in a stark contrast to Sophie's finesse, he scrambled over too.

Holding her smart phone in front of her, Sophie led them towards the fire exit at the corner of the lot.

'Wait!' Brian put his hand on her shoulder. 'This is my game now.'

Sophie automatically went to argue but then realised he was right. Nodding her assent, she stepped aside.

*

The image staring out from the restroom mirror looked as though it had been dragged through a hedge backwards. External appearances of matted hair and a dirty face were nothing compared to the throbbing headache and chapped lips she was now suffering though. Janet washed her face thoroughly then drank deeply from the cold stream of water from the tap. She knew her broken lips and headache were most likely down to dehydration caused by the anaesthetic they had used on her.

An idea of locking herself into the bathroom in the hope someone might come and rescue her flickered across her mind but she dismissed it immediately. The flimsy lock would never stop a child let alone a full grown man intent on gaining his millions. There was a knock at the door.

'Janet, it's time.'

The sound of Sam's voice made her blood boil but she wasn't going to give him the satisfaction of showing him any fear. Unlocking the flimsy latch, Janet stepped out into the dim corridor, lit only by the emergency fire exit sign at the far end. As they were most likely the only ones in the building, it must have been their attempt not to attract any extra attention from outside, Janet thought.

Sam stood there waiting with an irritating smirk

across his face. At first Janet presumed his amusement was born out of victory but then she noticed he held something in his right hand. Dread washed over her as she realised it was the same hood they had tied around her neck the first time they kidnapped her.

'There are some who don't want you to see their faces,' Sam explained, as if she was an idiot.

The mask augmented the spark of hope that they were going to release her again, but she wasn't totally convinced. After a moment of stand-off, she relented and pulled the loose fitting black hood over her head. A faint smell of tobacco smoke hung within the fabric. She couldn't be sure if it was the same hood they had used on her before but if it was, had they used on others since. Maybe they kidnapped people regularly, she mused?

More and more crazy thoughts began to swirl around inside Janet's head as the darkness of the hood engulfed her once more. Where did they even get hoods from? It wasn't as if they could pop down to their local clothes store and ask for a "One size fits all kidnapping hood, please," or maybe a granny belonging to one of the kidnappers had sat carefully sewing at the seams one afternoon between watching daytime TV and baking cakes. She realised her mind was starting to run away again.

Sam's hand touched her elbow in order to guide her. Her first instinct was to pull away from him but she knew, if she did, she would just end up bumping into things. Janet had to trust him for now. Even though he had used her to gain access to the Fletcher Rosworth files, he had never yet hurt her. Christ, what was she thinking? Was she coming down with a case of Stockholm syndrome?

She reminded herself; this bastard had been responsible for Marie and Rebecca's little "accident" as he had put it. He was nothing more than a greedy, ruthless crook. They paused momentarily as Sam opened the door at the end of the corridor. Janet heard the sound of several voices within the room before all went silent. She didn't need to be a rocket scientist to realise that all eyes had now turned towards her. She continued to allowed herself be led through a maze of turns before eventually, Sam told her to sit. Cautiously she felt for a chair then sat.

*

Brian signalled the other two to hang back a little as he flattened himself against the wall and approached the fire exit. There was no way of knowing if anyone was keeping watch, or even how many they were going up against, but they had committed to this now. Seeing no shadows or any visible movement behind the door, he silently moved himself to just below the square window. With the pump action shotgun at the ready, he gently pushed against the door a little to make sure it hadn't been barred on the other side. The intumescent fire strips around the door let out a snake like hiss as they parted.

The noise seemed deafening in contrast to the complete silence of the deserted parking lot. Anyone within the stairwell couldn't have failed to hear them but no alarm was raised. Brian paused and took a questioning look back at the others. Ron nodded his assent that he was ready. There would be no turning back from this point.

Brian cautiously edged the door open a little more, keeping his body out of the potential line of fire, then quickly stepped into the bottom of the stairway. He made a brief check for any blind spots then he waved the others to follow.

The dead of night silence is a tricky beast. Each step, each rustle of clothing, stood out as if someone had been playing the sounds through an amplifier, especially within the confines of the stairway. The only saving grace was it worked both ways. They strained to hear any sounds from the levels above. Finally, satisfied they had gone undetected, Brian edged up the first flight of stairs.

A partially glazed, ground floor emergency exit door displayed a complete lack of activity outside on the street. Brian had anticipated they would need to make a decision by the time they reached the next landing to either search that level first or the one above but someone had made that choice easy for them.

A small wedge of wood had been placed within the frame to prevent the stairway door slamming shut. Brian looked behind him to see if the others had spotted it. Ron nodded. Most likely, some poorly paid janitor had been given a sizeable sum just to leave doors unlocked. Maybe it was the difference between a holiday for his family or not, who knew. Either way, it was becoming obvious that Janet had been brought into the building this way.

Brian peered carefully through the narrow window of the first floor fire door. On the other side, the long, dimly lit corridor, with its scuffed and dirty magnolia walls, showed no sign of activity. Once in there, he knew they would have no place to hide if anyone emerged from any of the adjoining offices.

'There are five doors, Janet must be behind one of them. Can you tell which?' Brian called Sophie over to look down the corridor.

Moving alongside Brian, she held up her phone in front of them. He could see the clear outline of the main building on the little screen. Although it showed no internal walls, a green dot blinked somewhere towards the end of the block.

'It has to be one of those last offices on the left,' Sophie offered. 'I will know for sure when we get closer to the doors,' she added quickly, detecting Brian's reluctance to let her follow.

Brian knew he had somehow manoeuvred himself into the middle of a shit show of his own creation. He was just about to make an unlawful entry into an unknown environment. He didn't know how many were behind the door but he was pretty sure they would be armed. What's more, he was doing it with two civilians. He sighed. What could possibly go wrong, he asked himself?

'If it's locked, I'm going to shoot the lock, then we go in hard and loud to keep the element of surprise on our side. I'll go first, you two follow as crowd control, got it?'

It was crude, but any plan was better than none.

'Ready?' Brian looked for confirmation.

'Ready,' they both answered.

'OK then, let's go,' Brian said, pushing the door open.

A faint smell of photocopier ink, combined with cheap aftershave, lingered in the air as Brian ran towards the furthest of the office doors.

Without warning, an ape-like arm wrapped itself around Ron's neck then completely lifted him off the floor. Somehow they had managed to miss the heavily muscled man lurking within an alcove at the other end of the corridor.

On hearing the sudden movement behind her, Sophie turned in time to witness Ron's feet leave the floor. At a height of six, six and weighing two hundred and eighty pounds, the guy must have lived inside a gym. She realised, if she didn't do something quickly, the giant would crush Ron's airway.

Frantically lashing out with his feet, Ron was attempting to push against the wall to unsteady his attacker but he was too far from it. Without hesitation, Sophie launched a searing kick, straight into the attacker's groin. The giant let out a high pitched whimper but much to Sophie's surprise, Mr Muscles failed to go down. It was enough to make him loosen the throat hold though, allowing Ron to drop free.

Brian had almost reached the end of the corridor before he realised something was going on behind him. He turned and began to run back.

'Go, I can handle this,' Ron said, gasping for air and rubbing some feeling back into his neck. A moment of indecision passed over Sophie as she first looked to Ron, then back to the giant cradling his broken baby maker. It wouldn't be long before the behemoth regained his composure but if they didn't act now, the noise would surely spoil their element of surprise.

Brian didn't need telling twice. He nodded his affirmation, then raced back down the hall. Sophie hesitated a moment longer, still unsure.

'Go!' Ron urged her.

'Be careful,' Sophie warned, then turned and raced after Brian.

By the time she caught up with him, Brian had paused between the last two doors and was looking to Sophie to identify the locator.

'This one,' Sophie pointed to the second from last door.

A brass plaque on the wall next to the door indicated "Births & Deaths". Brian hoped that wasn't some sort of bad omen.

Crashing sounds rumbled on from the far end of the corridor as Ron and the muscle mountain set about expressing their conflict of interests. Ordinarily, Ron was more than capable of handling himself but Brian had serious doubts about the outcome this time. There was nothing he could do about it right now and they needed to act fast.

Turning his attention back to their own task, Brian quietly pushed the handle down then slammed his shoulder against the heavy door. The spring loaded door closer thwarted his attempt to burst in quickly but it also resulted in a much quieter entry than anticipated. Rather than opening into a large office as expected, they found themselves standing within another internal corridor. Three doors stood on their right. A bathroom, a store cupboard and a small kitchen. The door at the far end had to be the main office area.

Now, with his adrenaline levels sky high, Brian made it to the last door in half a dozen steps, pressed the handle and heaved the door open with as much force as possible. He had tried to compensate for another door closer but this time, there wasn't one. The door offered no resistance and slammed against the wall, sending a metal waste paper basket spinning across the room. Brian's unchecked momentum sent him stumbling into the office a little before he eventually gained his footing.

Instantly, he assessed the situation and levelled the shotgun at the two men and a woman standing around a hooded figure seated at a desk. Brian recognised none of those in the room, but he assumed the hooded figure was Janet.

'Hands where I can see them,' he shouted, casting his eyes around the office for additional people.

Brian would have no hesitation dropping any of them if they made one wrong move and the kidnappers sensed it. The man standing just behind Janet was tall and gangly looking. He was middle aged, dark skinned and sported a bushy moustache. The other man was slightly younger but he was of a stockier build and wore his hair cropped as if he belonged to one of the armed forces. The third person was woman who had short, dark hair and was around the same age as the taller guy but she carried a menacing, almost spiteful, glint in her eye.

A few moments passed as the situation sank in but it was the tall moustached man who slowly raised his hands in compliance first. The other two hesitated a little but the sudden appearance of Sophie at Brian's side, wielding her Glock purposefully, convinced them that surrender was the safest option.

'You, with your left hand remove the gun and drop it on the floor,' Brian instructed the military looking guy.

The straps of his shoulder holster were clearly visible and the unmistakable bulge of a weapon on the guy's left side screamed danger to Brian. Right handed people wore their holster on the left, enabling an easy draw of the weapon. Without trained backup, things could quickly take a turn for the worse. He carefully watched the guy slowly slip his jacket open and unclip the weapon's restraining strap with his left hand. The movement appeared far less awkward than Brian had hoped for but the guy obviously knew, he would be dead before he could try anything.

With a silky smooth action, he slid a rather clumsy looking Desert Eagle from the holster and dropped it to the floor. The guy looked slightly embarrassed as he momentarily met Brian's eyes. With its enormous barrel, large elephant stopping calibre and rugged looks, those in the know understood the user must be compensating for something.

Brian resisted the urge to comment on the weapon. 'Any more?' He looked to the other two questioningly. They shook their heads in unison. He would have to watch them closely until Ron came back

'Over there,' Brian signalled with the barrel of the shotgun to an open space within the office. Chest high, blue partition panels dissected the office space into a large horse shoe shape but they offered no means of cover should the kidnappers attempt to make a run for it.

'Untie Janet and call the police,' Brian instructed Sophie, without taking his eyes off the kidnappers. It would be a tense few minutes before the police arrived and he still couldn't help worrying why Ron hadn't come back yet.

*

'Put the phone down.'

The cold tone of Sam's voice and what she presumed was the barrel of a gun pressing against the back of her head made Sophie shudder.

Sam had been in the bathroom when they had crashed their way into the office. Rather than rush out with guns blazing, he had waited patiently until he could get down the corridor undetected. But now, he had the cold barrel of his gun pressed against Sophie's head. Sophie slowly replaced the telephone receiver back on the hook.

Even though Brian knew they had lost the game, he still kept the shotgun trained on the others. Within his mind he frantically searched for a way out.

'We both know you're not going to let any of us walk free from here,' Brian said, his only bargaining chip now being the lives of Sam's contacts.

'What do you have in mind?' Sam held almost all the cards but he chose to indulge Brian a little.

'My life for theirs. Let them go and you keep me. I can even be used for a sizeable ransom I should imagine,' Brian offered.

Sam grinned, 'OK, drop the shotgun and they can go.'

Brian laughed a sour laugh, 'Yeh, I suppose I have your word on that.'

'What choice do you have?' Sam snarled.

Brian carefully weighed up his options. The three in front of him posed no immediate threat but he knew he couldn't turn quickly enough to stop Sam putting a bullet in Sophie first. If he dropped the shotgun, all three of them would surely die. There was also the possibility Sam wouldn't waste time shooting Sophie first, he would know Brian would try something. As if reading Brian's thoughts, Sam turned Sophie so that she was within Brian's line of fire.

'What's it to be, Brian?' Sam spoke through gritted teeth.

There was nothing left. Brian held up a hand in surrender and began lowering the shotgun. The moment it touched the floor, a deafening shot rang out, causing Brian to flinch as a spray of crimson filled the air and covered his face. Instinctively, he drew his Glock and spun around just in time to see Janet crash backwards against a desk, sending a computer monitor flying to the floor.

Sitrep. His combat training had taught him to react instinctively but this scenario was a new one to him. No one had afforded the mild and meek Janet a second thought but she had decided, enough was enough. Picking up the discarded Desert Eagle hand canon, she had aimed it at Sam Young's head and pulled the trigger. The .44 magnum round missed Sam's head but hit him directly in his left shoulder joint, separating his arm from body by all but a few stringy bits. Brian realised that it had been Sam's blood that had sprayed into his face but he had also witnessed Sophie fall to the floor.

The deafening shot within the confines of the office had taken them all by surprise and only now did each of them start to understand the situation.

Brian's thoughts quickly returned to the other three kidnappers and he brought his gun back around towards his forgotten targets. It was a fraction too late. As he turned, his hand was met with a kick from the guy with the cropped hair, sending the Glock falling to the floor and sliding under a computer table. A second kick hit Brian in the ribs but he had already started to roll with it. Even so, it knocked the wind out of him a little but his adrenaline masked the pain well.

The tall guy, sporting the dodgy moustache, stood as if he was an innocent bystander watching a playground fight.

The woman who had masqueraded as the shopper also acted fast and lunged for the fallen shotgun. She had just laid her fingers on the stock when a hand grabbed a fist full of hair and yanked her head back.

'No you don't bitch,' Sophie screamed. Her shoulder was now hurting like hell but Janet's bullet had only grazed her as it passed through Sam.

Tables, chairs and flimsy partitions flew in all directions as two separate conflicts now took place.

Brian's shoulder instantly went numb as a lucky blow hit him squarely on his recent wound. The excruciating pain made him gasp and he tried to roll away but the kidnapper followed and dealt a series of blows to the back of his head. Pulling a blade from the harness around his ankle the stocky man drew his arm back, ready to plunge it into Brian's neck. Just as he was about to deal the deadly blow, a red fire extinguisher come into sight and his world went dark.

'Miss me?' Ron asked, standing over Brian, a fire extinguisher hanging from his blooded fist. Brian rolled onto his back, panting, and saw his saviour standing over him grinning.

'What could go wrong, huh?' he reiterated. 'Best stop your girlfriend from killing the prisoner,' he quickly added, turning his head towards the commotion at the other end of the office. Sophie was in the process of bouncing the female kidnapper's head off a nearby desk even though she was almost unconscious.

No doubt, some poor office worker would find tufts of hair and dried blood on their files on Monday morning.

Ron laid a hand on Sophie's arm, 'I think she's about done now, honey.' He watched the feral hatred slowly ebb away as she realised who had touched her arm.

'Christ, I thought that big fucker had killed you,' she said, discarding her enemy and throwing her arms around his neck.

He winced but didn't pull back as her weight pressed against his ribs.

'Told you I'd handle him, didn't I?' Ron smiled down at her.

'Took your time though.' Sophie nestled her head into his shoulder. A sudden weariness swept over her as the adrenaline rush began leaving her body.

'Figured you two had this all under control,' Ron looked around the office, observing the signs of carnage.

A faint moan, followed by the sound of a waste paper bin clattering against a steel filing cabinet, turned their attentions towards the corner of the office. Janet climbed to her feet. A thin cut to her forehead and swelling around her right eye bore testimony to the Desert Eagle's massive recoil. Even though she had never even held a gun, let alone fired one before, sheer desperation combined with the hatred for Sam Young had prompted her to shoot the bastard. He would never kidnap her again. It was only pure luck the bullet hadn't passed through him and killed Sophie.

Sophie hadn't escaped the shot completely. A piece of the hollow point bullet had broken off as it passed through Sam and grazed the top of her shoulder.

Combined with the weight of Sam falling on her, she had been pinned to the floor for a while.

Brian retrieved his shotgun and instructed the tall guy to sit down on a swivel chair, while Ron tied his hands behind his back with a length of computer cord. Sam lay in a spreading pool of blood and groaned as approaching sirens grew louder.

ELEVEN

Ron took a sip from his complimentary coffee as he sat in the reception area of Drug-U-Like once more. The kidnapping drama had taken its toll on all of them. As soon as it became known that a member of the National Security team had been involved in selling secrets, the FBI jumped in and left no stone unturned.

Ron's sketchy past and his weak cover story of being a maintenance man had been met derisively but they did acknowledge he had been acting in the country's best interests. Eventually he had been forced to call Frank Landon in to smooth things over from one government department to another. According to Charlotte, Landon had been livid for getting summoned by the FBI to explain Ron's activities. Even though he had no idea what Ron had been mixed up in, Landon had assured them he had been acting for the Federal Bureau for the Prevention of Interactive Service team.

Sophie, on the other hand, had stirred up a lot more curiosity amongst the Feds. Even though they had acknowledged she had played a pivotal role in bringing the blackmailers to justice, they wanted to know how she had come by her information. Under cries of protest from Sophie, they took her phone, lap-top and tablet away and tried to access her files and programs. Although the best of their technicians worked tirelessly on the devices, they still couldn't find anything untoward. After two weeks of analysis, they reluctantly admitted there was no illegal software or information that breached government security so handed them back. A week later, all the files that had been copied, mysteriously disappeared from the FBI database.

Brian tried his best to urge the Feds to lay off Sophie and Ron but there was no putting the stopper back in the bottle. Two of Sam's former team members had been found to have rather more money in their bank accounts than they should have but it wasn't enough to charge them with anything. The most Brian could do was to fire them on the grounds of national security.

Fletcher Rosworth immediately ordered an inquiry into their security system. They sold the idea to their clients by announcing that it was just another upgrade in customer confidentiality.

The thin, tall guy, sporting the bushy moustache, turned out to be of Egyptian nationality, going under the name of Tarik Mahmood. He had been hired to oversee the technical side of the optical scanner and file downloads. At first, he tried to claim immunity as an Egyptian diplomat but his request never reached the Egyptian consulate. Once Mahmood realised his Government had made no attempt to locate him, he became extremely willing to talk. He led the Feds to the technical accomplice who had helped carry out the file extraction at Fletcher Rosworth. He also led them to an overseas bank account with twenty million dollars in it. There should have been twenty-five million in it but an unknown person had withdrawn a large portion of it a day prior, into an untraceable account.

Sam Young's greed meant he would now grow old inside a federal prison. He had mistakenly believed himself to be a major player in the operation when, in reality, he was no better than the security guard at Fletcher Rosworth who had been paid to look the other way. None of those arrested turned out to have any knowledge of who was pulling the strings at the head of the operation.

The loss of blood that Sam Young suffered from Janet's Wild West shooting had almost cost him his life. Ironically, it was also Janet's concern for his life that prompted her to call the paramedics, who arrived just in time.

'Mr Morris will see you now,' the young receptionist announced, bringing Ron back from his thoughts. Ron smiled back at the young lady as she stood at the edge of the reception area, waiting to guide him to her boss's office.

'Ah, Mr Hawley,' the middle aged managing director cautiously offered a handshake. 'Sally says that you are a friend of Rachael?' he asked.

Ron could immediately sense Mr Morris wasn't going to give out information freely. 'Sort of,' he said, knowing he would have to lay his cards on the table from the start. Mr Morris lifted an eyebrow as he waited for Ron to elaborate. 'I believe Rachael has got herself into trouble since she left here,' Ron began.

The look of concern on Mr Morris's face indicated he already suspected what the visit was about. 'How exactly do you know Rachael?' he asked, deciding it was time for straight talking.

'We believe she has become a vigilante, going around spraying anyone who creates a mess on the streets with an industrial strength lavender substance,' Ron said.

'We?' Richard Morris asked, completely ignoring the other details.

Ron paused momentarily as he considered how much he should reveal. 'I work for a little known branch of the government, set up to discreetly eradicate vigilantes known amongst the media as Min-heroes.'

Mr Morris frowned, 'Eradicate? How?'

'That, Mr Morris, is left to my own discretion,' Ron revealed.

Rachael's ex boss looked incredulous. 'And you think I'm going to reveal where she lives?'

'I already know where she lives. I'm just trying to find a way of stopping her before she goes too far. It won't be long before she sprays that chemical into a child's eyes and blinds them,' Ron replied.

'You can't help her, no one can,' Richard Morris said, miserably. He knew Ron was right but he was at a loss as to what could be done. 'The only one who had any success with Rachael was her therapist but she has since married and moved to Canada.'

'Has Drug-U-Like got any pharmaceutical laboratories over there?' Ron queried.

'Of course, we are a global corporation. We have laboratories in twenty-seven different countries. Had I known that she was going to go off the rails, I would have re-located Rachael there straight away. Now, I fear it is too late,' Mr Morris shook his head in despair.

'You leave that to me. You arrange a transfer for her, set up a meeting with her therapist, and I'll sort the rest out,' Ron said. 'I may also require a few sedatives,' Ron added, as his thought process slowly caught up.

'I can't force the girl to move to Canada,' Richard Morris gasped.

'Understand, if I don't sort this out my way, someone else will. They won't care about how they eradicate Rachael though,' Ron warned.

Mr Morris looked crestfallen, 'I'll make the arrangements.'

*

'Let's get out of here,' Sophie said, straddling Ron's lap and looking him square in the face.

Ron looked up into her hazel eyes. 'Out of here as in go out somewhere for food or the big, out of here?' He knew the answer but just wanted to check, in case he had read her wrong.

'The Feds have kept us under surveillance since we got Janet back. They constantly try hacking my emails and I can guarantee, *you* don't fart without them knowing. If we stay here, they will never leave us alone and we'll always be looking over our shoulders,' Sophie said.

'What do you have in mind?' Ron asked. It didn't really matter to him where they went but he asked out of curiosity anyway. He knew they were under surveillance but he had hoped they would eventually give up.

'Amsterdam,' Sophie replied, without a moment's hesitation.

'I can only speak English, of a sorts.' Ron feared being completely isolated in a foreign land and not being able to communicate. He knew the Europeans spoke all sorts of gobble-de-goo. It amazed him how so many separate countries, all bordering each other, could end up speaking so many different languages. He'd read somewhere that Germany had nine other countries attached to its borders. In the States you could drive right across the continent without needing anything other than English.

'The majority of them can speak English,' Sophie reassured. 'We could buy an old barge and you can fix it up,' Sophie could picture it in her mind.

'OK then, let's do it,' Ron said, still uncertain but liking the sound of going back to doing something he loved. 'Will you help me with Rachael first though?' He had told Sophie all about Lavender Girl and how she had gone over the edge.

'You're just a big softie,' Sophie said, hugging Ron tight. In truth, she saw it as one of his most endearing traits but she could see how it always got him into trouble. 'Of course I'll help.'

*

Rachael opened her eyes and slowly gazed around the sterile looking room. The only furnishings were a single bedside cabinet with nothing on it, a desk dead centre along a wall with a high backed chair neatly positioned against it, and a plain blind covering a large window. She knew she should feel panicky for not knowing where she was but the simplicity of the décor somehow made her feel relaxed.

As she swung her legs over the edge of the bed, her feet brushed the soft cream carpet, causing her to flinch and lift them up again. Although she had just woken in an unfamiliar room, without any knowledge of getting there, her primary concern was not having her slippers. Even though the carpet was brand new, in her mind, slippers were the only barrier between her feet becoming contaminated from the filth on the floor.

Gradually, it dawned on Rachael that she had

been kidnapped and moved to new surroundings but she remained calm. It didn't really matter. The only dilemma facing her at the moment was, she needed to pee. The closed door in the corner of the room had a shower symbol on it, indicating it was the room she needed. Although no more than half a dozen steps away, she still couldn't bring herself to put her bare feet to the floor.

A knock came from the door at the other side of the room.

'Come in,' Rachael called out, unsure of what else to say.

'Good morning, Rachael, how lovely it is to see you again,' Susan Willoughby said, walking into the room, a genuine smile on her face.

Rachael just stared in disbelief for a moment, then burst into tears. Abandoning all fears of contaminating her feet, she leapt from her bed, flung her arms around her doctor and sobbed.

A few moments passed, then Dr Willoughby pulled away from Rachael's embrace and held up a new pair of slippers.

'I thought you might like these,' she smiled. 'You will find new clothes in the wardrobe once you have showered, then I'll send someone to escort you to my office later,' she added.

Rachael took the proffered slippers and held them to her dearly. She felt safe once more.

*

Tears ran from Ron's eyes as he wound the window down a few more inches, in a desperate bid to blow away the fumes from the chemicals on his face. Sophie just laughed. Even though they had ambushed Rachael as she exited her apartment, they had not been quick enough to stop Lavender Girl turning within Ron's grasp and spraying him with the industrial scent.

Sophie suspected it was more down to Ron's reluctance to use too much force when he restrained her but she didn't push the issue. The eye watering chemical was enough chastisement in itself. Sophie had jumped in and administered the sedative through the epi-pen, but it had taken a while before Rachael calmed down. Richard Morris had already put his career on the line by agreeing to supply the drug but he had refused, point blank, to give them anything too powerful, just in case Rachael reacted badly to it.

Ron pulled onto the motel parking lot and parked next to Sophie's Toyota. If all went well, this was going to be the last time he used the truck and he felt a pang of sorrow for leaving the best vehicle he'd ever had. Tomorrow was going to be the start of a whole new life though and the loss of a truck was insignificant in comparison.

'You'd best get in the shower for an hour or two. I'll sort some food out for us.' Sophie said, laying a cautious kiss on Ron's cheek, avoiding as much of the chemical as possible.

They had booked and pre-paid the room for six nights in advance, that way there would be no suspicions raised for a while when Ron's truck remained in the parking lot.

In the morning, they would drive to Las Vegas in Sophie's Toyota, spend a night there, then fly to Europe. Ron didn't know how but Sophie had managed to come up with a new passport for him. The only difference from his original, was his last name was now going to be Howard instead of Hawley. The name change didn't bother him at all. It wasn't as if he was desperate to keep the family lineage going. Even with a new passport, he still feared the agency would somehow track him down and prevent him from leaving though.

*

'So, we just leave our stuff, jump on a plane and start a new life?' Ron knew that was the plan but couldn't quite believe it was about to happen.

'Having second thoughts?' Sophie questioned.

'Hell no. It's not as if there is anything here for me.' Ron bundled his rucksack onto the back seat of Sophie's car as a sign he was ready to take the leap.

Like Ron, Sophie had no ties. Brian had again begged her to come and work for him as the head of his cyber security team but she had flatly refused. Not only would be it be impossible to conform to their strict rules and regulations, the work would also be mundane and stifling. Besides, with her recently obtained financial windfall, a steady wage was no longer necessary.

'Let's go then,' Sophie said, climbing behind the wheel.

*

No one paid the slightest bit of attention to the light blue Toyota as it pulled of the Honey Tree Motel's parking lot on the damp and windy December morning. Ron's pickup remained outside room 47, his phone inside the glove box, and his keys lay in the room's bedside cabinet, ready for the cleaners to find in a week's time.

The plan was to drive across to Las Vegas, have

some fun along the way, then hop onto a flight to New Zealand. Once safely out of the states, they would country hop until they came to Europe. Without officially being on any wanted list, it wouldn't take them long to disappear completely.

Ron pushed his seat back as far as it would go and stretched out his legs. Sophie's little Toyota was deceptively spacious on the inside. The clever automotive designers had realised that compact cars only ever carried one or two people most of the time. On the rare occasion they did carry more passengers, however, it might necessitate the removal of all lower limbs.

He glanced over at Sophie and noticed she was looking intently in her mirrors.

'Expecting company?'

'Always,' she replied, forcing a smile.

Ron slipped his trainers off and allowed his toes a wiggle at their new found freedom. The lingering lavender scent on Ron still couldn't quite mask the aroma of sweaty feet that filled the little car.

Sophie looked across at Ron, 'Maybe we should stop off first to buy you some new socks,' she hinted.

Ron just grinned as he stared out of the window.

*

It took four days of hard driving in order for them to reach Vegas but they had fun along the way. During those long days of being bound together, rather than getting on each other's nerves, their similarities brought them closer. Sophie slowly begun to open up about her past. Ron's nature not to press for information made her more relaxed and able to talk. Ron also shared stories of his own life and due to his rocky history, he would regularly have Sophie doubling up in laughter.

Sophie chose a few short stop offs for them to break up the monotony of the journey. Some would prompt childhood memories for her, mostly of her father. Excitedly, she had dragged him to a place where a line of Cadillacs had been buried end on in the dirt in the name of art. Apparently, her father had sprayed her name on the roof of the last one in the line when she had been just a baby. Rather than an act of vandalism, he had claimed it to be his one and only contribution to art. Even though Sophie didn't hold out much hope that her name would still be there, it didn't stop her from eagerly combing the fresh artwork that others had contributed. Her passion had been infectious and Ron found himself searching the old scrap Caddies for remnants of her father's art but to no avail. Before leaving, Sophie sprayed their names on the last Caddie's roof with an old discarded spray can as a tribute to her late father's rebellious streak.

Once back on the road, Sophie talked more about her memories of her father. She even spoke a little about the darker years when her parents broke up. Eventually, the memories became too painful and she clammed up once more. Ron didn't push her.

They spent hour after hour either driving in a comfortable silence or listening to songs on the radio. Throughout the day, one would drive as the other took a nap, only stopping for gas and a motel for the night.

*

Even though Ron had been to Vegas once before, he had only just turned eighteen. As with so many other events in his life though, it had been a big mistake. Already towering over most folk, he had believed he would pass the scrutiny of the casino's security guards. After slipping into one of the casinos, he had been busy playing the slot machines when a guard had first challenged him for ID. Having been ejected from several casinos, word quickly spread that an underage kid was trying it on. With nowhere else to go, he had ended up confined to a motel room, drinking whiskey from a bottle that he had bribed a hobo into buying for him. Ron just hoped he would fare better this time.

Even as they entered the outer limits of the city, it quickly became a sharp contrast to the quiet roads of route sixty six they had been used to. Although still daylight, bright artificial lights illuminating burger joints, motels and even seven-eleven stores, started to spring up ever more. It seemed that if you didn't have enough bright lights in Vegas, you didn't exist.

Either the place had changed beyond all recognition or Ron's memories had failed him completely. Either way, it was as if he was seeing it for the first time as they slowly drove down the slip. Casinos were everywhere. If it wasn't a casino, it was most likely a steak house, out to entice tourists to part with their hard earned dollars. Biggest was best became the theme. The casinos offered the biggest jackpots and the steak houses offered the biggest slabs of meat.

They drove along the whole length of the strip and out the other side again, emerging at the far end where they found themselves a tidy little motel just on the outskirts. It was a modest establishment, probably the result of some private individual investing his life savings to get on the Las Vegas band wagon. Even though it was far from the city centre, in another ten years time it would get swallowed up by expansion and the owner would most likely receive a lucrative buyout.

After checking in at *The Safe Bet* motel, the receptionist, who was barely out of high school, handed them a credit size door card and directed them to an upper chalet overlooking the parking lot. The room was nothing special but at least it had all the usual comforts of an out of town motel. A colour TV the size of a laptop screen, an empty fridge and tea and coffee making facilities. The door at the rear opened into a cramped shower room, sporting out dated fixtures and a mildewing shower curtain. It wasn't luxury like the sign said but it would do for a couple of nights, then they would be off on their way to a new life.

Neither of them had wanted to stay too close to the clutch of the bright lights and the constant noise of the gambling capital. It would be just as easy to hop onto a bus for a short ride into the madness, then slip away once the insanity grew too loud. A much needed shower was in order first.

*

'I think it's time that we left now,' Ron said, in a tone more suited to an order rather than a request. If Sophie was offended, she showed no sign whatsoever.

'Just a few more goes,' she uttered, as the machine in front of her paid out yet another jackpot, it's lights and sirens alerting all around that you *could* win if you pumped enough money into it first.

The worrying thing was, Sophie hadn't pumped enough money into the machine and this was the fourth one within the casino that she had emptied.

Ron's personal experiences of good luck were few and far between. It was something others experienced mainly but he knew, even those blessed with good luck didn't win four jackpots in a night, not honestly anyway. Even though he had watched her like a hawk to see how she was doing it, there genuinely appeared to be no foul play. Now, as the sounds of the thirty two thousand dollar Klaxon filled the air again, he realised she was attracting the wrong sort of interest.

It wasn't the look of hatred and envy on the faces of her fellow gamblers that concerned him. It was more to do with the circle of rather poorly disguised plain clothed security staff who had begun to take an interest in her run of good "luck".

'We should leave. Now!' Ron said again, laying a firm hand on hers, as she bent down to load her winnings into the canvas bag provided especially for lucky guests.

Sophie stared at the hand resting on hers and was just about to protest when she noticed Ron's projected gaze. Following his line of sight, she suddenly picked up on his meaning.

'Oh, you could be right,' she nodded, in a small token of acknowledgement, then crammed a few of the silver dollars she had just won back into the machine.

'Seriously?' Ron hissed in her ear. A look of incredulity filled his face. His arms were already weighted down with coins, equivalent to that of a small child.

'Trust me,' Sophie offered him a small wink, then continued tapping repeatedly on the giant buttons.

This time, however, the machine refused to pay out. Eventually, after pumping in another hundred dollars worth of coins, Sophie shrugged her shoulders and pushed her bottom lip out in a display of mock indignation at having lost part of her booty.

From the corner of his eye, Ron noticed that the end of Sophie's winning streak must have been enough to satisfy most of the security staff and some of them started to drift away. A few members remained close by, nonchalantly pretending to take an interest in anything other than the two hauling their winnings towards the cashier. Although they could plainly see the lucky pair heading towards the door, those same security staff followed at a discrete distance to witness them leave their establishment.

It was a stark contrast between the outside and inside of the casino. The carefully controlled environment within the building was designed to eliminate any indication of time. With no windows to the outside, bright lighting throughout and not a clock to be seen anywhere within, people were lulled into feeding machines and playing games as long as they could keep their eyes open.

Outside, an icy night time wind blew across the desert, biting into their exposed flesh. Had there not been so much light pollution, the stars would surely have filled the clear sky. The bustling night life suddenly made Ron a little nervous of the thick wads of hundred dollar bills bulging in his pockets. He was still in the process of assessing their danger of being mugged when Sophie tugged on his sleeve and guided him over to a waiting taxi.

'Let's go get some food,' she said, pulling the cab's door open and climbing in.

Ron didn't need telling twice. Quickly, he slid alongside Sophie and pulled the door to the outside world shut.

'Take us to a really good steakhouse, but well away from all these crowds,' Sophie instructed the driver.

'I know just the place.' The cab driver lifted his head a little so he could smile at his new fare through his mirror, then pulled away from the kerbside and into the steady stream of traffic. As they slowly made their way along the strip, the driver struck up a one sided monologue of how his cousin worked at this great place which served the best steaks in the whole of Vegas, but the story fell on deaf ears.

Sophie leant back in the seat and ran her fingers through her tangle of wild, windswept hair.

'You were attracting a lot of attention from the security back there with that run of good *luck,*' Ron said, emphasising the word "Luck". He cast a glance across at Sophie to see if she had picked up on the insinuation.

'You think I was cheating?' she asked, raising her eyebrows and daring him to challenge her.

Ron laughed. He wasn't stupid enough to believe it was all down to luck but he wasn't clever enough to find out how she had kept winning either.

'I'll believe whatever you tell me,' he said, raising his hands to placate her. 'What I do know though, is if we had stayed there much longer they would have frog marched us into a quiet back room and asked us some serious questions,' he added.

Sophie nodded, 'I guess you're right,' she said, realising she had probably pushed her luck a bit too far.

'I can't believe you played on, knowing all those eyes were on you though.' Ron leaned his head back and smiled at the thought.

'They would have been more suspicious had I just walked away,' Sophie said.

Ron gave her a puzzled look.

'No gambler would have walked away passing up the chance of a "hold" just after the machine had paid out,' she added in a quieter voice, now realising the driver had stopped talking.

Ron nodded at her logic. He was just glad to be out of the place.

'You just tell them that "Al" brought you here and my cousin will look after you real good,' the driver said as he pulled onto the restaurant's parking lot and made his way closer to the entrance. Signs backing up Al's boast of the "best steaks in Vegas" could be clearly seen plastering the inside of the windows as they drew to a halt just outside.

'Thanks Al,' Sophie said, pushing the fare and a very generous tip into the driver's hand before getting out.

As they watched the cab drive off, the cold desert air once again began to bite. Sophie noticed Ron looking across the half full parking lot. It seemed that even in the early hours of the morning, it was never too late for a steak in Vegas.

'Ready to eat?' Sophie grasped his arm for the modicum of extra heat.

'Sure am,' he said, wrapping his arm around her waist and guiding her towards the entrance. 'Don't look over your shoulder now but we have company,' he said in a low voice even though there was no one near to hear them.

An old beige Ford Fairmont doing a sharp U-turn had caught his eye earlier as the cab had driven away from the casino. There was nothing unusual about that in itself and he wouldn't have paid it any attention had he not owned an identical one as a kid. It was too much of a coincidence that the same car was now parked at the far end of the lot with two figures sitting in it. The large wads of bills, bulging in their pockets, reminded him of their vulnerability.

The entrance to the diner was positioned just on the far corner of the building and Ron suspected that the large sign with the establishment's name on it would briefly obscure their followers line of sight.

'Keep walking,' Ron said, guiding Sophie straight past the entrance and along the side the big steak house. A dimly lit service path led them down to a small, fenced off compound containing a line of dumpsters, filled with empty beer bottles. Within the small compound, a kitchen fire exit door had been propped open with a broom in order to let some of the stifling heat out. Along with the emanating heat, the smell of enticing food touched their noses.

'You really know how to show a girl a good time,' Sophie said, as Ron helped her up onto the top of the dumpsters.

From the top of the plastic recycling bins, they climbed over the high chain link fence and silently dropped down into the sandy desert. With no one around to see them, they first skirted the rear of the adjacent budget car rental and then a nearby all night convenience store before rejoining the main street. By the time they reached the pavement once more, they were well away from the diner.

'Think they were out to mug us?' Sophie asked, as they cautiously made their way across a piece of waste ground.

'I hope so,' Ron replied.

Sophie initially frowned at the reply but quickly realised what he meant. She knew he was still worried they would track him down and bring him back.

'Quick, let's catch this bus,' Sophie said, spotting a golden bus approaching. They ran the remaining short distance to the stop just in time.

Dropping down into seats halfway along the nearly empty bus, Ron pressed his head against the window to see if there were any signs of the beige Ford following.

'See anything?' Sophie asked.

'No, they are too far away. They must think we have gone inside the diner.' He leant back in his seat and relaxed a little.

'Let's just grab a burger and go back to our room.' Sophie could see he was still worried.

The following day, they decided not to risk going into the city again, instead opting to stay at the motel, playing pool and watching the little TV in their room. Although Sophie believed Ron was being a little paranoid, she was more than happy to stay away from the city for the sake of just one more day. With their flight due to leave in the morning and a whole life ahead of them, a day of quiet time would be welcome. As the evening drew on, they sat in the little hotel bar, drinking overpriced beer and talking about their future.

'Where are we going to live when we get to Amsterdam?' Ron asked, setting down another two bottles of beer on the table. He was more than happy to leave the arrangements to Sophie but he wasn't keen on being a kept man all his life. 'I'll also need to get a job eventually,' he added, huddling up to Sophie.

Ron knew the casino cash would sustain them for a few years but he wasn't sure how long they could survive once it ran out. Sophie had money tucked away, that was obvious, but even though he strived to be a modern man, of sorts, deep down he realised he was still a caveman at heart.

Sophie turned and stared at Ron. He could see she was bubbling inside and wanted to tell him something. Then, with a beaming smile she came to a decision and began rummaging about in her bag for something. Eventually, she pulled out an envelope from one of the side pockets and handed it to Ron.

'What's this?' Ron asked, a puzzled expression all over his face.

'I wasn't going to give it you yet but I can't wait any longer.'

Ron pulled a piece of paper from the envelope and read it in disbelief.

'Is this ours?' he questioned.

'Yep, it's going to need a lot of work on it but I figured if I shopped around a little I might find a good carpenter to fix it up,' she smiled mischievously.

Ron looked at the piece of paper in his hands once more. On the front was a bill of sale for a large Dutch barge and on the back was a photograph of the original ad. At ninety foot long and fourteen feet wide it would have swamped both of their apartments together. He shook his head in disbelief, lowered the paper and embraced Sophie tightly.

*

Like any other airport around the world, McCarran airport is decorated with neon information boards displaying departure and arrival times for every scheduled flight. The difference with the Las Vegas airport is, it doesn't let you leave quietly. The gambling machines that litter the waiting areas are occupied almost twenty-four hours a day with visitors parting with any last change. Those just arriving in Vegas could be forgiven for thinking that they had landed directly inside a casino. The revenue from the 1400 slot machines alone raises over $30 million a year, even though they are known for their poor payouts. Ron had to hand it to them, they certainly knew how to squeeze every last cent out of the tourists.

Sophie headed straight over to the check in desk to pick up their tickets. Once checked in, they would be able to relax a little and hide themselves away inside a restaurant until boarding time.

At the passport control, Ron desperately tried not to appear guilty of some imagined crime as he underwent scrutiny. The constant flick of the woman's stare between his passport and his face would have sent a saint into a sudden bout of confession but Ron held his nerve. Eventually, satisfied he was who his documents said he was, the clerk suddenly manufactured a smile and handed his passport back.

'Hell, that was intense,' Ron quipped, as they headed towards the nearest bar.

'That's it, all we have to do now is jump on the plane when it's ready,' Sophie replied, relieved just as much as Ron. She knew they had just crossed the biggest hurdle. If they were under surveillance, they would have been stopped at that point.

The next hour flew by as they sat and talked

about all the things they wanted to see on their way to a new life. Sophie talked mainly but Ron was just happy to sit and listen to the excitement in her voice. No longer in a dark place, she bubbled with all the energy of a teenager. Ron too allowed himself to imagine a future where he wasn't always looking over his shoulder.

The airport speakers burst into life with a loud ding, followed by the usual muffled announcement, telling them it was time to board the plane. They were grinning like teenagers as they took a long slow walk to their boarding gate. By the time they reached the gate, the majority of passengers had already crammed themselves onto the plane. They knew it would be the usual routine of passengers standing in the isles trying to fill overhead lockers with bags of cheap souvenirs.

Ron still carried a big grin as staff checked his boarding pass then waved him through. Sophie did the same.

'Miss Parker, could you come with us please?' The voice at Sophie's shoulder made her spin around in shock. A man in a dark suit was holding up his FBI identification in a pre-emptive manoeuvre to stifle the anticipated protests while his partner stood by.

In all their excitement, they had failed to spot the two agents, in their unmistakable suits, waiting at the gate.

'Stop!' Sophie called out, not to the agents but to a very serious looking Ron as he bounded towards them. He paused, just the other side of the gate, much to the relief of the nervous looking gate staff, but he still carried the look of a raging bull.

'What's going on?' he demanded.

'This is a federal matter sir, please don't try to

interfere,' the Fed spoke in his best authoritative voice, but he couldn't quite mask the concern written across his face.

The balance between Ron doing something really stupid and listening to Sophie was on a knife's edge.

'Go, I'll catch up with you later, I promise.' Sophie leant over the barrier, pushed the receipt for their boat into his hand and kissed him on the cheek. 'I know where to find you,' she whispered in his ear, smiled, then turned away. It hurt like hell to watch her leave but he knew she was right, he would only make things worse if he made a scene. All along, Ron had believed that it would be Landon who would send people to bring him back. He should have realised, it was the FBI who was never going to let Sophie out of their sights. As Ron watched the two agents lead her away, he wondered, would ever see her again?

ABOUT THE AUTHOR

Philip Payne

About the author

Having left secondary school in 1981 with a handful of middle of the road CSE's (the precursor of GCSE's), writing a book was as likely as flying to the moon. I had spent my first twelve months of secondary school in what at the time was referred to as the remedial class. In those days we cruelly called it the "dummy's class" but most of us wore the title with some degree of rebellious pride. Looking back, I realise it just wasn't my time to learn.

As with most school leavers with my level of academic achievement, I ended up working in a menial job. Even though I had to work sixty hours serving petrol for my £54 a week, I was happy to have money in my pocket. I eventually became a plumber and remained so for the next 37 years.

At the age of 51, I underwent open heart surgery and, maybe suffering from the realisation that I wasn't immortal, decided to write a book. All my life, I've loved reading books, so I figured, nothing ventured, nothing gained.

As you can guess, equipped with just my 36 year old English CSE it wasn't going to be an easy task. Fortunately, limited academic qualifications doesn't restrict a sense of imagination and with the aid of Spellcheck, my three wonderful children and my very patient friends to help me edit, I give you “Ron”

Printed in Great Britain
by Amazon

27718118R00209